The Magical Mancer Novels of

DON CALLANDER

The adventures begin when a young man answers a strange advertisement: APPRENTICE WANTED to learn the MYSTERIES and SECRETS of WIZARDRY in the Discipline of FIRE . . .

PYROMANCER

"The sorcerer's animated kitchen is a delight, as is his brassy bronze owl . . . There are nice original touches here."
—PIERS ANTHONY

Then the young Pyromancer meets his match—a beautiful and beguiling apprentice learning the Mysteries of WATER . . .

AQUAMANCER

"Amusing . . . delightful talking animals and fish!" —*Locus*

The Pyromancer and Aquamancer try to free a tribe of men enslaved in stone by a treacherous Master of the EARTH . . .

GEOMANCER

"Readers who have followed the Fire Adept's progress . . . will welcome familiar characters and cozy settings in the latest entry in this light fantasy series for fans of all ages."
—*Booklist*

The Mancer novels are "delightful . . . fun to read!"
—*South Florida SF Society*

Ace Books by Don Callander

DRAGON COMPANION
DRAGON RESCUE
PYROMANCER
AQUAMANCER
GEOMANCER
AEROMANCER

AEROMANCER

DON CALLANDER

ACE BOOKS, NEW YORK

This book is an Ace original edition,
and has never been previously published.

AEROMANCER

An Ace Book / published by arrangement with
the author

PRINTING HISTORY
Ace edition / September 1997

The Putnam Berkley World Wide Web site address is
http://www.berkley.com

Make sure to check out *PB Plug*,
the science fiction/fantasy newsletter, at
http://www.pbplug.com

ISBN: 0–441–00472–5

ACE®
Ace Books are published by The Berkley Publishing Group, a member
of Penguin Putnam Inc.
200 Madison Avenue, New York, NY 10016.
ACE and the "A" design are trademarks
belonging to Charter Communications, Inc.

PRINTED IN THE UNITED STATES OF AMERICA

10 9 8 7 6 5 4 3 2 1

Chief among those who give me their unqualified support, and quite a few very good suggestions, too, is Andrew Morgan Callander, my grandson.

Andy loves a good fantasy. He's thinking of writing some of his own, one of these days . . . when he's not busy being a Boy Scout, learning to fence, doing very well in middle school, working (and playing) on his father's computer, taking care of his cats . . . and looking forward to this, his very own book.

—Don Callander
May 1994
Pineedle Point
Longwood, Florida

"The profession of Aeromancer—skill in working spells by the virtues of air and other gases, as opposed, say, to an Aquamancer, who works magics using the powers of water in its several forms—has fallen into disrepute in recent centuries, mainly because of a renegade Wizard named Frigeon.

"A new Air Adept, once the apprentice of the aforementioned Frigeon of Eternal Ice, has risen to Journeyman in recent years, accomplishing much to reestablish the good repute of the Craft of Aeromancy.

"He is Cribblon of Farflung . . ."

> —Myrn Manstar Brightglade of Flowring Isle
> Master Aquamancer
> *An Examination of the Current Status of Wizardry*

"A *Wizard's* work is never done, either!"

> —Flarman Flowerstalk
> before a Conventicle of Faerie Scholars

AEROMANCER

Chapter One

Little Lost Filly

"THE trouble with you Geomancers," maintained Journeyman Aeromancer Cribblon of Farflung, flipping an eight-inch flapjack deftly into the air and catching it neatly again in Griddle, "is you want everything immutable, solid as the hills . . . engraved in stone, as it were."

"Of course!" agreed Geomancer Lithold Stonebreaker of Wyvern Hills in the Serecomba Desert of Choin. "How else may one deal with history, geography, economics, politics, sociology, geology, and the other, younger branches of science—such as your own, my dear Cribblon?"

"My own feeling, if I may say so, gracious lady," put in Marbleheart Sea Otter, polishing off his third flapjack stack with thick, amber maple syrup and sweet Valley butter—some of which was still dripping from his long gray whiskers, "is that one can be *too* hard-set in one's expectations. It's a changeling and changeable world, I've observed."

Fire Wizard Douglas Brightglade sat on the edge of the firelight, his son Brand sprawling across one knee and Brand's twin sister Brenda perched on the other, listening to his friends arguing amiably.

His pretty wife, dark-haired Myrn Manstar Brightglade, merely listened and nodded her head when she agreed with a good point. She kept a sharp eye on the twins—in happy contemplation of their daughter and their son at this early-summer-evening picnic, the twins' first ever—on the wide, gently sloping front lawn of Wizards' High beside the ancient Fairy Well.

In a World where you could expect high adventures and sudden disturbances to pop out of just about anywhere, Myrn was most content. Her own Examination for Advancement to full Mastery only lacked a suitable Journey in her Craft. Her Examination could be set as early as Midsummer's Eve, yet a month and three weeks off.

She'd wed her beloved Douglas, completed her studies of her Master's books and demonstrations of Aquamancy atop the high Water Tower of Waterand Palace, and conceived, borne, and greatly enjoyed her twins, all in the space of three hectic years.

Myrn was supremely happy just listening to the good-natured banter between the Journeyman Aeromancer and the Lady Geomancer while finishing the latest two pancakes from cast-iron Griddle nestling cozily in the embers.

As for Flarman Flowerstalk—the famous Pyromancer—he appeared to be sound asleep, having recently devoured a round half-dozen flapjacks. His eyes were closed and his hands were clasped loosely over his ample tummy. He leaned comfortably against the ancient fieldstone curbing of Fairy Well, only half-aware of the pleasant drone of conversation.

The Sea Otter, Douglas's Familiar, lay curled into a furry ball near the fire. Not far off the elder Pyromancer's own Familiar, the tomcat Black Flame, solemnly instructed four of his youngest sons and daughters in the fine feline art of stalking fireflies.

The glowing insects enjoyed the chase at least as much as the kittens.

Black Flame's wives, Pert and Party, rested contentedly on the still sun-warmed stone curbing of the ancient well, watching the Beginner's Class in Stalking . . . and purring compliments to each other on their latest litters.

An errant breeze, called forth by the nighttime cooling of the eastward hills overlooking broad Valley of Dukedom, fanned the fire. Flarman stirred and sat half-erect. Marbleheart and the seven cats stood suddenly very still and turned their heads to listen to what the wind was sighing.

Douglas caught Brand just as he was about to tumble to the grass and held him and his sister close while he turned his inner Wizard's ear into the wind.

Lithold and Cribblon paused in their banter.

Myrn laughed in delight. " 'Tis my Master, come from Warm Seas for a bite of pancake picnic and cool Dukedom evening, I believe!''

As they turned to look at each other in pleasured wonder, a darker part of the night swirled soundlessly against the stars and Augurian of Waterand suddenly appeared in the soft circle of firelight.

"Welcome, Water Adept!" hailed Flarman, sitting straighter yet and beginning to rise.

"Magister!" Douglas and Myrn called in unison.

"Pfumph!" shouted young Brand, waving his arms delightedly.

"Don't get up, please," begged the tall, spare Water Adept, smiling warmly at everyone but especially on his Apprentice. He bent to give her a kiss on the forehead, and then kissed the twins on their rosy cheeks, ignoring the traces of maple syrup still adhering there

Brenda cooed sleepily, and smiled up at him. Brand gurgled in delight again.

They made him comfortable against the well curbing next to his very best friend, Flarman. The cats came to pay their respects, along with the Sea Otter.

Cribblon bowed and shook the Water Adept's hand firmly, beaming with pleasure.

And Lithold, as he sat beside her in the grass, kissed him quickly but firmly on the left cheek.

"Everybody here?" Augurian asked, looking about himself and beaming happily at them all.

"We can call for Wong, if you wish. He could be here by breakfast-time tomorrow, I'm sure," Flarman told his friend.

"No need, Fire Eater. Leave the poor old Choinese gentleman to his stone trees and tea plantations. Doing well, I do believe, even without our intervention, is the Emperor's Foremost Magician?''

"Right as spring rain!" agreed Flarman, sharing a pillow

with his oldest friend. "We didn't expect you just now, Waterman. But you're always welcome ... of that there's no doubt. I even think our Air Adept might find a bit more batter in his bowl to make you some flapjacks—if you're hungry."

Augurian made himself comfortable and agreed that he had come away from Waterand without breaking his fast, so Cribblon busied himself once more cooking the last of the pancakes.

Marbleheart searched the night sky until he saw, as he'd expected, a silently circling smudge of gray-white, high overhead.

"Ho! Ha! Come on down, Featherbrain," he called, standing on his hind legs and waving both forepaws. "You could use some pancakes, too, I imagine!"

Stormy Petrel, Augurian's silent, shy Familiar, needed no further urging, and shortly both the bird and his Master were busy eating pancakes, which were delicious, light, and fluffy, as only an Air Adept can make them.

"How now?" asked Flarman Flowerstalk when the newcomers had finished eating and settled back to enjoy the company, the cool night breeze, and the countless stars wheeling overhead.

"Even a Wizard gets lonely," admitted Augurian with a slow smile.

Across the fire from him Stormy Petrel nodded emphatically.

"I was looking into reports of several of old Frigeon's lost enchantments," the Water Adept continued. "We can discuss them in the morning, if you'll lend me a bit of your hottest spelling, Firebrand."

"Serenit lose track of some of his enchantments?" asked Myrn, shaking her head.

"He was banging them out so fast and so furious for a while there," her Master explained, "that he kept almost no records at all. He now recalls them piecemeal. These spellings he remembered when he started to build a levee to control the spring flooding of the New River a few weeks ago."

"This has been going on and on," Douglas observed. "Maybe we ought to make an audit with Serenit-that-was-Frigeon, to make sure we haven't missed anyone."

"I've been doing just that," admitted Flarman, nodding his

head at his former Apprentice. "It'll be several years yet before we get them all, I'm afraid."

"But I'm *determined* to get them all," insisted Augurian.
"As I need special help, be sure I'll call on you, individually
or as a group."

Flarman sighed and rested his head against the stone curbing.

"Time to get some aspiring young Wizardlings into their
cribs," decided Myrn, rising reluctantly.

"I'll keep an eye on them until they're full asleep," Marbleheart offered.

He and his young Master's wife went off, each bearing a
sleepy toddler, into the High cottage, heading for the double
crib old Michael Wroughter had whipped together on almost
no notice when the word had first spread of the births of *twins*
to the popular young Brightglades.

The older Wizards finally wended their sleepy ways off to
their beds, leaving Douglas and Myrn, returned from bedding
her twins, to quench the cooking fire (which Douglas did with
a gentle word and a gesture of thanks) and pick up stray scraps
of pancake to feed to the hens and their chicks in the morning.

Despite many adventures together, a happy marriage, difficult studies, and the birth of their son and daughter, in many
ways the young couple acted as if they had just met and first
fallen in love.

The low new moon was so romantic and the air so soft after
the sharp nip of winter, and the stars so thunderously silent
above all, they took advantage of the very late evening hour
to sit on the edge of the lawn above Crooked Brook talking
of absolutely nothing important at all.

As the young Fire Adept rose at last to suggest bed, his wife
placed her hand on his sleeve. Following her gaze he sensed
rather than saw, at first, a large and darkling figure moving
along River Road on the far side of the Brook.

"Dwarf?" wondered Myrn. "Goblin, perhaps?"

"Neither Goblin nor Hobgoblin, I'm sure," murmured her
husband. "It came from Precious's house. Yes, I see . . . it *is*
Precious . . . and someone else. A pony, perhaps?"

The confusion wrought by the thin moonlight and deep
shadows under the apple trees was resolved when the figures

stepped onto the loose planks of Old Bridge and the young
Wizards could hear the sounds of a pair of heavy farm-boots
and four dainty hooves drumming on the wood.

"Who've you got there, Grandfather?" Douglas called, in
case the old farmer couldn't make them out in the dappled
moonlight by the old Fairy Well.

"Ah! Douglas!" called Precious. "A friend, I deem! Someone come to ask for your assistance, I suspect."

"At this time of night?" yawned Myrn. "I'm sorry! I didn't
intend to be rude but it's well after midnight and I'm very
sleepy."

"Sleepy comes easy with twin babies," chuckled the orchardman.

Now that they were closer, Douglas and Myrn saw more
clearly who it was accompanied Precious—a small, dark gray
horse dappled with paler patches.

"This is . . . ?" asked Douglas when Precious and his companion drew up before them.

"Drat 'f I know, Wizard!" laughed the orchardman with a
shrug. "Came to the barn over to our place long after I'd fed
the stock. To stay the night with my old Jennifer, I guess. I
heard them two whinnying and snuffling up a storm a few
moments back and went out to see was someone hurting or
affrighted."

"And it was this adorable little pony?" cried Myrn,
charmed by the perfect tininess of the animal. "Hello, my
darling! Welcome to Valley and to Wizards' High!"

"Thing is," Precious went on, speaking softly as he might
of someone with a serious illness. "Thing is she can't—or
won't—talk! Nary a word out of her mouth since I found her
in the stalls with Jennifer and her Roland. Tame enough, and
intelligent, I daresay, but not a word out of her."

Myrn approached the filly carefully, so as not to startle her,
and stroked her neck, running her hands through her long, soft
mane, and clucking consolingly to her all the while.

"Not a *wild* horse, I'd say," guessed Douglas. "Or she'd
not come so close to be petted, not even by Myrn. Shod, too,
I see. And her coat's quite smooth and hardly damaged by
rough travel."

"She's not of Valley," Precious said firmly. "I know every

stallion, mare, colt, filly, mule, and donkey in three days' ride of here. Stranger, she certainly is.''

''Not really a wild pony, by the looks of her,'' agreed Myrn thoughtfully.

She stroked the horse's forelock and smoothed down her silky flank. ''Not really a pony at all. A youngish girl-horse, I'd guess. She's not quite full grown, still very young, don't you think, Precious? She hasn't the too-long legs of a foal.''

Precious leaned thoughtfully against the well curbing and examined the creature in the light of the moon, which was now slipping fast down toward the western horizon.

''A very young lass, but a filly, for a' that,'' he agreed. ''But from whence d'you think she's come?''

''We can ask Captain Possumtail or Squire Frenstil later in the morning,'' decided Douglas, yawning. ''They know more about horses than I or my Sea-sailor lady, I think.''

He let the tiny horse, which stood at her shoulder only as high as his chest, sniff his right palm and wrist.

''Come with us, pretty horseling!'' he urged her gently. ''We've a warm, dry byre with six lady cows and two new calves to keep you company. In the bright of morning, perhaps we can find where you hail from—and why you've come here.''

The tiny beast sniffed at his hand again and nodded her immediate assent.

Observed Myrn, falling in on the other side of the animal, ''She shows clear signs of good breeding. Coming up to the High with us, Precious?''

''No, Mistress Myrn, me dearest! Must return to me good-wife, Lilac. Left her sound asleep abed and if she wakens, it might startle her to find me gone and no sign of me in barn or milk shed, although dawn's only a few hours away.''

He bade them a fond good night . . . ''Or what's left of it!'' . . . and turned back down the sloping lawn toward Old Bridge.

The Wizards led the dainty filly between them up the lawn and around the cottage, hearing old Precious's boots ring solidly on the bridge planks behind them as he recrossed to his fields and orchards and sleeping wife.

Flarman Flowerstalk rose early, despite the lateness of the pancake picnic the evening before, and tended his dairy cows

and chickens, rather than awaken his former Apprentice and
now Master-Wizard-in-his-own-right.

Black Flame accompanied the older Pyromancer to the byre
under the High and watched as Flarman oversaw the milking
of the four High cows (leaving a generous portion for the two
newborn calves), swept out yesterday's bedding with a gesture
that called upon a stray breeze, and waved down fragrant fresh
hay from the loft. The Ladies of the Byre had already filed
out across the cobbled yard and through the gate into the early-
summer meadow just beyond.

Flarman had been startled for a moment at the sight of the
tiny horse, but a few kind words and a handful of last summer's barleycorn mixed with rich Valley oats won her trust
and approval.

"You'll be more comfortable without that blanket, I think,"
Flarman suggested.

He unbuckled the thick leather strap that held a gray blanket
in place across her back. She gave a grateful shake and shed
the covering—and Flarman gasped in surprise!

For the blanket had hidden a pair of beautiful, sturdy wings,
reaching up higher than the horse was tall at the shoulder.
Their feathers were of shimmering gold and pale cream, in
contrast to her gray-and-dapple coat.

The filly shook her wings with evident relief and swung
them up and then down to loosen crimped feathers, almost
sweeping the Wizard off his feet at her first eager flap.

"Oh, I say!" he said with a laugh, catching himself from
falling against a bale of wheat straw, on which he then sat
suddenly. "What a beauty you are, indeed!"

Black Flame jumped on his shoulder, both to assure himself
the old Wizard was unhurt and to get a finer view of the newcomer, who was looking at Flarman apologetically.

"Where did you come from?" asked Flarman, but the pony
merely shook her head sadly and nosed gently against his arm.

"Well then—finish your breakfast," the Wizard advised.
"I'll leave the gate open so you can stretch your legs and
wings in the warm meadow air while we're breaking our own
fast."

The gray-and-gold horseling nodded happily and trotted
from the byre into the morning sunshine; in unspoken thanks

at being unconfined at last, her wings glistened and flashed in
the sun.

"Where in World did she come from?" Flarman asked his
young friend and pupil, Douglas Brightglade.

"The horse?" asked Douglas, reaching for a piece of
golden-brown toast and watching while Butterknife jumped
forward to spread it with creamery butter. Jam Pot stood ready
to add her own sweet strawberry contribution as soon as the
butter was spread and melted in to Butterknife's satisfaction.

"The *flying* horse, you should say," said Flarman.

He described the little animal's golden wings, unfurled in
the bright meadow morning light.

Douglas accepted a generous dollop of strawberry jam from
Jam Pot.

"Precious brought her over early this morning, sir. She
came to seek shelter in his barn sometime late last evening."

"Good old Precious! Never could turn away a stray,"
laughed the older Pyromancer.

"But I must have been half-asleep last night . . . this morning . . . for I didn't notice any wings," Douglas added.

"They only came to light when I unbuckled her saddle-
blanket," Flarman explained.

Myrn Brightglade came singing down the winding stair,
bearing both of her children, one on each hip, bright-eyed
Brenda and sleepy-eyed Brand.

"A *flying* horse!" she exclaimed, popping each twin into a
high chair on either side of her before she sat down. "Must've
been too sleepy to notice!"

"A flying *horse*!" exclaimed Marbleheart, bursting into the
big sunny kitchen from the courtyard. "There's a flying horse
circling the High!"

Douglas and Myrn rushed out to look. Flarman stayed to
watch the twins, who squealed in delight at the antics of Salt
and Pepper fighting a mock duel with shining, sharp fruit
knives in the center of the vast kitchen table for their amusement.

"I discovered her wings when I took off her blanket," explained the older Wizard when the young couple returned.

"She's exercising them, just now," Myrn said with a nod.
"So beautiful! We just waved at her. No need to interrupt,

especially if her wings have been bound for very long under a blanket.''

''I never heard of any such beast in this part of World,'' mused her husband.

Quickly checking the breakfasting progress of his children, he fell to eating his oatmeal with a will. The strawberry-jammed toast quickly disappeared, to be replaced by a second cup of steaming coffee with heavy cream and a plate of scrambled eggs and sausages, all hot and savory.

''I've read of them in my studies,'' Myrn told them, following her husband's lead, but keeping an eye on the twins at the same time. ''They're not native to this part of World, are they? I seem to recall mention of them in the distant Grasslands.''

''I think you have it, there,'' agreed Flarman, tucking into a bowl of sliced peaches. ''I know I've never seen one outside of books, nor heard of one in this part of World. What do you say about it, Rainman?''

This last was directed to Augurian, who just then entered the kitchen from the hall.

''Flying horses?'' he asked, sitting at the table opposite Flarman. ''Cream, please! I've heard of them . . . but never in our corner of World.''

Creamer dashed over to the Water Adept's place and tilted a generous dollop into his coffee. Sugar Caster was standing right behind Creamer. The Water Adept loved sweet and creamy coffee with his breakfast.

Blue Teakettle, supervising breakfast preparations from her usual perch on the front of Range, clucked impatiently at Griddle. He'd spent the night producing perfect pancakes over an open fire and now was being asked to grill rashers of hickory-smoked bacon and patties of pork sausage for the people of Wizards' High and their guests, but with good will and savory results.

''Have you ever seen one, Magister?'' asked Myrn of Augurian.

Brand decided it was time to feed his mother's left ear some oat porridge, but she deftly managed to forestall catastrophe and guide the spoon back to its proper orifice.

''Only from a distance,'' Augurian replied thoughtfully. ''Once, long ago, when my travels took me into the Nearer East for a short while.''

"Never been that far east, myself," murmured Flarman, pushing back his empty porridge bowl and reaching for another piece of hot buttered toast. "What's it like?"

"Mountainous. Dry. Sandy desert or endless grassy steppes. Sparsely inhabited," replied Augurian. "Interesting *flora* and *fauna*—of which flying horses are only one of many. I spent little time there, unfortunately. The War against The Darkness interfered with youthful wanderings, just as it did yours, Firestarter."

"Are all animals there mute?" wondered his pretty pupil, rejoining the conversation now that her twins were actively engaged in feeding themselves, not each other . . . nor the kittens waiting expectantly for droppings on the floor under their high chairs.

"No, I don't recall any dumb animals among those I encountered there. But I never really met a *pegasus* close-to," admitted the Water Adept. "They must speak, for they are known far and wide for their classical poetry, I've heard."

"I think I'll look into that question this very morning," murmured Douglas. "I've a feeling this horse-with-wings has a tale to tell, if she could or would talk."

"I agree," said Flarman. "I, too, will pursue some investigations in that line, m'boy. Let's agree to compare notes over lunch, eh?"

Douglas and Flarman left the Water Adepts . . . Douglas to climb to the library at the top of the stairs, and the older Fire Wizard for his workshop under Wizards' High.

"Have you an assignment for me?" asked Myrn, gathering up her children.

"No," replied Augurian. "I'm going to do some research on the subject, myself. I'd like to discuss it with you, once you've settled our young persons."

He tickled Brand under the chin, much to the boy's glee, ignoring the oatmeal that had lodged there during the baby's attempts to feed himself.

"Uncle!" cried his twin sister, and the Water Adept paused to give her a kiss and a pat. She was much the neater eater of the two, he noticed.

"After your baths," Myrn told her twins with a warm smile, "I understand Bronze Owl'll talk to you of fairies, goblins, and banshees and such."

"Nanshees!" crowed two-year-old Brand gleefully. "Bronze Owl'll tell us of Nanshees!"

"Nothing frightens these two," Augurian chuckled. "Join me when you can, Journeyman. We must speak of your Journeying."

Myrn threw him a kiss and nodded eagerly.

"Come along, little Banshees," she said to her babes. "No, this time you shall walk. Flying spells are all very well, but they don't do anything to develop strong young legs, do they?"

While the several Wizards went off to research the origins of the little winged horse, Marbleheart Sea Otter headed for the still-icy waters of Crooked Brook, intending to swim a bit and check on the development of a bed of freshwater oysters he'd planted in the shadowed water under Old Bridge.

On the way he stopped to greet the Ladies of the Byre, contentedly cropping tender spring grasses and watching their two calves cavort in the sunshine.

"What do you think of this winged horse?" Marbleheart asked the Matriarch of the Milch Cows.

She lowered her head to look the Otter in the eye and then shook her horns.

"No comment, eh?" the web-footed animal said, sighing. "Well, that makes it more difficult, doesn't it? She not being able or willing to speak, as it were."

The beautiful little horse trotted over to greet him shyly, nodding and pawing the damp earth in a pleased-to-meet-you fashion.

"Is it that you *can't* speak?" Marbleheart wondered. "Or that you don't *care* to?"

The horse, given the choice, managed to indicate her complete inability to speak.

"Was it ever thus?" asked the Otter, shaking his head sadly.

The filly shook her head also.

"You could once talk? Is that it?"

The little horse nodded vigorously.

"And you miss it, don't you?"

The horse signaled a definite "Yes!" by bobbing her head up and down several times.

"Well, the 'mancers'll fix you up, never fear—if it's possible for their powers of Wizardry. We've got a whole bunch of expert Wizards here, you see. You came to the right place!''

He *galumped* off to check on his oysters and when he looked back later, he noticed the little horse looking much more chipper than she had, teaching the calves to jump over stones on the bank of the Brook as their mothers and aunts looked on contentedly.

''There's a story in yon pretty head,'' Marbleheart said to Augurian's Familiar, Stormy Petrel, who'd come to watch his good friend swim and dive.

Stormy nodded judiciously.

Chapter Two

Journeying

AS it turned out, the discussion of the flying horse was delayed.

In midday when Douglas came down from the library seeking his lunch he found Prince Bryarmote seated at the big kitchen table, calmly munching one of Blue Teakettle's best molasses cookies and sipping steaming tea.

"Ho!" cried the young Wizard, clapping the burly Dwarf on his broad and muscular back. "Well met! How're the cookies?"

"None better!" Bryarmote said with a laugh, giving the young Pyromancer a rib-rattling hug. "Have one! Take two!"

Douglas took a pair of the delicious dark brown wafers marked with artistic cross-hatchings and swirls of white frosting by a certain artistic Fork, and called for a glass of milk.

Milk Pitcher waddled across the wide tabletop on her short legs to fill his glass. Blue Teakettle signaled to Dinner Bell to make an appeal, calling everyone to the midday meal.

"What brings you here?" Douglas asked his old friend. "You're certainly looking fit and fiddled!"

"Never better," agreed Bryarmote. "Marriage does agree with us both, I see. Where's your bride and the little Wizardlings? I didn't see them when I arrived a few minutes ago."

"The children are in the charge of Bronze Owl, who's giving them early lessons on fairy-folk and half-worldlings," mumbled Douglas around the second bite of molasses cookie. "Owl'll bring them to lunch now that Bell has pealed."

Sure enough, within two minutes the entire company of residents and guests of Wizards' High appeared from all directions, for lunch was a time to discuss the morning's activities and prepare for afternoon's work.

Flarman, the last to arrive, wiped a smudge of soot from his nose and plumped down in his chair at the head of the long table, greeting his old friend the Dwarf most heartily.

"Welcome, Delver!" he cried. "I should have known you were coming, for I noticed in late morning that Blue Teakettle set an extra place at table."

"She always knows, somehow, doesn't she?" marveled the Dwarf in admiration.

From her perch on the front edge of Range, Blue Teakettle burbled happily and bobbed a thank-you curtsy to the Dwarf, spilling drops of hot water which sizzled merrily when they struck the hot stovetop.

Everyone wanted to know how Princess Cristol fared these days, and whether she was yet with child. Bryarmote and Cristol had been married for several years.

"These things take considerably longer for Dwarfs than for you Humans," Bryarmote insisted with a bright crimson blush, but he was pleased that they'd asked. "All in good time, dear friends!"

"Why do you come at this time?" asked Douglas at last, no longer able to control his large Bump of Curiosity. Flarman nodded eagerly and Myrn clapped her hands softly.

"Nothing World-shaking, probably," replied the Dwarf. "A matter of a missing neighbor, only."

"Neighbor?" asked Flarman, leaning forward. "Who? Not someone of Fairstrand, surely. They're your nearest neighbors."

"No, not a Fairstrander, although they first brought it to my attention when they delivered fresh fish to my kitchens, as is their weekly habit. Captain Beckett of Fairstrand personally came to me three . . . no, four . . . days back. He'd called at New Land's Flarmansport—"

"Named for a certain World-famous Fire Wizard, you know," said Flarman Flowerstalk with a chuckle.

"As we all well know," agreed the Dwarf dryly. "Clangeon told Captain Beckett that Serenit has gone missing!"

"Serenit! Missing?" cried Cribblon. "That's not like Serenit."

"But true," insisted Bryarmote. "He hasn't been seen in his home or valley since last Saturday morning, according to Clangeon."

"That's not like Serenit," echoed Lithold Stonebreaker, frowning.

Douglas and Myrn nodded agreement.

"It is, however, very much like his *old* self . . . Frigeon," said Bronze Owl solemnly.

"No, I don't think that," Douglas said sternly. "Besides, Serenit lost all Frigeon's wizardly powers when he was defeated."

"Still . . ." The Owl shrugged with a soft clash of metal pinions.

"Much more likely he was stolen away or led astray," considered Augurian. "What does Clangeon think?"

"He's beside himself! Not much help, I have to admit," said Bryarmote sourly.

"Is it possible," said Cribblon, looking very concerned, "that Serenit has backslid? Is it?"

"Possible . . . but I don't believe it for a minute!" cried Douglas. "He has no Magical Powers, as I said."

"If he got 'em once," Bryarmote growled darkly, "he could get 'em again."

"Not without our noticing," Myrn insisted, quite firmly. "No, I don't think Serenit's backslid. He's become lost . . . or captured . . . or something like."

The company at the luncheon table was silent for a time before Myrn laid aside her napkin and said, "Well!"

"What's in your pretty head, my dear?" Lithold asked.

"I believe in Serenit, as Douglas does. If he's disappeared, there's a good . . . or a bad . . . reason for it, Magisters!"

Flarman pushed back from his place, leaving his lunch half-finished.

"I'll have a look into this at once, if you'll excuse me. I feel responsible to and for Serenit."

"As do I," agreed Augurian. "I'll come help you, if I may."

"Come and most welcome," replied the Fire Wizard. "Douglas? Myrn?"

"Go ahead, beloved," said Myrn to Douglas. "I'll see the twins put down for their nap, and join you in the workshop."

By the time she arrived, the Wizards and Familiars had cleared a large space on Flarman's vast and cluttered work-table and were watching him set up a complicated arrangement of flasks, glass and rubber tubing, spiraled condensers, metal stands, petcocks, clamps, and a large crystal retort half-filled with an oily orange liquid that roiled and burbled of its own volition.

"We're setting up a Tracer Spell on Serenit," explained Douglas in a whisper to his wife, so as not to disturb the working Wizard. "Watch now!"

Flarman lighted the spirit lamp under the retort with a flick of his right index finger. The bright blue-and-yellow flame caressed the round bottom of the retort and the orange liquid began at once to boil and give off tendrils of pinkish steam.

"It'll turn pale yellow as the Essence of Searching passes into steam," Augurian murmured. "Now. . . ."

The long, tapered spout of the retort directed pink steam into the coiled glass condenser, where, in the bottom of each coil, a pale yellow liquid began to condense, pushed onward by the force of more steam from the retort.

This yellow liquid dropped steadily from the end of the retort's long spout into a small glass beaker. With each additional drop the matter in the beaker became darker and bluer, until it took on the hue of pure indigo.

Douglas handed his Master a pair of thick gloves and, when the older Wizard had donned them, a burning spill of clean pinewood.

"Watch your eyes!" warned Flarman as he reached for the beaker.

He waited until they were ready, then touched the burning splinter to the deep blue liquid.

There was a brilliant flash of light, and the entire workshop filled with an acrid, heavy gray smoke which felt bitterly cold on their hands and faces.

Myrn gasped and Douglas threw his cloak about her shoulders, for the temperature in the workshop suddenly plunged close to freezing.

Flarman, at a critical juncture, cried out three words of powerful magic.

"Argamon! Freestatic! Grabbleo!"

The smoke flinched, as if a fresh, warm breeze had blown through it, and retreated quickly to a far, dark corner, the dimmest part of the large workshop, where it hung thickly in the air, turning and twisting about—in the vague shape, suddenly, of a cloaked figure.

Two burning points of light appeared when the figure's head lifted to look at them. The "eyes" blinked three times, slowly.

"A Spector!" murmured Douglas to Myrn, who was clinging tightly to his arm. "A Watcher . . . I think."

"Yes, a Watcher," agreed Flarman, removing the heavy gloves. "We can ask it questions . . . for a while. It must answer the truth. But stick to the matter at hand. Time is limited!"

He turned to face the ghostly Spector.

"Where is Serenit, First Citizen of New Land?" he demanded without preamble.

The Watcher wavered for a moment before the answer came, in a thin, chilly voice from a great distance.

"Do you mean the former Aeromancer known as Frigeon?" it asked.

"Call me 'sir,' " Flarman demanded sharply. "You know my rank!"

"Sir!" said the apparition rather sullenly.

"Serenit *was* Frigeon, of course," Flarman said steadily. "Now he is Serenit. Where is he?

Again the smoky figure paused, turning as if consulting unseen others behind him in the deepest darkness.

"Serenit-that-was-Frigeon, if that is he of whom you inquire, sir, is beyond our ken," the Spector said slowly. "I can't help you except to say he went east, not north, south, or west . . . nor up nor down, for that matter. Seek him eastward . . . sir!"

"Good enough!" said Flarman with some satisfaction. "Tell me, did he leave of his own desire?"

Again a long pause, but Flarman and his friends waited patiently.

"No, Serenit was carried off against his will, sir!" said the smoke figure at last, precisely, coldly.

Flarman paused, glanced at Augurian, then at Douglas, Myrn, and the others in turn.

"You cannot say exactly where he is?" asked Augurian. "Just that he is in the east?"

The dim figure turned to face his new questioner, bowing slightly to the Water Adept, recognizing his Powers.

"He was taken against his will. He is somewhere in the Nearer East. He has no Powers of his own to project his location to you, sirs! Yet he needs assistance, and quickly."

"Who holds him?" asked Douglas.

The Spector considered the young Wizard for a moment before bowing.

"I cannot say, young Pyromancer. If I could, I would . . . for you and your Masters are worthy of the Light and I am pledged to assist your cause, if and as well as I can, I and my . . . sensors."

He paused, hooded head cocked sideways, as if listening again to someone behind him.

"I add only that he's held by a force I cannot comprehend at all. If I could, I would tell you, sirs."

There was a long silence following this statement.

"Tell us," Myrn Brightglade broke into the silence. "Is Serenit in danger? Does his capture bode ill for World?"

The smoke figure shivered and began to thin. Only the burning eyes remained, regarding the pretty young Journeyman steadily, but not with hostility.

If anything, with deep, deep sadness.

"I can help you no further, Mistress. Except to say . . ."

His figure was all but invisible, like smoke dispersing in a gentle breeze.

". . . it bodes ill for World and the Light. Someone must go to this . . . Serenit's . . . rescue . . ."

Myrn leaned forward to hear his last words.

". . . a long, dangerous Journey!"

And the eyes blinked and the thinning smoke swirled and trailed out the open transom above the workshop door.

The company sat in silence.

"I had . . . other questions to ask it," said Myrn, unsteadily. "Can you call it back, Magister?"

"I cannot," said Flarman, looking quite weary.

Augurian said, "Perhaps if *I* tried?"

"It's not your *forte*," said Flarman, flatly. "He has said Myrn is the best one to rescue poor Serenit. I just wish the apparition could have told us more of the nature of his captors."

"Is it necessary to rescue Serenit?" asked Marbleheart, speaking for the first time. "Maybe we should just . . . let him go?"

"Nonsense!" cried Myrn. "He may have been the worst of wicked Magickers once but he's been a good friend since he reformed."

"True," Douglas said, nodding, "and I have a strong feeling that the danger is as much to the rest us as it is to Serenit of New Land."

"I have to agree," said the Lady Geomancer. "Flarman? Myrn must go on this Journeying. Do you agree?"

"Entirely." Flarman sighed. "Little we can do to make it easier or safer, except the things we've tried to teach and show her. Not even Douglas can assist, I'm afraid, beyond love and good advice."

"It's something must be done," decided Douglas, taking Myrn's hand in his own and looking into her Sea-green eyes. "Do you agree, companion?"

"I agree, understand, and expect the restrictions, just as you did in the very dangerous matter of the Witches of Coven," answered Myrn, sitting straighter on her stool. "I'll prepare myself and leave at once!"

Actually it was three days before she managed to get away.

There were the twins to see to.

And her husband to reassure.

And spells to review and to discuss with her Master.

And so many people to bespeak and arrangements to make, as well.

When it came to the twins, she and her husband considered taking them to stay with her mother and father on distant Flowering Isle in the midst of Warm Sea. But they decided to leave them in the care of Douglas's mother, Glorianna, and ship-wright father, at nearby Perthside.

"If it takes longer than a few weeks," Myrn said to Douglas as he prepared to take the twins to his mother's house overlooking Farango Waters, "you must arrange for my mother to share the care of our precious babes, Douglas."

"I'll do that. Don't worry, sweetheart! There are fifty or a hundred beings within call who'd move World to protect and care for our children."

"I know," said the mother with a deep sigh. "But I still feel only you and I can do the job properly. I don't want them to forget me!"

"No fear of that," said Douglas, kissing her on the forehead. "You're quite unforgettable, believe me!"

She spent a half-day alone with her Master, Augurian of Waterand. They reviewed the Aquamantic Arts the fisher-lass from Flowering Isle had learned in three years of his careful instruction, to make sure there were no voids in her water-lore.

"The most useful spells you already know quite well and use almost every day," Augurian said calmly. "Your best equipments will be a cool head and a large dose of common sense, my dear stepdaughter."

Yet, she could tell he was upset and worried . . . although *that* she'd always expected of him, when the time came for her Journeying.

"Magister . . . beloved teacher and great friend! Everything you've taught me is engraved on my heart and mind, believe me. I'll be just fine!"

"In my mind I know it." Augurian sighed, then shed a tear, something she had never seen from him before. "It's in my heart that I have fears."

Flarman sat her on a tall, three-legged stool in the underhill workshop. The day after their interview with the smoke Spector had turned hot and thundery, but here in the Wizard's workrooms it remained cool, dry, and still.

"I know you've the knowledge and skills to do even the most difficult jobs," Flarman told her. "I can't give you much magical help, under the rules, but I don't need to. Here . . ."

He laid in her hand a round ivory box with a tight-fitted lid.

Opening it, Myrn found that it was a simple magnetic compass. The needle was painted black on one end and was clear silver on the other. It jiggled nervously back and forth as she moved it.

"It'll tell you which way to turn," Flarman explained solemnly. "And bring you safely home, no matter how far you wander."

"Magister . . . I . . . ," began the young lady.

She exclaimed in surprised delight as he produced a scroll of fine, paper-thin parchment, rolled inside a silver tube tied with red silk tassels at either end.

Her Journeyman's certificate!

"Don't need to carry it with you," Flarman told her. "Douglas always keeps his here, hidden in the stair newel-post. Even when he went to Old Kingdom to take on those wicked Witches of Coven. Actually it isn't worth anything, except to apprise World of your schooling in the Powers."

"I'll put mine in the newel-post, too," decided Myrn. "With Douglas's Certificate of Mastery."

Flarman laughed.

"No one will ever doubt your Powers or good training, beautiful child! You know that we'll be keeping as close an eye on you as Wizardly possible, within the rules?"

"I expect that," said Myrn with a pleased nod.

"And we'll try to catch you if you should trip. I only wish we knew what it is you're facing. At least Douglas had a fairly good idea about the Witches of Coven before he tackled them."

"No reason to worry," insisted Myrn. "I'm no grand heroine, Magister! If it becomes too much for me I'll call for help, you can be sure."

"That's the best thing you could have said to calm my fears," cried Flarman. "Let's go get hot chocolate and some of Blue's special pecan cookies!"

The moon was beginning to show signs of shrinking to half-full when Myrn and Douglas perched together on the curb of the Fairy Well on the sheep-cropped front lawn of the High.

It was close upon midnight.

Tomorrow Myrn would leave for the Nearer East.

They said little, occasionally squeezed one another's hand or gave a loving pat or a kiss.

The twins were long asleep. In the morning Douglas would take them on horseback down along Crooked Brook, through Trunkety Town and on to Perthside and his father's shipyards and his mother's sunny home above busy Farango Waters.

Glorianna and the older Douglas would be ecstatic. Their grandchildren would be absolutely delighted to have a large number of new playmates from the families of ship's carpenters in their grandfather's yards and among the busy nuns of Glothersome Abbey. They would run and shout, do easy chores, go to school, climb trees, and swim and boat in the long, narrow Waters.

Douglas reminded her, "And I'll see them every weekend, while I can. The change will be good for them, Myrn."

"I tell myself that, too. But it isn't easy to leave one's husband and one's children, even in such good company and in such good cause."

Douglas nodded but had the good sense to say no more.

"If you need me . . . forget the Journeying," he added at last. "You've plenty of time for that. Call me and I'll come by fastest means."

"Of course I will," his wife said. "I'm no bedtime-book heroine, believe me."

"Well, you really are, if you look at yourself from outside," said her young husband and dearest friend. "But that shouldn't surprise anyone."

"You'll write my mother and father?" she asked, changing the subject.

"Of course. And we'll go and spend some time with them on Flowring Isle, after Midsummer's Eve," Douglas promised. "You should be finished in Nearer East long before then."

"I hope this Journeying doesn't delay my Examination," worried Myrn. "I so wanted to get it behind me."

"It'll come anytime you're ready, sweetheart. I promise you!"

The gibbous moon reached its zenith and began to tumble down toward the western horizon.

Douglas clasped his wife's hands, looked at her beautiful face in the moonlight, and said, "I love you, Myrn Manstar!"

"And I do so love *you,* Douglas Brightglade, husband and

lover! I'm so very happy that we met and loved and married."

"You'll be just fine," he insisted, and this time he sounded as if he really meant it.

The problem of exactly where to go (the Nearer East was a huge, rather underpopulated area on the far shore of Sea) was finally decided by the elder Wizards after much magical tracery and long computations.

"Serenit did manage to leave a faint trail," explained Flarman, speaking for himself, for Lithold, and for Augurian. "A person of his former powers always leaves traces, even when he doesn't intend to."

"Do I leave traces, too?" asked Myrn, startled at the thought.

"Of course! Like your perfume or the smell of vanilla when you've been baking a cake," Lithold said. "I can always tell where you are, somehow. You have a special aura, and so do Flarman and Douglas and Augurian . . . even Marbleheart. But you, especially."

"That's comforting, anyway," decided the new Journeyman Aquamancer. "But how do I get started?"

"Fairly easy," replied Augurian.

He reached in his wide left sleeve and withdrew a single strand of pearls of graduated size, from a single large, perfectly round and pure white gem in the middle of the string down to tiny pinkish-gray seed-pearls at either end.

"This I was saving for you when you'd gained Mastery, but now is a better time," he explained, fastening the gold clasp about her neck. "These are Pearls of Passage. I collected them over the years . . . centuries, in fact. I intended to give them to my own bride, if I ever found one. . . ."

"Then you must keep them for her," insisted Myrn, shaking her head. "You're still young enough to marry, Magister! And someday you will, I'm sure."

"In that case, *you* can give them to my chosen bride," said Augurian, chuckling and putting his hands behind his back. "*You* need them now. And if I ever meet the lady I wish to marry, I'll have other gifts to present to her . . . one of which will be you, as a stepdaughter!"

He steadfastly refused to take the pearls back, although Myrn continued to insist.

"They'll carry you to far places and bring you safely home," Augurian explained after she'd at last agreed to accept his gift. "Unlike the Feather Pin Bryarmote's mother gave you and which you gave to Douglas, this talisman will serve you, or anyone who knows how to use it, for as long as you wear it. You can give it away, and take it back again, and it will work for you the second time, too."

"It's truly beautiful!" exclaimed Myrn. "How does it work?"

"Much like the Feather Pin," replied the Water Wizard. "Merely say, *'Pearly, Pearly, Do!'* and make a travel wish ... and you're on your way! Not instantaneous translation, mind you, but quicker than quick! Just tell it where you wish to go."

"And were *do* I wish to go?" Myrn asked, fingering the lustrous gems about her neck.

"Port of Samarca," Flarman advised. "That's the last place with any trace of Serenit's passing. We can't give you much help beyond that ... at least not yet."

"Keep in touch!" advised her Master, giving her a tight embrace.

"Write if you can," begged Douglas. "Mother'll take good care of our babies and won't let them forget you for a minute!"

"Douglas is going to be busy tracing these new enchantments Serenit recently remembered," explained Flarman. "We'll all be on call, if and when you need us."

"Wish I were going along." Marbleheart sighed, then sniffled just a bit. "I yearn to travel again, to swim in new oceans and rivers."

"Sweet, silly Familiar!" Myrn laughed, and ruffled the soft fur behind his ears. "Your Master'll be flying you off somewhere shortly, if I know my husband. And if I call him, I'll need you too, dearest Rockhead."

They stood on the front stoop of Wizards' High, always a good departure point for any trip.

Myrn had said good-bye to Blue Teakettle and all the kitchen utensils, as well as the Ladies of the Byre and the High's chickens, too, early that morning. Pert and Party came to see her off, leading their kittens to get a parting scratch on

their backs, arching with pleasure. Black Flame stood proudly
by and accepted a loving caress, also.

"Well, I better get going," said the Journeyman Aquamancer. She took a deep breath to say the Pearls' magic words. . . .

She felt a warm, moist touch on her arm and, looking about,
found the little gray horse had appeared beside her.

"My dear little flier!" she exclaimed. "Do you come to say
good-bye, too?"

The horseling shook her head; definitely no!

"Then *what*?" Myrn wondered.

The little horse pushed against Myrn's left hip and tossed
her head twice, pointing her pink nose eastward.

"I think she wants you to take her along," Douglas guessed.

"Yes, indeed, that's just what she wants," agreed Flarman.
"She's heard you're going toward her homeland."

"Good company!" Myrn laughed and then, seating herself
gracefully on the little horse, sidesaddle, spoke the words that
would propel them both into distant adventure.

Chapter Three

Port of Samarca

A grizzled Wayness Seacaptain named Mallet strove to hold his hot temper in check.

"It does no good to get angry at such landlubberly governmental *flunkies*," he rumbled in an aside to his ship's clerk. "They just get more and more righteously stubborn, I've found."

"Now, Sir Port Master," he began again, even managing to smile ingratiatingly at the pompous, portly Port official, "explain what it is you require. Do I misunderstand? We must wait *five full days* before we can set foot ashore?"

"Truly, that *is* the law," murmured the plump bureaucrat, nodding his turbaned head gravely. "Five nightfalls at anchor here . . . *then* you may came ashore. After that, I *may* give permission for your crew to take their leisure in our city."

He spoke softly but firmly, paused, then said, as quietly, "Of course, I *may* be able to hasten permission for yourself. Unfortunately, I'm a rather busy man. . . ."

"How much?" Mallet ground out, trying very hard to maintain his pleasant smile.

The Port Master diffidently named a medium-sized sum. Mallet gave in after a bit more polite demur.

"New places . . . new ploys!" he quoted to his First Officer, a younger Westonguer appropriately named Pilot. "Two nights to wait! Well, break the news gently to the crew. We'll have a landfall party here aboard, tonight. Extra ration of rum. Tomorrow we'll paint and scrub and mend-and-make to pass the time . . . and impress the locals.''

Pilot grinned broadly. He was the kind of First Mate who enjoyed nothing better than a good field-day. There were always so many extra things that needed to be done to clean, improve, and repair a sailing ship like the two-masted fore-and-aft-rigged *Encounter* after a month's Sea voyage.

"What can we expect, once we've . . . ah . . . observed the required formalities?'' Mallet asked the Samarcan official.

"I will publish your name and post your cargo list, as is my duty,'' replied the Port Master blandly. "On the appointed morning, if all goes well, I will meet you ashore below the Great Bastion, there, and accompany you to Merchant's Hall. There you will meet our merchants and be able to sell and buy, to our mutual benefit, it is to be hoped.''

He reached into his robe and produced a packet of papers bound with yellow silk cording.

"You should study our Port Regulations,'' he went on, handing the file to the Seacaptain. "Notice there are certain . . . ah . . . imports which are *strictly* prohibited. If you have such on board, keep them locked in your holds, please, honored Captain. Do not mention them at any time to the Merchants of Samarca. Regulations will warn you of the penalties for illegal importation of forbidden goods. I assure you they are swift and . . . effective.''

Mallet nodded his understanding and thumbed through the sheaf of papers quickly, noting frequent headings warning "PROHIBITED GOODS—*Import on Penalty of Instant Confiscation, Incarceration, & Possible Execution.*''

"Of course, we do not wish to make any trouble for ourselves or for you, Sir Port Master,'' he assured the chubby little man. "May I offer you a cup of tea, or a sip of *fungwah*? That's a brandy produced in the northern part of the great Choin Empire. Most heartwarming, if I may say so.''

The Port Master, whose name was Alama Sheik, licked his thick lips in sudden interest.

"A *taste* of the brandy, honored Captain, but no more! You will note that all fermented and distilled beverages are strictly prohibited entry to Samarca . . . on pain of bodily dismemberment!''

Nevertheless, when he'd tasted the excellent and powerful liquor of Choin, he politely asked for a second glass, which he downed at a gulp, making sure none of his marines, standing at attention at the accommodation ladder, could see him.

''Quite—ah—*wicked*!'' He coughed, handing the ship's steward his empty tumbler. ''Ah . . . I may require a second visit to your *Encounter* on tomorrow evening, good Captain!''

Aha! thought Mallet.

He bowed deeply to the bureaucrat and assured him he would be welcome aboard *Encounter* any day or any hour.

''Unfortunately, my duties . . . you understand?'' said the official, forgetting to appear stiff and formal. ''I . . . ah . . . may be required to reinspect your Bill of Health tomorrow evening.''

''Anytime, Revered Port Master,'' repeated Mallet blandly. ''Merely send us a few minutes' warning so we may properly prepare for your visits.''

''It'll probably be well after dark,'' warned the Port Master in a whisper. ''Press of daily business, you understand.''

''Perfectly,'' replied the Wayness Seacaptain dryly.

Two evenings later—the intervening day having been spent in scraping, painting, mending, remaking, rerigging, and scrubbing until *Encounter* shone like a new-launched flagship and all but sparkled on the clear green waters of Samarca Harbor— the lookout hailed the quarterdeck. A sailing skiff, which the locals called *''dhow,''* stood off a short distance in the gloaming, flashing a signal for permission to come alongside.

''Ho!'' snorted Mallet. ''Our good, portly, pickled Port Master, I'll wager! Come to sample forbidden *fungwah* again . . . and again, without soldiers and underflunkies.''

''No bet! 'Tis a sure thing,'' his First Mate said, grinning. ''Shall I signal him to come aboard, Skipper?''

''Of course! He's undoubtedly an important official of the Sultanate, or whatever they call their fancy government here. But, quick and quiet! No need to tell the entire harbor about it.''

After the first appreciative nip of *fungwah,* the official relaxed and examined the sparse comfort of *Encounter*'s small main cabin.

"You may come ashore to meet the Merchants tomorrow morning at the third hour, Seacaptain," he announced rather pompously. "There's considerable interest in trading with Dukedom, especially in the fine hempen rope and the iron implements you've brought for sale."

"Will I be permitted to bring samples ashore to Merchant's Hall tomorrow?" inquired Mallet, carefully refilling the Port Master's glass to the brim.

"Oh yes! Whatever permitted goods you wish!" cried the official, sipping the *fungwah* eagerly.

Now he drank more appreciatively, savoring the mellow old brandy on his tongue. Mallet poured a half-glass for himself. They were alone in the main cabin, for the official had come in mufti—unofficially and without his usual armed guards and attendants.

"This is wonderfully excellent . . . ah . . . refreshment," commented Alama Sheik. "I sincerely regret it must, by decree of our idealistic young Sultan, be forbidden to our shores."

"Yet, it's wonderfully . . . *medicinal,* you might say," suggested the Seacaptain. "Guaranteed to relax one and put one's troubles in perspective, I'm told, if used with moderation . . . and circumspection."

"Medicinal?" considered the Port Master, taking a tiny sip more. "I fear that ruse has been overused in the past by unscrupulous traders. No, you would have to obtain the *approval* of a licensed physician . . ."

Mallet shook his head, sadly.

"I'm at a disadvantage there, worthy Port Master. I wouldn't know how to contact a licensed physician here. I've only met the youthful Quarantine Doctor. I don't suppose he . . . ?"

'No, no! I see I must come to your assistance, good Captain Mallet! Let me see . . . do I know a fully licensed physician who could attest to the . . . ah . . . therapeutic properties of your *fungwah*?"

Captain Mallet took a tiny sip of the Choin brandy. It burned pleasantly down toward his stomach.

"Oh, what *is* the matter with my memory these days!" cried

the official. "A very good, old friend, one Saleem Abala, has just returned to the Port from the Sultanic Presence. Having been a Physician in service to our gracious Sultan for two years, he needs to recoup lost fees. I think we might . . . ah . . . *persuade* him of the . . . er . . . *medicinal* value of this *fungwah*. In fact, I'm quite sure of it!"

"Could I offer a friendly gift to the good Physician, in token of my gratitude?" asked the Seacaptain with exaggerated politeness.

"Heavens, no! No, Dr. Abala will charge only the usual Inspection Portion—one-fiftieth part of the value of the . . . medicine. His lawful fee for consultation, of course."

"One *fiftieth*!" Mallet choked. "Ah, well, if that's the custom here, Honored Guest. I have no desire to circumvent Sultanic law, of course."

"Of course not!" the other said with a chuckle, polishing off his third portion of *fungwah*. "If you will place the matter of this quite potent *medicine*, which has amazingly and suddenly cured several of my own personal maladies, with me I will certainly, in my poor fumbling way, make the proper and quite legal arrangements."

"Whew!" breathed Mallet to his second-in-command after the tipsy Port functionary had rolled over the side and been lowered carefully into his waiting *dhow*. "I thought only the servants of the Empire of Choin were so sticky in the palms!"

"According to what I've heard from the bumboat-men who sold us fruits and vegetables—as well as information—yestere'en and this morning, this is the safest way to proceed in Samarca, Captain."

"It doesn't surprise me," rumbled Mallet, wiping his forehead, for the cabin had become stuffy and hot. "I must keep my eyes open, and my ears, too, about this distant Sultan and his servants. What have you learned so far?"

The Mate sipped a bit of the powerful brandy, nodding his head all the time.

"He makes his capital three or four days distant, inland, this Sultan Trobuk. A fair and just young ruler, I'm told, but that may be just local flummery. Still, so far no one has gainsaid his power . . . or his popularity."

"He's ill-served by such as our friend the Port Master,"
growled the Westonguer.

"Not really! It's rather the way of life and business here in
the Nearer East," First Officer Pilot maintained.

"We'll learn their ways soon enough," decided Mallet. "I
wish you could come with me tomorrow morning, but I'll feel
much safer if you remain in command here while I'm ashore."

He went on deck for a breath of fresh air. The Mate considered the half-inch of brandy left in the *fungwah* flask, but
shook his head, corked the flask tightly, and followed his captain up onto the quarterdeck.

The official shore-going of *Encounter*'s Captain completely
obscured the arrival, the next forenoontide, of Myrn and the
winged filly, whom Myrn had decided to call Nameless.

The eyes of hangers-about along the docks and even of the
watchful Sultanate Guards were drawn to the colorful pag-
eantry on the landing below Great Bastion, the squat stone fort
of obviously great strength on the northern edge of the inner
harbor.

Word of the arrival of the captain of a ship from Dukedom—the first such arrival in over two centuries—had spread
far and wide, attracting all eyes to the ceremonial welcoming.

Captain Mallet, carefully trimmed and combed and dressed
in his best uniform of gold-and-blue broadcloth edged with
tastefully subdued white lace, wearing a ceremonial sword at
his side and a cocked hat on his head, stepped ashore from
Encounter's quarter-boat to the ringing salutes of long, up-
curving, polished-brass trumpets, to the roar of copper kettledrums, and to the eager shouts of the watching throng.

"Welcome to Samarca, Sir Captain Mallet!" cried Alama
Sheik in a shrill, loud voice. "May this be the first of many
such happy arrivals! In the name of the Great and Powerful
Sultan Trobuk, the Munificent, the Opener of Doors, the Master of Blue Seas, Golden Deserts, and Green Hills, welcome
to Samarca and to the Empire of the Midday Sun!"

Mallet bowed deeply, first to the gold-and-green-and-blue
banner representing Sultan Trobuk, as he had been instructed,
and then to the Sultan's splendidly overdressed representative,
Alama Sheik.

The battery of twenty-five kettledrums drowned out the rest

of the formal greetings, followed by an even louder trumpet voluntary. The onlookers cheered and waved arms, hats, and turbans enthusiastically. Between shouts of approval, the crowd speculated at great length on what sorts of goods the strange vessel had brought.

Alama led the bearded Seacaptain across the wide, granite-paved plaza under the fortress walls to Merchant's Hall.

"You will here meet and greet Samarca's leading Merchant Princes," he explained again, puffing at the unaccustomed exercise of walking a hundred yards to the Hall's wide portico. "There will be refreshments"—the thought of which perked him up considerably—"and then you can all sit down together and discuss business."

Seacaptain Mallet glanced behind as they crossed the fore-court of the vast and ornate Merchant's Hall. The bales and boxes of sample goods he'd brought with him, mostly iron hardware and sturdy woolen cloth in bolts, had been set ashore and were being guarded by his sailors on the dock.

"They'll not be molested," Alama assured him, following his glance. "When we begin to speak of selling and buying, you may order the samples brought into the Hall and your men will be entertained as befits welcome customers. Dancing girls and witty songs . . . cool drinks and a hearty luncheon!"

Chattering breathlessly, the chubby Sheik led Mallet, accompanied only by *Encounter*'s young factor, Simon Threadneedle, into the inner courtyard of Merchant's Hall.

They were greeted there by a dozen or more men of all ages, shapes, and sizes who shared one common characteristic—they were all most richly dressed in reds, golds, luxurious blue linen, and heavy silks in a rainbow of softer colors.

"Here's our Chairman of the Merchant's Guild," Alama said to Mallet, "Lesser Sheik Abdulla Farr. Sheik . . . Seacaptain Mallet of *Encounter* out of Westongue in Dukedom."

The Seacaptain and his young factor bowed, and the Chairman of the Merchant's Guild, a man of forty or so summers dressed in rich fabrics and heavy golden bangles, returned their courtesy with a bow and a broad smile.

"Allow me to introduce my fellow Merchant Princes," he said to Captain Mallet. "With the Port Master's kind permission, of course."

Alama Sheik nodded pleasantly but with a court functionary's pretended lofty disinterest in mere—if extremely wealthy—merchants.

Myrn's arrival went entirely unremarked.

The Pearls' magic set her and the horseling in a pleasant residential square in the very heart of the upper part of the city. The square was cooled by a tall fountain and shaded by lofty, feathery palms and wide-spreading, red-flowering vines trained on ornate trellises. Their blossoms filled the warm air with a pleasant, peppery perfume.

Seated on the carved stone curbing of the fountain in the center of the square were two small children who regarded the sudden appearance of a beautiful young lady and a horse with mingled surprise, awe, and fear.

"Don't be alarmed, my dears," called Myrn, smiling warmly at them. "I'm a Journeyman Wizard and I often arrive unexpectedly this way, you see."

"A—a W-W-Wizard?" squeaked the boy. "Oh, help!"

"Now, now, Farrouki!" the girl beside him soothed his fear solemnly. "She's the good sort of Wizard, I can tell."

Farrouki looked rather doubtful about that, but the little girl rose, bobbed a deep curtsy to the newcomer, and said, "I am Farianah, daughter of Farrouk the Camel Merchant of Balistan. This is my little brother Farrouki. Welcome, Lady Wizard!"

"How nicely you greet me! May we drink from your fountain?"

The children moved aside and watched while first Myrn and then the winged horse slaked their thirst with the cool water.

"Do you live nearby?" asked Myrn, seating herself on the marble curbing so she could talk to the children at their own eye level. "It's certainly a very quiet, pretty neighborhood, I must say."

"That's our house," said Farrouki, pointing to the four-storey building across the court from the fountain. "We live here with Mother and Father and. . . ."

"And your papa's a camel merchant?" asked Myrn, drawing them close to her side with her warm smile and friendly words.

"Yes . . . but he's away just now," Farrouki told her, frowning at the thought.

"Oh, Farri!" gasped his sister. "You're not supposed to tell that to strangers!"

"Well, *everybody* knows it, don't they? Even the beggars know when they come to the gate asking for alms!"

Her brother's frankness about family business obviously embarrassed his older sister. She changed the subject quickly.

"Where are you at home, Lady Wizard?" she asked.

"My name is Myrn Manstar Brightglade. Just call me Myrn, dear children. I come from an island in Sea called Flowring. Have you ever heard of it, Farianah?"

"No ... but girls don't get to study geography," she admitted. "Only boys!"

"*I've* seen it on maps!" claimed her brother importantly. "Somewhere! I don't remember where, however."

"Come sit here in the shade and I'll tell you all about it and about my winged horse ... and why I've come to Samarca," Myrn said to them solemnly. "If you'd like to hear."

The children eagerly settled on the curbing on either side of her. Farrouki reached up to stroke the winged horse's soft, pink-gray nose. The horse allowed the caress for a moment, then drew gently away.

"What's your horse's name?" the little boy asked.

"I don't know," replied the Journeyman Aquamancer, frowning. "I call her Nameless. She can't speak, you see. Or won't."

"If you can speak and won't," said Farianah to the little horse, "it's not very nice of you!"

The little horse hung her head—in shame, it seemed, so Myrn reached up to give her a hug around the neck.

"It's all right, little one!" she soothed. "We'll learn your name in good time."

Her words perked the filly up at once and she moved closer to the fountain curb to allow the children to stroke her neck and pat her dappled flanks, nuzzling them back as if to say, "I'll forgive you if you'll forgive my silence."

Myrn described Flowring Isle for the children and told of her life there as a fisherman's daughter. There, she said, she'd met and married Douglas Brightglade, the famous Pyromancer.

"Where is Master Douglas, then?" asked Farianah, interrupting her tale.

"At home, taking care of our twin babies," Myrn explained.

"Brand's a boy . . . and Brenda's a little girl baby."

"Which came first?" wondered Farianah.

"Silly," said her brother, snorting, "they're *twins*. They were born at the same time."

"*We're* not twins," his sister countered with a sniff. "I was born first by a twelve-month!"

"Well, that's so," Farrouki admitted.

"In our case, Brand was born first, but his sister arrived only a short time after," Myrn hastened to explain.

It was quite hot in the walled courtyard, as the sun had climbed into the middle of the sky. The children invited their new and interesting friends into a smaller, walled water-garden off to one side, surrounded by two wings of their father's house and shaded with brightly striped awnings.

The filly followed them into the garden and began daintily sampling the greenery. Then, as the children and Myrn talked, the horse lowered her head and dozed.

"Will you stay in Samarca now?" asked Farianah. "We used to live in Kultrana where the white grapes grow and they dry them into the most delicious raisins anywhere! But Papa moved us here, hoping he could sell camels to the people on the coast. But they prefer horses here, he says."

"Camels are smelly and always bad-tempered," chimed in her brother. "You have to know how to handle them very firmly. Papa is off looking for a better market."

He was quite well informed about his father's camel-trading business, it seemed.

"Where do you live?" Farianah asked Myrn again.

"With my husband Douglas and our children in a place called Valley, in Dukedom," explained Myrn. "In a wonderful cottage under a tall hill named Wizards' High, beside a brook called Crooked."

She reached down and drew, in the sand of the garden path, a crude map of Sea and its surrounding lands and the islands in the middle, naming them as she talked.

She was still explaining World geography and history when a door to the Camel Merchant's house opened and a young woman, dressed in flowing cream-colored robes and wearing a gauzy veil across her nose and mouth, emerged carrying a large earthenware jar balanced easily on her head.

"Farri! Farianah? Who is your guest? You should invite her inside, where it's much cooler."

"This is our mama," announced Farianah proudly. "Her name is Shadizar and she is the most beautiful lady in the whole Sultanate."

Lady Shadizar blushed with pleasure and modest confusion at her daughter's words. Not to be outdone, her son took her hand and led her to meet the Wizard.

"My mother is not afraid of Wizards, I can tell you!" he cried.

"Not that Myrn is a Wizard to fear," added his sister.

"All Wizards are to be feared, at times," warned their mother, bowing courteously to the stranger in her garden. "So be careful how you act around this pretty Wizard, children!"

She smiled brightly at Myrn to show she was teasing . . . mostly.

"Will you come within, Mistress? We're about to sit down to a light midday meal and you are most cordially invited to join us."

Myrn accepted graciously and Shadizar, after filling her water jug at the fountain, led her across the garden to the door. The children whooped in delight and ran before them to hold the door wide.

"There is little for me to do to pass the days," admitted Shadizar to Myrn. "The people of this place are slow to make friends, I fear, and there are very few ladies who come to call. Most stay hidden away, you see. Local custom . . . which I so far have been forced to follow. Much too confining! I was born in the high grasslands, a daughter of the fresh, open air, sweet pastures, forests, and vineyards of my homeland."

"I agree with you, Lady Shadizar!" Myrn laughed. "I, too, was brought up in the open, on Sea and on island beaches, forests, and rocky headlands."

By the time they'd finished the meal of cold, spiced lamb in a piquant sauce, served with plump raisins and round, crisp-crusted loaves of bread, downed with cups of fresh goat's milk that Myrn, hesitant at first, found richly delicious and refreshing, Myrn and her hostess were fast becoming close friends.

Shadizar told of her childhood on her father's station in the southern grasslands. Myrn regaled the children and their mother with her story of young Douglas Brightglade's first arrival on her home island, of the oh-so-slow Horniads, and the precious blue coral and pearl-oyster beds.

A maid came to take the children off for their afternoon nap, and her hostess led Myrn to the second floor of the large, airy house, where they sat on a balcony overlooking the shady street, screened from the afternoon sun and eyes on the street below by a lattice decorated with intricately carved butterflies.

"Why do you visit our country just now, Myrn?" asked Shadizar. "If you care to tell me, that is. I understand that Wizards have secrets they must keep."

"No secret, really. I came to rescue a friend named Serenit of New Land who was, we fear, captured and brought to this part of World against his will. He's known to have passed through this city a few days ago. We fear he's in grave danger."

" 'We' being you and your husband Douglas?" asked the lady, handing Myrn a palm-leaf fan with which to cool herself, for it was now the hottest part of the day.

"Yes, Douglas and I . . . plus several other members of what's known as the Fellowship of Light. My own teacher is the Aquamancer Augurian of Waterand Island, and my husband's former master is Flarman Flowerstalk, a Fire Wizard."

"Names quite strange to me, I fear," admitted Shadizar. "I listen to the gossips in the marketplaces but I haven't heard of a captive of that nature in our city. I'm afraid I cannot help you."

"You can help by telling me of the ways and beliefs of your countrymen," Myrn urged. "I know a little from my studies, but not enough, by far."

"I'd be delighted," cried Shadizar, smiling. "Stay with us this night and tomorrow and we'll make inquiries. I assume you would prefer them to be . . . quietly made?"

"It would seem best." Myrn sighed. "From what you've said, this is evidently a man's country. A lone girl, even though a Journeyman Wizard, might have trouble finding out about a captive like Serenit."

"Tell me the story from the beginning, then," urged the Camel Trader's lady.

She had long since removed her veil, and Myrn envied her loose, light clothing. The afternoon air was hot, still, and humid—too much so for Myrn, even in her summery dress. With three or four simple gestures she re-formed her costume to look much like Shadizar's loose attire. This done, she summoned a soft, cool breeze off Sea.

The Camel Trader's wife watched in awe and delight, making a suggestion here or a comment there.

A maidservant brought a pitcher of an iced concoction of tea, pineapple, and orange juices, which Myrn found most refreshing.

"Let me see," she considered. "I should begin at the very start, when Douglas arrived on Flowring Isle. The poor man had fallen overboard from a ship at Sea. . . ."

After a long day of polite sparring and intense haggling with the Merchant Princes of Samarca in their Hall, Mallet and Simon Threadneedle were escorted by a committee of Merchants to the fleet landing, where *Encounter*'s quarter-boat and her crew waited patiently in the shade of a brightly striped awning.

"We will resume discussions and business tomorrow," Alfara, the Chief of the Merchant's Guild, promised. He'd become increasingly cordial as the day had worn on and prospects for profits had mounted dizzyingly. "Would the fourth hour of the morning be suitable for you, honored Captain?"

"Quite suitable, and pleasant as well," replied Mallet, who well knew how to be cordial when profitable trading demanded he be. "I'll come ashore at that hour, if that is your desire, dear sir. Now . . . I've kept you from family and dinner much too long. I bid you a fine evening and a quiet night!"

The Merchant Princes bowed deeply and Mallet returned their parting salutes. Young Simon bowed and nodded and the quarter-boat's crew gave a lusty cheer, both to thank the Merchants for the hospitality and to show their relief over the end of a long, hot day of waiting.

"Oh, I almost forgot," added the Head Merchant, turning back to Mallet. "The Port Master, before he went off, told me to say you may send your crew ashore this evening. The Sultan's Guards have given their assent, as long as your men stay within the posted confines of the lower city."

"Excellent!" said Mallet. "In that case, I'll send my Starboard Watch ashore after evening mess."

"They should be recalled to your ship before midnight," warned the Head Merchant, grinning broadly. "A foreigner ashore after that hour will be housed in the city lockup and must be redeemed . . . at no small cost!"

"I'll see to it they all know," Mallet agreed, nodding, "and will make sure all are back aboard before curfew."

The Merchants and the Seacaptain parted, the former dispersing to their homes higher in the city while *Encounter*'s quarter-boat whisked away Mallet and Simon, both feeling rather pleased, if hot and tired after their day's work.

"Ahoy the boat!" came a familiar hail out of the gathering gloom over the harbor.

"Encounter!" Simon yelled back, indicating to the watch aboard that their Captain was returning.

There came the sound of bare feet running, muffled orders, and a rattle of weapons and harness—all the watch on duty had been issued cutlasses and billies on the off chance that waterfront thieves might try to sneak aboard during the hours of darkness.

Side boys stiffened to attention at a word from the gnarled Bos'n when Mallet's head appeared above the deck as he clambered up the accommodation ladder. The Bos'n's Mates twittered a shrill greeting in unison on their silver pipes and the afterguard presented arms as best as they remembered how.

"All went well, then?" asked Pilot when the salutes were finished and the afterguard and the boat's crew had been sent below to dinner.

"Very well, indeed!" replied his Captain. "We'll send the Starboard Watch ashore after mess, until an hour before midnight, First Mate. Warn them strongly not to leave the harbor precinct—plenty of amusements there for everyone, I'm told—and to be *sure* to make the final liberty boat before it leaves at the change to the Mid Watch! After that, it's swim out to us or spend the night in the local brig ashore and lose three months' pay in ransom."

"Aye, aye, sir!" the First Mate said, grinning approvingly.

That's the way things *should* be run by landlubbers, his smile implied.

"Get your rest," added Mallet, yawning mightily. "You'll go ashore with us tomorrow morning at the fourth hour after sunrise. Plenty of profits to be made, and we'll both keep busy."

"Aye!" responded Pilot.

"You be ready, too," said the Captain to his clerk, who had caught the yawns and was standing by, gaping and gasping and rubbing his tired eyes.

Mallet went to his tiny sleeping cabin only after a careful circuit of *Encounter*'s spotless deck, inspecting and checking, making sure the Duty Watch was wide awake.

Just before he stepped down into the quarter-boat the following morning, Mallet was stopped by the rapid approach of a small rowboat-taxi. Its single passenger was a slight, brown-skinned young man in pea-green livery, looking very important but not a little awed by the beautiful ship and the strange sailors staring at him over the schooner's rail.

"Message for Captain Mallet!" he called in answer to the Bos'n's warning hail. "From my Mistress, the Lady Farrouk!"

"Lay alongside," Mallet ordered. "I am here."

Once hooked onto the quarter-boat's side by a grinning Seaman, the youth stood in the rocking bottom of the little rowing dinghy to hand up a folded parchment that was sealed, Mallet could see even from some distance away, by a blue-green wax impression the size of a large coin and the shape of a cockle shell.

"Give the lad a quarter-ducat," he ordered his Coxs'n gruffly, "and tell him to give way. We shan't keep the Chief of the Merchant's Guild waiting."

As the dinghy scooted hurriedly off, Mallet handed the message to his clerk, after closely inspecting the seal.

"From an Aquamancer, by the looks of it," he muttered in surprise. "What's it say, Simon?"

"It reads," the clerk intoned:

"To Captain Mallet of Encounter *schooner:*

Welcome to the Port of Samarca. A friend wishes to greet you when you have a few moments free. Come to the House of Farrouk the Camel Seller on the Street of Bitter Oranges. At your leisure and pleasure. Anyone can give you directions from the strand."

"It's signed 'Shadizar, wife of Farrouk—on behalf of another better-known to you,' " Simon finished, handing the note back to his captain.

"Might be Augurian of Waterand," considered the Seacaptain. "Wonder why he wants to remain unnamed."

He nodded to his Coxs'n to unhook from *Encounter*'s chains and give way for the shore. The boat's oarsmen heaved lustily on their sweeps and the Coxs'n swung the tiller over.

"Answer to the Camel Merchant's wife's message, sir?" prompted Simon.

The young man in his water-taxi was hovering nearby, obviously waiting.

"Eh? Well, I guess so," said Mallet, distracted by the sights and sounds of the busy harbor. "Yes. Find out where this Farrouk person lives and write his wife a note saying I'll wait upon her and her . . . guest . . . before sunset this evening. As soon as we can get away from these Merchant Princes."

"Aye, aye, sir!"

He waved to the water-taxi to follow them ashore and, once there, handed the reply to the dark-skinned youngster, making a mental note to find out what he could about this Farrouk while negotiations were going on that day at Merchant's Hall.

Chapter Four

Rolling Stones

DOUGLAS Brightglade wet a handful of smooth, flat, blue-gray gabro pebbles by dipping them in the frigid ice-melt water of New River.

Cribblon and Marbleheart watched with keen professional interest. The pale northern sun washed over the wide glacial valley, busy reviving summer colors of young birch and poplars after a long, snowy winter.

Far down the steep-sided fjord a small fleet of fishing smacks was busy setting purse-nets. In the clear, cool air overhead a flock of gray-and-white Northland Seagulls mewed plaintively, wheeled, and dipped, anticipating a very good meal from the remnants of the cleaning of the fishermen's catch later in the day.

Douglas ignored them all—friend, Familiar, birds, and boats—concentrating on the shiny-wet pebbles in the palm of his right hand.

He murmured a short string of spell words, of which Marbleheart caught only a few—*"Faghalenty sus su'-russ. Minory bel amnor. Pluanget a rur!"*

With this last he suddenly flung the seven smooth stones high into the air, letting them fall into the center of a smoothed-out space in the fine, dry river-mouth sand. The soft sand kept the ice-polished pebbles from scattering or rolling about.

In fact, they half-buried themselves in the sand and came to rest almost at once.

"Good cast!" murmured the Sea Otter in approval.

Cribblon nodded agreement.

Douglas studied the arrangement of stones for a long and silent moment before looking to his companions.

"What do *you* see, Marbleheart? Even a Familiar should be able to read the outlines, at least."

"Who, me?" squeaked Marbleheart in mock-surprise. "I haven't even got the hang of reading tea-leavings, Master!"

"Theory is similar, if not the exact same," Douglas assured his furry Familiar with a shrug. "You should make *some* sense of the stones, at least, old Stick-in-the-Mud!"

He shook his head slightly to the Journeyman Aeromancer not to interfere, giving the Sea Otter a chance to read the pattern of the stones for himself.

"Well, hummm! *Huh?* Ah, er . . . and, I vow," muttered Marbleheart. "Hey, this looks like a job for Lithold Stone-breaker, I must say!"

"These are stony signs and placings even you should know, Marbleheart!" cried Douglas, pretending disappointment. "Try harder!"

"Hum," muttered the Sea Otter, touching several of the stones in order.

"Well!" he repeated. "Ah, yes! Well, here's a symbol for the sun. I recognize that one. I really do!"

"Good, so far," chuckled Cribblon. "That *is* a symbol for a sun of some sort. . . ."

"Let him figure it out," Douglas cautioned, settling back against a large boulder torn ages before from the valley's side, carried miles downstream by the grinding ice, and polished smoothly rounded. Its sun-warmth felt good on his back. Spring, nearly finished in Valley, was just beginning here in the Northland.

"A rising sun . . . indicating . . . the direction east?" asked Marbleheart, frowning fiercely in concentration. "Yes, I should think so! And here's a configuration for Sea-travel, I see."

Douglas and Cribblon nodded silently.

"Oh, come *on*, fellas!" objected the Otter. "I'm pretty new to this descrying business, you know. How about a hint or two?"

"That's the rising sun; you're right about that," said Douglas, pointing. "Indicates direction. And the symbol for a dire spelling is clear, you see? That says . . . what?"

Marbleheart frowned even more deeply, then clapped his forepaws as the answer came to him.

"Frigeon's old evil magicking! Obviously the spellbounders we seek are off to the *east* of us. But there's nothing there but jumbles of rock and old lava beds and deep Sea inlets filled with mewling Seabirds, Master!"

"You aren't looking far enough, Here! What do you make of this?"

He indicated one of the smooth blue stones leaning against its neighbor.

"That would be an indication of distance, not direction, I think," said Marbleheart, looking up at Douglas after a moment.

"Correct! And how far away is the missing victim?"

"Oh, pretty far!" the Otter thought aloud. "Fifty leagues?"

"You're guessing," Douglas accused sternly. "Observe the angle of declination, please."

"More than a hundred and fifty leagues!" cried the long, sleek water mammal. "And there are . . . what? . . . seven miles to a league? Seven times a hundred and fifty miles . . . at least a thousand miles to the east! Am I right?"

"Perfectly right," Cribblon laughed, for the Otter's figures agreed with his own quite perfectly.

"And well to the south," added Douglas thoughtfully.

He stood and brushed the fine glacial sand from his trouser knees, then glanced up at the pale noonday sun and out over the chill, blue fjord to the fishing fleet.

"A thousand miles!" the Sea Otter was saying to himself. "East by a good bit south? Isn't that where Myrn is Journeying to look for old Serenit? Nearer East, as I recall."

"It's where the stones say to seek Frigeon's lost enchantments," agreed the Aeromancer, also climbing to his feet. "Perhaps Serenit, too? Is there anything else there, Douglas? Have we missed anything in the portents?"

Douglas considered. "No, I don't believe so. Stone-casting

gives only compass direction and leagues-distant, remember. There's no indication of what to look for, once we get there.''

''Well, the sooner we get going, the better, then,'' said Marbleheart, busily brushing sand from his thick coat. ''The only question is: *how* shall we go?''

The fastest way would be to use the Feather Pin's magic, Douglas knew. The easiest way would be to find a ship going east and ask for passage. No Westonguer nor Waynessman vessel, nor Highlandorm swift longboat, nor junk of Imperial Choin, nor the sailing canoes of Warm Sea, would refuse, if asked, to carry them wherever they wanted to go on Wizard's business.

''But I feel a need for speed,'' Douglas told his companions. ''Myrn is there well ahead of us. While following our lost king's trail. It might well be practical to be closer, in case she runs into trouble on her Journeying.''

''But we'd interfere at some risk to her qualification,'' objected Cribblon.

They returned toward Serenit's rambling, steep-roofed, log-and-stone house overlooking the confluence of New River and the fjord.

''*I* could help her out,'' Marbleheart suggested. ''As I assisted you in the matter of Coven. And Cribblon could help, also,'' he added, remembering past adventures.

''But I'm a Journeyman myself now,'' the Aeromancer objected. ''Wouldn't it disqualify Myrn, if I helped?''

''Have to ask Flarman or Augurian for a ruling,'' decided Douglas. ''Although they never objected to your helping me in Old Kingdom, did they?''

''But I was just a middle-aged *Apprentice* then,'' Cribblon reminded him. ''Now I'm a full-rigged, middle-aged Journeyman.''

''Recall that Flarman and Augurian, when they were Journeymen, cooperated on their own Journeyings,'' Marbleheart put in quickly. ''How could they object if Cribblon helped Myrn on *her* Journeying?''

''But I myself must be careful, mustn't I?'' asked Douglas, waving to Clangeon, awaiting them on the wide front porch of Serenit's house. ''Still . . . I've a feeling Myrn may have bitten off more than she can easily chew, as Flarman says at times of me. It would be . . ."

". . . convenient," his Familiar finished his dangling sentence for him, "for us to be close. Just in case."

Douglas was quiet during supper, half-listening to Clangeon's worried chatter, Marbleheart's optimistic reassurances, and Cribblon's calm words of advice. The Steward's cooking was almost as inspired as that of Blue Teakettle (he was one of her best pupils, when it came to that), and the roast wild duck with black raspberry compote and toasted wild onions were superb.

"We'll leave at dawn the second morning from now, gentlemen. Caspar is bringing *Donation* here. In fact, we should see his topsails down the fjord by dawn's light," Douglas announced at last, pushing back from his place. "A magnificent dinner, Clang! You are an apt pupil of Blue Teakettle."

"And your goodwife, Myrn, too," said the Steward, much pleased by the young Wizard's compliment. "And your goodlady mother, also . . . and Mistress Manstar, Myrn's mother on Flowring Isle, too. In this near-wilderness, being a good cook is very important, as my good master says."

"He's right!" cried Marbleheart, scrubbing stray raspberry seeds from his whiskers with a napkin. "Now, old Clangeon, you can place the whole matter safely in our hands. Why, with two Journeymen and me, the world's greatest Familiar, working on his kidnapping, old Serenit's as good as rescued."

"I feel a great deal better knowing Mistress Brightglade is looking for him," admitted Clangeon, smiling gratefully at the Otter. "And that you will be near to hand, should she need help, Douglas."

"We must get some sleep," decided Douglas, patting the Steward on the shoulder. "We'll be hot on the trail of the missing spellbound victims in a few days."

"Could I go with you?" begged Clangeon, "Maybe *I* could help your beautiful wife?"

"Better stay here and take good care of your pioneers and the Stones," Douglas recommended, referring to the tribe of warriors who'd recently settled in the glacial valley. "If Myrn needs help, 'twill be the kind Wizards—and their Familiars— can best provide."

"I suppose you're right," said Clangeon, sighing. "Let me bring some lanterns to light you to your beds, sirs and Otter."

As soft evening fell over the Port of Samarca, Mallet and Simon drifted away from the crowd leaving Merchant's Hall and made their way up the slope of the shore into the heart of the lower city.

Torches and lamps lighted the streets, and the smells of spicy cooking and strong coffee filled the warm evening air. The Port Watch from *Encounter* filled smoky taverns and gaudily decorated cafes; their boisterous laughter and applause for scantily clad dancers shook the air and made the townspeople pleased and friendly.

Beyond a certain point the street they followed became lined with shuttered shops and offices guarded by men in black *khaftans* hefting heavy, curve-bladed scimitars, and eyeing the pedestrians silently.

Mallet thrust his cloak aside to show the quality of his clothing and weapons.

"Think they'll stop us?" inquired his young clerk, uneasily.

"Not if they're like policemen everywhere," muttered his Captain. "They'll allow Quality to go unchallenged, for fear of reprimand if they get in the way of someone important."

It proved so. The guards noted the passage of the two Westonguers with polite nods but without comment. Climbing the steep street to another level, Mallet and Simon found themselves passing taller, more severely decorated buildings—banks and counting houses—interspersed with the offices of wealthy lawyers and importers' showrooms.

"Up the next street," whispered Simon, who had gotten directions from a servant at the Hall. "Near the top of the hill. Red-brown-and-blue-striped flag out front. House of the Camel Merchant."

"There 'tis!" cried Mallet, who detested whispering anywhere. "Yes, the cressets on the roof light the house flag quite well."

He strode to the closed and barred iron gate in the center of the Camel Merchant's house facade and jerked on a bell-rope hanging from the balcony overhead.

Muted bells tolled far within. Soft footsteps sounded, slip-

pers on stone flooring beyond the gate, and a woman's voice
through a wicket asked their business.

"Seacaptain Mallet of *Encounter* schooner," Mallet announced firmly. "To see your mistress, the wife of the Camel
Merchant Farrouk . . . at her own invitation."

"And who accompanies you, brave Captain?" asked the
female voice.

"My clerk, one Simon Threadneedle of Wayness Isles,"
replied Mallet.

"Oh! Please . . . come within," said the servant, and the
gate swung silently open, allowing the men to cross the thresh-
old into a small, tiled, lantern-lit vestibule.

"Please wait here momentarily," requested the veiled maid
when the gate was closed again.

She disappeared into the shadows at the other end of the
anteroom.

"Did you notice how she was *dressed*?" murmured Simon,
his voice betraying shock and surprise.

"Normal for women in this place," grunted his more experienced Captain. "Rather sensible, if you think of it. It's
bloody hot!"

He would have taken off his wool Sea cape if there had
been anywhere to hang it.

"I'm not sure they'd allow such skimpy covering in Westongue, even if it *was* warm enough," said his clerk with a
nervous chuckle.

Before the Seacaptain could reply, the young woman returned.

"Please come within, Seacaptain Mallet and Clerk Threadneedle of *Encounter*," she said, pointing the way through the
inner doorway.

They followed her into a wider, well-lighted hallway beyond
the vestibule. As the curtain fell into place the woman's great,
dark eyes smiled welcomingly at them.

She announced politely, "My mistress takes her ease in the
fountain court in the early evening."

Their guide led them down the hall toward the back of the
house. Mallet had little time to glance at the rich tapestries
and sculptures and paintings that adorned the walls and cub-
bies they passed. The overall impression was one of quiet,
comfortable wealth, without undue show.

The servant girl opened a solid door which let out a spill of brighter lantern light to dazzle them for a moment. When the two Seamen stepped through, blinking, they were met by a smiling Myrn, a second lady, and two small children who looked up at the rough-looking sailors in some awe.

"Here's my old shipmate, Mallet of Wayness!" cried the Journeyman Water Adept. "Welcome, welcome! This is Farianah and this is my young friend Farrouki, children of our host and hostess. Greet Lady Shadizar, whose house this is. It's so good to see you, Seacaptain. Hello, Simon! I remember meeting you at Westongue. Come in and shed shoes and your hot cloaks."

Myrn gave them both a firm hug and the Captain a kiss on the cheek.

"Mistress Brightglade!" Mallet exclaimed. "How came you here? I heard from Thornwood Duke just before I last sailed from Westongue that you had borne two lusty younguns. Congratulations!"

"I forgot; you've been at Sea for long months, Mallet," said Myrn. "Yes, Douglas and I are proud parents. We named them Brand and Brenda, in honor of Douglas's Fire Mastery."

She waited while the children politely bowed and greeted their guests, then led them all out into the fountain garden. A supper had been laid upon a low table, awaiting them, and three young men dressed in green livery strummed guitars and hummed pleasant evening melodies intended to fill the background but not to distract attention from conversation.

"A very great pleasure and an honor, ma'am," said Mallet with a surprisingly graceful bow to Shadizar. He introduced the ship's factor.

"Your business is going well?" inquired Shadizar, knowing from long experience how to put men at ease in early conversation. "I heard last evening an account of your first meeting with our Merchant Princes, from a friend. They say, in the marketplace, that the Princes were very pleased with what you brought to sell."

"I'm certain of it, ma'am," said the Seacaptain, accepting a seat on a stone bench near the fountain basin. It was cool and pleasant in the water garden, and the sound of the softly falling spray allowed them to talk without fear of being overheard from without, or even by the servants.

"What shall I eat first?" Myrn asked Farianah and Farrouki. "It all looks so delicious and lovely!"

"Don't let the fancy things distract you, Myrn," advised the boy, earnestly. "I like the honey-barbecued morsels of lamb, myself. Cook makes them so very tender and good!"

Myrn, allowing Mallet and his clerk time to feel at ease in a strange situation, tried some of the lamb rolled in savory, tender leaves, and pronounced it to be absolutely delicious.

"Try this *sukki*," urged the little girl Farianah, presenting a tray to her new friend. "Taste it first and then I'll tell you what's in it . . . and who made it!"

Myrn accepted a tidbit from the proffered plate and popped it into her mouth.

"Oh! *Ah! Hot!*" she gasped, sucking air into her mouth in quick gasps. "But delicious, nevertheless! What is it? May I have another?"

The little girl flushed with pleasure and her brother laughed delightedly.

" 'Tis spiced and marinated tongue," explained Farianah, "and I made it myself."

"*I* don't like it," exclaimed Farrouki.

"I can see why you might not, being so young and tender," laughed Myrn. "But an old, toughened Wizard like me . . . I think it's *wonderful!*"

She asked Farianah for the recipe, intending to prepare the dish for her young husband, who didn't usually like tongue, first chance she got. Douglas did love fiery foods, being a Fire Wizard by profession.

When the evening grew dark outside and the modest feast was consumed down to the fruit ices and candied figs and dates, the children were wafted away on a cloud of satisfaction and goodwill to their beds. Myrn, Shadizar, and the Weston-guers sat near the fountain, enjoying the cool, moist air.

"May I ask what you do here, Mistress?" asked Mallet, sipping the thick, strong coffee flavored with clove.

"It's no secret, Seacaptain," answered the Journeyman Aquamancer. "I'm Journeying in my Craft . . . that is, I've accepted the task of finding our old friend, Serenit of New Land, who's gone missing. We fear he was kidnapped by someone, but so far I don't know to where or by whom."

"A serious undertaking for one so young and pretty," said Mallet, shaking his head.

"Not for Myrn," spoke up his ship's clerk. "She can do *anything*!"

"Ah, you have an ardent admirer in my young factor here." Mallet laughed.

"We're old friends," said the Flowring lass.

"She got me my first berth aboard a Westongue ship," Simon explained proudly.

"Well and well!" exclaimed Mallet. "We have *you* to thank for Simon then, mistress? He's been more than just able aboard my ship. On this voyage alone his efforts will increase our profits by ten or twelve percent."

"I'm not surprised," murmured Myrn, smiling at the young man. "He'll be one of your best captains, one of these days."

The four of them sat in friendly conversation for an hour or more longer before Shadizar rose and excused herself.

"You have things to discuss with Captain Mallet, I know," she said to Myrn. "I'll go see to the children and leave you alone as long as you like."

"No, no!" Myrn protested. "We'll need your advice and ideas, Shadizar. See to the little ones, then return to us; you have better information about local conditions than any of us, I know."

So, when the young mother had tucked her little ones safely into bed and come back to the quiet garden, Myrn explained her mission to them all.

"Serenit was obviously kidnapped . . . by someone we haven't yet been able to name," she ended her story. "I have reason to believe he passed through Port here, and that's the last I know of him."

"There're a lot of places his captors could have dragged him from here," said Shadizar. "But the most likely, I think, would be into, or across, High Desert. 'Tis an empty, wide, hot, dry, and sometimes dangerous land. I know, for I lived on its edges all my childhood."

"Empty? How?" asked Mallet.

He had traded several times in New Land and liked the First Citizen, for all that he drove stiff bargains for his timber, barrels of pitch, and fine building stone.

"As empty as Sea," replied Shadizar, smiling at him, "but much, much drier. Little or nothing lives there other than snakes and lizards and a few tough horses and wild camels which my kinsmen capture to tame and ride."

"That's how they live, then, your kinsmen?" wondered Simon. "Raising beasts of burden, I mean?"

"That . . . and by robbing each other, mostly," admitted Shadizar. She shook her dark head rather sadly. "Or they sweep down on caravans going to the mines on the far side of High Desert. Westbound caravans are seldom bothered, for they carry heavy ingots of smelted copper and pigs of tin and a little gold and silver from the Darkest Mountains mines. No, the marauders usually seek to waylay the eastbound caravans loaded with food and tools to support the mines in the barren mountains. Little grows there. Water's very scarce and scarcely palatable."

"See?" cried Myrn, "I knew I needed your advice and experience in my quest. Thank you, Shadizar-sister!"

"From my short experience at trading here," said Mallet, "I would say all metals are quite scarce and very dear here in the Nearer East, as we call this shore."

"That's true," the lady of the house nodded. "Iron is almost as dear as silver. When you offer iron implements for sale in Merchant's Hall, the Princes see yours as a better, cheaper alternative to the far-off mines under the Darkest Mountains."

"But that area," put in Simon thoughtfully, "sounds like a good place for a . . . *twisted* Magician, for example, to hide himself."

"What are you thinking, Clerk?" his captain asked.

"Such a lonely place would have beckoned to, say, a Dark Enemy fleeing Last Battle."

Myrn arched her black eyebrows but said nothing for a moment.

"Well, that suggests a connection with Serenit, who has been kidnapped to somewhere beyond the desert, I now believe. As the Air Wizard Frigeon he was a feared enemy to the Darkness, two centuries back. Might some creature of the Darkness have captured him, Captain?"

"You must know more of such wicked things than I, my dear Journeyman. Ask Lord Augurian or Flarman Flowerstalk.

Wizards have more information on the Enemy following Last Battle than ever I heard.''

Myrn sighed. ''Well, I must find out as much as I can and, if necessary, I can call on the Fellowship for assistance. But I'd like at least to rescue our friend Serenit . . . for that's my assigned task, you know.''

''And you must do this dangerous task unassisted,'' cried Shadizar. ''It seems very difficult for a full Fellowship of Wizards, let alone a single, young Wizardling like you, my dear!''

''It isn't *supposed* to be easy,'' said Myrn stoutly. ''And who knows—I may pull it off better than all the others. Would the Dark Enemy suspect a mere lass? As far as that goes, my task in this is to rescue poor Serenit—not to conquer a powerful Dark Enemy single-handedly!''

''And rescue him you will, Myrn,'' said their hostess. ''But now, gentlemen, it approaches midnight and I must warn you that no stranger is allowed freedom of our streets after that hour. . . .''

''So we've heard,'' the Seacaptain said with a nod.

''Yes, the Sultan's Guards have standing orders from the Sultan himself to arrest anyone caught abroad between midnight and dawn prayer-call. I must admit I approve of the regulation. Before, no one was safe in the nighttime streets from bandits and purse-snatchers and such.''

She shivered slightly.

''You are most welcome to spend the night here, of course,'' Shadizar added.

''Most kind of you to offer but I must return to *Encounter*,'' said Mallet.

''Let's plan to meet tomorrow after you've completed your business,'' Myrn suggested.

''We're nearly finished,'' Simon pointed out. ''A half-day tomorrow to agree on the value of a Dukedom ducat compared to that of your *rupee* and we'll have sent ashore every bit of our cargo . . . including some things supposedly highly illegal.''

''Ah.'' Shadizar laughed, ''So Port Master Alama Sheik has found a way to acquire your alcoholic beverages, eh? No surprise—I suspect not even to the Sultan himself.''

''A strange way to do business, at very least,'' thought Mallet aloud, rising to go. ''But, in strange lands they often have strange ways, and on the whole I approve of as little spirituous liquor at low prices as possible myself. Seaman's bane, we calls it!''

Myrn and Shadizar escorted the men to the front door. Somewhere above them in the warm, starry night a high, nasal voice sang a wavering melody.

"Prayer-singer," explained the lady of the house. "He calls on people to repent of their sins and come to worship before all doors are locked at curfew. It means, Captain Mallet, that you and Master Simon have just a half hour to reach the fleet landing and embark on the harbor waters. Once one's afloat, the laws of the Sultan's Admiralty apply, and they know no curfew."

"We'll hurry. I've no desire to sit in a Samarcan jail overnight," Mallet assured her. "Besides, what would my men say when they heard of it?"

Shadizar summoned the young man who'd brought her message to *Encounter* earlier in the day.

"This is my most excellent factotum, Groat," she introduced him. "He's completely reliable and will be crafty enough to return home before the Guards sweep the streets for stragglers . . . or to hide in the black shadows, won't you, Groat?"

"Of course, ma'am!" replied the grinning steward. "I've met the good Seacaptain on his beautiful ship already. Will you allow me to escort you, Captain Mallet?"

"Keep me out of jail and I'll follow you willingly," said a laughing Mallet, who liked the cheerful young man. "If we run behind-times, you may sleep on *Encounter* in a hammock overnight, and let the harbor swells rock you to slumber as it does us sailors."

"I will if I must," said the factotum, pulling a wry face. "Although I have a horror of deep waters."

"My Lady Brightglade," said Mallet, turning to Myrn, "I'll send a message to you here in mid-morning, as soon as I know when I'll be free. There's no reason to hide our acquaintance, is there?"

"None that I know of," answered Myrn. "However, I would just as lief the authorities here do not know too much of me or my mission. Who knows whether Serenit's kidnappers have friends or informants here?"

"Wise enough!" The Seacaptain nodded, giving her a parting bow. "We'll serve you as ever we can, of course. Until tomorrow, then, Lady Shadizar. Know that I greatly enjoyed your house, your children, your table, and your beauty and wisdom!"

"Good night . . . and walk fast," advised Shadizar. "Bail is expensive in our lockup. Especially for you, who will be considered wealthy, on the evidence of your tall sailing ship."

"We're off!" cried Mallet, bowing again quickly, and he and Simon, led by the factotum, disappeared into the darkness of the street.

Chapter Five

Invitation from the Sultan

JUST before noon the following day Mallet wrote a short note to Lady Shadizar and gave it to a street urchin to deliver.

"My Lady," he wrote—

"As it might become a matter of malicious gossip for me too often to visit your home in the absence of your good husband, may I suggest you meet me at the fleet landing two hours after high noon, accompanied, of course, by a suitable escort. It would be my pleasure to conduct you on a tour of my ship Encounter, *and provide an interesting supper on her deck. Reply by this bright young man, who has been promised double his stipend if he brings your reply to me within the hour.*

> *Mallet*
> *Captain of* Encounter
> *At anchor in the Port of Samarca"*

Shadizar's reply was warmly favorable, and when the business meeting at Merchant's Hall broke up after a congratulatory luncheon Mallet found her, accompanied by her son, daughter, and Groat, waiting for him beside *Encounter*'s quarter-boat, being politely ogled by its oarsmen.

"Good!" cried Mallet, remembering to bow deeply to the lady. "I'm delighted you've brought your bright, beautiful children. They remind me of my own sons and daughters, whom I see all too seldom, being so much at Sea, M'lady!"

"And here is my secretary, whom you have met, and the children's *amah*," said Shadizar. "You'll remember meeting her yester-eve?"

"Ah, yes. Charmed!" said the Seacaptain, trying very hard not to seem too interested in the *"amah"*—Myrn Brightglade, dressed appropriately in a style halfway between that of a servant and a poor relative.

"A pleasure, sir," murmured Myrn, bowing her head in the manner of the women of Samarca, hands pressed palm-to-palm in front of her mouth.

Mallet stifled a deep chuckle and said gruffly instead, "Keep a close eye on the young-uns, mistress. There're far too many ways for curious fingers to be hurt aboard a ship."

Myrn bowed submissively once more, murmuring, "I am a daughter of Seafarers myself, Revered Seacaptain. You can trust me not to allow the children to come to harm."

Once in the quarter-boat, as the crew pulled lustily for *Encounter,* the public formality of their meeting disappeared and the children, wild with excitement at being taken aboard a sailing ship, plied Myrn, Mallet, and their mother with questions and observations that kept them all busy.

Warned of his Captain's guests by a shout from the quarter-boat's Coxs'n, First Mate Pilot had rigged a bos'n's chair over the side in which Lady Shadizar and her children . . . and their *"amah"* . . . were hoisted primly aboard, it not being considered proper for highborn ladies to climb accommodation ladders.

"I could have climbed the foremast easily," Myrn told Farianah. "I was born a sailor. Climbing shrouds is second nature to me."

"How fortunate you are!" said little Farrouki, sighing. "I've never been aboard a *felucca*, let alone a huge vessel like this."

"Well, son," said one of the Seamen, "I hears your pa's a dealer in them weird-looking humpty camels I saw ashore last evening?"

"Papa's a Camel Merchant, and quite successful at it," replied Farrouki. "Why?"

"Just that you can probably ride one of them awful beasts with great ease."

"I've ridden camels since I was old enough to hold reins," Farrouki boasted.

"If you were to put me an one of them there *cambels*," moaned the sailor with a very real shudder of revulsion, "I'd be very likely to faint dead away!"

Farrouki and his sister thought this most strange, but before the afternoon was over, the sailors had the children climbing to the foretruck crowsnest—a full fifteen feet above the foredeck!—and talking of steerage and rights of way, of dunnage and tonnage, of sails and running and standing rigging, and of other Seamanly things.

"Have you never been aboard a ship, ma'am?" Mallet asked when their mother set firm foot on the deck after her swing up from the boat. It almost took her breath away and colored her cheeks most attractively, every one of the watching Dukedom crewmen thought.

"Never!" She gazed in awe around the spotless main deck.

"Then allow me to give you a first lesson in Seamanship," said the Seacaptain, grinning broadly. "You never know when it might come in handy!"

While they were shown about *Encounter*, Myrn kept to her role as the children's nurse, although she was amused to overhear remarks some of the bolder sailors made when they saw her rather scanty costume and veiled face.

"You scurvy swabs!" she growled at last, choking with laughter at the sight of their shocked faces. "That's no way to speak of any lady guest! Stow it! Next man to make such bloody-awful remarks in my hearing'll spend his homeward voyage pumping the bilges . . . by hand!"

After that, as word spread that the *amah* was not exactly what she seemed, the sailors treated her with considerably more respect.

Especially when she was included in the party at the Captain's supper table and sat at his left hand, rather than at the far end of the table.

■　　■　　■

"I've received a summons—an invitation, if you prefer—
to the court of your Sultan, What's-His-Name," announced
Mallet as the steward poured the sweet dessert wine to be
drunk with an excellent plum duff.

"Sultan Trobuk, you mean?" asked Shadizar, brightening
at the news. "I've met him once myself, and his young only-
wife, the Sultana Nioba."

"Tell me about them then, please," requested Mallet. "I've
never been summoned to the presence of a Sultan before."

Shadizar thought for a moment before she said, "I like our
Sultan, although he is quite young. No more than twenty-two
summers, I do believe. He succeeded to the Divan upon the
death of his grandfather, a fierce old desert chieftain named
Fadouzal."

She paused to nibble a bit of the duff, which was delicious.

"He's quite handsome, our young Sultan, and very polite
and mild-mannered. I've heard that his ascent to the Royal
Divan was marked with great ceremony and a few quiet ar-
rests. His father and grandfather were not ones for the niceties
of law and had kept some real rascals about them. A few were
relatives of mine, you know, but I couldn't really blame the
new Sultan for sending them away . . . or having them be-
headed."

"Executed!" cried Myrn. "Were they that evil, then?"

"Without a doubt," Shadizar admitted.

A quartet of *Encounter* Seamen with concertinas, a fiddle,
and a homemade sort of xylophone began to play sentimental
Sea-songs just then, and conversation lagged for a while.

With the music came a treat: strawberry ice cream made
possible by Thornwood Duke's thoughtfulness in providing
Encounter several of the famous Cold Boxes designed by Flarman Flowerstalk and built by Wayness craftsman Michael
Wroughter. No Waynesser nor Westongue ship sailed without
at least one Cold Box these days, Mallet told his guests
proudly.

"We eat Valley beef three months at Sea!" he boasted.
"And the boxes keep milk fresh as morning's milking for
weeks after it's taken from the cows."

"Your Seamen eat better than some Sheiks I know," exclaimed the amazed Shadizar. "I well remember what caravan
riders must eat after a week out on the desert. Dried beans or

peas and barbecued-dry mutton so hard a rider has to have good teeth and strong jaws just to get his meal out of it—and that's after boiling it for half a day!''

Dusk fell and a cool breeze sprang up from Sea. Mallet suggested they make themselves comfortable on the quarterdeck, to enjoy the evening until it was time to go ashore.

Lanterns were rigged from the yards and the crew gathered in the waist to sing rollicking old songs in four-part harmony and perform feats of strength and agility for their guests. Everyone enjoyed the sweet, hard-fleshed pears and pomegranates Shadizar had brought out from the fruit sellers ashore.

At last Myrn said, ''Tell us about your invitation, Mallet.''

''I'm bidden to the capital,'' said Mallet. ''I'm advised not to refuse, for the sake of trade between us and Samarca, although I don't like leaving my ship for that long.''

''It's common for Sultans to do thus,'' Shadizar nodded. ''You'll be safe and well received, I know. Sultans use such summonses to learn of matters beyond Samarca's borders and shores. Trobuk is eager to establish trade and communications with the West, I've heard.''

''You must go then,'' said Myrn from her seat on a cushion at Shadizar's feet.

''I'll depart tomorrow at turn of the forenoon watch. If this suits your own plans,'' he said to Myrn.

''I'll go with you, Mallet, old canvas-puncher, but it's best I travel in disguise.''

''I've no objection,'' declared the Seacaptain. ''In fact, I'm delighted! Can you be ready by mid-morn? I could easily put off my departure. . . .''

''No, that shouldn't be necessary,'' Myrn declared. ''With the help of my friend Shadizar and her young factotum here, who seems to know almost everything that goes on in Port, I've learned that Serenit was indeed brought here by a strange ship some days ago and taken on eastward . . . probably to the Sultan's capital. And the ways and means suggest to me he's captive, as we suspected, of Darkness agents. When I get a bit closer, I can tell better about that.''

''Isn't this getting rather dangerous for you, Myrn?'' asked Shadizar, shaking her pretty head in worry. ''Shouldn't you seek help from your Wizard friends?''

''Perhaps I should . . . ,'' replied the Journeyman Aquamancer thoughtfully. "I certainly could use Douglas about now! But I don't think I should delay longer in closing with Serenit's captors."

"I'm ready to serve you in any way I can, you know," Mallet vowed.

"Just take me with you to the Sultan. Does his capital city have a name?"

"Oh, yes, it's called Balistan," answered Farrouk's wife. "It was once the property of my husband's family, until the old Sultan preempted it. A very nice, really delightful place, cool in summer and well watered."

Myrn thanked her and Shadizar returned her smile threefold, saying, "You've quickly become a dear friend, Myrn Brightglade. I wish I could do more for you!"

Myrn thanked her again, adding a kiss on her cheek, followed by kisses on the cheeks of both children, who were close to sleep now that the heat of day had passed.

Guards on the walls and streets of the Port watched *Encounter*'s quarter-boat deposit the Camel Merchant's family and their retinue at the landing below the great fortress, never noticing that the party was one short of what it had been when it had arrived in mid-afternoon.

A party of ten sailors, agog to see the forbidden upper part of the city, formed an armed escort and marched with the Camel Merchant's lady, her children, and their servants right to her door.

They returned just in time to escape the Guards attentions as the prayer-caller finished his eerie late-night chant from the tower of the mosque.

Chapter Six

Balistan

TRAVEL from the Port of Samarca to the capital at Balistan was pleasant and quite safe, according to both Shadizar and Port Master Alama. The road eastward climbed in easy switchbacks over the low Shorn Hills, then wound down a long, shallow, well-watered valley which in time merged into a pleasant green farmland along both sides of the river El Shatt.

Two days' additional journey by camel-drawn river-barge, Alama had assured Mallet, would take them to the Sultan's beautiful capital, located across the shallow, freshwater Lake Balissa.

"On the other side of that begins High Desert," Shadizar had said. "My husband can put you in touch with the desert chieftains, if you require assistance beyond there."

"I may need that," Myrn said with a nod.

They rode on horses in a fair-sized caravan, for on Lady Shadizar's advice Mallet took with him a party of experienced and armed petty officers, as well as Simon Threadneedle and several young Midshipmen who would serve their Seacaptain as formal attendants.

"I would have preferred to travel alone, or just with Simon," Mallet said, a bit grumpily.

"In this land," Shadizar advised him, "you are judged by

three things: your clothing, your weapons, and the size of your train. To do less than your very best would mean being looked down upon by many at the court of the Sultan.''

''Well . . . if you say so,'' said the Seacaptain, sighing.

''Besides, your young men will enjoy the trip as a change from standing watch in Port and going on liberty ashore,'' Myrn told him. ''An important part of their education in their profession, don't you think?''

This thought brightened Mallet's outlook, and by the time they'd ridden horses, provided by the Sultanate, over the ridge of coastal hills, the party was happy and very excited by the pleasant country through which it rode.

That evening they came to an inn, or *caravansary*, run by the Sultanate for wayfarers. This establishment provided clean and comfortable quarters for masters and servants alike, as well as for their horses, mules, and camels.

Included among the party's horses was the tiny (compared with the sturdy mares and geldings of the Sultan's transport service) and silent filly, Nameless, her spectacular wings once again hidden under a drab saddle cloth.

The horseling at first kept timidly to herself. Soon, however, the sturdy post mares took her into their care and protected her from the dangers of the road.

''We sensed at once her Quality,'' one of the mares told Myrn the second morning on the road. ''She's not your usual filly-daughter, we all recognized at once.''

''I deeply appreciate your taking care of her,'' replied Myrn, conjuring a handful of sugar cubes from her left sleeve as a treat for the hardworking packhorses. ''I know she seems a bit strange, but time and kindness may cure her silence.''

During the hot days—it was well into summer here in the Nearer East—Nameless trotted in the shade of Myrn's saddle mare or between two of the friendly baggage animals, who treated her with considerable deference, as if they thought her royalty.

The second evening after leaving the Port, the Seacaptain's party reached the banks of a clear, sand-bottomed river and gave up their mounts for a large, shallow-draft, single-sailed barge on which they would float in comfort down to the lake and across to the Sultan's capital on the far shore.

Myrn and Nameless bid a fond good-bye to the saddle mares and a thank-you to the pack animals.

"It's an easy life and we appreciate the fact, but it can be rather boring," admitted one horse, bumping Myrn's arm with her nose in friendly fashion. "If you come back this way, we'll carry you again, swiftly and gladly. You've been most pleasant and understanding, mistress. We won't remark on your disguise. Your secrets are quite safe with us."

Myrn didn't know whether to laugh or shiver at her words. She'd spent three days trying very hard not to be noticed by even the *Encounter* sailors, some of whom had seen her in Westongue in the past.

"Oh, nobody else noticed you in this crowd of Men," another mare assured her. "But we saddle mares know a thing or two about good breeding. We recognize highborn ladies when we carry them. A soft but firm hand on the reins. A dainty spurring heel. Quiet command in the voice. Sure signs of Quality, my dear!"

It took another two days, sailing downstream aboard the barge, to reach the calm, blue-green waters of Lake Balissa. Here they transferred to a larger, single-sailed felucca which carried them in wide tacks, a half a day across the shallow lake. By hot mid-afternoon they came in sight of the city of Balistan, situated on a long, low, palm-scattered hill which rose between the lake and the western edge of endless-seeming dunes. High Desert rose to the distant horizon beyond that in smoothly curved ridges and pyramids of dun and entirely empty sand.

On the far eastern horizon Myrn made out a serrated line of purple mountains.

"Those," explained a barge sailor, seeing her gaze turned that way, "are the fearsome Darkest Mountains. Beyond them is Ebony Sea, I hear. Never seen it myself."

"Maybe you'll see Ebony Sea yet," Myrn teased. "You'll be one of the best-traveled young men in Samarca."

"Go you to that desolate part of the Sultanate?" groaned the lad with a sour grimace. "No, not for me the High Desert. I prefer the river or the lake!"

"Meanwhile," Myrn said soberly, "what's this fast-flying craft bearing down on us?"

"The good Sultan's guardboat—or one of them," replied

the youth. "They'll check Captain Mallet's papers and escort you to the Sultan's palace. Nothing to fear, Mistress! The Sultan's a law-abiding man, and he expects his subjects to be so, also."

The rakish galley came swiftly up to them, propelled by banks of long, black sweeps moving in precise unison. A quarter-mile off the oars, at a shouted order, suddenly churned the water, halting the ship's headlong progress in the space of less than twice the galley's length—a considerable feat of strength and Seamanly skill, Myrn knew from experience.

"Hail, travelers!" came a cry from the guard-galley. "State your names, titles, and business in Balistan, in the name of the Great Sultan."

The crew of the *felucca* scrambled to haul down her single great sail, quickly lashing it about its massive boom. Her way carried her closer to the motionless galley.

"I be Mallet of Wayness, Seacaptain of Dukedom and Dukedom's Thornwood Duke, commanding His Grace's sloop *Encounter*," roared Mallet in answer, as at home with shouted communications as any sailor would be.

"Welcome to Balistan, Seacaptain!" came the answer from an officer in the forepeak of the guardship. "His Sublime Majesty the Sultan Trobuk bids us greet you! Have your boatmen follow me under oars, if you please, Honored Sir. Reception has been prepared for you at the royal pier—over yonder, you see, where the Sultan's green-and-white pennants fly from tall masts."

"We'll follow ye in then," agreed Mallet easily. "And thank you!"

The guardship's oarsmen spun her on her heel and pulled for the near shore. The ferryboat crew quickly ran out their own long sweeps and began the grueling task of rowing the heavy *felucca*, chuffing and chanting in rhythm.

Mallet came to where Myrn stood by the rail in the bow.

"What do you make of this city?" he asked.

"The Sultan has decreed that most buildings here shall be no more than three stories tall," replied the Journeyman, who had inquired of the crewmen. "Taller buildings would block the prevailing winds, and wind is important for cooling the royal brow and keeping the Sultan's air fresh."

"I wondered why there were so few towers or tall keeps," said Mallet, nodding his understanding. "What features attracted the old Sultan to this place, I wonder. It seems a bit out of the way to me."

"Well, sir," replied Myrn, "they say it's actually almost exactly central to the whole country. No one tribal or city Sheik can claim the Sultan favors him by living nearer to his lands than to those of others, you see. And it's warm here in winter but not overly hot in midsummer."

"Besides that," the Seaman murmured, "the Desert Sheiks are this Trobuk's people. He has his roots under the dunes, as they say."

"Well, it's very pretty; very romantic," decided Myrn, shading her eyes against the sun's sparkle on the blue-green water. "Master Augurian says palm trees always make a place seem quite exotic, and I guess he's right."

"I wonder what it's like with a strong east wind," Mallet asked no one in particular. "Pretty gritty, I'd guess."

"I hear, Captain, that great sandstorms are the bane of wintertime living here in Balistan," Myrn agreed soberly. Then she broke into a wide grin and chuckled. "I'm told one of the Great Sultan's harsher punishments is banishment into the desert in the chill and blustery winters."

"The good gentleman seems to have a fine sense of proportion," noted Mallet. "Personally, I hope to be safe in Westongue Harbor or at sunny Wayness Isles with my family before winter comes again."

They were met at the royal dock by a large crowd of waving and cheering people, mostly men. When the mooring lines were tossed up on the long stone pier, eager hands gathered them in and quickly tied the ship up, with due regard for the prevailing wind.

"A brassy band, even!" Simon laughed. "We're to be honored guests, I see."

"There's the Grand Vizier," the ferry captain noted, sounding a bit sour. "His name is Kalinort. The one dressed all in richest black, I mean. A beetling-browed and ill-natured nobleman, I've heard. Turns on smiles and scowls like a *fellahin* opens and closes an irrigation sluice."

The Grand Vizier waited until Captain Mallet stepped ashore, then greeted him gravely and with all signs of respect.

After some ceremonial speeches and a fanfare or two from the long brass trumpets, Mallet's party fell in behind the Seacaptain and the Grand Vizier and moved between lines of the Sultan's cheering subjects up the stone-paved strand and through the wide-open gates of the city.

Myrn moved ahead to be close enough to Mallet to hear what was said in the lead party, just following the six *Encounter* Midshipmen.

"His Worship the Sultan Trobuk will greet you in person this evening at a private supper," the black-clad Vizier was saying to Mallet. "Until then, I am to show you to suitable quarters and provide all comforts and services you may require, Honored Seacaptain. We will walk, if you have no objection. The palace precincts are less than a thousand paces up this gentle slope, on the brow of the hill."

"A bath would be welcome, and fresh clothing," considered Mallet, seemingly unperturbed by the elaborate formality of his welcome. "We eagerly look forward to meeting His Sublime Excellency the Sultan, my dear Grand Vizier. We are entirely at his pleasure, of course. Our business in Samarca was satisfactorily completed five days ago in Port."

"Ah! But perhaps you would recommend some trade goods, in which we could invest . . . things imported from your far shores of Sea," said the officer of the court. "In fair exchange for ours."

"It'll be my great pleasure to do so," replied the Seacaptain. "I can recommend to your weavers our superior woolen yarns or to your best tailors, tent-, and sail-makers the famous Wayness-cotton canvases and tarpaulins. Or, perhaps, straight, sturdy pine timbers for shipbuilding or construction, fresh-cut in New Land?"

"Those, certainly, and perhaps much, much more," agreed the Vizier. "There'll be plenty of time to go into the details, tomorrow. Tonight, you are to be the Great Sultan's guest, and he will be most pleased if you will relax and enjoy his hospitality."

"Seems sort of oily, doesn't he?" Myrn whispered to Simon, who was walking just in front of her.

"Speak carefully, Mistress Myrn," warned *Encounter*'s factor. "No telling whose ears are turned toward us in this crowd!"

"You're right, of course," agreed Myrn.

The party moved through an ornate gate into the palace grounds, immaculately tailored and pleasantly filled with alternate squares of closely trimmed lawn and bright flower gardens, splashing fountains and deep ponds.

"I shall watch and listen."

She pursed her lips behind her veil and gazed about her with interest at the Sultan's palace.

"Will your . . . er, the young maiden . . . share your quarters?" asked Grand Vizier Kalinort suddenly. They had reached the visitors' wing of the palace and an efficient staff was busy assigning rooms.

Caught by surprise, Mallet cleared his throat.

"Oh, ah . . . no! She's not really a . . . personal servant nor a slave," he stammered. "Ah . . . daughter of an old business associate I've agreed to allow to travel with me. She should have quarters of her own."

Kalinort nodded his head, showing no surprise.

"Then perhaps you'll allow me to quarter her in the *hareem*, good Captain. She'll be quite safe there and much more comfortable. My own daughter resides therein. 'Tis a man's world else, as you may have noticed."

Mallet caught Myrn's slight nod and said, "Of course. Whatever you think proper, Grand Vizier."

Behind the official's back he frowned at Myrn, not happy to have her too far separated from him. Myrn smiled slightly but made no comment when a liveried manservant approached to lead her down an arcaded way toward another part of the huge, pleasant sprawl of palace.

"She'll be under the care of Her Divine Highness the Sultana Nioba," she heard the Grand Vizier explain to Mallet. "Most comfortable and honored, you may be sure. Sultana Nioba will make her feel as if she were at home."

The turbaned servant waited patiently, giving no sign of approval or disapproval, then led Myrn through an elaborately carved—and obviously closely guarded—door into the Sultan's seraglio.

Chapter Seven

The Sultana

THE silent manservant escorted Myrn no farther than a large, high-ceilinged anteroom just within the sturdy entryway to the *hareem*. Here he introduced her to a middle-aged, rather plump and motherly woman named Aeasha.

Lady Aeasha bowed deeply to Myrn, wished her a long and pleasant stay in Balistan, and led her through a long series of ornate public rooms without further comment.

"How beautiful!" exclaimed Myrn. "And so very comfortable, I must say also."

"Thank you, Mistress Brightglade," said the woman over her shoulder. "It's the finest *hareem* anywhere in Nearer East, or so I'm told. Come this way, please!"

She gestured to a husky female archer armed with a long recurved bow and a short, straight sword. With a salute, the soldier opened another heavy door and Lady Aeasha led the Journeyman Aquamancer through, around an open garden court with a fountain-fed pool in its center, to a door on the far side.

"These will be your apartments, Lady Brightglade," she said to Myrn, bowing again at the open door. "If it pleases you, that is. Will you inspect my choice?"

Myrn entered the apartment and allowed Aeasha to show her the six big, high-ceilinged, elaborately decorated rooms, most with windows overlooking Lake Balissa and the green hills to the west.

"*Most* comfortable!" Myrn approved. "Far too fine for me, I'm sure, but I'll accept them with great pleasure, good Lady Aeasha. Is this the bedchamber? It's almost as large as my parents' whole cottage at home on Flowring Isle!"

Myrn inspected the luxurious bedroom and the sumptuous bath beyond, a private sitting room to one side, a large formal parlor on the other, a wide balcony overlooking the lake, and a private dining room.

The sixth room seemed to be a study. It was lined on three walls with rows of shelves filled to overflowing with imposing-looking books and parchment scrolls, and chests under deep-set, latticed windows which held a selection of fine musical instruments and a wide variety of toys made of gold, silver, ivory, and sweet-smelling woods.

"This is your dayroom," explained Lady Aeasha, sweeping her arm about to show it off. "Of course, if there's anything else you might require or desire to make your stay content and comfortable, you have but to ask."

She explained that each room was equipped with a gong which, when struck, would bring one or more servants—herself, chambermaids, parlor maids, cooks, musicians, dancers, storytellers, hairdressers, butlers, and so on, a list which quite took Myrn's breath away.

"Are there other residents in the . . . er . . . seraglio?" she asked at last.

"Oh my, yes! The Sultan has but one wife and the Royal Couple are, as yet, childless, but a number of Sultana Nioba's close lady friends and personal attendants come frequently to keep her company. And, of course, there is the Lady Gerhana, over on the desert-view side."

"Gerhana? Who is she, pray tell?" wondered Myrn, trying one of the soft, bouncy divans in the sitting room.

"Ah . . ." Aeasha hesitated. "She's the daughter of the Grand Vizier."

The matronly seraglio mistress glanced about quickly before she added, "A rather sullen sort of child, poor Lady Gerhana. Just into her teens, and . . . well . . . *difficult,* at times."

It was all Aeasha would say about the Grand Vizier's daughter.

"And the *rules*?" asked Myrn. "I assume, this being a seraglio, there are some very firm regulations."

"Oh, not so strict as some, nor so strict as they once were, bless you, my lady! His Peerless Sublimity the Sultan has relaxed or done away with many of the old *Rules of Proper Conduct for Royal Concubines and Wives*. Well, Sultana Nioba is his *only* wife, you see. In the days of the old Sultan, the young Sultan's grandfather, twelve wives and forty-seven children lived here at one time or another."

"Forty-seven children!" exclaimed Myrn, sitting up straight. "Will he—will His Majesty the Sultan, that is . . . eventually take more than the one wife?"

"It used to be common practice," Aeasha admitted in a whisper, "but Sultan Trobuk has been heard to say he intends to do away with the old marriage customs. He's quite deeply in love with his Sultana. But between you and me and this mute wall here, I believe the Grand Vizier intends to break his resolve on that point. He would like his own daughter . . . but I've said far too much already."

"Tell me which rules apply, then," begged Myrn, for the woman showed signs of retreating in some confusion.

"Oh, well . . . not many apply to you. You should not leave the *hareem* unannounced, but inform me, or the Grand Vizier, or the Sultan himself, first. Then you may go almost anywhere in the palace you desire . . . with the exception of the Sultan's own suite, of course. Unless he invites you—in which case he'll send a servant to escort you past his guards."

"Little chance of that," said Myrn, thinking aloud. "What else?"

"Well, let me see," said the plump Aeasha. "Ah, you must dress properly, modestly, outside the seraglio walls, of course. Veils are no longer required, but bare . . . er . . . bosoms and bare feet are *strictly* forbidden! And your head should be covered, but that's only loosely held to, you'll find. A light scarf over your hair is simply polite, if you are unmarried."

"Even for a guest?" asked Myrn, shaking her head. She seldom wore any sort of hat, except at Sea when bad weather made it desirable. "Besides, I'm married and the mother of two."

"It's for your own protection, you see. Even for me! And no man has thought me attractive in fifteen years."

This last was so sadly said that Myrn touched her companion's arm in sympathy.

"Now, I doubt that!" she said. "I think you're quite handsome, and I know quite a few gentlemen who would agree."

"You . . . you . . . are *most* kind," said Lady Aeasha, sighing, then recovering her composure with a struggle. "You see, I was betrothed in marriage once, fifteen years ago, but my intended husband was killed in a fall from his horse. Custom doomed me to life as a widow. I'm most fortunate that the Sultan, who is a very kind young man, took pity on me and appointed me to this post . . . long before there were royal wives to care for, in fact. He was then yet little more than a child himself."

Myrn patted Aeasha's plump hand.

"Maybe if Sultana Nioba were to tell her husband of your unhappiness . . ."

"Oh, am I really unhappy, for all that?" asked the Seraglio Mistress. "I have very important duties to attend to and the sweet, good Sultana and even poor young Lady Gerhana to look after and mother. They are both really most kind and generous. . . ."

"How do I seek permission to leave the apartments, then?" asked the Aquamancer, changing the subject.

"Call me, and I'll arrange for an escort, if you need one. The palace at Balistan and its grounds are vast and beautiful, and there's much to see and do. Not to mention the city beyond the walls—the bazaars, the cafes, the theaters, the lake for fishing and boating, and secluded beaches for bathing. Adventurous souls ride out on the dunes to picnic or visit wandering Sheiks . . . but I don't recommend that without a trusted guide, at least until you're more familiar with the ways of the desert. In fall and winter there're often quite terrible sandstorms which can be *very* dangerous."

"A sea of sand doesn't particularly worry me," decided Myrn as the Seraglio Mistress started again toward the front door. "Maybe I'll try swimming in the lake. Is it safe?"

"Safe as kittens," the woman assured her. "Thank you, dear Mistress Brightglade. Pull on the red cord whenever you wish me to come. I'll be here at once, unless I'm called first to attend on the Sultana."

"Tell me one other thing," said Myrn as they neared the

door to the apartment. "What sort of person is Sultana Nioba? When do you think I could greet her?"

"There's no kinder, gentler, more affectionate, more sweet-tempered lady in the whole of Samarca! If you like, I'll tell her that you wish to meet her privately. She's sure to agree, for she is . . . well, although I shouldn't say it . . . lonely, despite her friends here and her husband the Sultan just at the other end of the palace."

"Do that, Aeasha," murmured Myrn. "I should pay my respects to her, at any rate. She sounds like a very nice person."

"Oh, she is that," Aeasha assured her from the doorway. "Good afternoon, Lady Myrn! Now, strike the blue gong and your own servants will come to you. As for me, ring the red bell when I can help you further."

And she whisked out and down the hall, as if she feared she had said much too much already.

Myrn amused herself by exploring the large, airy apartment in depth, not just looking at the luxurious furniture and fine furnishings, but probing for secrets using certain Wizardly skills she'd learned from Augurian, long ago.

She soon discovered a hidden passageway within the thick wall between her bedroom and the sitting room, complete with hidden peepholes through which to watch and hear anyone in either room. A spy could reach this secret passage from a linen closet in the hall outside, and presumably reach other passages overlooking the several adjacent empty apartments as well.

"Inches deep in drifted sand and dust," she muttered to herself. "And the hinges haven't been oiled in years! Nobody's used these secret ways to spy on the Sultan's *hareem* in a long, long time. Good!"

Just to be sure, she installed some simple Confusion Spells. When she was finished, no intruder could use the secret passages without her knowing of it, and once he got inside, the spy holes would be very difficult to use due to an excess of spiderwebs in the proper places.

Myrn opened a wide, latticed door and went onto the private terrace. She was gazing out over the lake and wishing Douglas were with her when there came a discreet knock on the apartment's front door.

She started to utter a charm for door-opening, but stopped herself in time.

No use giving myself away just yet, she mused.

She walked to the door and peeped through its own hidden spy hole. Lady Aeasha waited patiently on her doorstep, hands demurely folded.

"Her Majesty the Sultana would be pleased if you could come see her, now," she called to Myrn through the panels. "There'll be very little time later."

"Well, if she doesn't mind a little dust and sweat...," Myrn said, laughing as she opened the door for Aeasha. "I haven't had a bath yet."

"Of course, you *should* bathe...," began the Seraglio Mistress. "But if you don't come soon, who knows when 'later' will be. Tomorrow, perhaps?"

"I'll come now, then, dirt, dust, sweat, and all," decided Myrn. "Let me run a comb through my hair and splash my face with cool water."

In less than five minutes Myrn had followed the Seraglio Mistress around the center court to the southern wing of the seraglio.

"This wing is mostly empty, of course," Lady Aeasha told her, speaking softly. "In the old days..."

"Grandfather had a number of wives, I gather," said Myrn matter-of-factly. "How'd he manage it, I wonder, Aeasha. Personally, I can't think of anything more boring than a whole wing filled with women with little to do but get into mischief."

"I wasn't here then, of course," said the Seraglio Mistress. "I have *heard* such tales, m'lady! Makes you think maybe the young Sultan is wisest after all, holding his wives to one nice lady like our Sultana!"

She paused at a door at the end of the hallway and knocked twice, softly.

In a moment the door swung wide and they were admitted by a girl in a rather brief costume consisting of a pair of trousers of clinging, transparent material and a bodice of the same flimsy cloth wrapped loosely about her breasts several times and tied behind her neck.

"Her Majesty awaits you, ladies!" The maid bobbed and smiled. "This way, please."

Myrn and Aeasha followed her through a large, ornately decorated reception room, down a short, mirrored hall, and out onto an open balcony shaded from the afternoon sun with green-and-white striped awnings—the royal colors, Myrn guessed, for they had appeared on all the flags flying at the royal dock when the Seacaptain's party had landed.

Seated on a low couch against the curving balcony baluster was a beautiful and somewhat wistful-looking young woman with light brown skin and the largest, clearest, most appealing brown eyes Myrn had ever seen.

"Her Highness the Sultana Nioba, First and Forever Wife of our Gracious and Gifted Sultan Trobuk," Lady Aeasha announced, dropping a deep courtesy. "Your Majesty, may I present Lady Myrn Manstar Brightglade of Waterand and Flowring Islands in western Great Sea?"

The Sultana nodded her head pleasantly to Myrn's own, respectful bow.

"Welcome to our palace and our country, Lady Myrn."

"Very pleased to meet Your Majesty," replied the Aquamancer, bowing again gravely. "Forgive me if I don't know quite the protocol for meeting a Sultana. You're the very first I've ever seen."

Sultana Nioba laughed. Her smile lit up her heart-shaped face like a beacon from within.

"No formalities are needed, Lady Myrn. I'm so pleased you wished to meet me privately. Official functions never do much for getting acquainted with one's guests, I find. Please have a seat and let us become friends."

She patted the cushions beside her. Myrn seated herself at once.

"Leave us, if you wish, Aeasha," said the Sultana. "I know you have much to do, even in this empty *hareem*."

The Seraglio Mistress bowed twice, smiled encouragingly at Myrn, and left the two young ladies alone on the balcony.

"Or will she listen from inside the walls, Majesty?" Myrn wondered aloud.

"Not Aeasha!" The Sultana laughed aloud. "I don't think it has ever occurred to Aeasha to spy on me—or on anyone else, for that matter. I'm very fond of Aeasha. I sometimes wish she were a bit more . . . well, *assertive*!"

"I know what you mean, Your Highness." chuckled Myrn.

"Tell me of yourself—your origins, your education, your travels," Nioba begged, leaning forward eagerly. "I would love to travel, but there has been little opportunity so far. Where is your Isle of Flowring? Is that right? Flowring? A strange name."

"Don't they teach even future Sultanas practical stuff like geography?" Myrn asked. "No? Well, let me give you your first lesson."

She drew a piece of chalk from her wide left sleeve and began to draw the outlines of Sea on the blue-tiled floor at their feet, showing, one by one, the locations of Old Kingdom, Dukedom, Highlandorm, the Empire of Choin, and, across the lower edge, the vast desert Serecomba.

"This is now called New Land," Myrn said, drawing in the long course of New River. "A few years ago it ceased to be Eternal Ice Glacier when the ice began to melt."

"A river of ice!" exclaimed Nioba. "It's hard to imagine."

"Very cold and rather uncomfortable, if you don't dress warmly," Myrn added. "But true! Actually, I was prisoner there for several days, four years ago. It took my best efforts to keep from turning quite blue."

The Sultana begged eagerly for the story and when her women came to bathe and dress her for dinner, the two girls were chattering and laughing like old school friends.

"You must tell me more of your wonderful Wizard husband and beautiful children and the dear old Wizards!" cried the Sultana, rising reluctantly. "Later. I'll have you seated next to me at dinner. Your stories are better than my grandmother's fantasies of *djinni* and wicked sorcerers!"

"My pleasure, Your Majesty," said Myrn rather formally now that the servants were within earshot. "My very great pleasure!"

No one came to show Myrn back to her apartment but she had a Wizard's bravery and a Seaman's sense of direction, so found her way without a faltering step. She pulled the blue cord which called her chambermaids, stripped off her dusty traveling clothes, and slid gratefully into a hot, perfumed bath.

She noted a new costume laid out for her on the bed.

"I see they didn't give me anything in green." She laughed aloud, working up a mound of fragrant lather with the vial of scented soap she found in a silver tray beside the pool. "Green must be the *royal* color here. No matter! Blue's my best color anyway."

Aeasha came to escort Myrn to the Sultan's private dinner party, giving her an approving glance and a timid smile.

"We'll walk slowly, as we're a bit early," she told the Aquamancer, holding the door wide. "What a becoming necklace of strange white stones! What are they, please?"

"Pearls," Myrn explained. "Haven't you ever seen pearls before?"

"Never!" cried the Seraglio Mistress. "Pearls? They must come from very far away."

"Never seen pearls before?" wondered the Aquamancer aloud. "They aren't earth gems, like your own rubies and amethysts. They're water jewels, grown by Sea creatures called oysters."

" 'Oysters'?"

Myrn used their leisurely stroll from the seraglio through the main palace to the Sultan's private wing to explain the origins and uses of pearls.

"I never heard of such a wondrous thing," exclaimed the Seraglio Mistress. "And I've had to become an expert on rare jewels and precious metals in my position."

She left Myrn in the charge of a tall, silent Guardsman at the entrance to the Sultan's private apartment.

"I'll come or send someone to escort you back to your apartment when the dinner ends," she told Myrn.

"You aren't invited to dinner?" Myrn asked in surprise.

"No. I've my duties to attend to, of course. With you and the Sultana here, and Lady Gerhana also, my *hareem* is empty except for servants. I'll have a pleasant meal with my chief assistants, and we'll conduct business and perhaps play draughts later in my own little apartment on the desert side. Have a splendid evening, Mistress!"

And she disappeared as quickly as that.

Myrn found she had arrived, as Aeasha had implied, well in advance of the other guests at the Sultan's party. While she waited in a richly decorated anteroom, she spent the time examining the shelves of books and scrolls around the walls, trying to decipher their strange titles and wondering if any of them contained pictures. She reached for a large, leather-bound volume, intending to leaf through it.

"A most ponderous and learned treatise on civil engineering," said a voice behind her.

Turning, Myrn smiled at a rather dour girl with heavy, reddish-brown hair and a bad case of acne on her chin.

She was dressed as frumpily as possible for one wearing the light, loose clothing of the women of Samarca. She was tall and gangly, perhaps thirteen years of age, with practically no figure at all. Her brown-yellow evening robe fell straight from her thin shoulders to the floor.

"I'm Myrn Brightglade," the Journeyman said at once, smiling warmly and nodding her head. "I guess you're the Vizier's daughter, Lady Gerhana, aren't you? Someone told me you also lived in the *hareem*."

"I am the *Grand* Vizier's daughter," declared the young lady, touching Myrn's extended hand tentatively. "I am . . . pleased to meet you, a stranger from over Sea!"

"*Grand,* then," said Myrn with a laugh. "I've met your father, of course. And heard a little about you, Gerhana, my dear. How old are you?"

Gerhana blushed bright red and admitted to being almost fourteen years of age.

"A difficult age for us girls," Myrn sympathized. "I remember being thirteen. I wanted desperately to be a boy like my brothers. But I found later that being a girl had overwhelming compensations."

"If you say so, Mistress Brightglade," replied the Vizier's— *Grand* Vizier's—daughter with a sad little sigh.

"I say it, but you'll have to experience it for yourself, Gerhana. Tell me about yourself! I haven't seen many . . . in fact, I've seen *no* young people your age here since I arrived."

"Oh, there're plenty of them about the palace and out in the city," offered Gerhana, showing a glint of enthusiasm for the first time. "Unfortunately, my father—"

She closed her mouth with a snap as several men appeared in the doorway, talking animatedly and laughing. Among them was Captain Mallet, who broke away from his new friends and came to greet Myrn with some relief.

"My brand-new friend, Lady Gerhana, the Grand Vizier's

daughter," Myrn introduced them. "Captain Mallet is commander of the sloop *Encounter*," she explained to Gerhana. "A good friend and trusted guardian, I can attest."

"You are not his concubine, then?" Gerhana asked with disturbing directness.

"Not . . . what . . . ?" began Mallet, surprised by the blunt question from one so young.

"No, Captain Mallet was kind enough to allow me to travel with him to this place," Myrn said. "I'll explain it to you later, if you'd like. Captain Mallet is a good friend of mine, and of my husband's, also."

Gerhana frowned for a moment, then said, "That explains why you are housed in the seraglio, rather than sharing a bed with the good Captain."

A splendidly dressed and beturbaned young man with a carefully curled and trimmed short beard and long mustaches waxed into magnificent curves on either side of his smiling mouth came in, greeting Gerhana with a cordial bow and clapping Mallet on the shoulder.

The Grand Vizier's daughter bowed deeply and Myrn followed her lead.

"Is this your ward, then, Captain Mallet?"

"This is Mistress Myrn Manstar Brightglade, Sire," Mallet introduced her. "From the island called Flowring in South Seas. Wife of a very good friend of mine, Fire Wizard Douglas Brightglade of Wizards' High in Dukedom. Myrn, my dear, this is His Most Solemn Majesty, the Sultan Trobuk of this land Samarca. He's our host and the sole ruler of this beautiful country."

Myrn managed another graceful curtsy and a brilliant smile.

"I've had the pleasure of meeting your beautiful Sultana, sir," she said. "We are already good friends, I think."

"Ah, my Nioba! She should be here momentarily. It is protocol for the Sultana to arrive last, you understand."

"That explains why Lady Aeasha made sure I arrived early," said Myrn.

"I'm sure of it. Tell me, Mistress, have you been in our country long?"

"Only a very short while, sir," admitted Myrn.

"And how do you find it?" the Sultan inquired.

"Delightful, Your Majesty." Myrn answered. "Absolutely delightful!"

Just then the outer door was swung wide by a pair of young men in splendid green-and-white livery who bowed deeply to the assembled company and then, turning to flank the door, bowed even more deeply to the latest arrival, the Sultana Nioba.

"My dear!" cried Sultan Trobuk, glowing suddenly with obvious pride and affection. "Come and meet out new friends from the far West."

"Sultan-husband!" murmured Nioba, bowing. "Yes, I've already met the delightful Lady Myrn, thank you. And this must be the Seacaptain of whom she told me ... Mallet of Wayness?"

Mallet bowed extra deeply, a bit flustered by the appearance of the beautiful young Sultana.

A red-turbaned court functionary appeared at an inner door, announcing supper. Further conversation was lost in a general movement toward the dining room.

"You've met Gerhana, the daughter of our Grand Vizier?" Nioba asked Myrn once they were settled at their table.

"We've had but a few moments to chat, Your Highness," replied Myrn, smiling at the girl warmly. "I look forward to talking to her much more."

"We're fellow inmates of the seraglio," Gerhana said a bit sourly. "We'll have plenty of time to get to know each other."

The Sultan and the male members of the dinner party were seated at a large, well-laden table on the terrace looking out over the lake, where the sun was setting. Gerhana's father arrived just then, bowing and scraping, ignoring the ladies except for a perfunctory nod in their direction.

The few other ladies present, wives of the Sultan's ministers, were seated with the Sultana, Myrn, and Gerhana at a smaller table indoors.

Servants immediately entered through a hidden doorway, bearing pitchers of iced fruit nectar and, Myrn suspected, wines and aperitifs for the men to accompany the first course, a dark green ice decorated with delicate rosettes of mint and spearmint leaves.

The ladies' table got only the fruit nectar to drink, which pleased Myrn well, for it was delicious.

"If you desire wine, Lady Myrn," said Nioba, "I'll ask the steward to serve it to you."

"Women," said Gerhana with a grimace, "are not supposed to be able to control themselves after a sip of anything with alcohol in it."

"I *prefer* fruit nectar, actually." Myrn said lightly, sipping from her goblet. "Thank you anyway, ladies."

At the main table the men talked of trade and Sea routes, laughing and drinking what proved to be Choin *fungwah* and, when the first course was paraded from the butler's pantry, commenting on the flavors, colors, and textures of the dishes.

At the ladies' table, Sultana Nioba guided both the choices of food and conversation. She was kind to Gerhana, who was rather too quiet under the sharp eyes of her father, and managed to include her pleasantly in the conversation.

"I love most of all to ride out on the desert," Nioba told Myrn. "I was born on the wide grasslands, you know, and rode a horse as soon as I could stay in a saddle."

"I'm absolutely no good on a horse for anything but slow riding," admitted the Journeyman Aquamancer. "My chosen element is water."

"I never even learned to swim," confided the Sultana with a sigh. "I never *saw* a body of water bigger than a bathtub before I married. The lake here is quite frightening to me."

"I swim in the lake every day, when I can get away from the seraglio," put in Gerhana, joining in the conversation for the first time. Nioba had probably chosen the subject of swimming to include the young girl, Myrn thought.

"Do you sail?" she asked Gerhana.

"No, I've never been in any sort of boat, except for the barges crossing the lake," Gerhana admitted.

"I'm completely at a loss on the lake myself," the Sultana said. "Perhaps between you and Mistress Brightglade, you can teach me to swim, Hana?"

"My pleasure, indeed," Myrn said.

"And mine. Anytime at all!" replied the girl, obviously pleased. "I know a nice, secluded beach, not far south of the city. It would be a pleasant picnic outing for you, Highness."

"I'll arrange it, then," decided Nioba with a quick nod.

"My husband swims every other day or so, I know. I should *try* to learn, at least."

"He's the one who should teach you to swim," Myrn suggested.

"Oh, it's just not done!" cried young Hana, sincerely shocked at the idea.

Nioba blushed crimson and changed the subject to horses.

"I have with me a remarkable little horse I call Nameless," said Myrn to the other ladies. "She's stabled with your own horses, I understand, Highness. Quite unusual, and very pretty, too!"

"Then we shall go riding in the morning . . . and swimming lessons and a picnic lunch on the beach," Nioba decided.

Chapter Eight

New Arrivals

AEASHA was waiting nervously in the Sultan's antechamber when the dinner party ended just before midnight. She bowed to the Sultana and then to Gerhana, whose sullen look had disappeared since the beginning of the dinner party, and finally to Myrn.

"May I escort you to your apartments, Sultana and ladies?" she asked.

"How nice!" exclaimed Myrn. "Your palace is so enormous that I wouldn't be surprised to get lost."

"The palace is a man's world," sniffed Hana, but she softened her remark with a grin. "We would greatly appreciate your seeing us safely home, Lady Aeasha."

Sultana Nioba smiled at them all, gave the Seraglio Mistress a fond hug, and motioned to the Captain of her personal Guard to precede them down the lantern-lit corridor.

"They're all such *nice* young men," she said to Myrn. "It's part of their training to escort me anywhere I go outside the *hareem,* you see. It can be a nuisance for them, of course, but my dear Trobuk has limited their duties to relatively formal occasions like this."

The four of them walked abreast down the wide corridor, chatting of dinner and the guests and their outing on the morrow. Nioba gave the Seraglio Mistress orders for the picnic, and suggested which horses she would choose for their morning ride on the desert.

Myrn reluctantly decided that little Nameless would not be suited to such a ride.

"I'll inform the Guard Officer," promised Aeasha solemnly. "It's the rule. . . ."

"I should have asked my husband to rescind that rule about having an armed escort while riding outside the palace. Oh, well . . . just mention it to the Captain, up ahead, before they leave us at the *hareem* door, please, will you? We shall not require them at the picnic on the shore, of course. That'll be private . . . for just us ladies, I think."

Aeasha nodded agreement, and shortly she moved ahead to speak to the Captain of the Escort.

"I'm certainly glad I don't have to have an armed escort to go everywhere," said Myrn. "How do you stand it, Majesty?"

"Just call me Nioba when we're not in formal company," begged the Sultana. "I get so tired of formalities! Actually a guard or two will be comforting when we ride out on the sands. It's so easy to get lost, and there are wandering tribes who come close in the night—mostly out of curiosity, I think."

The guard formed two lines to see them through the seraglio door, saluting and wishing the ladies a good night.

Myrn thought Hana glanced a bit more lingeringly at the last Guardsman in line . . . and that the soldier smiled under his dark mustache at her for a brief moment.

"A friend?" she whispered to the girl.

"Hardly!" sniffed the Grand Vizier's daughter, but she colored quite prettily as they passed through the heavy door before it was closed behind them by the female soldiers on duty within.

Myrn and Hana escorted the Sultana to her apartment and stood talking at the door for some minutes, loath to let a pleasant evening end.

"I'll send word to you about our starting hour tomorrow morning," Nioba said to them both.

"I suppose someone can provide a suitable riding habit for me?" said Myrn. "And a swimming costume, also? I'm afraid I didn't bring either."

The Sultana laughed. "You'll have them both in large choice before we ride out."

She kissed them both good night, smiled, and waved as they turned to go back to their own suites down the long corridor.

"Do you like the Sultana?" Hana asked when they were well out of hearing.

"Oh, very much indeed," Myrn told her. "And I know *you* like her, also."

"I love her very much. My mother died when I was still a baby, you see. Although my father is quite coldly formal to Nioba, I regard her secretly as my second mother. She's very kind to me, while my ambitious father is interested in me only as a gaming piece."

"Here's my door," said Myrn. "Come in for a while to talk? I'm not tired myself, as yet."

Gerhana hesitated a moment, and then nodded.

"There's so much about you that I don't know," she told Myrn.

"I'll tell all, right from the beginning. There's no reason to hide anything."

"I won't tell anyone, even so," promised the girl, plumping down on a silk brocade hassock and tossing her heavy veil on the floor with a sigh.

"Let's begin by practicing smiling," declared Myrn. "Are you always so glum?"

Gerhana groaned in comic despair.

"*Ugly,* you mean! I feel like a . . . a . . . camel! I'm so skinny! And nothing seems to help these awful blemishes!"

"Let me see if I can do something for them, for I've made a special study of such things. I remember the skin problems I suffered when I was your age." Myrn laughed at the memory. "Don't look so surprised! You must have guessed by now that I'm a Journeyman Wizard."

"I . . . guessed something like that," said the girl, looking a little worried. "Nobody said it as a fact."

"Well, it's true! I'm a Journeyman Aquamancer. Among other things, we Water Wizards specialize in good feelings, such as you get from a nice, hot bath or a bracing swim in clear water. Your problem is, when you get right down to it, a matter of how you feel about yourself."

■   ■   ■

When she eventually sent the girl off to bed in her own suite, Myrn called her attendants—not so much because she needed help, but because she had no idea where her nightgown had been stored away.

"Cucumber slices for skin blemishes are an Aquamancy I've recommended to that lonely young girl," she told her hairdresser, who was running a brush through her lustrous black hair preparatory to braiding it for bed. "I think that would work quite well for our Hana, don't you?"

The hairdresser smiled at her own girlhood memories and said, "My mother used cucumber poultices on my face when I was that girl's age, Mistress. The secret is to use them in a *regular* nightly regimen, you know. Once a week or so doesn't do much good. I found that out the hard way. And you must scrub your face beforehand with the purest soaps, also, my mama insisted."

"Wise mama! I must remember to mention soap to Hana. What we won't do for our beauty," said the sleepy Aquamancer, yawning.

Douglas Brightglade and Cribblon came on deck to stretch their legs and fill their lungs with the cool air of early morning. The misty rain of the days before had blown away on a warm southerly wind and the sun was gem-bright as it rose from beyond the coastal hills of the Nearer East.

Marbleheart thumped down beside them on the still-damp deck.

"What in World are you doing?" Douglas asked, surprised by his Familiar's sudden appearance from above.

"Checking out the view," Marbleheart explained. He pointed upward. "From the main top, way up there!"

Douglas leaned back and glanced past the great, billowing main sail and the main tops'l above it. Beyond that a skys'l looked even brighter and cleaner than the more frequently spread canvas below.

"I didn't know you were a climber," Cribblon said to the Sea Otter.

"I can climb with the best of 'em," Marbleheart maintained stoutly. "But in this case I flew, thanks to a Short-Hop Spell Douglas taught me. We're coming to a harbor ahead, mates. I thought you'd like to know."

Just then a hail came from the foremasthead.

"Deck there! Bay entrance and a good-sized city, dead ahead!" the lookout called.

A flurry of activity ended the early-morning calm. Deckhands appeared at the sound of the Bos'n's pipe shrilling and shouted orders from the Officer of the Deck. Captain Caspar Marlin popped from the companionway under the poop, still drawing on his jacket and wiping at a fluff of shaving soap from beneath his chin.

He nodded to Douglas, Cribblon, and Marbleheart and turned about to glance at the ship's suit of sails, the clouds, and the nearing shoreline.

"Take in skys'ls, royals, and tops'ls!" he ordered his First Mate.

To the helmsman he gave a slight change in course, heading *Donation* more exactly toward the center of the wide, rock-framed entrance to the Port of Samarca.

"Ever been here before, Captain?" Douglas asked Caspar once the change of course and shortened sails had been accomplished and all off-duty hands had trooped below to breakfast.

"No, but I wouldn't be surprised if someone else from Wayness or Westongue has been here before us. Thornwood Duke intends to open all the old trading ports in this part of Sea. Reestablish trade and such."

Douglas nodded.

"Not a small place, at that," Caspar went on, studying the opening harbor through his glass. "Well, that figures! The old sailing instructions Thornwood unearthed from Dukedom's archives say it's the single port for a sizable country. Name of . . . Samarca, I believe."

"It was here that we lost track of Serenit, then?" asked Cribblon.

"And it was from here we last heard from Myrn." Douglas nodded his head. "She's no longer here, though."

"How do you know?" chirped the Otter. "Oh, by Wizard-to-Wizard Empathy! Yes, I fail to sense her anywhere about, but . . . yes, she *has* been here, and recently."

"Possibly. Surely," said his young Master. "We'll stay out of your way, Caspar. Until you get her into harbor."

Donation's crew dashed about in organized confusion. Sails were further shortened or lowered and bundled away into sail lockers, or furled neatly to their yards. *Donation*'s speed dropped quickly until she was wafting slowly along between the rocky headlands into the broad bay of Port.

"Hoist colors!" Caspar ordered. "Keep an open eye, up there! Anything happens, I want to know of it *at once,* hear ye?"

"Aye, aye, sir!" came the voice of the maintruck lookout. "Ah, Captain? There's a handsome sloop anchored in the roadstead. Looks to be a Waynessman! Probably . . . yes, 'tis *Encounter!*"

"Ah, Mallet's command," cried Caspar at once. "He's been to Sea for these nine months or more, touching many places here in eastern Sea last I heard."

"*Encounter*'s salutin' us," called the lookout. "Dips her ensign thrice, she does!"

"Signals, there! Give her the proper reply."

The signalman and his mates jumped to their flag bags and loosened the hoists, ready to bend on the bright flags as ordered.

"All clear over there, then," decided Douglas. "I think that fort ashore is signaling us, also."

"Sharp eye, m'lad!" cried Captain Marlin, for Douglas's words had hardly been spoken when the lookout called the same news of the flag hoist at the top of the low, round fort dominating the anchorage.

"I don't know that signal at all," complained the First Mate, a grizzled, middle-aged officer named Parmenter. "This here signal book says that hoist signifies 'Send over all prisoners!' But I don't . . ."

"Stand by to heave-to," snapped Captain Marlin. "We'll take no undue chances. Signals! Make 'Hail and well met' over my pennant, now. I'll let Mallet know who's come to join him, at least."

Douglas went below to change to his best Wizard's coat, in case he would be required to meet officialdom from ashore. Marbleheart flew again to the foremast crosstree, carefully staying clear of working parties just completing a neat heave-to.

In ten minutes the lookout reported a *dhow* sailing swiftly toward them.

"Friendly, do ye think?" inquired Douglas, returning to deck as he fastened his wide leather belt.

"No doubt friendly but being cautious," replied Caspar, studying the approaching boat through his glass. "There's armed men aboard her, but not enough to worry about, if they think to be aggressive, I'd say. Formal greeting party, more'n likely, Douglas. They'll hail us soon. . . ."

"*Donation* from *Encounter*," roared the signal yeoman. "*Encounter* says, 'Welcome to . . . ah . . . Samarca,' I guess he's saying, sir."

"Properly signaled! He says all is well, but Mallet's not aboard," Caspar relayed to Douglas.

He clapped his fancy, gold-laced tricorn hat on his head and strode over to the rail to watch the guardboat approach. " '*Dhow*' is what they calls 'em, these easterly people, as I recall. Handy little boats under sweeps or a single great triangular sail. For her length and draft, a useful guardboat, I'd say."

The *dhow* swung about broadside within hailing distance as her oarsmen hauled their sweeps in a dash of salt spray and let the craft drift sideways slowly toward the Waynessman on the easy harbor swell.

"Aboard the ship!" came a hail from her waist. "Welcome to Port of Samarca. Thank you for heaving-to. Give us your name and port of origin, please."

"Five whole days!" Caspar sputtered. "Never heard of such! What am I supposed to do for five days, sirrah? My men are already wild to set foot ashore here!"

"The Medical Officer must come aboard first, and we must complete certain . . . er . . . formalities, Captain," explained the young Coast Guard officer rather stiffly.

"Are there ways to speed things up, eh?" Caspar inquired.

"Not for me to say," replied the officer. "The worthy Port Master has been notified and will be along directly. After the Port Doctor has given your ship a clean bill of health, Port Master *may* shorten your quarantine by a bit. I can't promise a thing, sir."

Douglas smiled warmly at the earnest young man.

"You'll do everything you can to speed things up, won't you, Captain?"

"Ah, er . . . yes, good Master. Of course! It's my job," replied the officer, evidently a bit flustered. "I'll signal ashore to speed the Port Master. It's the best I can do."

"I understand," murmured the Master Pyromancer. "Meanwhile, may our compatriot over there visit us? We'll want to exchange greetings and mail."

"Well, really," protested the Guard Captain uneasily, glancing back over his shoulder at the fort. "Well . . . I don't see why not, Master."

"We'll so signal *Encounter,* then," said Douglas, gesturing toward the Wayness schooner. "Captain Marlin here will wait on His Excellency the Port Master, as soon as he can get here."

"Ah, yes, of course, sir," exclaimed the soldier. "There! I see His Excellency's *dhow* setting out from the landing, even now. I'll signal him all is well here aboard . . . *Donation,* did you say she's called?"

He turned to shout an order to a Guardsman, who ran to the rail and waved red-and-white semaphore flags about for a minute or two. Someone on the Port Master's boat acknowledged the flag signals and the large, ornate barge was propelled toward *Donation.*

"Talk to the Port Master first," Douglas said quietly to Caspar, "and then call whoever commands aboard *Encounter* to come report."

"Good enough, Fire Wizard," Caspar agreed.

He nodded to the Coast Guard officer. "Tell the good Port Master he is most welcome to board. Maybe your men would like a bit of—"

"No, we must stand off now and await the Port Master's signal that all is well, Captain. Maybe next time? Appreciate it, sir!"

He saluted and dropped down the accommodation ladder into his waiting boat, followed by his signalman, and ordered his oarsmen to give way.

"Play it coolly, then," Douglas advised Caspar. "Mallet and *Encounter* have been here for some days, I believe. We're not entirely a surprise. Just need to hear what's happened from *Encounter.*"

"I'll speak to the Port Master like a rich Wayness uncle, then," chuckled the Seacaptain. "We'll straighten out this pesky quarantine business right quickly. Five days! 'Tain't civilized, says I.''

But he waited patiently for the Port Master's boat to slide alongside, putting on his most agreeable, most diplomatic face.

Port Master Alama Sheik clambered laboriously up *Donation*'s accommodation ladder, puffing and spluttering the whole way. Behind him his crew carefully suppressed grins. A fine sweet-sour alcoholic vapor preceded the official onto *Donation*'s freshly holystoned quarterdeck.

"I will never understand why ships must come a-calling here at such unholy hours," the official growled at Caspar over the sound of the Bos'n's whistles, ignoring the salutes of the ship's officers and sideboys. "Who are you, sirrah? My head is splitting! Can't we sit down and get this over with?"

Caspar Marlin, at a loss for words, held his tongue and showed the obviously hungover Port official to a chair under an awning already spread to protect the visiting official from the hot morning sun.

"Conditions at Sea set the hour of our arrival . . . ," he began to explain to the landsman.

"Be ye rested, Port Master!" Douglas interrupted, touching the fat little Sheik's left elbow lightly. "Here! Take a cup of tea. It'll drive away your aches and the pains of official worry at once."

Alama frowned sourly at the young man but accepted the steaming cup from a steward and gulped at it, gingerly.

After a second and a third swallow, he heaved a tremulous sigh, shook his head, and smiled at the Wizard.

"Many thanks, young sir," he cried, wiping his lips on the back of his hand. "I feel revived already! My name's Alama. Good tea, this!"

"Our pleasure," murmured Douglas. "May I present Captain Marlin of *Donation* of Wayness and Westongue in Dukedom? I am Master Pyromancer Douglas Brightglade."

"A Wizard," exclaimed Alama, after bowing to Caspar and then to Douglas. "Am I right?"

"Yes—a Wizard of Fire, you understand. Most pleased to meet you in your beautiful Port of Samarca, Port Master."

"Wizards are few and far between here in Nearer East," observed the Sheik. "Welcome, at any rate, my dear sirs! May I ask your purposes in visiting our Sultan's Port and domain?

We welcome honest traders, of course. We've already been doing very brisk business with your sister-ship *Encounter* and with Captain Mallet.''

"So we surmised," put in Caspar. "A beautiful harbor! We hope to see it busy with out trade in a few short months."

"You don't happen to have any of the Choinese *fungwah*?" asked the Port Master, a trifle plaintively. "I feel the need to be restored somewhat and it's a remarkable tonic, I've been told."

Douglas took the Sheik's hand and touched his shoulder for a brief moment, looking the official directly in his bleared eyes.

"There's plenty of such medicine aboard, of course, but I don't see any signs of sickness in you, my dear Alama. Steady of hand! Clear of eye! You are, I'm sure, a trifle overweight, but one can understand that, you being in a sedentary sort of position."

Alama opened his mouth to protest but closed it again in some surprise.

"You know, I *do* feel rather fine, now. A momentary indisposition, I imagine. May I have another cup of your fine tea, instead? It has ... something else in it than just brewed leaves, perhaps? I own several thousand acres of upland coffee plantation and am something of an expert on drinking ... coffee, I mean."

"We get this tea from our friends in Choin," said Caspar. "May we sit down with you, Port Master?"

"Of course. And let us all enjoy some more of your Choinese tea. Quite bracing."

After several minutes of polite conversation in which the Port Master became increasingly friendly and talkative, thanks in part to the quality of the Choinese brew but helped a bit by some judicious magic, Alama turned to business.

"I could sit here in the shade on your spotless deck for hours, just chatting," offered the Port Master jovially. "But I know you're eager to come ashore and see what our Merchant Princes have to offer for sale and might wish to buy. I understand from my good friend Seacaptain Mallet that your wise Duke is seeking to reopen trade with this part of World."

He mentioned the five-day quarantine but hastened to say

he was empowered by the Sultan to reduce it to two days and one night in certain worthy cases.

"I've a warehouse packed to the rafters with green coffee beans waiting for a buyer. I fear that a day or two longer and they'll begin to sprout, at great cost to myself," Alama said sadly.

"Between us, *Encounter* and *Donation,* we can probably take all the coffee you have . . . at a reasonable price, of course," said Caspar, drawing out his well-thumbed notebook. "We can carry . . ."

The Seacaptain and the Port official entered into brisk discussion of coffee prices and delivery conditions. At the end of a half hour both parties were satisfied, the one to get a good price for coffee beans which might otherwise soon spoil, and the other to get a cargo with huge potential for profits in the West.

"As for the . . . ah . . . quarantine," said Alama, leaning back and reaching for a fourth cup of tea, "I can, on my own recognizance, reduce it to the two days and a night. That puts your official landing at the Port on tomorrow morning. I'd like you to meet with a delegation of our Merchant Princes. They represent our business community, you see. I assume you have other goods to trade, in addition to the tea leaves and the glass goods you mentioned?"

"Glass is the largest part of our cargo," said Caspar. "It comes from Old Kingdom and is the best quality I've seen in our part of World in my lifetime."

"Old Kingdom . . . a name we hear only in ancient romances, I fear," said the Port Master "We used to get all sorts of interesting and valuable goods from that quarter, before my day. I think you'll find markets here for many cargoes, Captain. I'll go ashore and arrange a meeting with the Merchant Princes, if we're done here. A Port Doctor is waiting to inspect your log and look at the health of your sailors. His fee is nominal . . . a fiftieth part of the value of the cargo you will have sold here, only."

"A reasonable fee, of course," said Caspar, wincing. "Anything else we should know?"

"Oh, yes! Here!" He drew a thick sheaf of papers bound with a green ribbon from his inner pocket and handed it over. "Port Regulations drawn up by our young Sultan Trobuk.

Note that import of alcoholic beverages is strictly forbidden. Please leave any you have aboard under lock and key.''

"I don't really have all that much, except a small supply for our own consumption," admitted Caspar. "May I offer you a dram or two, good Port Master Alama?"

Alama seemed about to accept, then looked quite surprised.

"No! I've no taste for liquors . . . and they are, after all, forbidden by law. Others may try to get you to sell what little you have, for liquors are scarce and bring good prices. I advise you to obtain our Sultan's permission before you do so. The penalties for illegal importation of alcoholic beverages are quite heavy."

"We'll be careful, then, and tell others to be careful when they call here," said Douglas, who had sat with the negotiators but said little until this moment. "For now, I suppose there is no objection if we signal *Encounter*'s Captain to report to us here?"

"No problem, Wizardly sir. Captain Mallet, my very good friend, is being entertained by our Sultan at his capital. Meanwhile, if you desire to visit Port before your quarantine is fully expired, you have but to send for me to arrange it. There would be a small . . . er . . . *administrative fee,* of course."

He departed, stone sober for a change yet feeling quite jolly, much to the surprise of his clerks, sailors, and marines, promising to come to call in the morning with full details of their official welcome.

Within a half hour of his departure Acting-Captain Pilot arrived by quarter-boat from *Encounter* to report to Captain Marlin, as requested by a fresh flurry of signal flags.

The morning ride was very pleasant, thanks to the company of the Sultana and Hana, who delighted in the freedom of the open High Desert. They never left sight of the low, square towers of Balistan Palace. The huge expanse of sand dunes was empty, hot, dry, and monotonous to Myrn . . . although, if challenged, she'd have had to admit it was very similar to being at Sea.

"Look there,' called out Hana, who'd ridden ahead to the top of a tall dune.

"What have you found?" Nioba called.

"Come see," answered the Grand Vizier's daughter.

They spurred to join her, followed by their guard of six soldiers, fully armed and looking rather hot and dusty.

Beyond the dune Gerhana had found signs of a campsite in the sand. Marks on the ground clearly showed where desert nomads had pitched their tents and tethered their camels.

"One of the wandering tribes, I suppose," said Nioba, drawing on her reins. "They enjoy complete freedom of High Desert, according to old custom and Sultanic law. My husband is a son of one of the most powerful desert clans, the Grearhs. Your father, Hana, claims they spy on us, but the Sultan says they're merely keeping an eye on the wastelands."

"Last March a nomad band rode right into Balistan to warn us of a great, late sandstorm coming," Hana told Myrn. "I've had that argument with Father, many times. I've given up on it! It just makes him colder and angrier at me than usual."

She shook her head sadly. The three women sat on their mounts for a moment, studying the traces of the nomad's night camp. It was already being effaced by drifting sand.

"Where do they go from here, then?" Myrn asked, easing herself in her saddle. Even the ride from Port of Samarca had not made her a happy equestrienne. She did enjoy the sense of freedom, however, after the carefully guarded *hareem.*

"It wouldn't mean much to you if I could tell you," laughed the Sultana. "Between our towers and the eastern mountains our desert men travel by the stars, for there are few landmarks."

" 'The way of a Desert Tribe in the sand and the way of a maid with a man,' " quoted Hana, " 'are among the greatest mysteries of the land.' "

Myrn urged her mare down the easy windward slope of the dune, where, in the midst of the campsite, she dismounted, studying the signs of occupancy left behind by the wanderers.

"A small group, actually," she announced, straightening up.

"You can read their signs?" asked Hana, obviously impressed.

"Partly. My husband Douglas is much better at it. I would guess . . . perhaps fifteen adults, and almost as many children, although it's hard to tell from *their* signs. Forty or so camels. They rode in from the northeast yester-evening and departed early this morning toward the south. Where do they find water, I wonder. There's no water nearer here than the lake."

"Perhaps they circled Balistan and filled their water skins from the lake waters during the night," Nioba guessed, riding down to Myrn's side.

"Still," said Myrn thoughtfully, studying the ground about them, "I would stake my advancement to full Aquamancy there's water not far underground here, if one would dig for it."

"No nomad would stoop to digging—not even for water," snorted Hana.

"Now, my dear, that isn't so," Nioba told her sternly. "There are places where nomads have dug great cisterns to reach water deep under the sand. I've seen them."

"I must believe you, Majesty," said the young girl with a sniff, "but it's hard to imagine the desert people actually *digging* for water . . . or anything else."

"Hana's not a desert child herself," Nioba explained to Myrn as they turned their horses back up the slope of the dune. "Coastal people never have much use for the sand tribes, I'm afraid."

"I would have thought the Grand Vizier—what's Hana's father's name? Kalinort?—I would have guessed he was of the same tribe or family as your husband."

"Not so! Kalinort is from a wealthy coast family. He's as capable as the day is long in summer," maintained the Sultana, "or so Trobuk insists. I sometimes wonder, myself. A prideful man, it's sure."

"For certain," Hana agreed emphatically. "And he's my own father."

The party rode a bit farther south, then turned due west, leaving their escort behind on the southern edge of Balistan. Met there by Aeasha and four maidservants, they made their way down to the shore of Lake Balissa, where the cool, green-blue waters lapped contentedly on sugar-white sand or splashed over half-submerged rocks.

Between two such rocks, each as big as small houses, the Sultana called a halt. Aeasha and her girls quickly erected a white canvas pavilion against the soft wind and bright sun—and against the eyes of passersby—so Myrn and her companions could slip out of their riding costumes and into bathing attire.

"Must be careful not to sunburn," Aeasha warned them.

"Here, rub a bit of this ointment upon your skin, especially on your shoulders and faces.

She produced a pleasant-smelling ointment in a silver-topped jar and showed them how to apply it.

"I never worried about sun burning before," protested Nioba.

Her skin was light milk chocolate in color, even where it was usually covered by her clothing.

"You haven't been out in the sun for weeks, at least," Hana told her. "Even *I* burn if I stay in the sun long enough."

"At least Aeasha's ointment smells much better than the wool-fat the desert people use to the same purpose," Nioba considered. "Who shall go in the water first? Myrn, my dear? You're the Water Adept!"

"I'll swim a bit for you to watch. Check out the local creatures at the same time—a good idea in strange waters," said the Journeyman. "Watch me, then, and see how I do it. Swimming's no difficult task, believe me! The bottom's quite filled with beautiful corals and speckled rocks, colored plants and very interesting fishes."

"Ugh," gasped Hana, making an ugly face. "Creepy-crawly, nasty, slimy things!"

"Not really! Most of 'em are entirely harmless, and the few harmful ones are the easiest to spot, so brightly colored are they. Sea creatures almost always give fair warning."

Chapter Nine

On the Trail

DOUGLAS, Cribblon, and Marbleheart found the Captain of the Sultan's Guard, a tall, rather an esthetic-looking man with a neatly trimmed black beard and a pale blue turban. His name was Aliada.

"We're looking for a missing friend. We believe he was kidnapped in the far northwest and brought through your city a few days back."

"These things happen, *effendi*," the Guard shrugged. "Your Wayness ships are not the only ones to call at Port of Samarca, you must understand. Our responsibility is to protect the lives and property of our citizens, not to keep track of strayed or stolen strangers."

Douglas nodded. "I imagine you take notice of almost everyone who comes to or passes through the Port, however."

The tall Guard nodded solemnly. A subordinate, a younger man, stood several paces away, watching and listening but saying nothing.

"If you could describe your friend's appearance, perhaps? Or that of his captors?"

"We don't know who captured him ... or why. Serenit himself is almost as tall as you, rather thinner, with short white hair. Light blue eyes. He'd be pale, unless they allowed him to become sunburned on the voyage hither from New Land.

He was wearing, when last seen, a woolen cloak of pale blue and a close-fitting cap of brown leather lined with lamb's wool. I *hope* his captors allowed him to take the warm surcoat off by the time they arrived here.''

"Certainly anyone dressed like that would be very noticeable," admitted Aliada with a small smile. "If his captors wished to conceal him, they would have taken his heavy clothing from him, I would think. No, I have no report of such a man here. White hair is very common. Pale blue eyes and pale skin . . . not nearly so common."

"As a Wizard," Douglas said, letting his glance sweep the entire waterfront from the top of the fortress wall where he'd been granted the interview by the Captain of the Sultan's Guard, "I sense his late presence, although his scent's perhaps two weeks old by now. My . . . informant . . . thought he was not held here long but passed through quickly."

"The highway east toward Balistan is the best road," Aliada volunteered. "Or, of course, his captors may have taken him north or south from here by ship. The desert stretches hundreds of miles both ways, north and south also."

"And in the east? There are mountains, I know, and then Ebony Sea, I think you call it, beyond?"

"Ebony Sea, yes, *effendi*, and on its near shore, the Darkest Mountains. There are some small mining settlements in those highlands, but it's inhospitable country, I hear."

Douglas nodded again. Cribblon changed the subject.

"The Seacaptain from Dukedom? The commander of *Encounter* sloop? His name is . . ."

'Ah, Captain Mallet! I'm aware of him, sir.''

"His second-in-command says he was called to the court of the Sultan."

"Yes, sir! He's gone to Balistan at the command of Sultan Trobuk. He and his party left . . . when was it, Frasci? Six days back? As it would take them only five days at most to reach the Sultan's palace, I'm safe in saying they've arrived there by now."

"Who was in Captain Mallet's party?" asked Marbleheart.

The Guard officer regarded the Sea Otter with some bemusement for the space of a breath.

"His party consisted of six young officers—Midshipmen, I believe they're called—and about the same number of Seamen, as servants and armed escorts," answered Frasci. "And a servant girl evidently loaned to the Seacaptain by Lady Shadizar, wife of Camel Merchant Farrouk."

"Farrouk?" asked Douglas. "That's a name new to me."

"The Seacaptain befriended Farrouk's family early in his stay," explained Aliada. "A bit of a scandal, actually. The Camel Trader is not at home."

"I understand," Douglas said, smiling. "Well and good! Perhaps we should seek an introduction to the Camel Merchant's wife? Do you see any objection to that course?"

"In the old Sultan's day it would have been unthinkable," the senior Guard considered slowly. "But this Shadizar and her husband are among the younger, less inhibited generation. May I have Officer Frasci show you the Camel Merchant's home? It is not far away, in the upper part of the city."

"I'll send her a note first, I believe," Douglas decided. "So as not to intrude on her privacy."

Frasci and his superior nodded, pleased by the Wizard's tact.

"I'll be pleased to take your message to Lady Shadizar's house, if you wish," volunteered Frasci, after a glance at his superior for approval.

"A shortish note, then," decided Douglas, drawing a pad of paper and a pen case from his wide left sleeve. "It'll take me just a moment."

When he'd written the note—

"My Lady Shadizar, wife of Farrouk the Camel Merchant—

A friend of Seacaptain Mallet respectfully requests the honor of a short interview at your convenience.

*Douglas Brightglade, Pyromancer
of Wizards' High, Dukedom."*

—and given it to the younger Guard, the Wizard, the Journeyman, and the Otter accepted an invitation from Captain Aliada to wait in the austere headquarters within the fortress wall until the subordinate returned.

They sipped sweet iced coffee and talked about the Great War, the struggle with The Darkness, and especially of the Fellowship of Wizards. Douglas outlined the history of the

West in the last two centuries while Nearer East had been cut off. Aliada listened carefully.

"We have had virtually no news of happenings in the West," Aliada explained. "It's good to know, now that we will be trading again with your countrymen. I've heard a bit of what you're telling me, of course. The Merchant Princes learned it from Seacaptain Mallet."

"I can see how, in your line of work, knowing something of our history would be useful," Douglas said dryly.

"Our tasks are to preserve order, of course, and protect his subjects in the name of the reigning Sultan," the Guard explained. "It's easier if we know the backgrounds of strangers we must deal with, as you can easily understand."

Frasci returned from his errand within the hour, bearing a note to Douglas from Lady Shadizar.

"My Good Pyromancer Douglas Brightglade," it said—,

"Please join me for midday luncheon at my home. It is possible I have more current news of your friend than others in this city. You will be most welcome!

> *Shadizar*
> *Wife of Farrouk and*
> *Friend of Myrn, you honored wife."*

"We'll go, of course," said the young Pyromancer, rising. "Many thanks for your hospitality and cooperation, Captain Aliada. If I can be of any assistance to you, please call on me at once."

Aliada smiled and saluted courteously.

"Show them the way, Officer Frasci. It has been a great pleasure, Wizard of Fire."

Shadizar and her children greeted Douglas in her cool fountain garden.

"I *know* you to be Pyromancer Douglas Brightglade, for your Myrn carefully described you to me," she said, showing him to a seat. "Children, this is Myrn's husband, the Wizard Brightglade. . . ."

"Please, call me Douglas, m'lady," Douglas protested. "And this is Cribblon, a Journeyman Aeromancer."

"You will honor us by using our given names, also," said Shadizar. "And this is . . . don't tell me! I recall . . . Marblehead?"

"*Marbleheart,* to be sure!" chuckled the sleek, six-foot mammal with a pleased grin.

Farrouki and Farianah were shy at first, but the Otter soon won them over. He was delighted with the courtyard fountain pool and asked permission to splash in it.

"The heat here tends to dry my skin terribly," he explained.

The children watched in amazement. Then their eyes opened even wider when, after his bath, Marbleheart showed them his Drying Spell.

"I am, of course, seeking Myrn," said Douglas to his hostess. "Although I may not assist her or risk forfeiting her Journeying, you understand, I would feel better knowing where she is . . . just in case."

Shadizar laughed.

"It's just as Myrn said!" she told him. "She knew you would not be far behind . . . just in case."

"I guess I'm pretty obvious," admitted Douglas, blushing. "But Journeying can be quite dangerous."

"But 'Wizards must learn to fend for themselves,' " Shadizar quoted Myrn. "And I have much confidence in your young lady-wife to overcome even the most terrible odds."

"Well, I do also," claimed Douglas. "But . . . it's good to be as *sure* as possible."

Shadizar laughed again and signaled to her servants to begin serving luncheon beside the playing fountain, amid the beds of bright poppies and nodding tulips.

An hour of swimming lessons whetted their appetites and cemented their growing friendships. Aeasha and her assistants had spread an elaborate picnic lunch on a smoothly flat table-sized rock in the shade of the pavilion. The three swimmers, dried quickly by the desert breezes, sat on soft cushions in the sand to enjoy their meal.

"Come, eat with us," the Sultana called to her servants. "We are all children of the desert here! This business of being subservient is carried much too far, I believe. As does my husband Trobuk."

The seven of them sat around the smooth, black rock, chattering and telling stories, at which Aeasha, with her hidden sense of humor, was the acknowledged specialist.

The food was light and refreshing, suited for a very hot day. The beat of the westering sun prompted them to remain at table long after the last sweetmeat was devoured and the last of the iced fruit juices drunk.

"I must return to the palace," Nioba said at last. "My husband has asked me to be with him tonight."

"I wish to stop at the stables to see if my little filly is well," decided Myrn, reaching for her clothing. "It has been a *most* pleasant afternoon and morning, Nioba. You've given me much more time than I deserve. I know you're busy."

"Not nearly so busy as I'd like to be," the Sultana admitted. "I love to be with Trobuk, and we often use these intimate evenings to discuss matters of importance. I will tell him of you, Myrn, if I may."

Chatting pleasantly the three ladies and their attendants rode back into the city. Myrn observed the people they met on the road, especially in the crowded evening market near the southern gate of the Sultan's palace, and decided that Nioba was admired and even loved by her husband's subjects. While many of the glances that followed their progress were filled merely with curiosity, not a few in the crowds looked on the Sultana with genuine affection, she thought.

"Do you ride out from the palace often like this?" she asked Nioba.

"Almost daily."

"She's being much too modest," Hana interjected. "She attends constantly to the welfare of the poor and has built a healing hospital for all, under her direct supervision."

"Indeed!" exclaimed Myrn. "I admire you for that, Highness."

Nioba blushed with pleasure and smiled at the Guards at the south gate to her husband's palace, who saluted courteously with their long pikes as the ladies rode through.

Myrn left Nioba and the rest of the ladies at the entrance to the *hareem,* and rode on with the grooms who'd come to lead their mounts to the stables at the rear of the palace compound.

Here she found Nameless, looking newly bathed, brushed, fit, and rested.

"I've had a most pleasant day," Myrn told the filly. "I should have arranged for you to join us, my dear. I apologize."

Nameless pushed her pink nose into Myrn's shoulder.

"Let's walk about the exercise yard for a while," Myrn suggested, and the filly followed her out into the first shadows of early evening.

"Have you been treated well?" Myrn asked.

The horse nodded her head yes.

"I must now get busy about rescuing our friend Serenit."

Nameless shook her head as if to say, Well, of course!

They enjoyed the cool of evening for a while in silence. The large, sand-floored exercise yard was empty for the moment, as the Sultan's horses were at that hour being watered and fed. The palace itself was a-hum with voices and the sounds of people at work or play, the smells of evening meals being prepared, the songs of young maids, and the laughter of house-boys busy at various evening tasks.

"A most pleasant place, considering its size," Myrn said. The little filly nodded.

A liveried servant came into the yard and approached them, bowing deeply.

"Mistress Brightglade?"

"I am Myrn Brightglade," answered the Journeyman Aquamancer.

"My Master's respects," said the servant, bowing again. "He prays a moment of your time, if you can spare it to him."

'Who *is* your Master?" Myrn asked.

"Your pardon, Mistress. I serve His Excellency, the Grand Vizier Kalinort."

"Ah, yes," said Myrn. "Well, I suppose his wish is very nearly a command around here. Lead the way."

She waved farewell to the little horse, who stood at the gate of the stable yard watching Myrn follow the splendidly dressed servitor through an archway into the palace proper.

"Through here, please, Mistress," said the manservant, bowing her ahead of himself through a small door within the archway.

"The Grand Vizier is within?" Myrn asked, stepping ahead of him into the dark doorway. "I—"

A heavy blanket was flung over her head and she was swept off her feet by a pair of strong arms. It happened so quickly and unexpectedly that Myrn had no chance to cry out or resist.

"Take her away," she heard a muffled voice growl nearby. "Carry her to the Stone Trees straightaway."

Myrn considered a half-dozen quick spells that would have set her free instantly, but the attack was perhaps her first lead to the missing First Citizen.

She felt herself being folded over a saddle, and the horse beneath her was led away, hooves clacking on pavement for a short distance.

Then they passed through a doorway . . . archway? . . . gateway? . . . and the air she breathed through the loosely woven cloth smelled of night-blooming jasmine, frying meat, and hot, freshly baked bread.

It feels of the outside, somehow, she decided, and she settled down as comfortably as the hard saddle allowed.

Spelling could wait.

Nameless caught a glimpse of Myrn's sudden capture and snorted angrily, but just then a stable hand came by with a halter and a smile.

"Here alone, little one?" he crooned. "Come . . . !"

And before she could pull away he had slipped a halter loosely over her ears and led her off toward her stall. Nameless shook her head sharply. The halter slipped off and fell to the ground.

Before the boy could recover, the horse shook free of her blanket, spread her shimmering wings, and snapped them downward, stirring up a whirlwind of sand which blinded the hapless stable lad.

By the time he'd brushed the painful sand from his eyes and cried out for help, the little horse was gone.

Chapter Ten

A Step Behind!

"A strange young man who says he's a Fire Wizard has come asking an audience, Sire," said a Guard Officer to Sultan Trobuk. "We thought it wise to at least tell you of his request."

Trobuk waved away his barber, who had just finished trimming the young Sultan's elegant mustaches and beard.

"A Fire Wizard? Did he give a name?"

"He says he is Douglas Brightglade of Wizards' High in Dukedom," replied the soldier, bowing again.

"Dukedom! Ask him to wait a moment longer and send quickly for Captain Mallet. He might know of this Wizard."

Mallet arrived somewhat out of breath three minutes later.

"Douglas? Here? Yes, I know him well, Sire. An old friend, in fact, although I had no idea he was in the Nearer East."

"You advise me to see him then?"

"If you will! He and his friends are well thought of in the West, Sire. He's very close to our Thornwood Duke . . . who would undoubtedly consider it a personal favor if you would receive Douglas Brightglade."

"Show him in, then," Trobuk ordered the Guardsman. "Stay here with me, please, Captain."

Douglas entered through the door, followed by four archers

with notched arrows and half-drawn bows who watched him very carefully.

"Hail, Wizard Brightglade!" said the Sultan formally.

Douglas bowed respectfully, smiled, and nodded to Mallet.

"This is Douglas Brightglade, the younger Fire Wizard of whom we spoke, Lord Sultan," the Seacaptain said at once, grinning back at Douglas. "You may recall I spoke of his role in defeating Ice King Frigeon some years ago."

"I do recall," said Trobuk. "Welcome to Samarca, Fire Wizard! It's a great pleasure to meet you, having heard of your adventures from the good Seacaptain."

"I'm flattered, to say the least," Douglas chuckled, bowing again. "I'm sorry that I'd no chance to warn you of my coming, Your Majesty. I came in a bit of a hurry. We of the Fellowship of Wizards are still engaged in important rescues and repairs arising from the misdeeds of the wicked Ice King."

"Ah! That is what our friend Mallet was telling us," exclaimed Trobuk. "As well as something about a Coven of Witches?"

"Exactly," agreed Mallet.

"Come and sit with us and tell us what we can do to help you in your difficult tasks," the Sultan cordially suggested, leading the way into his inner parlor. The latticed widows had been thrown wide open and a dry evening breeze blew strongly from the east, billowing the draperies and bringing the clean, hot scent of the desert.

"Well, sir, I have *two* tasks at the moment," Douglas began, accepting a glass of iced fruit juice from a bowing servitor. "I came to Samarca specifically to locate and arrange disenchantment of a certain King Priad and people. . . ."

"I've heard of Priad," Trobuk said, frowning in thought. "King Priad's small realm was just south, along our Seacoast. But he and his family disappeared centuries ago! Their land is now empty waste. Its people scattered into High Desert, according to all the old stories."

"Priad somehow incurred the wrath—or the fear—of the Ice King," Douglas explained. "He was enchanted by Frigeon and somehow hidden away. For a number of years since the defeat of Frigeon, our Fellowship has devoted much of its time to tracing down and resolving such wicked, old enchantments."

"I was taught we, here in the East weren't affected by Frigeon's magics."

"As far as we can tell, Frigeon had little time or interest to expend toward this part of World," Douglas agreed. "In fact, this's the first time we've traced a Frigeonic spell here, which explains why we know so very little about King Priad's enchanting. Now that Frigeon is defeated and reformed, as Serenit of New Land he finds it difficult to remember the details of his former wickednesses."

A disturbance at the door heralded the arrival of a darkly beautiful young woman with shining black hair and a rich brown complexion, attended by a motherly-looking woman of middle years.

"Ah! My one-wife Nioba! Come in, my beloved, and greet the Wizard Douglas Brightglade."

Nioba bowed deeply to her husband, then kissed him before turning to greet Douglas.

"I've heard a great deal about you, Douglas Brightglade," she said, smiling and returning the young Wizard's bow. "Your goodwife Myrn and I talked of little else all day long today."

"Now I am *really* flattered," Douglas said, laughing. "The other part of my mission—if I may call it that, Sultana—here in your land was to keep a loving eye on my wife on her professional Journeying." He then explained to the royal couple the importance of Journeying for a Wizardry candidate.

After Nioba sent off to the *hareem* for Myrn, Douglas asked permission to present his companions. Cribblon and Marbleheart were admitted to the Sultan's private apartment, introduced to the Sultan and the Sultana, and warmly welcomed.

The Sultan asked Marbleheart to sit beside him where he could admire his sleek, soft fur and bright face.

"Forgive my curiosity, but I don't think anyone in Samarca has ever seen such a remarkable creature," he exclaimed.

"I'm not at all surprised, Sir Sultan," replied the Otter. "We Sea Otters mainly stay where a fur coat is not such a dratted, hot nuisance. Would you mind terribly if, later on, I slipped into your pool to cool off? *Whew!*"

At the Sultana's request, Cribblon explained his magical specialty, Aeromancy.

"I'm particularly interested in phenomena and magical

properties of the air all about us. And related other gases, of course," Cribblon said, modestly.

"You command the winds?" asked Sultana Nioba.

"More than just that, really, ma'am!" Cribblon said earnestly. "My earliest lessons were in weather—and nullifying noxious airs and directing the flow of winds. Weather is a major concern of an Aeromancer, of course."

"What sort of weather can we expect here tomorrow, I wonder," mused Trobuk aloud.

"Well," said Cribblon, screwing up his face, "I can tell you the wind is shifting to the southeast and will shortly bring unwelcome blowing sand and dust upon your beautiful city. But I have to assume you are accustomed to such storms here."

"It's always useful to know when these High Desert storms will hit," considered the young Sultan. "To have one at this time is rather unusual, as they come most often in the winter months. Every year we lose a few head of sheep and horses or even a poor nomad or two when they're caught in unexpected sandstorms."

As if to underline Cribblon's storm warning, just then a servant opened the door to the outer room, admitting a hot, turbulent burst of wind. The lamp-flames jumped high and a bank of candles was snuffed at once.

"I beg your pardon most humbly, Great Sultan!" cried the servant as he fell to his knees before Trobuk and Nioba. "Desert wind is rising. . . ."

"So I see," said Trobuk.

To Cribblon he nodded and said, "Your foreseeing is already coming to pass, Aeromancer."

"This is just the beginning, sir. I would spread a warning, if I may advise you on the matter. This storm bids fair to blow all night and half of tomorrow."

"Issue a storm warning!" Trobuk called to one of his attendants. "Sound the storm alarms at once! And somebody cover the windows!"

The servant sent to fetch Myrn entered and fell to his knees before the divan, an action evidently required, Marbleheart decided, of one bearing bad news.

"Sire! Majesties! I am unable to find the Lady Myrn!"

"What do you say?" cried Nioba sharply. "I myself left

her at the *hareem* gate not two hours past, sirrah.''

''Your Guards say she never returned to the seraglio, Highness,'' gulped the servant, wringing his hands. ''And the hostlers never saw her at all, they say.''

''Myrn missing,'' Nioba gasped to Douglas, laying her hand on his arm.

The Pyromancer narrowed his eyes thoughtfully and hummed a bit of a tune to himself.

''I feel no call from my wife, nor detect any magical danger,'' he said slowly. ''Wherever she's gone, she went willingly.''

''She went to the stable to visit the filly who came to this place with her,'' the Sultana remembered. ''My husband, we must search for her.''

''At once,'' agreed the Sultan. ''Anyone can become lost in my grandsire's vast palace, of course.''

Before the Sultan could order a search, however, a tremendous gust of hot wind rattled the heavy shutters which had been drawn over the windows. Heavy doors shook on their hinges, open windows banged, and shouts of servants startled by tumbling potted plants and cries of surprised Guards came from all sides.

''Storm has arrived,'' announced Cribblon.

At the first strong gust of sand-laden wind, the three High Desert horsemen who'd carried Myrn off angled away from their path into the lee of a steep-sided dune.

The wind and sand hissed across the dune-top, making an eerie sound akin to one made by blowing steadily across the top of an empty bottle, but *much* louder, Myrn thought. The rumble of rushing sand increased in volume until it became a booming roar.

Goodness, thought the Journeyman Aquamancer. *A sandstorm!*

But she soon realized that her captors, familiar with such sudden storms here on the desert, had headed their horses into the wind-shadow of the tall dunes and laid the beasts down, wrapping loose cloths about their heads to filter the blown sand.

The men themselves withdrew into the deepest shadow of

the tall dune, taking the Aquamancer, still wrapped in her covering blanket, with them.

"Stay down," one shouted in her ear. "This will pass after a time."

Myrn nodded, not sure her captors even saw the gesture, and wedged herself between the leader of the captors and his horse.

A murmured spell or two ensured her comfort and safety through the rest of the long, loud night on the roaring desert.

After a time, she slept.

Nameless, following traces of the three kidnappers by flying across the desert some distance behind them, was forced to land and seek shelter also. Skirting a series of low, sandy hills being blown to sharp, flying fragments, grain by grain, she came suddenly upon a solid wall of dressed white stones.

A low, wide door in the wall gaped, inviting the flying horse inside a black hole without windows.

Any port in a storm, she thought, entering the corridor beyond the doorway. *This is somewhat better!*

The wind didn't blow here at all and, as the horseling trotted a few paces down a broad corridor, even the shrilling of the wind and the rushing-rumbling of flying sand faded to a murmur.

A number of other fugitives had taken refuge in the stone building, which otherwise appeared to be empty of Men or their devices.

A family of gray-and-white rabbits passed Nameless, heading for the innermost parts. The father paused politely to beg Nameless's pardon for going on ahead.

"Plenty of room for us all here," he said.

When the horse merely nodded, he waved his family on—five half-grown baby rabbits and their blonde-furred doe-mother.

Nameless shook her wings to dislodge the sand stuck in her feathers and carefully folded them over her back, tucking the tips under her tummy. At first the passage she followed was blacker than the night outside. She moved forward slowly, guided by the sounds of tiny desert animals and an occasional lizard or long-legged bird moving past her, deeper into the structure.

Shortly she realized her eyes were becoming adjusted to the dark. She shied nervously when a sleek leopard bumped into her from behind, murmuring apologies as she passed.

The corridor changed direction suddenly, then jogged back in the original direction. Nameless walked more and more slowly now, with her right shoulder brushing the wall. She found the floor of the passage clear of debris and smoothly paved.

Another sharp turn. Suddenly the passageway became much lighter. A warm glow ahead, as of embers in a banked fire, showed her a wide, high room whose distant walls could be only dimly seen. The sounds of the storm were now but a quiet murmur, far behind.

She saw, in the middle of this vast room, a jumbled pile of faintly shining metallic plates that were somehow providing the dim lighting. A strange, not unpleasant, melange of odors reached the horseling and she stopped, trying to pierce the gloom.

One end of the metallic pile reared suddenly upward and two huge, golden eyes regarded her sleepily, blinked twice, and widened.

"A flying horse, by Krupp," said a rumbling voice.

Below the eyes a flicker of bluish-orange flame showed a mouth wide open in surprise.

"Now, now, little horse," the voice boomed. "Come closer! It gets quite cold here during a sandy-wind like this. At the least I can keep you warm until it's over."

Fear clutched at the filly's wildly beating heart, but she noticed that many of the animals who'd passed her in the corridor had taken refuge in the—whatever it was—a cave or a building cut from or built of solid stone?

The animals had gathered quietly about the huge beast she'd at first taken to be a loose pile of metal. They were settling down on the smooth sand drifted across the floor, showing no fear of their strange host and polite interest in the newcomer.

"Allow me to introduce myself," said the voice from below the great yellow eyes. The beast emitted a spear of pale yellow flame. "I am known as Lesser Dragon. Who are you, then, my dear?"

The silent horse came closer, shaking her head and tossing her cream-colored mane.

"A flying horse, as I live long and breath fire," exclaimed Lesser Dragon. "Don't fear, dear filly. We won't harm you. Sit here by my side until the storm falls off, and let me introduce you to my friends. . . ."

The Dragon's head turned and as he named the beasts about him, his words were delivered with short, pale flashes of pure flame and welcome warmth.

"Here's an old friend: Riantor the Jackal. He lives in the heart of High Desert and raises his family on its hot sands."

The striped, black-and-yellow doglike beast grinned broadly at the horse and nodded in greeting. Beyond him were his mate and a litter of lately born puppies, gazing at the horse over their mother's ruffled mane. They grinned and chuckled softly.

"By my right hind-leg is Oliver, Patriarch of all the High Desert Hares, and his six wives and twenty-seven *kinder*," continued the Dragon, puffing pink, peppermint-scented smoke rings their way. "An old friend. And here is . . ."

He introduced a dozen other animals, all of whom nodded and spoke to the little horse pleasantly, urging her to come close and settle down near the Dragon.

"Without young Lesser here," explained the mother of a large family of desert rats, "well, some of us would not survive these storms, and it's so much more pleasant to be here with our friend, safe and warm."

Nameless was soon satisfied the Dragon, for all his size and awesome fires, was friendly. She nodded pleasantly at each introduction and settled down between a pair of prong-horn antelopes and near three spotted ocelots who purred a welcome and snuggled cozily against the flying horse's flank to share their warmth.

"Not *too* long to wait, actually, I should judge," chatted Lesser Dragon to no one in particular. "Might as well snooze. I'll wake you when the wind dies down in the morning."

The strangely assorted group of antelopes, zebras, wild goats (they had a rather strong odor but were actually quite pleasant, Nameless found), and even an elderly, rather arthritic lion named Fidellio, along with assorted jackals, hyenas, several families of rabbits, and a brace of tiny, delicate dik-diks, settled down to sleep the storm away.

"Silent one," said the Dragon sleepily. "Can you speak? Or are you sorely enchanted?"

Nameless nodded into the half-darkness, then put her head down between her folded forelegs and fell asleep. Through the stone of the ancient structure that sheltered them, she could hear the storm wind roaring without cease.

Chapter Eleven

After the Storm

THE wind thundered until well after time for sunrise. The graying of the sky in mid-morning at last provided some welcome visibility.

Myrn awoke to find soft sand piled smoothly about her and a new dune built behind them by sand blown from the crest of the older dune that had protected them.

"Breakfast time," she called brightly, sitting up and throwing off sand and blanket. "Anyone hungry?"

The kidnappers sat up and looked at her in surprise. The wind had settled down to a chilly breeze.

"A fire . . . in the manner of us Brightglades, good sirs," Myrn announced, making a pass over a patch of smooth sand between them. A cheery fire sprang to life, filling the area between the tall dunes with the smell of fragrant wood smoke.

Myrn removed a package from her left sleeve (all Wizards use the voluminous sleeves of their robes to carry useful and important items) and unwrapped its waxed-linen covering.

A delicious scent, a bit like fresh-baked bread but rather more sugary and spicy, filled the air, and the desert riders drew closer to Myrn's fire, despite their fear of magic.

Myrn quickly tore off half the loaf and neatly divided the Faerie waybread among them.

"This'll fill your middles," she told them, "and make you

forget our missed dinner last night, too. There's plenty more
. . . if you want it."

The leader of the band introduced himself, quite politely, as
Alabar the Mercenary, and his two fellows, Flicker and Salaman. The seven—men, Journeyman, and horses—sat or stood
in the wind-shade of the thirty-foot dune, enjoying one of
World's most satisfying foods, Faerie waybread, which never
spoiled nor ran out if it was willingly shared.

"May I ask where you're taking me?" Myrn asked at last,
folding the waybread packet carefully and resealing the waxed
covering before slipping it back into her sleeve. Its bulk had
hardly been diminished by their ample meal the men noticed
with wonder. They exchanged uneasy glances but had to admit
the waybread was most deliciously satisfying.

"We're under orders to deliver you to Stone Trees," re-
vealed Alabar the Mercenary. "Once we start out now we'll
be there before dark."

"I don't suppose you'd care to give me the name of whoever contracted with you to carry me off?" Myrn asked
sweetly. "I wasn't aware of any enemies in this part of
World."

"Well . . . perhaps later, when you're safely in charge of the
Slavers," said the leader.

"No harm telling her now, is there?" asked Flicker with a
nervous laugh.

"No, I suppose not," conceded Alabar, nodding his head
reluctantly. "We're too far out on the sand for escape. Still, I
suspect his name is better left unsaid, even now, little mistress.
We strongly advise you to submit to your fate and come along
willingly. Even with a mount—which you don't have—you'd
soon become completely and hopelessly lost out here and perhaps die of thirst or hunger, or worse."

"Maybe . . . and maybe not," replied the Journeyman. "Deserts hold little threat for an Aquamancer."

With a quick gesture she produced an earthenware quart jug,
from which she streamed clear, cool water for the horses and
their riders. All drank thirstily and the men filled their clay
water bottles, nodding to her in gratitude.

"I don't intend to escape, I promise you . . . at least not just
yet, anyway," Myrn told them.

"Do us all a great favor," pleaded the bandit leader, "and

don't try to escape until we've turned you over to the Slave Dealers. Once we've their silver safely in hand, you can run away from *them,* if you want.''

''I was told slavery had been outlawed in Samarca,'' Myrn commented as they prepared to mount, Myrn riding astride behind Alabar.

''That's so, but our young Sultan is pledged to keep out of Desert Tribe business, you see. The Slavers don't actually *defy* his will . . . or so they claim. I know the Sultan has banned *involuntary* slavery everywhere in the Sultanate.''

''Except for marriage,'' put in Salamar with a dry chuckle. ''You can still buy yourself a pretty, strong, hardworking young wife, if you have the ready cash or convenient credit . . . even in Balistan itself!''

''The practice is dying away, even so,'' insisted his chief. ''Along with the practice of having more than one wife.''

''I know . . . the Sultan himself has only one wife. I've met her,'' said Myrn.

''Yes, the Singular Sultana Nioba we calls her! They say he'll hold to her and to her alone. And who'll blame him? We lesser men, however, must content ourselves with lesser women.''

''An old argument among us,'' admitted Flicker to Myrn, shaking his head. ''Personally, I'm fully content with just my one wife. Begging your pardon, Mistress Brightglade, but one woman is *more than enough* for me.''

Talking thus they rode east and a bit to the north over the trackless sand until long past noon, up and down the marching lines of dunes, occasionally following dry *wadis* half-drifted full.

''Another two or three hours,'' estimated Alabar when they stopped to rest and water their mounts from their waterjugs in the scant shade of another overbearing dune. At its foot Myrn examined a tiny patch of cacti and green-gray succulents growing among rounded stones.

''There is certainly water not far underfoot,'' she told her captors. ''And, see? Where it's close to the surface it fosters greenery.''

''Who can eat cactus!'' scoffed Alabar.

''*Something* is dining on these succulents, you can see,'' Myrn pointed out. ''Rabbits or such.''

"Desert hares! Food for starving slaves, only," exclaimed Flicker.

"Why, not so," cried his companion Salaman. "My mother makes a right tasty stew of them flop-eared desert hares, I knows well. People come from miles around to taste it."

"As a Water Adept," Myrn told them, "I believe much of this land could flower, given a little moisture."

"If there *was* water to dig deep for," Salaman said with a bitter laugh, "the farmers would push us wanderers into the stark Darkest, for sure."

"You prefer desert land, Salaman, and no water to drink, then?" scoffed Alabar. "Not me! If I could grow a little barley, a little sorghum, and a coconut palm or three . . . and had water left over for growing grass for grazing stock, I'd settle down at once. Rich as a sultan! Only total fools or hopeless dreamers *prefer* the desert life."

"And give up being a marauder?" Myrn wondered, innocently.

"No doubt about it. Do you suppose I *enjoy* carrying off maidens into slavery? The pay ain't that good, either, says I."

"And if I point out that I'm no maiden? I'm the mother of two beautiful children . . . and the wife of a Fire Wizard, too."

"All the more reason to get you quickly to Stone Trees Oasis," muttered Alabar, frowning. "Then we can go back home to our tattered tents, whining wives and skinny children, and always-thirsty horses and camels and chickens."

A few hours later they sighted the grove of Stone Trees and, among them, a group of gaudy orange-and-white-striped tents above which long green pennants snapped in the last of the southeasterly breezes.

"The Slavers . . . or at least their tents," announced Alabar, drawing on his reins. "Slavers are a secretive, dour lot, even for desert people."

"Slavers anywhere are seldom fat and cheerful, I've heard," observed Myrn. "Such men hide their faces and names."

The desert riders nodded their heads, almost in unison.

"You'll soon discover for yourself, Mistress Myrn," their leader promised, touching his mount with his heel to send the horse down a long slope of sand to the edge of the grove of petrified trees. "*Too* soon, I should imagine, for your own liking."

"Can't you turn storm winds aside?" Douglas Brightglade had asked Cribblon late the night before.

They sat on a glassed-in balcony, looking out at the solid brown overcast of blowing sand.

"*Could,* I suppose," replied the Journeyman Aeromancer after some thought. "But not a good idea! There are immense Powers of Air behind such storms, Douglas. Powers'd have to be channeled elsewhere, were I to force them to subside before-time hereabouts. Might do even more harm there than good here, you see."

"Yes, of course; I realize that," Douglas said with a weary nod. "We should get some sleep against the end of the storm, I guess. At least there are no warnings of danger to Myrn, at the moment."

Marbleheart had already found a convenient pile of plump, silken cushions in which to nest, and he was fast asleep.

"Once the storm wind dies down on its own, the desert air will be cool and clear—ideal for tracking Myrn across High Desert, if that's what you plan. By late morning the air should be still," the Air Adept observed.

"What is it I *really* want t'do, however?" Douglas asked the darkness beyond the windows. "I must give it careful thought. Meanwhile, we might as well get some sleep, old boy."

"If it's any consolation, Douglas," Cribblon grumbled, allowing himself to fall on one of the low beds, "whoever stole Myrn must surely be a local and therefore more accustomed to these storms than others not born here. Desert people know how to ride out a sandstorm, just as sailors know what to do in a gale at Sea."

"I'm not really worried about Myrn," Douglas protested.

Cribblon grunted . . . a sound which Douglas decided was one of agreement.

Flarman Flowerstalk pushed back his second cup of black coffee and glanced sharply across the kitchen table at his companions, Augurian and Lithold, who were still dawdling over

the rich chocolate pudding and cream Blue Teakettle had
whipped up for a luncheon sweet.

"We can polish off the Farbwelt disenchantment in a few
hours," the Aquamancer said, feeling Flarman's gaze upon
him. "Lithold and I, I mean. A little water, a little of the lore
of stones, I should think."

"How did you know I was thinking of taking the afternoon
off?" cried the Pyromancer, rising from his chair.

His Napkin shook itself free of crumbs and folded itself
neatly into a square. Flarman's Plate, Cup, and Silverware
jumped up and scooted away to steaming Dishpan, which
greeted them all with a bubbly gurgle.

"My dear Flarman!" The Earth Wizard laughed, sending
her empty dessert plate after Flarman's. "Your attention's
been wandering since yesterday's message from Douglas. At
the moment, I don't really see how we could assist either the
young Fire Wizard or his bride. But if you feel you must . . ."

"I thought . . . just to take a peek or two?" murmured Flarman. "You two go ahead and complete the disenchantment. I
intend to do some long-looking while the atmospherics are
suitable. The thunderstorms yesterday clouded the best
views."

He nodded his excuses and disappeared through the kitchen
door. They heard his quick footsteps cross the sun-warmed
cobbles of the courtyard, where the High's hens and their yellow chicks were resting in the shade of the kitchen wellhouse.

"Sometimes," the Geomancer sighed, "I think you menfolk
lack complete confidence in your own students. Myrn will do
just fine. And young Douglas, if anything, is better suited for
such adventures than any of us older magickers, Augurian."

"Still . . ." The Water Adept sighed.

A disturbance in the air in the darkest far corner of the
kitchen heralded the arrival of Deka the Wraith. When she had
firmed her embodiment, she smiled dazzlingly at the Wizards
and flowed across to them.

"Welcome, far traveler," called Lithold.

"Have a seat, here, my dear," Augurian echoed her greeting. "Here is some mousse left from luncheon. I think you'll
find it most sustaining after your journey from . . . where? The
Nearer East?"

"Now the thundering's passed northeastward," said the

Wraith, hovering daintily before occupying one of the Chairs. "Atmospherics were quite disturbing, if not dangerous."

Lithold Stonebreaker served her a dish of pudding and gestured to Creamer to come forth. Silver Pitcher poured the Wraith messenger a small glass of chilled *miscytwine*. Deka laughed happily and tasted the pudding.

"Any news?" prompted Augurian.

"Nothing new to report, Water Wizard," answered the Wraith, looking more substantial now that she'd had a mouthful or two of the pudding and a swallow of Blue Teakettle's best lemonade. "Douglas, Marbleheart, and Cribblon have arrived in a place called Balistan—the Sultan's capital in Samarca—but Myrn, who'd been there before them, has gone off into High Desert."

"You make no estimate of their progress?" Lithold inquired.

"No, ma'am. That's not my task. I was to be careful only to observe, as I was asked."

"Of course," cried the tall, lean Aquamancer, nodding his head. "Journeying's always harder on those who must stay t'home. As you say, Myrn is both quite adept and quick as a dolphin. And Douglas, also."

"Still," admitted Lithold, "it'd be very nice to *know*. Shall we go up to the library? We have the problem of Farbwelt to attend to, you know. Those poor elephants have been sorely enchanted for *far* too long as it is."

The Wraith finished her pudding, daintily drank a bit more of the tart-sweet *miscytwine,* and shimmered through the kitchen wall, avoiding the sunniest part of the courtyard, and appeared in Flarman's workshop under the High.

The Pyromancer looked up at her entrance and smiled warmly.

"Ah! Good! I was just about to call you, Wraith. Welcome, once again."

"I do so love this dim and richly fragrant place, Fire Wizard," said the Wraith, settling on a proffered stool beside the Wizard's long worktable.

"All goes well over in Nearer East?" Flarman inquired.

"Well as can be, when it comes to Wizards and Journeymen and such," said the Wraith with a wry smile.

"Douglas and Myrn are together, then?" Flarman asked, anxiously.

"Not yet, Magister. But they're close in miles and will be reunited shortly, I'm sure."

"Well . . . so! They can handle themselves, even if there is a nasty Servant of Darkness in those far mountains somewhere. I've just learned of it myself. We'll keep an eye on them all, won't we?"

"Certainly, Pyromancer," the Wraith said.

Chapter Twelve

Stone Trees Oasis

"THE Grand Vizier has sent us a prize, I see," said one of the Slave Dealers, examining Myrn thoughtfully. "Worth the silver asked and given, I'd say, wouldn't you?"

The second, younger Dealer nodded silently.

Myrn smiled and pirouetted gracefully, her arms outstretched.

"I can sing and play a few musical instruments fairly well," she said. "And cook up a storm, diaper babies, and—"

"Not required," interrupted the younger Dealer sharply. "A pretty face. Clean limbs. No visible scars—at least I've seen none as yet. She must be examined more closely, Brother."

Myrn shook her head.

"I wouldn't advise closer examination," she said evenly.

"Ah, but we really must," cried the older man. "What if your backside were striped with many whippings? A sensible buyer would think you were unruly and thus too expensive, were he to purchase you. Our customers demand perfection."

"Well, there you are bound for disappointment, I guess." The Journeyman Aquamancer grinned. "You'll have to take my word for it. No scars nor stripes! Just a little cicatrix on my right calf, where I was bitten by a startled baby tiger shark a long time since, Master."

129

The two black-clad Dealers stared at her, their eyes narrowed and calculating.

"Slaves are property," the older Dealer told her at last. "We'll see you as we please, young woman! Disrobe, now . . . or suffer very unpleasant consequences!"

Myrn drew herself up to her full five feet, eight inches.

"What you see is what you get," she snapped. "I'll disrobe for no man here!"

She stood her ground as the two men advanced warily, reaching for her arms and shoulders.

Myrn murmured a quiet spell word and clapped her palms together softly.

"Yes, well, *I* am satisfied," said the older Slaver, stepping back and dusting his hands together. "And you, Brint? She's perfect, I'd say."

"Oh, yes . . . quite perfect," agreed the other, blinking, and falling back also. "And surprisingly intelligent, too, I would add. Should bring a good profit to the Company, I'd venture."

Myrn smiled at them brightly, unmoving, waiting.

"Well, as I said . . . where were we? She shouldn't need to be chained, do you think?"

"No one can escape your captivity, way out here on the empty High Desert," suggested the Aquamancer. "Why bother with chains?"

"Yes, why chains . . . which might leave unsightly marks and maybe suggest untoward behavior," considered the older Slaver. "No chains, then! Take her to a holding tent, Brint. I'll send the sempstress to examine her clothing and perhaps arrange something more . . . suitable."

Brint nodded gravely and gestured to the Journeyman to follow him, the matters of searching and chaining clearly forgotten.

"Tell me about yourself, kind sir," Myrn said as they crossed from the large main residence tent to a smaller, less decorated pavilion on the other side of the Slavers' compound. "You name is Brint, I gather. My name, in case anyone should ask, is Myrn Manstar Brightglade."

The young Dealer stopped, seeming a bit confused. "Oh, yes . . . Brint. The other is Master Burnt. He's manager of our enterprise, you see."

"Is it my imagination, or is this business of slaving—buying and selling people, I mean—seeing difficult days? I heard the Sultan has no favor for it,'' Myrn asked, laying her hand on the young Dealer's arm.

Brint colored, swallowed, then turned away to hold open the gauze curtain that veiled the entrance to the tent.

''There're still plenty of . . . wealthy customers . . . for pretty girls and talented entertainers, and strong workers,'' he sputtered.

Myrn entered the tent and glanced about.

The dim, dusty interior was cluttered with dirty old rugs and empty wooden cases, and overall, it smelt strongly of unwashed bodies punctuated with sharp whiffs of camel and horse dung.

''*Ugh!* You expect a proper young lady like me to make my bed *here*? This place hasn't been properly cleaned in months,'' she snorted. ''Look at the dirt! Those boxes should have been burned for fuel ages ago, Master Brint.''

''You won't be here very long,'' explained the young man. ''The sales commence in the morning. Put up with the discomfort for a night. Your new master will undoubtedly accommodate you in greater comfort.''

''I'd rather sleep on the cold sand under those stone trees,'' scoffed the Journeyman. ''*Phew!* You say I'm valuable merchandise, yet expect me to lie down in this sty? Any Man with common sense would refuse to buy a field hand who smelled like this, I'm sure. Would you?''

''Never thought about it that way,'' admitted the young Slaver. ''You *will* be given the chance to bathe, of course. Tomorrow at dawn. Until then—''

''Well! If you haven't the pride to offer your merchandise a clean place to rest and recover from an arduous trip across the windy desert, maybe you'll allow me to do some tent-cleaning for myself.''

Not waiting for his permission, Myrn pushed up her sleeves and gestured sharply at a pile of wooden crates near the entrance. At once they rose in the air and flung themselves out the open tent flap, whistling cheerfully as they hurtled through the air.

''Look out!'' cried Brint sharply as one box narrowly missed his shins. ''What do you do? Stop at once!''

''Not until I've made this hovel a suitable place in which a lady can sleep," snapped Myrn. "Make a clear path, Slave Dealer! I'll have this place spotless in a few shakes."

As good as her word, she quickly cleared out the trash and moldy old straw, then conjured a stiff breeze heavy with moisture to blow the loose chaff and dust from the old carpets that covered the tent floor.

"Shampooing would be a good idea," she added, with evident satisfaction.

Brint jumped out of the way when she pulled a large bucket of soapy, hot water from thin air and set it to swirling frantically over the carpets and up the side walls of the tent.

"No time at all, you see." Myrn sniffed. "Smells much better already. What were you keeping in here, anyway, Brint? Pigs would have been neater, I swear! These pillows need a good airing and fluffing. . . ."

She whisked the down pillows up and out, where she arranged them in a slowly whirling circle about the tent peak, shaking their dust and fluffing their feathers vigorously.

"Help! What are you doing?" cried the Dealer, wide-eyed with disbelief.

"Cleaning house, of course," replied Myrn. "If old Dicksey at the Trunkety General Store offered his goods in such disreputable conditions, the housewives of Valley would've driven him out of town years since! When you've things to offer for sale, my dear sir, you must present them in the best manner possible. Lesson number one of sensible, successful marketing, I'd say."

"I never heard of such a thing," cried the young man, stepping back to avoid the swirling waters as they flowed out of the tent and quickly sank into the sand. "I don't think—"

"Obviously, none of you ever *did* think," said Myrn with a shake of her finger. "Well, I won't allow such a dirty mess. Watch out for the divan! *Whew!* What a sorry business!"

Gathering his black robes around his knees, the Dealer turned and trotted off toward the residence tent.

Myrn shook her head as she watched him go.

"Come back in a half hour," she called after her captor. "I'll have things quite presentable by then."

Brint had disappeared into the other tent.

"She's a *genie* of whirlwinds, I swear, Brother!" he said to his superior. "She must be some sort of a witch or. . . . I never *saw* such a thing!"

"Nonsense, Brother!" scoffed Burnt. "She's just a snippy little girl. We've housed and sold a thousand just like her."

"Not like *this* one," muttered his subordinate. "Well, she can't get away—can she?—so I intend to stay far away from her until her cleaning is finished."

"Best advice," murmured Burnt, who was busily writing items and prices in his ledgers, ignoring the sounds from across the way . . . sounds of water cascading and bubbling, hot breezes *shooshing*, and Myrn singing a lively song:

> *"This's a way we clean our house,*
> *Sweep outdoors,*
> *Rinse our floors!*
> *So early in the morning!"*

"Although," Myrn's pleasant voice said cheerfully, "I admit it's rather late in the day for such an early-morning song!"

When the storm finally subsided, Nameless awoke, shook loose sand from her mane, and climbed to her feet.

Most of the animals who'd shared the ancient temple overnight had already departed. They'd breakfasts and schoolchildren to see to. A pair of young leopards still slept in the far corner of the large room, hunting in their morning dreams, softly snarling, and twitching their whiskers and paws.

"Well, horseling!" said Lesser Dragon, opening his luminous eyes. "Did you sleep well? Do you have a place to go? I'll be happy to set you on your way, if you're lost."

Nameless nodded her head and shook her long main, as if to say, I have places to go and things to do, friend Dragon. I appreciate your kind hospitality, but . . .

"I understand," said Lesser, nodding his enormous head. "Well, if you could tell me where you wanted to go . . ."

Nameless shrugged.

"Still silent? That makes it difficult—but not impossible. Come outside and we'll try to decide which way you'll fly, now that the storm has passed."

He poked one of the sleeping leopards with the pointed tip

of his tail. The cat sprang awake at once, whipping about to see who had prodded him in the haunch.

"Now, Spots . . . you can stay as long as you like, of course," said Lesser in a kindly tone. "But I wanted to mention that the morning hunting hours are nearly over, if you want to do some breakfasting before the heat of day."

"Is it?" cried the spotted cat. "I don't suppose the little horse is fair game? Looks quite tender and delicious to me."

"None of that!" The Dragon snorted a puff of acrid blue smoke. "What you seek for your lunch is *your* business, but the flying horse is my guest. You know my house rules!"

"Just asking," said the cat, sulking a bit. "Here, Ruff! Time to be on our way."

With that, the sleek young cats nodded to the Dragon and Nameless in thanks and left without a backward glance.

"Nice people, really," the Dragon insisted, "though I can't always agree with their ideas of proper cuisine. . . ."

When they reached the outer doorway the leopards were nowhere in sight. Nameless looked about in curiosity, then turned to Lesser, her eyes asking many unspoken questions.

"This place? Used to be the grand temple of a sect that worshipped their own ancestors, I believe. Long since gone— when I took it over for a lair there were no longer any worshippers, nor ancestors left to worship."

He stretched himself to full length in the bright, warm morning sun, groaning deeply with pleasure.

"Nice desert day! A bit cool for this time of year. I prefer it really hot, of course. Cold leaves me . . . cold, to tell you the absolute truth. Now, what's to do with you, my girl?"

He led the flying horse up to the top of a nearby dune that hid the City of the Disappeared, as he called his place, from sight. The view was wonderful . . . and long, as well. In the west they could just glimpse the tips of the Sultan's palace towers at Balistan and the glint of sun on the lake. In the distant east, gray, blue, and brown peaks fretted the horizon in the clear desert air.

"Not that way, then?" the Dragon asked, pointing toward the palace. "Then, toward the Darkest Mountains? Not much there, even of wildlife. Some of my friends have warned of a strange being hiding there, however. I wish you could tell me what you're seeking."

The little horse considered the Dragon's words for a moment, then began to draw with her right fore-hoof in the wind-smoothed sand. Circles interlinked with circles, a dozen or more circles . . . a chain.

"Chain? Ah, yes, I see I've hit on it," cried Lesser.

Nameless nodded enthusiastically, and then carefully added a stick figure of what was evidently a human female attached to the far end of the chain.

"A woman? On a chain, I see. *Ahhhh,*" whistled Lesser softly. "You're interested in the Slave Traders, perhaps? One of their female goods?"

Nameless nodded vigorously.

"The Slavers! Of course! They'd be at the Stone Trees just now. Do you see that peak on the horizon? The one with a deep notch in the top? Locals call it Horn of Dilemma, although I must admit I don't really think the name is appropriate." The Dragon laughed. "If you were to keep yonder Horn in front of you and travel just a hair to the north—or left—of a direct line from here to the Horn, in time you'll come to a grove of petrified trees."

Nameless nodded eagerly.

"Under Stone Trees you'll find the camp of the Slave Dealers at this time of the year. They buy and sell poor people, dancing girls, metal workers, and such, just as herders buy and sell cows and camels. Nasty business!"

Nameless studied the horizon for a long moment, then nodded in decision.

"You'll go that way, then? Tell you what . . . since I've nothing very important to do, may I go along to make sure nothing ill happens to you?"

The flying horse nodded, grinned (as best a horse can grin), and gestured with her head, Come along, and welcome!

"There're a few damp, grassy spots on the way that I know of, so we can get something to eat, I s'pose, if the new-blown sand hasn't covered them over," Lesser said as they flew off side by side, the huge winged Dragon and the tiny winged horse. "Well, I guess we big, strong animals can go a day without fodder, if need be!"

The Dragon flew quite easily and lightly for one so large.

"I must admit it's curiosity that moves me to accompany

you," Lesser said after a while. "Although friendly interest has a large part in it, too."

Nameless nickered pleasantly.

To the Dragon it sounded very much like a pleased chuckle.

Douglas went to the door of the suite, leaving the Air Wizard behind in their room, still sleeping. He'd always heard that Aeromancers are notorious snorers, and now he'd found it to be true.

Marbleheart was already off on his own, snooping about the vast palace, talking to the people sweeping deep sand from the hallways and clearing the myriad courtyards and flat rooftops.

"May I speak to His Majesty, the Sultan?" Douglas asked a Lieutenant of the Sultan's Guard.

"I'll inquire," replied the turbaned Guard politely.

He passed the young Wizard's request on to an impressive Major, who in turn whispered it to the Colonel of The Guard just inside the Sultan's door.

In a few moments the big, ornate doors, which were closed tight only at night, swung wide and the Sultan himself, smiling and pleased, came out to greet the youthful Pyromancer.

"No real damage was done," Trobuk reported happily. "I've known these desert storms to dump three to five feet of sand on the roofs and threaten to collapse them."

"Things are almost back to normal, then?" asked Douglas.

They went into Trobuk's private sitting room. The awnings had been reinstalled and the shutters folded away to admit the late-morning sun. The air was cool and crisp—quite pleasant for Douglas, but obviously still rather chilly for the Sultan's servants, busily shivering and sweeping sand from the parlor floor.

"It'll be normal in a few minutes," Trobuk promised. "But the young lady, your wife, has completely disappeared! I asked the palace and town Guards to keep searching for her, but there's no sign of her anywhere in the palace. It's a large town, Balistan, and she may have gotten lost in the darkness of the storm . . . slept in some hidden corner overnight."

His words were intended to reassure the missing lady's husband, but Douglas shook his head.

"She's no longer here . . . nor anywhere in Balistan, sir. She went east and a bit north early yester-evening, just before my friends and I arrived.''

"Then she was benighted by the storm, I fear," Trobuk decided. "I'll call out my Camel Corps! They can sweep the desert to the east of here for signs of her.''

Douglas shook his head.

"No, I'll follow her trail myself. What I wonder now is did she go on her own? Or did someone carry her off? It isn't like Myrn to go off into a strange and dangerous land without good reason and some word to her hostess. And the Sultana was as surprised as anyone she had gone.''

"I'll make inquiry, nevertheless," insisted Trobuk. "It reflects on my hospitality, to have her disappear from my very palace!''

None of his servants remembered seeing the lady the previous evening.

"She left us when we returned from the picnic," recalled Lady Aeasha, looking even more worried than Douglas. "She said she'd look in on her horse in the royal stables. That's the last time she was seen, I believe.''

Nioba confirmed the *hareem* mistress's words.

"She left us at the south door of the seraglio," she told her husband and Douglas. "I've asked the stable workers and grooms, and none of them remember seeing her—but the little horse she brought with her is missing, also!''

"Ah, we make progress!" Trobuk said, giving his pretty wife a quick hug. "She obviously rides her own horse. Unfortunately, the night's winds will have covered any tracks or scent.''

"If we could just discover," Nioba frowned, speaking softly, "what led her to go out in a coming storm, unescorted. She saw what the desert, even here close to our palace, is like in daytime. Surely she would never go alone at night, and in a sandstorm, without maps or escort!''

"Perhaps not," said Douglas. "I feel I should start at once to follow. If only we knew where she was headed . . .''

"There are only a few sensible destinations in that direction," Nioba said. "She either went to search for one of the bands of nomads, or she went to the Darkest Mountains. I know she was seeking someone. His name was . . . Serenit?''

"Of course! The captive First Citizen," Douglas replied.

"That was my understanding," the Sultana said with a wan smile. "Perhaps she heard word of him and felt she should leave at once, without saying why or telling where she went."

"My wife has more sense than that," Douglas firmly insisted, "but it seems like our only clue. Well, we'll go east toward the Darkest Mountains, then. No, Lord Sultan, I won't need any assistance or soldiers. My companions and I will leave at once."

He sent for Marbleheart and the Air Adept, and moments later, in the growing noontime warmth, they stood on the Sultan's balcony overlooking the shimmering sand. Douglas took from his pocket a delicate golden pin in the shape of a curved feather and fastened it to his shirt lapel very carefully.

"We'll head for the only real landmark Trobuk can think of on our way to the mountains," he explained to his companions. "A grove of petrified trees near the foothills of the Darkest. Slave Traders camp there this time of year, he says. They might have seen Myrn pass by. Everybody ready?"

"I hate to leave so soon." Marbleheart sighed, then tucked his tail beneath his tummy to keep it out of the way as they took off. "The people here have been most hospitable."

"Yes, they have," agreed Cribblon, making sure his Journeyman's cap was secure on his head. "Thank you so very much, Lord Sultan and Lady Sultana!"

"We'll return soon with good news," Douglas promised, shaking Trobuk by the hand and bowing to Nioba. "We'll see you then!"

He spoke the feather's magic words. The three friends rose at once into the air and flashed off east over the empty waste in the direction of Stone Trees Oasis.

The heavily armed guard saluted respectfully at the door to Dealer Burnt's tent.

"All is well at full nightfall, Elder. The Night Watch is on posts and wide awake."

Burnt, having removed his heavy black outer robes, hood, and scarf, was seated in the deep shadow of the raised tent flap, smoking an elaborate water pipe preparatory to crawling into his evening bath and waiting bed.

"The . . . woman who calls herself Myrn?" he asked the guard, peering up at him. "In the holding tent?"

"She's cooking herself a delicious-smelling dinner of some sort," replied the other. "You did say to leave her strictly alone, sir, so . . ."

"Yes, yes! For very good reason. I also ordered her not to be fed. Hungry slaves are much more tractable, I've always found."

"Whatever it is she's cooking," the soldier said stiffly, "it was nothing I recognized. Not from the camp larder, I'm sure. Some sort of toasted bread, I think. . . ."

"Well, no harm, I suppose. She's a dangerous one, Frimbor! Best left to herself. The sooner we sell her, the better. She's too smart to try to escape into the desert, especially at night. I think I heard a lion earlier."

"Lions and such. They're prowling for food after the storm covered their old tracks and trails."

Burnt nodded in dismissal.

"If a lion takes it into his head . . . a waste of good money, of course, but perhaps a good thing for us," muttered the senior Slaver. "Now, where's that vial of attar-of-rose soap I bought in Port bazaar last winter?"

"There's a fairly large camp there, under those bare trees," said Marbleheart, who had the best night vision of the three. "Strange-looking trees! Something familiar about them, however."

Douglas aimed their feather-flight down just behind the top of a dune overlooking the shadowy grove.

"We've seen petrified trees before, remember?" he told the Otter.

"Yes, around Lady Lithold's mountain fastness in the Serecomba Desert," the Otter remembered as they touched down on the hard-packed sand. "Any water nearby, do you think? I'm dry as salt cod!"

"Must be some water down there," said Cribblon, stretching his legs after their hours-long flight over the featureless desert.

"I'll slide and slither down for a sip and a look, then, if you don't object," offered the animal. He was always ready for new adventures, even in dead of moonless night. "Be right back to report what I see and hear."

And he was off, a slightly darker shadow over the sand.

Douglas and Cribblon found shelter in a slight hollow on the backside of the tall dune and settled down to eat a cold supper, rest, and wait for Marbleheart's return. They'd been aloft since midday, and it was close now upon midnight.

Chapter Thirteen

Auction Action

MYRN, an early riser by habit, left her tent wearing a long robe and carrying a fluffy white towel, her hairbrush, her toothbrush, and a vial of scented liquid soap, just as the sky over Stone Trees Oasis became light enough to show the way.

She stopped an armed guard to ask the way. He directed her away to the left, beyond the camp.

"Ah! Yes, I see the glint of the water now," Myrn cried, nodding her thanks.

"Don't wander off into the dunes," advised the young soldier gravely. "Customers arrive shortly and the auction will commence mid-morning."

"Thank you, sir! No, I merely wish to bathe and brush my hair," Myrn told him. "I don't intend to wander off, believe me."

She found the wide, still pool beyond the tallest of the strange Stone Trees. Douglas had told her of the stone grove surrounding the Geomancer's mountain in the middle of the Serecomba, but those trees, she recalled, were living entities, complete with jewel-like leaves.

These were bare, once-living oaks and walnuts, ages since turned to solid stone by volcanic action and water. Still, they had, she thought as she wound her way between them, a strange, everlasting kind of desert beauty.

141

She examined the great, shallow pool critically and decided it was clear and pure. Drinking water for the Slavers camp was drawn from the depths nearest the tents, so she walked around the sandy shore until she found a protected spot hidden from view by the columns of petrified trunks.

Slipping off her robe, she waded into the cool water and was soon lathering up and humming a song to herself. She soaped her hair generously, then gathered up a great shimmering globe of water (to the surprise of several small fishes who lived in the shallows) and dashed it over her head and shoulders to rinse the soapsuds from her long, black hair.

"Sorry!" she called out to the fish. "I should have warned you. Won't do it again."

"No problem, mistress," peeped one of the silvery pond-fish as the school swam out of range of the soap bubbles. "We were caught by surprise."

"Story of many a poor fish's life, I suspect," murmured Myrn to herself.

She waded out onto a tiny beach of fine, green gravel, ignoring a troop of a dozen soldiers coming just then from the camp on the far shore to fill water jars. She toweled her hair and her body vigorously, still humming. The desert air was so dry even the slight breeze that now blew was enough to dry her hair quickly.

She dressed herself in clean linen and a light, flowered frock, smelling of fresh air and fragrant Waterand soap made from the rich oil of coconuts.

"*Pssst!*" called a clump of low-growing palmettos a short distance away.

"Hey!" said the startled Journeyman Aquamancer, jumping slightly.

"Just me! Marbleheart!" came the voice from among the fronds. "We arrived an hour or two back. Douglas and Cribblon are on the far duneside, napping a bit, I suspect. . . ."

"Oh, Marblefoot!" cried Myrn, relieved. "No, don't come out! Remain hidden from the camp followers."

"I guess I understand that," the Sea Otter replied. "Well, no one has seen me yet, my dear Myrn. Nor will they, if you so wish. Only . . . tell me what you intend to do, so we'll know what to expect. I'm sure Douglas will ask me when I return to him."

"I would expect him to, yes," Myrn agreed.

She finished dressing, combed her hair, and transformed her frock into a softly flowing, ankle-length, dazzling white gown with wide sleeves, a cowl neck, and convenient, carefully hidden pockets.

On her feet she now wore sandals of gilded leather. As a finishing touch she wound a wide golden ribbon through her heavy, dark hair, to keep it from blowing about too wildly.

"A sight for sour pusses," chuckled Marbleheart, peeking through the fronds. "Can I come out now?"

"No, stay hidden! When I return to my tent, go to wherever our Douglas is resting and tell him I'm safe and sound. Understand?"

"I can see that for myself," Marbleheart said. "Pretty as ever!"

"Flatterer!" said Myrn, but she was pleased. "Now, listen, Marblebrain! Here's my plan—such as it is. . . ."

When her briefing was completed the Sea Otter slithered off around the nearest trees. Myrn walked slowly, thoughtfully, around the shore to camp, watched appreciatively by a dozen young camp workers who were supposed to be drawing water for the Slavers' horses.

Horseback and camelback riders were beginning to appear over the western horizon, riding in groups ranging from two or three to a dozen, many bearing lances or short bows in their hands. They were robed against the nighttime chill, which still lingered even though the sun was already clear of the horizon and beginning to warm the sand.

Although their clothing was mostly drab grays and dull yellows, on closer examination Myrn saw it was of rich fabrics and well sewn. The riders wore scarves about their heads, ends draped down over their shoulders, held in place by braided lengths of colorful silken cords.

Each group wore a different pattern of color-cording, Myrn realized as she stopped in the shade of her tent flap to watch them pass.

"Some sort of tribal or family insignia, I suppose," she decided.

Elder Burnt and several of his young assistants stood on the edge of camp to welcome arrivals. As each group approached, a Slaver lad was assigned to lead them across the coarse oasis

grass into the shade of a gaily striped awning stretched between several Stone Trees. Here the travelers dismounted and
tethered their mounts out of the fierce desert sun.

Attendants rushed to water and offer feed to the horses,
politely greeting the riders.

The customers were then escorted to a second pavilion
where they were served rich, savory coffee, salted nuts, and
honeyed fruit while seated upon richly colored carpets spread
on the grass, talking among themselves and greeting other
newcomers as they arrived.

By mid-morning fully two hundred customers had arrived
with their retinues and were milling about expectantly.

Elder Burnt moved slowly among them, greeting old and
welcoming new customers with grave courtesy.

"We shall begin as soon as our lookouts tell us everyone
is well arrived," he said in answer to repeated questions. "*Ah!*
I am signaled that no others are sighted on the trail for as far
as eye can see! We shall commence."

The men (there were no women among the customers at all)
gathered around him under the largest pavilion of them all,
whose sides had been hoisted to allow the dry desert breezes
access to the milling crowd. Assistants appeared with pillows
and carpets for those considered special guests, but most of
the men stood about easily, watching with interest as a Slave
Trader marked out a circle in the sand in the center of the
floor, beside which Burnt stood directing activities.

"As usual," he announced at last, "we will begin with the
indentured craftsmen and skilled laborers, good sirs! Pay heed,
for I will call them forth one at a time and detail their accom-
plishments and talents—and the beginning bids—for you."

"Do you vouch for their claims of ability?" called a young
man in the standing crowd.

Myrn recognized her husband's voice, although she had to
look twice to see where he stood. Douglas was dressed in a
red-and-yellow robe and a *jalabah* that threw his face and fair
hair into deep shadow.

"If anyone is dissatisfied," Burnt said with an ingratiating
smile, "we will refund all of your payment, with the exception
of a small service fee. Thus it has ever been at our auctions."

Myrn found a shaded spot, partially hidden from the throng,
in which to sit, legs crossed and her back against a Stone Tree

trunk. She pulled a thin white veil across her face, as was the custom in Nearer East among women in public places. The men nearby studiously ignored her, for the most part, and paid close attention to the Elder, who now began to chant in a high, nasal tone.

"I offer you for sale of term contract . . . Talabar the Tailor, a superior craftsman in the designing and fabrication of sturdy yet fashionable wool, silk, and cotton clothing! Talabar was one of the Sultan's court's most eagerly sought after artisans of the needle, scissors, and cloths, but he unfortunately—for himself—fell afoul of unpaid debts which required him to offer his services as an indentured servant by order of His Calm Supremacy, our beloved Sultan Trobuk."

Talabar the Tailor walked to the center of the circle beside Elder Burnt, where he bowed deeply to all sides, smiled confidently, and nodded to several people he recognized in the gathering.

There was a smattering of applause

"Indenture is for three full years or until outstanding debt is paid in full," droned the Elder. "Materials not included. Tools furnished by the craftsman. Here's a *bargain,* my dear sirs! I will begin the bidding at five hundred silver *dinari. . . .*"

Hearing the tailor's high asking price, some in the gathering moved away from the ring, shaking their heads. A surprisingly large number, however, pressed closer, listening closely, asking questions, and fingering their purses thoughtfully.

"A good tailor is worth his price in prestige alone," Burnt was chanting loudly. "He can clothe you and your whole family fit for the Sultan's court when you go to pay your respects or bring important petitions. Master Talabar knows the time-honored secrets of sewing hidden seams and cutting perfect, comfortable pantaloons, dear sirs! Not just a bargain but a true indication of his owner's taste, elegance, and wealth. The opening bid is . . . five hundred dinari!"

The crowd murmured for a moment and then an elegantly dressed young man raised his hand and bid five hundred *dinari.*

"Ah, a worthy bidder, who values quality of cloth, style, and cut, offers five hundred. Will someone offer five hundred and *ten* dinari?" the Slave Dealer asked gravely, bowing respectfully to the bidder.

"Five hundred!" repeated the auction bookkeeper, quickly jotting the bid in a ledger.

An older man raised both hands, fingers spread.

"The good Emir Sheoom bids five hundred and *ten*!" cried the Elder at once. "Anyone? Who will bid five-and-*twenty*?"

The bidding was lively for several minutes, but the elegant young courtier—certainly from one of the noble coastal families, not a rugged desert tribesman, Myrn decided—closed the deal with a final bid of six hundred and twenty *dinari*.

"Going to the young gentleman from . . . Port of Samarca, isn't it? Yes! Going once . . . and twice . . . and a final time . . . *Sold!*" intoned Burnt shrilly, clapping his hands to close the bidding.

The buyer nodded and moved to the cashier's table to lay down his money. The tailor, grinning both with pleasure and some relief, stepped forward and bowed to his new master.

"Tailor Talabar ran up a gambling debt of close to four hundred *dinari*, I overheard," said a voice close beside Myrn. "The Slave-sellers made a nice profit on him, I see."

"Cribblon? What in World are you supposed to be?" Myrn giggling.

"Douglas thought I'd be more helpful, should something go wrong, if I disguised myself as a caterpillar. Actually, he wanted me to be a butterfly, but I prefer to keep my feet on the ground," the Aeromancer-caterpillar explained. "There are too many hungry birds in the desert."

He was perched on her shoulder, bright green and yellow and black, not far from her left ear.

"This tailor—he will not be a lifelong slave, then?" Myrn asked him.

"No . . . he'll serve some months or years to repay his gambling debts. Seems only fair, when he's overstepped the bounds of sensible play," replied the caterpillar. "Interesting, nevertheless, isn't it? I wonder who'll go on the block next!"

"What has Douglas done with his Familiar?" the Journeyman Aquamancer asked quietly.

"Oh, he's turned Marbleheart into a small, black monkey." The caterpillar chuckled. "Marbleheart wanted to be a horse, but Douglas advised against it. If you look closely, you'll see our good Sea Otter perched on that pile of cloth boltings near his Master."

Myrn picked out the monkey-who-was-an-Otter among gaily colored bolts of cotton and linen cloth piled near the entrance.

"He makes a better monkey than a horse, anyway," she thought aloud, then fell silent as the dour Elder began to announce the next sale—a company of bankrupt tentmakers to serve a long sentence for their accumulated indebtedness.

Three hours later Elder Burnt called a recess for lunch.

The crowd moved off to sample the food and drink provided by the Slavers in a shaded clearing by the pool.

"Hungry?" Myrn asked the many-legged Cribblon.

"Famished!" admitted the enchanted Journeyman. "We caterpillars dote on tender leaves, of course, and petrified trees only put out stoney leaves. What's for lunch, fair Myrn?"

"Anything you desire! I don't suppose we should ask my handsome husband and Marbleheart the Monkey to join us."

"Better not! Might make the Slavers unhappy . . . and Douglas wishes to remain anonymous as long as possible," advised the caterpillar.

Myrn moved away to her tent, which was shaded by several of the Stone Tree trunks and was, therefore, relatively cool despite the noontime heat.

As they were finishing a light meal of mixed green salad and fresh-baked white bread, Marbleheart the Monkey appeared from above, where he'd been swinging from stony tree to tree.

"I could use a slice of your bread, Mistress," he said. "And a glass of cold milk would be nice. Should I pretend to beg, do you think?"

"No, just sit beside me, here," laughed his Master's good-wife.

She spread Blue Teakettle's crusty white bread with orange marmalade and poured the monkey a cup of milk fresh from the cows at Wizards' High.

"What does my husband eat this noontide?" she asked the disguised Otter.

"Oh, things like spiced goat's brain and fried bits of something I don't care to discuss or even think about. These desert nomads prefer *heavy* foods! Too much spicing for my tummy in this heat! This marmalade's wonderful—Blue Teakettle's?"

"Of course!" replied the Lady Aquamancer. "And some coconut ice cream to come, when you finish the marmalade sandwiches."

"Coconuts? From Waterand Island, I'd guess," crowed Marbleheart happily. *"Yummm!"*

A smiling group of lightly clad girls were set to dancing once the noon break was over. Four young men provided flute and drum music with a distinctively suggestive beat.

Burnt was replaced now as auctioneer by his young assistant, Brint, who had a more lively style of patter as he pointed out the charms and talents of the dancers.

"Musicians *included*!" he sang out. "Guar-an-teed! Sold as a set. Fresh from the far Southeast, Sirs! Beginning bid ... fifteen hundred *dinari*! A bargain, my dear sirs!"

"These are not the same as the indentured workers," observed the caterpillar dryly. "They're to be sold outright, I understand."

"Not my favorite thing, slavery," Myrn commented sourly. "I can perhaps understand indenturing for foolishly piled-up debts. But these poor little girls deserve better than a lifetime of slavery, don't you think?"

"You'll have to ask the girls, I guess," sighed the Journeyman Aeromancer, shrugging his three front-most pairs of shoulders. "They don't seem to be too distraught."

"When are *you* to go into the circle ... do you know?" Marbleheart asked.

"Nobody's told me a thing."

"They're probably saving you for the climax of the show," the Otter-Monkey decided. "I'll go and see if Douglas has any news on it. He'll want to know if you still intend to follow your plan, Myrn."

Myrn confirmed her plan, slightly modified by what she had seen that morning.

Marbleheart shook his head.

"It *might* work. We'll stand by in case it doesn't, of course. You realize that one pass, one gesture, one helpful spell from Douglas might keep you from achieving Mastery ... or is it Mistress-y?"

"I'm aware of it." Myrn sighed. "Tell my loving husband

that he's *not* to interfere with magic, unless it's a matter of death or dire injury. He'll understand.''

''Understand, maybe,'' sniffed the Monkey, ''but he'll not like it, I assure you.''

''If things fall apart,'' put in the Air Adept–caterpillar, ''Marbleheart and I are prepared to step in to help you, Myrn. That's allowed under Flarman's rules.''

''Thank you, sweethearts! I hope and believe I can take care of myself. Don't either of you do *anything* unless I ask, please.''

Marbleheart patted her gently on the cheek with a soft paw and leaped to catch the edge of the tent roof, swinging his lithe monkey body up onto the canvas.

He disappeared in the direction of his Master.

In the ring in the center of the tent the dancing troupe bowed, the crowd applauded enthusiastically, and the auctioneer called for opening bids. Action was lively for a while. Nobody noticed a black-furred monkey settling on the red-and-white-clad young man's shoulder and chattering excitedly in his ear.

Two experienced midwives, several expert cooks, a physician condemned for malpractice, four experienced well-diggers, an old man who made scented soaps, and a number of young serving girls and boys followed the dancers ... the latter group too young to have any real talents other than strong backs to offer a new master.

They all were quickly sold and went off with their purchasers, looking quite pleased with the results, and grateful to the Slavers as well. Not a few wept to say good-bye to their sellers.

Myrn, meanwhile, studied the buyers and consulted with several of the Traders' wives and daughters as they attended the female slaves, applying cosmetics and serving cool drinks to them or combing their hair and arranging their clothing, which was a nice mixture of modesty and enticement.

''That one ... Harroun? You say he's from the foothills of the Darkest Mountains?'' she asked a young Trader lass who was helping her arrange her hair.

''A bit old for you, if I may say so, dearie. He seeks such as you for his son, who's nearing marriage age, I hear.''

"He's been looking at me all afternoon," Myrn said thoughtfully. "I think he's planning to bid once I go into the circle."

"You could do worse," offered the girl with a shrug. "Much worse! Although mind you, I wouldn't want to live that near to the dangerous mountains. I prefer our nice, clean, level desert myself . . . if I can't have a rich coastal town."

"You fear the uplands, then?" Myrn asked.

"Not the mountains so much, but what lies beyond. Ebony Sea! There are terrifying and wicked . . . *things* along that shore, I've been told. By those who should know!"

She actually knew little more than that, Myrn found.

During a coffee break in mid-afternoon, Trader Brint came looking for Myrn.

"You'll go into the circle next . . . after coffee and cakes," he told her. "Step up when I call you, walk straight, and stand modestly in the center of yon circle with your eyes downcast. Unless I—or a customer—should speak to you, say nothing. Understand me, my girl? I'll attempt to get the very best place for you. We'll start you quite high. Any questions?"

"I want that older man—Harroun, I believe his name to be—so see if you can arrange that, please," Myrn told him.

Brint stroked his bearded chin, scratched at his rather hawk-like nose, and shook his head.

"Can't promise, mistress! Harroun Sheik is a good old sort, but not all that wealthy. He may bid—I've seen his eyes on you, too—but some of the coastal lordlings could overbid him without really trying."

"Start me in his direction if you can manage it," Myrn insisted. "Leave the outcome to me!"

"I don't agree with old Brother Burnt," Brint added as he turned away. "He pooh-poohed your powers and value from the first. He doesn't want me to mention your claim to being a witch."

"Wizard," Myrn corrected him sharply. "Look you, Trader! I need two things out of all this: to have a chance to talk to this Harroun at some length, and to travel to and over the Darkest Mountains, if he can be persuaded to take me home with him."

"I don't pretend to understand any of this." Brint sighed,

then shook his head. "But if I can help you, Mistress, you may count on me."

"I ask no more," said Myrn, giving him a smile and a quick wave as he left.

"Time to resume," young Brint grunted, coloring brightly. "Be ready!"

"She's up next," Marbleheart-monkey chattered in Douglas's left ear. "See that old countryman dressed in dusty dark green and dirty yellow? The one with the three-foot ostrich feather in his turban? He's the one, Myrn says. He lives nearest where we think Serenit's held. If she goes east as part of this Sheik's entourage, she thinks, she'll travel well hidden from the kidnappers' eyes and spies."

"Not bad thinking," Douglas agreed, nodding. "Well, she's nearly a full Wizard and has always been quick to catch on to such matters. Try as I might, I can't detect a trace of our poor First Citizen closer than just somewhere to the east. And there's the problem of this King Priad and his people to which I'm supposed to address myself."

"Myrn says not to worry," continued Marbleheart. "Do you want me here, Douglas, or should I go to Myrn? *With* Myrn, I should say."

"Just so," said Douglas, shaking his head uneasily. "Stick to my dear Aquamantic wife, Familiar! And let me know exactly what I can do for her as quickly as Otter legs can carry news. Or monkey legs, for that matter."

"Have no doubts about that!" cried the Monkey-Otter, and he was off once more over the hot tent tops.

"A most beautiful, talented, healthy, black-haired, green eyed wench, good sirs! A true bargain, for she is a trained Magicker . . . actually a practicing Aquamancer from the mysterious, far-off isles of Warm Seas! This one would be highly valuable on the desert, finding water in hidden wells deep under the sand," bawled Brint, enthusiastically waving both hands and gesturing at Myrn as she stepped into the circle.

She stood, smiling slightly, eyes looking boldly forward, despite the Slave Trader's instructions, and at once caught the elderly sheik's gaze.

He blinked in surprise. Myrn smiled warmly and nodded to him.

"A true bargain!" continued Brint, missing the byplay completely. "Beauty and skill in one very neat package, sirs! I invite your closest examination before you hear my starting price. Come forward and satisfy yourselves she is a bargain without equal at *any* price. I present to you . . . Myrn of Flowring Island, Water Adept!"

The crowd, most of them simply out of curiosity, edged forward to look more closely at the item for sale. They walked all about her, carefully noting her size and shape. A few asked Myrn questions, politely and quietly.

Douglas came close and smiled at her, but said nothing.

"Where is this Flowring Isle, sweetness?" asked one of the Seacoast dandies. "Don't believe I've ever heard of it."

"Three days' sail north and west of Waterand Island, my Master's home," replied Myrn. "Fourteen days' sail, I'm told, due west of Samarca. Some of you may have heard of our large and perfect pearls and our blue corals, sir. We're famous for supplying them to both East and West."

"Ah, yes," said Harroun, speaking for the first time, although he had been examining her as closely as any. "You young bucks won't remember, but there was a time in my great-great-grandfather's youth when rare Flowring pearls were much in demand. Most beautiful, too!"

"Are you thinking of bidding on this beauty?" asked the young Port dandy who had earlier purchased the tailor's indenture. "A bit of comfort for your old age, eh?"

"I seek a suitable first-wife for my only son, rather," said the desert chieftain gravely. "He's of marriageable age, you see."

"You should let the boy pick his own first-bride," snorted the other. "He may not favor a foreign lass like this one. She appeals to me more directly! Name your asking price, Slave Trader! I'm eager to hear how you value this dark-haired enchantress."

"All in good time, worthy master," cried Brint. "Give those in the back a chance to view our offering more closely. Plenty of time for all, sirs!"

He deftly fended other price inquiries until all the buyers had looked to their heart's content. Surprisingly, none of the customers asked Myrn to demonstrate any magic spells.

Myrn stood, meeting their eyes, but smiling mostly at the elderly desert man from the dry foothills of the Darkest Mountains.

"My lands are broad, but mostly rocky," Harroun said to Myrn. "We aren't the richest sheikdom of fair Samarca, by any means. But my only son is quite handsome. I think you'll like him. He's kind and well educated, too."

"If it were up to me," Myrn whispered in reply, "I'd go with you immediately, good Harroun. You seem the decent sort to me."

"Let us bid!" called the elegant young fop from the coast. "The sun drops toward Sea, as 'tis. Many of us must return to Balistan tonight, and it's a longish night ride."

"Not for us of the desert," one of the desert chiefs laughed. "Night is a better time to cross hot sands, young sir."

"I prefer daylight for *my* traveling," insisted the man from Port of Samarca. "Let the sale begin!"

Myrn caught her husband's eye and nodded slightly. Douglas frowned just a bit but said nothing.

"Well, then . . . let us begin at a reasonable figure for this fair jewel of Sea named Myrn. A Water Wizard, remember! Highly trained," shouted Brint. "For this maid of the Warm Seas I ask . . . fifteen hundred *dinari*!"

Many in the crowd gasped at the steep price, shrugged their shoulders, shook their heads, and moved away, seeking the refreshment tent or preparing for departure.

A small group remained, some to listen and watch, and a few to offer bids.

"Fifteen hundred and one!" shouted the dandy, laughing and glancing around to see if he could determine who was serious, who'd stayed just to play games, and who was merely watching.

"Fifteen hundred and one *dinari!*" echoed the clerk, hurriedly writing down the opening bid.

"Who . . . ?" began Brint.

"And *five!*" said Harroun firmly.

"Ah! But, my dear old papa, consider whom you bid against! I am Badishah, son of Alama Sheik, the very wealthy Port Master of Port of Samarca, you should know!"

"I am greatly pleased to meet you, young sir," said Harroun, bowing calmly. "I remember your goodsire well. We fought side by side under old Sultan Fadouzal, long since. When you return to Port, give him my regards."

"You know of our wealth and influence, then?" asked the younger man, with a slight sneer. "No wealthier man exists in Samarca, I vow to you."

"That is true . . . of your good *father*," said a new voice.

Douglas stepped forward, bowing to the elderly Sheik and nodding coolly to the young man. "What of your *own* wealth, Master Badishah? How deeply into your father's pocket do your idle fingers reach, I wonder."

Badishah drew himself up—but still had to look above himself to stare at the stranger's face, for Douglas was five inches taller than he.

"My business is *my* business," he snapped. "Take care, whoever you are!"

"I'm called Douglas Brightglade, a traveler from . . . a far place," replied the Pyromancer, winking solemnly at Myrn. "I've enjoyed the Slave Traders' hospitality and their interesting show, and I feel it incumbent on myself to save them from being shortchanged. I bid fifteen hundred and twenty-five *dinari,* Auctioneer!"

The crowd, sensing an amusing confrontation and eager to see the supercilious young son of a wealthy sheik bested in a bargain, moved closer to the circle, calling out encouragement and a few ribald remarks.

"Easy! Easy!" cried Brint, holding up his hands. "All must get their chance to bid. Fifteen hundred and—"

"Fifty," Harroun said quickly.

"Fifteen hundred and fifty *dinari*!" responded Brint, quickly and a bit breathlessly.

His clerk scribbled furiously, recording the desert man's bid.

"Ah! You'd test my will and my purse?" Badishah snarled at Harroun. "Add another fifty dinari, Slave Trader!"

"Two thou—," began the recorder.

"And one!" Douglas said softly.

"And five!" retorted the elderly sheik, still calm as morning.

"Bah!" snapped Badishah. "Make that . . . *three thousand*!"

"I—I must sadly pass, then." Harroun sighed and shook

his head. "Three thousands *denari* . . . Why, my whole sheik-dom would yield little more than that!"

The crowd sighed, laughed aloud, and relaxed.

Brint took a deep breath. "Three thousand *dinari* are bid by the young gentleman from Port! Going for the first time! Going—"

"See his cash first," advised Douglas suddenly. "I wonder if he can pay the price."

"You have the . . . the *gall* to question my credit!" screamed Badishah. "I'm good for the price, Slave Trader! My credit is well established."

"But *I* will offer three thousand in hard cash . . . solid gold and silver *dinari*," the Pyromancer told the auctioneer. "*Real* money. Here and now!"

He shook his left sleeve over the sand floor and a long, gleaming stream of silver, along with a large handful of gold coins, fell out. The flow seemed to go on forever and ever.

"Cash takes preference over credit," ruled Brint in a choked voice. "You are called upon to produce . . . ah . . . three thousand *dinari* in cash, young Badishah. On this spot!"

"The terms, as explained to me earlier by this young Trader's older associate," Douglas explained, "are cash only. No credit! I offer three thousand . . . in this gold and silver."

He gestured at the considerable pile of bright metal at Myrn's feet.

"Forget the whole stinking thing!" blurted young Badishah. "I don't need a witch-woman, anyway, no matter how pretty and willing!"

"Then," said Brint, "going once . . . twice—"

"However, I don't want the girl on those terms," Douglas interrupted, shaking his head.

"Then . . . *what*?" sputtered the Slave Trader, at a loss for words for the first time.

"Harroun Sheik!" Douglas whispered to the old man. "I'll buy the lady for you, if you'll accept my terms. Not for your son to marry, but rather as your advisor."

"I've never heard of such a thing," the Sheik whispered back in a shocked voice.

The dwindling crowd moved back again toward the center of the floor, where Myrn stood before the considerable pile of gold and silver coins.

"Well . . . ah . . . *er* . . . ," gasped Harroun. "Well, my thanks, young sir, but—"

"Take the money," insisted the Pyromancer, leaning forward again to whisper in his ear. "The lady is my beloved wife and needs your protection. This will buy it . . . if you'll extend it for gold and silver. But you must decide at once, good sir!"

"I accept your very kind offer of a loan," Harroun said in a loud, carrying voice. "On your terms, sir!"

He turned to the Slaver, gesturing toward the coins. "There's your payment. I declare the sale closed!"

"Sold to Harroun Sheik of Hollow Hill!" cried Brint quickly, before anyone else could interfere.

The crowd cheered lustily while Badishah stomped angrily away, shouting to his servants that he would to return to Balistan at once.

"Thank you!" said Douglas to the elderly chieftain. "Come! I think the auction is well over. The sun will be setting in a few minutes, and you'll want to get an early start in the morning."

While Brint was supervising the stacking, counting, and sacking of the coins, Myrn flung her arms about her husband's neck and buried her head in his shoulder, laughing and weeping at the same time.

"Get a receipt!" Douglas advised the desert man. "Let's go somewhere and have a cool drink and talk business, sir!"

"Gladly!" replied the Sheik. "Gladly! I suspect I've failed to find young Saladim a wife, but I believe I may have found him a few powerful friends."

"Friends . . . wives . . . What's the difference!" Marbleheart the Monkey laughed aloud. "I think we managed that fairly well, Wizards all. Didn't even use any magic!"

"Oh? And where did all those shiny coins came from, may I ask?" Myrn wondered. "Flarman's treasury hidden deep under Wizards' High?"

"Well, Flarman won't mind, under the circumstances," Douglas insisted. "Flarman Flowerstalk has little use or time for money, anyway. What's for supper, may I ask, lady-wife?"

Myrn skipped happily along beside him and began to plan her menu aloud, much to the desert chieftain's amazement and Marbleheart's amusement.

"Roast lamb, done just the way you like it best, Harroun Sheik, and mashed potatoes? Or better . . . roasted potatoes with butter and chives. Sweet young peas and onions? Dessert? What's a good dessert on the desert, I wonder."

"Join us for supper," Douglas invited Harroun. "Sounds like it'll be a grand feast!"

"Apparently so," murmured Harroun, struggling not to laugh aloud and failing completely.

Chapter Fourteen

The Foothills

IN the last of High Desert's short twilight, Lesser Dragon and Nameless arrived and settled down behind the large dune overlooking the Slave Traders' busy, noisy encampment.

"Do you think she's there?" muttered Lesser. "Do you see her?"

Nameless nodded eagerly.

"Will you go down and join her, then?" the Dragon asked, a bit wistfully. "Would that be safe, do you think?"

The flying horse shook her head slowly. They stood watching the activity of the Slavers' camp for a long moment.

"It gets quite chilly very quickly out here," observed the filly's vast companion. "I'd better stay close, then. You can snuggle next to me and avoid any chills that might be lurking about."

The horse snorted and bumped her companion with her hip, as if to say, That's the idea, old chap! We'll watch through the long night together.

Lesser Dragon settled down, wriggling his hips, tail, legs, and shoulders until the soft sand flowed about him, hiding them both from all but the closest examination.

He closed his eyes and dozed. (It's the way of all Dragons to sleep whenever nothing presents itself for action.) After full dark, Nameless wandered slowly away to examine the guard outposts and study the stars, which were very bright in the deeply indigo sky.

Myrn and Douglas sat side by side eating the delicious roast, the minty sauce, and the roasted potatoes Blue Teakettle had sent them.

They had told Harroun Sheik their story—stories, rather—and explained their missions.

Marbleheart Sea Otter, taking a break from being a monkey, stretched himself full length in the still-warm sand, listening to their talk and putting in comments when he felt the conversation needed a boost.

The Journeyman Aeromancer, also restored to his proper shape, sat listening silently. His head nodded at times, for it had been a long, hot day. As a caterpillar he found he became uncommonly foot-weary by eventide.

"It'll take us three days to reach Hollow Hill, my home," Harroun explained, nibbling the raspberry ice Myrn had conjured a moment before. "Um! Delicious, my dear mistress . . . er, Myrn! If you can cook like this, my son will have lost a perfect, beautiful, and talented first-wife!"

"I cannot lie to you, Harroun." The Aquamancer laughed delightedly. "The whole dinner was prepared for us by a good friend and merely transported hither by a minor magic I mastered years ago. I'll mention your pleasure to Blue Teakettle, who prepared it all, when I see her again—which I hope will be sooner rather than later, Douglas! It's only twelve days until Summer Solstice, you realize."

"We're both closing in quickly on our goals." Douglas smiled back at his wife. "Three days for you to reach the foothills, you say, honored sir?"

"Yes, and please . . . call me Harroun," insisted the desert chief. "I never did go much for all these courtly titles and honorifics. I'm a simple country man."

"But have not always been such," observed Cribblon. "I heard you say that you once served under the old Sultan alongside such notables as the chubby Port Master."

"He was not always so overweight, nor as fond of strong drink," said Harroun, shaking his head sadly. "He and I were in the forefront of several terrible, splendid battles. When the fighting was over, Alama accepted from Sultan Fadouzal the post of Port Master, but I only wished to go home and raise my sheep, my goats, my horses, my camels, and my children. Unfortunately, perhaps, six of the seven last were daughters. . . . All but one girl and my lad have married well.''

"You son is your youngest child, then?'' Douglas asked.

"The very youngest!'' Harroun laughed. "And the apple of his sisters' and his father's and mother's eyes! He's but seventeen, is Saladim, and more of a poet than a warrior, I'm afraid. Having six doting older sisters, he's been slow to think of his own marriage. I would allow him his own choosing, if he'd shown any inclination that way.''

"I am only recently a husband and father myself,'' said Douglas. "Perhaps you should give him a few more years?''

"I've struggled with the idea of waiting, I admit.'' Harroun sighed, and finished his ice. "You may be right, Pyromancer. Certainly, aside from your fine Wizard-wife, here I saw no one I would have considered as daughter-in-law at the auction today.''

"There's plenty of time,'' Myrn said, thoughtfully picking at the last of her dessert with her spoon. "Have you left any of the sherbet, Marblehead?''

"I've had *more* than enough and am about to join our friend the Aeromancer in slumber.'' Marbleheart groaned sleepily. "What do you say, Masters? Shall we adjourn for the night?''

"For all your pranks and jokes, Familiar,'' Douglas said yawning, "I give you this: you know when to stop partying and go to bed.''

"It's a natural Otter talent,'' the water-animal said, then yawned.

Harroun chuckled and rose gracefully.

"I will seek my bed, also, friends,'' he said, yawning as well. "We will ride at dawn, Mistress Myrn. I'll send you my youngest and only remaining unwed daughter Marrah to fetch you when it's time to depart.''

"I'll be ready, good sir. My monkey and my caterpillar will accompany me, if you don't mind. As we explained, it's the nature of my Journeying that my wonderful, sleepy-eyed husband may not interfere.''

"What will you do then, Wizard?'' the chieftain asked Douglas.

"Oh, I'll be a distance behind, or maybe before, you. Not so far away that I cannot help if things go wrong, and yet not so close as to be judged interfering with Myrn's Journeying in her Craft.''

"You could join us in night camp, however?" Harroun asked. "You may trust my people to be discreet. I have a comfortable tent you can share with your goodwife, if you wish.''

"I'm greatly tempted," Douglas admitted, hugging Myrn about the waist. "But the people—the forces—we face are very good at noticing what happens at night. No, I'll remain unseen by you and by them for the moment.''

"If that's your decision, then," Harroun agreed. "I'll see you, Lady Myrn, in the earliest morning.''

"*Myrn in the Morn!*" Marbleheart began to hum from beyond the dying campfire. "Someone ought to set those words to music.''

The journey to the rugged, shadowy foothills of the Darkest Mountains passed without incident. Myrn was magically aware of her husband some miles behind them, but refrained from urging him to come closer, although she felt the need for his comfort and conversation.

She missed their children very much, too.

Marbleheart, again disguised as a black monkey, was all about the Sheik's caravan, making friends and chattering questions everywhere. Or he rode silently (which was unusual for him, for he loved good conversation almost as much as a good Seafood dinner) on Myrn's saddlebow.

The Journeyman Aeromancer had gladly given up the fuzzy form of a caterpillar and assumed that of a yellow-and-gray sand sparrow, in which form he acted as messenger between Myrn and Douglas. His sharp sparrow eyes would be useful, Douglas said, in what might lie ahead.

Myrn soon made a fast friend of Harroun's youngest daughter, Marrah, a lively, eager eighteen-year-old maiden who rode astride as if she were part of her horse and was filled with information about the sights and moods of High Desert and the animals, birds, and reptiles they saw along the trail.

"Marrah," cried Myrn early on the second afternoon. "I see a lake, off there!''

"You should know a heat mirage when you see one, being a Magician," the desert lass said with a laugh.

"Wizard!" Myrn corrected her. "Magicians are mere dabblers usually. Strictly entertainers! Nobody takes them all that seriously."

"Do you know any entertaining tricks, though?" the girl wondered, reaching over to ruffle the monkey's dark fur.

"Are you speaking to me or to Myrn?" asked the Otter-Monkey. "Yes, I know all sorts of amusing tricks and spells. I can start fires just about anywhere. I can make myself invisible, too. That's a very difficult spell to work, however. Other magicks cross with Invisibility Spells and one has to be very, very careful, my dear Mistress Marrah."

"I'd rather not be invisible," exclaimed Marrah. "Although, on second thought, it sounds quite exciting."

Myrn laughed and told her a story about her first experiments with Invisibility Spells, back on Waterand Island.

"I carefully fashioned a Cloak of Invisibility for myself, following an ancient Water Adept pattern. When it was finished, I put it on over my petticoat and walked down to the village below Waterand Palace."

"What fun!" said Marrah. "What did you do? Tweak someone's nose? Steal a pie from the baker's table?"

"I might have, except I realized very soon that I was invisible . . . but only *to the Menfolk*! The Waterand ladies saw me quite well. A girl rushed up to me and wanted to know why I was walking about in my shift! I was *so* embarrassed!"

"It could have been worse, of course," Marbleheart chortled. "It could have been the *men* who saw you in your underwear!"

Anecdotes helped fill the long, hot afternoon's ride.

"We'll camp tonight under yon outcrop," Harroun dropped back to say. "It must be a dry camping, however. No water within near on a day's ride of here, unfortunately."

"Yet I sense cool, clear water not far off," Myrn objected. "Aha! *Under* the sand and rocks, it is. Since coming to this desert land, I've sensed water a number of places where you would swear no water ever was."

"Even if there were water sufficient to drink and water our horses," the Sheik asked, "wouldn't this harsh soil be unsuitable for green crops? This desert is quite barren, I've always been told."

"I've been riding across your High Desert for a number of

days now, and I'm becoming increasingly convinced that there *is* water not far under the sand," Myrn insisted. "What's needed is a way to draw it to the surface and distribute it to gardens and fields. Did you know that the soil in a rain forest is poorer in nutrients than in most deserts? Master Augurian swears it's so! But, then, I've never been in a rain forest nor a true jungle."

"Nor have I," admitted Harroun, shaking his head, "and I find it hard to imagine such a place. Still, it might well be worth exploring the matter, if there *is* water not far beneath our sands. Even if the soil is poor, water would allow us to raise larger herds of goats or sheep. Maybe even cattle! Cows need a prodigious amount of water."

Conversing thus, the travelers rode toward the upthrusting bluish stone hills, the barren foothills of Darkest Mountains.

Early in the first day Douglas had been overtaken by the Dragon and Nameless.

As the Pyromancer followed the caravan of the Desert Sheik Harroun, the Dragon had *whooshed* down from the bright sky, nodding pleasantly and puffing a friendly wisp of greenish vapor.

Startled by the sudden appearance of a twenty-foot winged saurian, Douglas fell back two steps, but quickly recovered his presence of mind.

"Ah, a relative of my old friend Great Golden Dragon, aren't you? Yes, I see a family resemblance!"

"Let me introduce myself," said the Dragon. "Great Golden is my great-great-great-granduncle, of course. You already know my little flying friend here, do you not?"

"Yes, of course. Hello, Nameless! I'd almost forgotten you were with Myrn on her Journeying. Welcome to High Desert! Come around behind the hillock, won't you? I'm trailing that caravan ahead and wish to remain hidden, if I can."

They skirted the top of a low dune and, once they were hidden from view, Douglas asked the Dragon to scoop out a hollow in the sand that would protect them from the chill night wind and hide their fire from Harroun's outriders.

"I wish I could tell you I've heard all about you, but I haven't spoken nor written to Uncle Great Golden in some decades . . . and my little friend with the beautiful wings seems to be completely unable to speak.''

"Of course," said Douglas. "Do you like steak? I thought I'd indulge myself with tender sirloin and some crisp fried potatoes. A large lettuce salad will give Nameless something to enjoy more than the usual desert gleanings, I'm sure—as well as you and me."

Shortly they were settled down around his tiny fire, Dragon and Pyromancer eating juicy steaks and nibbling a huge tossed salad with pungent horseradish dressing on the side, which the little horse refused after a quick sniff, preferring her greenery without condiment.

Douglas had recounted his many adventures since the appearance of the winged horse at Wizards' High.

Lesser Dragon listened without comment, except for an occasional "*ah!*" or "*ooh!*" Nameless merely nodded her head from time to time.

"So, you see, I'm seeking this enchanted King Priad who was wickedly whisked away long ago by Frigeon. . . .''

At the name of the missing king, Nameless perked up her ears and looked startled.

"The name Priad means something to you?" Douglas asked. "Do you know anything of this enchanted king?"

The horse nodded eagerly, pawing the ground in frustration at not being able to speak.

"She really can't speak—a most wicked and pitiable enchantment!" cried the Dragon.

"It's time to do something about it," decided the Pyromancer. "It'll take a while, of course, but we've two days at least before Myrn and Harroun reach the Sheik's home. I should have done it before, I'm ashamed to admit. It would have been easier and more sure, done at Wizards' High. But then, we didn't know anything about Samarca, nor much about poor King Priad."

He considered the flying horse for a moment, then asked her, "With your permission, my girl?"

Nameless nodded even more vigorously than before. Clearing away the supper dishes with the wave of one hand, Douglas began examining her enchantment by the light of the little fire under the brow of the last, lofty dune.

Lesser Dragon, fascinated by the demonstration of de-spelling, curled himself about the fire, the Fire Wizard, and the flying filly, and prepared to guard and watch.

Douglas first drew a soft leather pouch from his right sleeve and emptied it on the sand before the fire. Leaning over his shoulder, the Dragon saw several flat sticks of glossy black wood, each about four inches long by an inch wide and thick, smoothly rounded at each end. There were also a number of bright metal stars of the sort that children play with, usually called "jacks."

Completing the Wizard's equipment was a small red rubber ball.

"These may look harmless," Douglas confided to the watching animals, "but, I assure you, in trained hands they can be *very* powerful!"

He picked up the black sticks and arranged them in the form of a six-pointed star—a hexagram, he called it—and carefully placed the seven silvery jacks in its center, just touching each other.

"Now!" exclaimed Douglas. "Sit quietly for a while. These jacks will tell us what I need to know about Nameless's enchantment—if she is enchanted, as we suspect."

For the better part of an hour he tossed the red ball in the air, again and again, snatched up the jacks, one or two or all at a time, and caught the ball again before it could touch the hard-packed sand.

At last he dropped ball and jacks outside the star and grinned happily.

"Well, that confirms *two* enchantments! You're doubly enchanted, Nameless, and very likely it was by Frigeon, for I recognize his signature in the forms of the spelling."

"But what good does this do us?" sniffed Lesser.

"It tells us what to do next," replied Douglas.

He returned the jacks, sticks, and ball to their leather bag and slid the pouch back into his wide right sleeve, drawing out in its place a crystal vial of clear liquid.

"Silence . . . and don't move for a while yet, please," he said to the two watchers. "This is the hardest part, especially where there's water but never was any ice."

"Ice?" wondered the Dragon. "Ah, I see . . . a part of the Ice King's magicking!"

"Exactly. Now, then . . . ," Douglas murmured, concentrating fiercely.

He poured the liquid from the vial into a flat ebony dish and placed the dish on a flat rock in front of the horse. They waited in silence until the water became perfectly still, reflecting the brightest stars on its surface.

At last the Pyromancer made a series of slow passes over the dish. Watching very closely, the Dragon saw no change, but when the Wizard carefully picked up the dish and shook it upside down over his left palm, the water, now a clear lens of ice, popped out.

A breath of frosty cold air rushed over them. Although the fire had nearly died, the lens glowed of its own light in Douglas's hand.

He grasped it carefully by its very edges and peered through it at the winged horse.

"Ah! So that's it! Clever of wicked, crafty old Frigeon, I must say," he murmured. "I wish Myrn were here to assist. Silently, now, friends! I know where to go from here but it'll take some time. Please don't speak aloud nor move quickly!"

For what seemed a very long time he sat perfectly still, studying the lens, unmoving and unspeaking. The Dragon resisted the urge to scratch an itch under his folded left wing. Nameless stood as still as a statue, hardly breathing, watching the young Wizard anxiously.

The slender new moon rose, swiftly at first, then more slowly as it reached its zenith, painting the desert pale silver and the shadows even blacker than before.

In the distance the young Dragon's sharp ears heard the sleepy snuffling and shuffling of the Sheik's horses on picket line under the shadow of a monolith. Everything else was quite still. Even the night breeze had died completely away with the rising of the new moon.

At last Douglas took a deep breath and blew on the lens, which quickly began to melt and dwindle into a puddle in his hand. He snatched up the vial and allowed the silvery liquid to flow into it, with not a drop lost.

"That was the hard part," he said quietly, but startlingly loud in the stillness of the night. "You can relax now."

He changed his own position and took a long drink from

his canteen, offering some to the little horse as well.

"I can tell you this—you *were* enchanted by old Frigeon. Part of it was to take away your power of speech . . . for what reason I can't imagine. Do you recall?"

"Yes, I do," said the horse, sounding a bit hoarse, as if she had caught a slight cold somewhere. "The Ice King—Frigeon—got very angry when I called him nasty and dastardly and some other very unladylike things!"

"Well, Frigeon always had a rather sudden temper, I know." Douglas laughed. "He took away your ability to speak?"

"Yes! As an example to my poor father and mother and our poor people, you see. They were not silenced, but refrained from speaking of the Ice King thereafter."

"Who *are* you, then?" asked Lesser, breathing a faint puff of startled steam into the air. "May I ask?"

"Of course, dear friend," the flying filly said with a throaty laugh and a bit of a sob. "I am called Indra. I'm the only child of King Priad of Tereniget."

"Tereniget? I've heard of it! South of here, was it not?" gasped the Dragon.

"South and east, I believe," answered the horse, nodding her pretty head. "But tell me, Master Brightglade—"

"Douglas," the Wizard insisted. "We're old friends, you and I, by now."

"Yes, old friends . . . you and your goodwife Myrn, too! But I wonder, if you will, why you stopped now short of disenchanting me fully? I truly appreciate your giving me back my voice, believe me. But I am, after all, a young woman. . . ."

"Of course! Well," Douglas explained, leaning forward to rest his back from the long spelling, "the Silence Spell was really quite simple to break, once I saw its shape. Your own shape, however, will take considerably longer disenchanting, and it seems it has to be carried out for all those under the same spell, at *one time,* or some will be lost forever! And who knows where your people are these days?"

"Well!" gasped Princess Indra.

"We'll have to locate Priad, then gather all his flying horse-people, get them safely in one place, and work their de-spelling all at once. Do you see?"

"I see . . . and agree!" cried the filly. "Of course!"

"Simply amazing," breathed the Dragon. "But what do we do in the meantime, pray?"

"There is the matter of watching out for Myrn," said the winged horseling. "She may need all of us if she runs afoul of whoever captured the terrible Frigeon."

"You must get used to calling him Serenit now," said Douglas, yawning despite himself. "A really quite nice old chap he turned out, once his powers were stripped away."

"I-I-I will have to work at that," admitted the horse. "Perhaps if I were to meet and talk to this Serenit I would feel more kindly toward him."

"That'll come, in time," the Pyromancer promised her. "Meanwhile, we need to get some sleep, good people. It's well after midnight. See, the new moon is ready to plunge into Sea!"

He scooped out a hollow place in the soft, still-warm sand next to the embers of his fire, lined it with blankets he conjured from somewhere, and settled down to sleep.

Lesser Dragon was already sound asleep, gently snoring soft puffs of greenish steam into the chill air.

Indra walked about on the dune slopes for a long time before she folded her legs and wings and closed her eyes for sleep, pressed against the Dragon's warm back.

"Do you see that flat-topped hill just ahead?" Harroun asked Myrn late the next day.

"Yes. It's somewhat strange—all the other hills are sharp-peaked."

"That's because my hill is hollowed out," the Sheik told her. "A natural fortress, you see. My great-grandfather hired a young Trollish prince to have his people excavate and shape it. Inside I stable my horses, fold my flocks, and pen my camels. I was raised there myself and have raised my own children there, too, in years past. We feel safe there. The sides are very tall, thick, and steep—impassable unless you know the secret way to enter."

The caravan wound up the lower slopes of the flat-topped hill the Sheik called Indigo Deep. It was much larger and loftier than Myrn had thought at first sight. The sun was almost setting when Harroun drew his horse to a halt on a flat shelf of rock at the base of the final, vertical cliff.

Above here the dark stone was perpendicular and polished smooth . . . unclimbable, Myrn decided.

Harroun sat on his horse facing the rock wall before him and clapped his hands loudly, three times.

The sheer wall before them split from top to bottom with a loud *snap* and the two valves drew apart with a soft, low rumble. Beyond in the twilight Myrn caught a glimpse of trees and rolling lawns, and the roof of a white building.

"Welcome to my beloved Deep!" cried Harroun, bowing in the saddle and gesturing Myrn to ride ahead of him through the gate. "Welcome to my home!"

"How beautiful! And here in the midst of High Desert," exclaimed the monkey Marbleheart. "Fountains and flowers and soft greensward! It even *feels* cooler than the desert behind us!"

Myrn sat on her horse admiring the hidden oasis in the deep center of the hill for a long moment before she urged her mount down a paved roadway that led to the white palace—there was no other word to describe it, although it was neither huge nor grand.

Herds of sheep grazed in the evening cool on the upper slopes within, while a large herd of beautiful horses gathered along the fence to greet the returned Sheik with prances, nods, and nickers of pleasure.

A dozen haughty camels left their own corral and plodded over to see what the commotion was, looking at the caravan warily and unsmiling at first, until they recognized the old Sheik, his servants, and their mounts.

Harroun led his guests—there was no thought, by now, of Myrn as anything other than an honored guest—toward the small palace.

"Those are my servants' and shepherds' homes," he explained, pointing off to the left. "And on the right are the dairy, the barns, stables, folds for the sheep, the blacksmith's, and the harness shops, and storage bins for hay and grain."

As they reached the portico at the front of the palace, the tall double doors swung wide, spilling out bright lantern light and a young man who dashed forth, waving gleefully to the arrivals.

"Father! Welcome home! Who is our guest? Wait until you

hear my new-written song, 'Maiden of the Sands'! 'Tis my very best yet!"

"My son Saladim," Harroun introduced the lad, after dismounting to embrace him and be embraced in return. "My boy, this is the Wizard Myrn Brightglade—"

"Most pleased to meet you, Mistress Wizard," interrupted the boy. "Wizard, did you say! *Ho!* I don't remember you ever speaking of knowing a Lady Wizard, Father!"

"A new and already much-admired acquaintance," his father explained.

He introduced Marbleheart the Monkey and the little sparrow Cribblon without explaining who or what they were.

"Come inside!" cried the lad. "Our lookouts reported your coming and I took the liberty of ordering supper, Father. The return of the Sheik is always pleasant excuse for a party," he bubbled. "And when he brings guests . . . all the more reason for a feast!"

He led his father and their guests inside the sprawling, comfortable, white stone manor.

Lesser Dragon studied the distant, flat-topped hill carefully. Of the three of them, he had the sharpest eyes over distance.

"They opened a great gate in the cliffs, quarter-way to the top. Very clever! A nice way to protect your home from wild beasts and desert marauders, I'd say."

Douglas nodded. He studied the sharply rising range of bare, dark mountains beyond the Sheik's hill. The sun had dipped under the horizon and the mountainous land had taken on a mysterious, almost sinister appearance, backlighted by early stars.

"We'll leave them at that, I think," he said to his companions. "Let's find a cozy place to camp out of the night's wind, overlooking Harroun's hill if possible."

Indra sniffed the air and stood looking about.

"There are lookout posts on the peaks, there and there. We'll have to give them wide berth if you don't wish them to know you're here," she told Douglas. "Why not just go up to the door and knock. We could sleep tonight in a real bed again."

"It probably'd be just fine, and a welcome bed and wife, too," Douglas responded. "But, no . . . even without his knowing it, Harroun may have spies in his household. We'll camp somewhere on a nearby mountainside and consider what's to do next.''

He led his friends in a wide circle, taking advantage of other hillocks and deep ravines to hide themselves from the Sheik's lookouts. It was long after full dark before the Dragon's keen night-sharp eyes found a shallow cave on the upper slope of one of the higher foothills.

''Reminds me of a cave we found, Marbleheart and I, near the Black Witch's Coven,'' Douglas murmured. ''It'll be rather cold, and the mouth doesn't face the Sheik's place as I'd like, but we've Dragon's body-heat for warmth. We'll be snug . . . and no one will notice us, perhaps.''

''I'll gather some fragrant grasses for beds,'' offered the Dragon. ''Take a quiet look about, too.''

''What would you like for supper?'' Douglas called after him.

''I'll find something in the hills,'' Lesser answered, heading out into the moonless dark. ''You take care of our little Princess.''

''Give me a task to do,'' begged Indra. ''I want to help, Douglas.''

''I could teach you some cooking . . . or rather, ordering. The grasses will serve as comfortable beds, when Lesser returns. However, you might like to pop over into Harroun's hill and tell Myrn where we are.''

''Delighted!'' cried the little horse.

''*She'll* be delighted to hear you talking, I'd think,'' Douglas said. ''In fact, stay with my wife tonight. Harroun's camp is probably a much safer place for you both than a bare mountain cave. This is no place for a Princess, even when she's a pretty filly!''

Although she denied it, it was clear the idea of sleeping that night in a castle—or a comfortable stable, at least—appealed more to the flying horse than sleeping on grass on a cold stone floor. She spread her wings, darting high into the air and disappearing in the direction of Harroun's foothill fortress.

Douglas wrote a detailed and long-overdue note to Flarman, detailing his and Myrn's adventures to date. Sealing it with a bit of fire-orange wax, he tossed the letter into the fire he'd set ablaze on the cave floor.

The letter disappeared in a quick flash and a slight pop.

He set about obtaining his own dinner, heaping platter of savory sausages, oven-baked brown beans, and chocolate layer cake for dessert.

When Lesser returned with a great double-armful of fresh valley grass, the Dragon ate the last of the cake in two gulps. Shortly they both—Lesser blocking the cave entrance, as secure a safeguard as any locked door—settled down to sleep.

Indra dropped quietly into the center of Harroun's sheikdom, pleased at its obvious comfort and country charm. She folded her wings and trotted up to the great double doors of the palace, then kicked her heels loudly several times on the thick panels.

A maidservant opened a postern to one side and stuck her head out inquiringly.

"A strange horse!" she called to someone behind her. "Why come to the house, pretty little thing? I should think a horse would prefer the stables. Around to the right, they are. You must belong to one of the our good Sheik's guests."

"Rather say I came to *see* one of them," replied Indra. "May I be taken to Mistress Myrn Brightglade? I'm her very close friend."

Something in the horse's manner caused the maid to bob a curtsy and invite her to enter at once.

"I'll take you to the Lady Wizard," the girl murmured, nodding to a Guard, armed with a long, curved scimitar, who stood beside her in the hall. "It's all right, Hakkim. Lady Myrn would have such an unusual friend, from what I've heard."

The guard nodded and the maid led the flying horse, who trod quietly and daintily as anyone could wish across the polished marble flooring, up a broad flight of stairs and down a wide corridor to the rooms that had been assigned to Myrn, her monkey, and her bird.

Supper was long over. Myrn was seated at a mirror brushing her thick, black hair, having just climbed from a delightfully hot, soapy bath.

"A visitor?" she called when her own maid answered the door. "Oh Nameless! I thought you were still safe in Balistan. Come in, my dearest! How came you here?"

The enchanted filly trotted in, looking around in curiosity

and nodding to the black monkey and the yellow-and-black sparrow in a friendly fashion.

"I followed you and found your husband Douglas," she explained, nuzzling the Aquamancer lovingly. "He has managed—"

"To restore your speech! How wonderful! Where is Douglas? Will he come tonight?"

"I'm afraid not, Mistress. . . ."

"No, it's Myrn! We're old friends, and should call each other by our first names. Which reminds me—what *is* your name? I can't keep calling you Nameless, now."

"I am Princess Indra of Tereniget," replied the horse, proudly. "But to you, I'll always answer to 'Nameless.' "

"No, no! Indra is beautiful! Tell me first what happened to you after I was stolen from the Sultan's palace. What did Douglas say and what does he plan to do?"

"He's but a short way off, watching and waiting on a cold mountainside," replied the filly. "He'd like to bespeak you, when you have a chance, and when he won't give you away to those who stole the First Citizen."

"Poor man! He could have come with you and slept in a bed with three soft mattresses, twelve silken pillows, a wonderful swan's-down coverlet . . . and me," cried Myrn.

Chapter Fifteen

Dangerous Ways

MYRN awoke and dressed in the darkness just before dawn. She left her companions fast asleep and walked softly down the broad stair to let herself out of the sally-port just as the sky began to brighten with morning.

As she turned to close the door, Marbleheart came *galumphing* along behind her, wriggling his long whiskers and pointing his sharp nose this way and that in curiosity.

"May I?" he asked Myrn. "If you'd rather be alone . . ."

"Nonsense!" said the Journeyman Aquamancer, laughing and patting the beast lovingly on the head. "I need to find a quiet place to bespeak Douglas for a moment."

"Up near the rim of this strange valley, perhaps. Everyone's asleep, except the guards, I see. Bit nippy, out here on High Desert in the morning! I'm glad I'm dressed as a Sea Otter, rather than as a flimsy monkey."

They crossed the level palace lawn, passed between rows of neat, flat-roofed dwellings of dressed stone and mortar with brightly striped awnings to keep off the sun's heat later in the day.

The whole floor of the roughly circular valley was delightfully landscaped with gardens of flowers; wide, sheep-cropped, green pastures; plots of vegetables; and rows of fruit trees, mostly oranges and lemons. Every few yards the two skirted small pools of clear water steaming slightly in the chill morning air.

"Springs, I gather," said Myrn, stopping to look with professional interest into the depths of one large pool of remarkable turquoise color.

"Smells rather familiar," Marbleheart remarked, sniffing and then sneezing. "*Ah-choo!* I've smelled this sort of sulfurous odor before . . . in the valley at the northern end of Eternal Glacier."

"Similar, at least," agreed Myrn. "And something about the rocks and the formations reminds me of Mount Blue Eye."

"A volcano, then?" Marbleheart asked, looking worried.

He knew from hard personal experience what a volcano can do, if it set its mind to it.

"I don't feel any tendency to erupt here . . . not like the feel of Blue Eye at all," Myrn reassured him. "The subterranean fires merely provide varying degrees of hot water for bathing, for laundry, and for castle-heating, I imagine."

Comparing their memories and experiences of volcanoes, the pair climbed a stairway cut into the inner side of Indigo Deep and in a short while reached a parapet that hung on the very rim, providing fabulous views all about, especially of sunrise over the sharply serrated peaks of the Darkest.

Marbleheart trotted along the parapet, sampling the air as well as the views in all directions, but Myrn stood and watched the sun free itself from the mountains, reaching out with her Aquamantic senses.

The Sea Otter settled down in an early spot of sunlight, eyes half-closed but senses alert. For the furred animal this was the best time of day in the desert. The air was yet cool and the new sun was just pleasantly warm.

"Awaken, sleepyhead!" he heard the girl call softly.

But when he raised his head to reply with a quip, he realized she'd spoken to another, not to him.

"Awaken, sweetheart," repeated Myrn with a low, love-filled chuckle. "I need to talk to you a moment, husband dear. Then you can go back to your comfortable grass bed and sleep the heat of day away!"

"I'm sorry . . . ," came Douglas's sleepy voice from the thin air over the desert. "I regret not coming to you last night with the Princess Indra."

"I'm delighted you were able to solve her enchantment and allow her to talk again. She would've kept us awake talking for hours, I fear, if I hadn't insisted we all needed a good night's sleep."

"I can imagine," said Douglas. "She's been under *that* part of her enchantment for over a century!"

"A hundred years! Then . . . she is one of Frigeon's spellbound? You saw through it and assisted her to recover?"

"There yet remains a much larger spell on the poor filly and her folks, to tackle when we have time," Douglas's voice said. "A moment, darling, please. I'll join you in more than just voice."

The air beside the stone parapet shimmered in the early sun, seemed to quake for a breathless moment, and suddenly the form of the young Pyromancer appeared standing beside his wife.

"Hello, Marbleheart!" Douglas said.

For several moments he devoted himself solely to Myrn while the Sea Otter watched, waiting for his own hug and rumple.

"Now!" gasped Myrn, drawing back a bit in Douglas's arms. "We really should talk about plans, shouldn't we, Douglas-my-dear?"

"I've given them some hours of thought—while I tried to sleep on fragrant grasses on the hard floor of a cave," her husband sniffed. Then, more gravely, "We've two different but closely related problems, as I see it."

"The matter of rescuing Serenit . . . and the matter of the flying horses?"

"Yes, we know now Frigeon and King Priad, Indra's father, had a disagreement some years ago. The Ice King sought to extend his hold to the eastern shores of Sea. Somehow Priad sought to block the Ice King in that, and Frigeon cast a spell that turned Priad, his wife and daughter, and a number of Priad's paladins and their ladies into flying horses. This was, I suspect, in the wastelands to the southeast."

"I see . . . ," Myrn murmured. "And when Frigeon fell, Indra set off to find someone to restore her people?"

"That's my guess. You can ask her about it when you return to Harroun's castle. She may be hazy about details, but you can guide her to full recall, if you have the time."

"What bothers me," put in Marbleheart, "is this: Myrn's task is to free our old chum Serenit from his captors, about whom we know virtually nothing. Our job, Douglas, is relatively easy: find and disenchant the people of this flying horse king. *Should* be fairly simple, what with Indra to assist. But Myrn's task isn't nearly as simple! To rescue old Serenit, she must face his unknown captors . . . and they sound pretty formidable, to me!"

"Yes, just so," said Douglas softly.

"Do you have any idea who Serenit's captors might be?" Myrn asked.

"I'm coming to see that he or they are—were?—minions of the Darkness, our foe at Last Battle," the Pyromancer explained.

Myrn hugged herself, shivering even though the sun by now had warmed the air about them quite pleasantly.

"Yes," her husband said with a nod. "The Darkness! But what part, and how powerful is it, I wonder?"

"Oh, I'll let you know, in time," said Myrn. "I imagine I'll find out when I seek for Frigeon . . . I mean Serenit."

Douglas shook his head.

"It's a much more difficult task you'd be facing. I wonder if we should switch our assignments, Myrn."

"No way that *I* know," answered his Journeyman-wife. "Besides, I'll have Cribblon to help. He's a very smart middle-aged Journeyman Aeromancer himself. And he doesn't outrank me, so he won't threaten my Journeying."

"But *I* would, eh? Well, I know that!" Douglas said, drawing down the corners of his mouth comically. "If you believe—"

"Believe? I'm certain of it!" cried the Aquamancer.

"So be it, then," Douglas decided. "But if you need me . . ."

"I'll not hesitate to call. More than just my Mastery depends on my completing my assigned task, of course. What was the Dark Servant's purpose in kidnapping the former Ice King? He—if he *is* a he—must be planning some sort of mischief. To hold the First Citizen as hostage?"

"I discount that," said Douglas, shaking his head, "or we'd have heard from him by now. No, I suspect he planned to steal Frigeon's Powers to rebuild his own! He *may* not yet have realized that Frigeon's Powers were dissipated along with his name and Ice Palace. When he finds out Serenit is Powerless . . .''

"Powerless he may be," said the Sea Otter, "but he knows enough about Wizardry to understand what this Darkness intends, I bet. Serenit's no fool, Master and Mistress! He'll masquerade as a full Wizard, just as long as he can."

"A good and useful thought." Douglas nodded in agreement. "Now, Myrn! Your task is only to rescue Serenit. *My* job is, if it comes to it, to tackle this Darkness thing. But we'll have to move fast!"

Myrn nodded, held up her hand for silence, and stood looking out over the mountains for a long moment. Douglas and Marbleheart allowed her the time to think.

"Yes," Myrn said at last. "You must send Nameless—Princess Indra, rather—to find her parents and the other flying horse people."

"As you suggest," agreed Douglas.

"Meanwhile, suppose you go openly into the mountains over there, sweet husband! You're a full Pyromancer, and this Darkness will be distracted by your appearance so near his haunt from a couple of mere Journeyman."

"Granted!"

"Marbleheart, Cribblon, and I will go into the mountains secretly, find Serenit, free him, and get out as quickly as possible, before the Servant even notices us."

"It'll still leave this Servant to deal with," objected her husband, shaking his head again. "We can't just leave him planning and doing mischiefs of all sorts."

"Once Serenit is safe," Myrn pointed out, "my assigned task will be finished. Cribblon and I will return to assist you in dealing with this Servant, whatever his-her-its name or nature might be."

"Well . . . ," Douglas hesitated. "Fine! I'll send a message this morning to Wizards' High, explaining the situation. We may need their assistance."

"But we daren't wait for them to arrive, do we?" asked Myrn. "So, I'll leave Harroun's valley later today. Will you come with me, Sea Otter?"

"Of course!" cried Marbleheart. "As a monkey, for the

moment. Monkeys are better suited to deserts and waterless mountains than us Sea Otters.''

"I'll try to keep an eye on you . . . and on this Servant, also,'' Douglas promised, taking his wife in his arms to say good-bye. ''I'll send you a message, after I send Deka the Wraith to the Wizards . . .''

"Cautiously! This Enemy might detect Deka and guess at your presence. Oh, Douglas! I'd much rather go into danger at your side. Or, better yet, sit on the front stoop of Wizards' High with our children and Bronze Owl and the cats . . . and watch the clouds make castles in the air over Valley.''

"Once this is done,'' her husband promised, smiling at her lovingly and longingly, ''we'll spend a whole fortnight doing nothing else, sweet wife!''

"I can hardly wait,'' murmured Myrn, and she lifted her face to be kissed once again.

When they returned to Harroun's house through the village and the gardens, the Aquamancer and the Sea Otter, who had resumed his disguise, were met at the front entrance by Saladim, Indra, and the sand sparrow.

"I thought I would show you and your friends about our place,'' Saladim told Myrn.

"Thank you, Saladim, but we'll be leaving as soon as I can make certain arrangements with your father.''

"I'm ready at any moment,'' chirped Cribblon, bobbing his head eagerly. Marbleheart and the flying horse nodded in agreement.

"You, Princess,'' Myrn said to the horse, ''must return to Douglas in his cave at once. He needs you to help him locate your parents.''

"At once!'' cried the filly, prancing with eagerness. ''If you're sure you can spare me, Myrn Brightglade, my best friend . . .''

"I'll manage. Douglas needs you,'' Myrn said. ''Will you go? Although how about some breakfast, first?''

"I've had food,'' the little horse assured her. ''Bamboo shoots and tender succulents grow beside the pools. There are advantages to being a horse!''

In a moment she'd said good-bye. Then spreading her bright wings, she shot into the air.

■   ■   ■

Flarman Flowerstalk whipped his trout line out over Crooked Brook, making his lure skip and wriggle like a real live fly by jiggling and jerking his long, flexible pole.

"Come to papa," he crooned to the trout, but Brook's surface remained undisturbed and the fish hidden deep within.

Black Flame appeared at his side, trying to hide his grin at the fly fisherman's lack of success.

"Deka has brought a message from Douglas? I'll come." The Pyromancer sighed, quickly reeling in his line. "I'm not doing much good here, except to amuse the sprats."

The cat regarded Brook's swift-running water as his Master wrapped up his fishing rod, stowed his lures, and lifted his empty creel.

"See what you can do, then," he murmured to his Familiar. "Trout for supper?"

"A promise! I'm an expert fisher-cat."

"Well, I suppose I *could* live with the envy," chuckled Flarman. "A nice, well-grilled fillet or two'd salve my disappointment pretty well, I suppose. A message from Douglas, you say? I'd better go at once!"

He climbed nimbly to Old River Road, then passed through the sagging front gate and up the curving brick walk to the front door of Wizards' High. Bronze Owl seemed to be dozing in the morning sun, hanging on his nail in the center of the right-hand valve.

"Messenger?" the Pyromancer asked him as he reached for the door handle.

"Inside," mumbled the Owl, nodding his head creakily. "From our wandering Wizardlings!"

He unhooked himself from his nail and flapped after Flarman down the center hallway into the kitchen, where they greeted the Wraith messenger as she floated over the end of the great table, on which Blue Teakettle had just set out a pitcher of iced lemonade and a plate of frosted oatmeal cookies.

"Where's Augurian?" Flarman asked Lithold, who'd just entered from the courtyard.

"He said he was going to sleep late," Lithold answered. "Shall I wake him?"

"No, let's hear what Douglas has to say first."

He sat facing Deka, greeting her affectionately by her name-for-friends-to-use.

"Such good victuals keep me going for eons and eons," the Wraith said, setting down her tumbler. "Greetings, Wizards both, and Bronze Owl! I have a message from the younger Pyromancer."

"So I heard," grunted the elder Pyromancer.

He waved to the Wraith to proceed.

"Master Pyromancer Douglas Brightglade," the Wraith recited in perfect imitation of Douglas's voice, "to the Wizards at Wizards' High. Greetings, Magisters!"

"Bother the formalities," sniffed Lithold. "What does Douglas have to say of himself and his lady?"

"That comes next, Stone Wizard," Deka said a bit tartly, for she hated to be interrupted. "Douglas begins:

"Masters and Mistress, friends all!
I am in a cave on the edge of High Desert of Samarca,
near the Darkest Mountains which separate us from Eb-
ony Sea to the east . . ."

The message was long but Deka recited it perfectly, without a mistake or misplaced emphasis. Flarman and Lithold (and everyone else in the kitchen) listened through to the end without comment.

"I think we'd better discuss this in council," Flarman decided when the Wraith had finished and picked up another cookie from the plate in front of her.

"Question is," said Lithold thoughtfully, "can Douglas, Myrn, and Cribblon, alone, face down a creature of The Darkness?"

"I'll waken the Water Adept, shall I?" asked Bronze Owl.

"No, let the man sleep an hour more," decided the senior Pyromancer. "I want to do some researching first. Like . . . what would be the quickest way to reach Samarca? Can you stay for our answer, Deka?"

"I'll return whenever you call, Flarman Firemaster, but I must be about my other tasks."

"Of course! Well, let's set a council for . . . ah . . . after lunch, in front of the Dwarf's Fireplace. Two o' the clock, that is."

"I think I'll do a little studying, also. I need to know more of these Darkest Mountains and the unexplored shores of Ebony Sea," Lithold decided.

When they looked back, the Wraith had disappeared, along with the rest of the oatmeal cookies. The *miscytwine* was long gone from Pitcher.

"If Flarman or Augurian were here they might give us some expert advice," Douglas said to Lesser Dragon and Princess Indra over his breakfasting. "I've looked and studied for an hour or two and I still only get a very dim outline of what opposes us—who holds Serenit captive, and where he's hidden among the peaks over there."

"Could I help?" asked the Dragon.

He lay prone on the rock ledge outside Douglas's cave, his scales blending so perfectly into the colors of the stones around and under him that even the birds circling the nearest hills didn't notice him. His head was inside the cave.

"I'm wasting time here," muttered Douglas, sounding more than a little disgusted with his lack of progress.

"Isn't it your goodwife's task to steal away the man Serenit?" the Dragon prompted him gently.

"Of course," said Douglas. "Perhaps if I do my own task I'll be more useful to Myrn, later on."

He turned to the flying horse, who rolled her eyes at him mischievously and cocked her head to one side.

"I'm sorry, Princess!" Douglas said, shaking his head. "I tend to worry about my beautiful wife, when I should be taking your problem to heart, as we agreed."

"Perfectly understandable," said the filly. "What do you need to know, Douglas?"

"Where will you find your father and mother and their people? It's time to arrange for their disenchantment."

"I can find them easily enough," replied the horse. "Papa'll have left word of their whereabouts at certain places we know of on the far shore of the Ebony."

"You'll go, then?" Douglas asked.

"Of course, Wizard."

"Next question is . . . how shall the Dragon and I go?"

"Fly, of course!" said Indra, with a surprised laugh.

"But everything I've ever been told about these Darkness

Servants warns me they can *smell* an enchanter or a Wizard when one gets close.''

"But you *want* him . . . her . . . it to detect you, I thought,'' said Lesser. "To mask Mistress Myrn's movements near its lair.''

"True—but not *too* soon, Dragon,'' said the Pyromancer. "I would rather not have to tackle a Dark Power until we know a bit more about it.''

"I've lived near the shores of the Ebony for more than a century,'' said Indra. "I never even knew there was such a *thing* as a. . . . a . . . Power of Darkness here!''

"Armed with more complete knowledge, we'd stand a better chance of forestalling any plots this wandered bit of Darkness may have hatched against Men and others who opposed The Darkness in Last Battle.''

"I see.'' Indra nodded.

She rose from her pile of dry hillside grass and stalked about the cave from side to side, deep in thought.

"Well,'' said Lesser, "I've been flying over the Darkest Mountains for close on a thousand years. This Dark Servant or whatever you want to call it will have observed me and will recognize me, I'd think. I can carry you to the Seashore to meet King Priad and maybe not be suspect. After all, thousands of birds and other things fly over this land daily. And there are Men—miners, I think—in the mountains, too. People tend to take us for granted.''

"You're right, of course,'' agreed Douglas.

"I'll go separately,'' declared Indra. "I'll find Papa and Mama. We'll then meet you in a preagreed place on the strand, out of sight of the Servant in the mountains.''

Douglas thought for a long moment, then nodded his head.

"Go ahead, Princess! Tell us where we're to meet you. We'll wait there, in case you have to go farther afield to find your family than you think. Bring them to meet us.''

Said the little horse at once, "Wait for us at Walrus Shingle. With the kind of racket those great Sea-going mammals make ashore, not even the most powerful Wizard or Sorcerer could eavesdrop.''

She squeezed past Lesser Dragon's shoulder and trotted out into the morning sun. Waving her tail at her companions, she launched herself into the sky.

"She didn't give us directions to this Walrus place," Douglas realized.

"I know where it is," Lesser Dragon said. "Hard to miss, what with all their yowling, grunting, and booming. Shall we wait for darkness, then? Time for a nap and a good, sustaining dinner first, I'd suggest. I'm becoming addicted to Blue Teakettle's home cooking!"

Chapter Sixteen

Afoot in the Darkest Mountains

"I don't dare use even the simplest Flying Spell, let alone Augurian's gift, the Traveling Pearls," Myrn explained. "Flarman says the Darkness Servants are very good at smelling spells. We'll have to go afoot."

"Ugh!" grumped the monkey, flopping down to blow a bit of sand from between the toes on his left hind foot. "Well, I climbed all over Blue Eye. Slid all over Eternal Ice, too. I guess I can climb these bad, old, dry mountains."

"Monkeys are considerably lighter than Sea Otters," Cribblon chirped. "Or . . . why not join me as a small bird?"

"No, *someone* has to keep his feet on the ground," retorted the Otter. "There might be all kinds of fierce beasts in those mountain fastnesses, you know! Hungry is the constant state of all wilderness beasts, I know from experience. A snow leopard once told me he expected to dine no more than once every two weeks, and I know snakes who go for months without a round meal."

"A quick pair of wings are better than size," Cribblon argued, but Marbleheart was determined to stay a monkey.

"Well, good-bye then, Harroun! We'll be back as soon as we can, of course," Myrn said, giving the old desert chief a warm hug and a kiss on the bearded cheek. "And young Saladim! I wish you could go along to help, but I fear what's

coming is going to be pretty much magical, requiring Wizard-
lore rather than bravery and good swordsmanship.''

"In the foothills we'd be as close as possible to you, should
you need us," Harroun suggested.

"No, stay here, please!" Myrn insisted. "I can call to you
here as well as up in the hills, anyhow. Good-bye, brave desert
men! Come along, beasts!"

The Sheik and his son watched them climb down the path
on the outside of the Deep and strike out toward the east.

"I wonder how the pretty little filly fares," Saladim said
wistfully as they turned to reenter the crater.

"You were really impressed with her, I'd say," his father
chuckled.

"She's a real Princess, Father! I wonder if she's as pretty
a girl as she is as a horse."

"Probably ugly as a she-goat," his father gently teased.

"You could turn me into a horse," suggested Marbleheart.

They'd walked their rough path for four hours and stopped
in the shade of an overhanging rock for lunch and a much-
needed breather. The sun was beginning to dip toward distant
Sea, far away to the west, and the air was very hot. Fortu-
nately, it was also very dry.

However, thunderheads were beginning to gather over the
Darkest peaks, threatening a storm.

"No!" Myrn said, a bit sharply. "Stop trying to protect me,
Marblehead! Magicking this close would be like a beacon at
moonless midnight if the Darkness thing is at all watchful."

"We should've thought of it earlier, I agree," said Cribblon
with a sigh.

He was fresh as a Valley morning himself. He flew ahead
and circled back to report on the steeply rising path, recom-
mending the best ways to go. He sought out timid mountain
mice and shy rock birds to come to tell Myrn what they knew
of the area and of the strange Darkness creature.

So far they'd brought only vague rumors and frightened
tales. As Myrn remarked while massaging her weary feet, few
of them had ever gone more than a mile or two from where
they'd been born or hatched.

"What we need is high-flying kinds of birds," suggested
Cribblon.

"Eagles and such?" asked the monkey.

He was holding up well, being small and light and agile. Dry heat doesn't bother monkeys at all.

The sparrow considered Otter's suggestion for a moment. "Eagles? Maybe gyrfalcons or kestrels. They're smaller and are as sharp-eyed as eagles, or so Bronze Owl once told me. Raptors have more curiosity, too, which is a good thing to have when you're small in a big, big country."

"But wouldn't they be dangerous?" Myrn wondered, interested in the idea despite her misgivings. "They might as easily eat you, Cribblon, as listen to you!"

"Some truth to that," the Journeyman Air Adept-sparrow agreed, solemnly. "But it may be worth the risk . . . and I'd be far away from you, Myrn, if I were forced to make a sudden shape-change in midair."

"If he . . . this Servant—I *do* wish he had a name—is watching Douglas he might not notice a tiny bit of magic like that," Myrn considered, slipping her stockings and shoes back on. "Wait 'til morning, Cribblon, if you're to do it. Somewhere I read that the first rays and the last rays of the sun tend to blind even the most powerful Watching Spells."

"Not much help if a hungry raptor stoops on you," grumbled Marbleheart. "Our Enemy is not the only danger here, Myrn."

"Worth the risk," Cribblon insisted. "Otherwise we're likely to be wandering about here in the mountains for days and days. What do you think, Myrn? It's *your* Journeying, after all."

"Be careful, Cribblon! I know you traveled alone all over Old Kingdom for years with a considerably smaller fund of magic than you have gained since, but still . . ."

"I'll wait until this storm passes," decided the middle-aged Journeyman, glancing at the towering black thunderhead above. "No sensible bird flies willingly in such inclement weather!"

Myrn and her party continued as long as they could, following steep-sided, rock-strewn gorges toward the high pass between the shoulders of two stark peaks. Soon the storm began, with fat, warm raindrops which were, at first, refreshing to the girl and the animals, but soon became a nuisance, making the trail slippery and the views uncertain.

"Time to camp for the night," Myrn decided at last.

"I've been looking for caves and such," Marbleheart told her. "No luck."

"There's an overhanging cliff up ahead," Cribblon said, landing on Myrn's left shoulder. "It'll be some protection . . . but not very much."

A great, blasting bolt of blue-white lightning flashed across the darkened sky and immediately the rain began to fall more heavily, as if the thunder had shaken it loose from the clouds.

Myrn calmly made a hand pass over her head and drew her companions close. The rain pelted all about them with ever-increasing fury, but only a few drops penetrated her Umbrella Spell. Lightning crashed and boomed almost without cease, shivering the air and shaking the ground.

"Now! While the lightning is playing," Myrn yelled to her two companions, "I'm going to carve us a hole in yon table rock. It'll just take a few seconds. Stand by!"

Using the tremendous roars and flashes of electricity from the low clouds to shield her magicking, Myrn quickly sliced into the stone wall she'd selected, carving a wide, barrel-vaulted passage into its lowest strata, until the three of them could easily walk within.

A few more moments and Myrn had set a fire, conjured up a hot meal, and made comfortable beds for them all, cozy as could be.

"With any luck at all," she puffed—the spelling had been arduous, if swiftly completed—"even a close watcher wouldn't have noticed."

"Ham and eggs!" exclaimed the Otter, delighted with the selection from Blue Teakettle's kitchen.

"*Argh!*" Cribblon made a wry grimace. "*Eggs!* I never really liked them before and I like them even less now that I know how a bird feels."

"No eggs for you, then, Airhead!" said the monkey. "More for us! Have a bit of this toasty-buttery corn fritter and some Valley ham—it's Blue at her very best!"

They settled down in some comfort, despite the tumult of the storm outside. The fire, tiny as it was, burned cheerfully, and the smell of hot cornbread and fried ham made them feel quite at home.

■　　　■　　　■

Douglas and Lesser Dragon had given Myrn's party several hours' head start. When they were ready to leave the cave at the edge of the foothills, twilight had fallen and the storm that had driven Myrn and her companions to shelter was flashing and rumbling across the face of the mountain range.

"We'll fly high, shall we?" asked the Dragon. "Take us a bit longer, but that'll just give our horseling more time to find her papa."

"The storm'll mask our movements, I should think," Douglas agreed. "Can you carry me or should I fly alongside?"

"Get aboard! No magic required! I can carry a much greater weight than a youthful Fire Wizard . . . and on my back you'll be quite invisible to anyone or anything below us."

Once Douglas was aboard, seated astride just in front of the beast's long, leathery wings, Lesser gave a warning grunt, a low shout, and flung his tremendous bulk off the cliff before the cave, catching a rushing updraft under his wings and letting it carry them high into the dark sky.

"These thunderheads must be close to five miles high, maybe more," he commented once they were well aloft. "It'll grow a little chilly, Pyromancer!"

Douglas drew a heavy, hooded, woolen cloak from his left sleeve and shrugged into it as the Dragon continued to beat his wings for altitude. Gusty winds shook the flying Dragon from all sides but Lesser flew steadily upward in great spirals, not allowing the vagaries of updrafts and downdrafts to turn him from his course.

The black and uproarious storm clouds towered like a cliff beside them, sheer from the foothills below. Lightning bolts crashed and roared every few seconds and dense cloud-masses charged upward and dropped suddenly down within the storm, flash-freezing rain into white pellets of hail and melting them back to rain once more. Where Lesser flew the air was rough but remained perfectly clear.

"Myrn is down there in the storm, somewhere," Douglas commented after a while. "She knows what to do to keep safe and dry, of course. Still . . ."

"Brave, capable lady, your wife, I understand from the little horse," rumbled the Dragon. "Must be terrible not to speak to her!"

"That's the worst part! And this storm roil makes any clear distant-sensing nearly impossible."

"The same should go for our Enemy, however," the Dragon pointed out. "There! We're nearing the roof of the storm!"

The sun, just below the western horizon at this altitude, struck long, golden beams across the flat, intensely black top of the thunderhead, throwing its writhing turmoil into sharp relief.

A spectacular sight, seldom seen by the ground-bound, Douglas thought, thrilled despite the bitterly cold and gusty air. He relaxed a bit, let the Dragon do the flying, and even enjoyed the view for some minutes as Lesser topped the miles-high column of storm wrack and began to glide over it toward the east. This high, the air was surprisingly calm.

"Walrus Shingle is a bit to the south, there, along the coast. See? With the Ebony beyond? Quite a sight!" the Dragon called over his shoulder.

He stretched his great wings out straight to either side and spiraled slowly downward, now well beyond the storm's eastern wall by a number of clear miles.

In a bit over an hour, with night fully fallen over Nearer East, the Dragon touched down on a flat, multilayered rock standing with its feet in the surf a bit offshore. He slid easily down the far side and ducked into a shallow undercut.

"No line of sight from our Enemy," he reported to his passenger. "Suit you as a camping spot until dawn, young Wizard?"

"Perfectly . . . dry, warm, and secure. You must be tired, after your high flight."

"A bit on the wing-weary side, I admit," said the Dragon. "A few hours' nap and I'll be just fine. That's Walrus Shingle, down there. Where the waves are breaking on the gravel beach. You see?"

"I think I see a few of the great tuskers, too," Douglas told him. "But they can wait until morning."

Lesser nodded, waited until the Pyromancer had dismounted and then wrapped himself in his cloak and found a soft chunk of sandstone for his pillow. The Dragon promptly half-buried himself in the warm sand and fell into deep slumber, snoring gently, exhaling occasional puffs of smoke that smelled,

Douglas thought, like Flarman's workshop under the High . . . sulfurous yet sweet, with hints of peat smoke and rain-washed clover.

The enormous Beachmaster opened his right eye to look at the dawn intruder, closed it again, and grunted disagreeably.

"Go 'way! Can't you see I'm sleeping."

"Sorry to bother you," Douglas answered pleasantly. "I just was wondering if you'd seen a flying horse about recently, sir. . . ."

The Walrus groaned, rolled a bit to his left, and reopened his right eye.

"Who are *you*? You don't live near here, I'm certain. Not many Men ever come to this side of the Darkest Mountains. I've seen your kind clambering about up there on the middle peaks. Puny little things! They wrench great hunks of rock from the mountains, pound them into gravel, and lug it off . . . for what reason I never could decide."

"Men do such strange, unaccountable things," Douglas agreed in a sympathetic tone. "Nice family you have here, sir! Do you live all year here beside the Ebony or . . . I'd have thought you'd prefer the colder waters of Sea, or the far north of the Ebony, maybe."

"Ha! No sensible, warm-blooded creature *prefers* Far North. It's a safe haven for birthing pups only, and catching delicious herring and pink salmon. My family has come here every summer long before Men ever did!"

Douglas walked around the pod of walruses, clucking in a friendly fashion to the huge females, who stared back at him uneasily, and chirping at the pups snuggled against their mothers' sides for safety.

He saw no sign of flying horses anywhere and shortly returned to the flat, smooth rock on which the Dragon was just awakening.

"I don't think they're here yet," the Wizard said to the Dragon. "Might as well find a sheltered spot and relax."

"I'll just sunbathe here for the morning," murmured Lesser sleepily. "Dragons require more sleep than you Men. Call me if you need me."

Taking the hint, Douglas walked some distance away and, finding a place where the stiff ocean breeze was partially

blocked by a golden sandstone outcrop, called upon Blue Teakettle's kitchen back at the High to provide blueberry waffles
and maple syrup and crisp strips of hickory-smoked bacon, to
be washed down by hot cocoa topped with sweet whipped
cream.

"A Wizard's life is not an easy one," he sighed aloud to
himself. "But there are compensations!"

The thunderstorm had long since cleared from the peaks and
in the glass-clear air he felt a distant tingle that meant Myrn
was awake and moving once again. With an effort he managed
not to project his thoughts toward her while sensing that she
was close to the saddle pass between two of the closer peaks.

There was another, darker feeling in the air, as well. A touch
of unease. An acrid whiff of ill will. A sour taint of uneasy
wickedness. It came, he decided, from the spear-sharp summit
of the tallest peak in the immediate vicinity, a twisted tower
of black rock overlooking everything else with a sort of rocky
sneer.

A wisp of dirty gray cloud clung tenaciously to its very tip,
like a soiled banner.

Up there, are you? Douglas thought. *Well, I'll keep an eye
on you from here!*

He settled down to compose a very minor Hiding Spell, just
in case the Dark Servant should happen to glance his way.
Nothing very strong nor too obvious—just a tiny bit of shadow
that might be lost in the wide, empty land and seascape.

He deployed Wizardly awareness to receive impressions but
not to project anything that might mark his location to a wake-
ful Darkness.

Ah! he thought. *Do I sense just a hint of poor old Serenit?
Yes!*

It came, he decided, from the middle slopes of the mountain
he dubbed Tallest Peak.

"*That's* where our friend is imprisoned," he decided.
"Now, if Myrn can just get close while things are still fairly
quiet . . ."

Myrn paused several times as they crept cautiously across
the barren stone shoulder between Tallest Peak and its shorter
neighbor, listening and searching with her Wizard's senses.

Marbleheart and Cribblon, both still in disguise, also

searched and observed, sniffing the cold air. The high pass was swept with a constant, chill breeze that brought to the Otter-monkey the familiar smells of saltwater, fish, Seabirds, beds of kelp, and . . . a Dragon and a Man, somewhere far below and to the south. If he hadn't known they were there, he'd never have recognized the faint scents.

"Douglas . . . over *that* way," he whispered to Myrn as she started off again, choosing her path carefully for safe footing as well as good cover.

"Yes, I feel him," the Journeyman Aquamancer replied softly. "He has sensed *us,* too. Careful now! A stray thought sent his way might establish a line the Servant could follow back to us. I'm positive the Dark Servant is already aware of Douglas. Do you feel it?"

Marbleheart nodded.

"But he's not yet discovered *us,*" chirped the sparrow. "We can't go much farther without being in full view, Myrn. Should I go ahead a bit and scout the eastern slopes? I'm small enough to go unnoticed among all the little birds and beasts now out enjoying morning's sun."

Myrn nodded.

"We'll head for that ragged patch of purple heather clinging to the rocks in that bit of tilted meadow. You see it? Off to the left a bit."

"I see it," replied the little bird. "I'll circle toward the base of the higher mountain on the left. My former Master is somewhere there, I sense. When you've lived near someone for years and years, you don't forget his aura. Meet you under the lip of the alpine meadow . . . noonish?"

"Go," urged Myrn. "It'll take us a couple of hours to reach the heather and find safe cover. What we need to determine is, first, the location of the Darkness Servant and, two, the exact location of Serenit's prison. If you find either, come back to us at once."

The tiny sparrow bobbed his head and darted off, hugging the dry, cold, rocky ground but skimming along at considerable speed. He tried to keep his eyes on the high, blue sky as he flew, to find a local raptor who might know of the Servant's presence . . . and perhaps the prison of the First Citizen of New Land, as well.

He couldn't watch above his head and under his belly at the same time.

It was a terrifying shock, therefore, when a silent shadow dropped suddenly over him and he felt sharp talons sink into the feathers on his neck and back.

"Gotcha!" rasped a voice just overhead.

Cribblon was whipped straight up, helpless in his efforts to free himself from a kestrel's wickedly curved killing claws.

Douglas leaped to his feet with a shout.

"Lesser! Fly out over the water. Make a grand fuss! Lots of smoke and fire!"

Lesser Dragon awoke and, without stopping to question, erupted from the sand and shot into the air with a thunderous crack of his leathery wings. In moments he was out over the rolling Ebony, scattering flocks of terns and gulls from his path, spurting reddish flame and sepia smoke.

"Out of my way!" he bellowed at the top of his considerable voice, making the cliffs behind him ring with echoes. "That's right! That's perfect! Make lots of fuss, you noisy oyster-snappers and clam-grabbers! *Ho! Ha!* Yoicks!"

Glancing up at the twisted top of Tallest Peak, Douglas saw a stirring, a changing.

"Hey! Look at *me,* blast you!" he thundered in a Wizardly roar.

He flung a handful of bright red fire onto the sand at his feet.

His Wizard's cloak flapped wildly in the stiff offshore breeze. He sent swift flashes of colored light up and out toward where the startled Servant crouched on its mountain peak.

Myrn leaped into the air also, snapping out a clear, short incantation that, before her jump had reached its apex, changed her from a dark-haired slip of a girl to bundle of streamlined, feathered fury.

"Find Serenit!" she screamed at the monkey as she shot upward into the bright air. "Get him out, if you can, and hide him somewhere!"

Marbleheart ducked away from the downdraft of the she-eagle's powerful wings and watched as Myrn climbed at tremendous speed after the kestrel and his struggling prey.

Turning away from the scene above, the Otter took the opportunity of the flurry of magic both close overhead and far below on the shore to shed his monkey form.

As a six-foot, sleek, swift Sea Otter, he plunged over the lip of the pass, slid between huge, tilted boulders, dashed through the patch of purple heather, and dropped, without stopping or even slowing, down a dry watercourse angling toward the shore far below.

The eagle, meanwhile, rapidly overtook the climbing kestrel and, screaming sharply, whizzed past him, missing his left wingtip feathers by less than a claw's length. The slipstream of her passage came close to knocking the kestrel out of the air altogether.

"Mine! Mine!" squawked the smaller raptor, startled. "My breakfast! Shear off! No fair! No fair!"

"Life's often unfair," Myrn shrieked at the top of her eagle's voice, twisting into a sharp turn. "Drop the sparrow, young kestrel! At once! I'll tear your eyes from your head!"

Fighting for flying room, the kestrel folded his wings along his sides and plummeted like a stone toward the mountainside below.

"No you don't," snarled Cribblon, finally freeing one wingtip long enough to make an appropriate Sign of Change.

The sparrow disappeared in a silent flash and in his place appeared a brown-and-white gyrfalcon. Before the kestrel could release his tight grip and swing away in panic, the gyrfalcon twisted over, breaking the grip on his back feathers, grasped the smaller raptor by neck and tail, and snapped out his own long pinions to slow their plunging descent.

"Mercy! Mercy!" mewed the thoroughly terrified kestrel, struggling to break Cribblon's tight grip. "Let me be, I pray! Let me go! I beg you!"

"Not just yet," hissed Cribblon, giving the smaller bird a sharp shake to settle him down. "Stop wriggling!"

The kestrel, recognizing a small hope in the gyrfalcon's words, froze in fear. Cribblon veered to the right and plunged to roost on a lonely rock pinnacle rising from the side of the southern mountain.

"Follow me when you can, Cribblon," called Myrn, dropping rapidly past them toward the rocky ground. "I'm going after the Otter to look for Serenit."

"Leave it to me," answered Cribblon. "Now! *You!* I'm going to let you go on this nice, quiet, peaceful pinnacle. Stay here to the count of a hundred before you move a single pinion. You *can* count to a hundred, can't you?"

He shook the smaller raptor vigorously.

"Yes, *yes!*" squeaked the kestrel. "Oh, please, sir! Let me go. I'll behave!"

"You'd better! Heed my advice, and stay clear of Darkest Mountains for a few days, kestrel. There're things about to happen here you don't want to catch you up, sirrah!"

Releasing his captive, Cribblon folded his wings and let his weight carry him straight down. At the last moment he snapped his wings flat out, fighting the pull of gravity with the push of the air on the underside of his pinions.

His streamlined body tipped, tilted, shuddered, and skimmed the rocky floor of the pass only a handful of feet above the scattered boulders. He caught a brief glimpse of the Myrn-eagle, far down the oceanward slope ahead of him.

"Right behind you, Myrn!" he screamed.

With the sure instincts of a longtime air-fighter, Lesser banked sharply, did a wing-over, and charged the great cloud of disturbed birds which had risen in his wake after his first pass.

"Move! *Move it!*" he bellowed, sending out a lurid spout of red-and-yellow flame and blue smoke. "Scatter!"

The birds screamed in fear and anger, then fled before the huge Dragon and his fiery breath. A few plunged into the waves below or flopped to the gravelly beach among the walruses, causing even greater tumults of bellowing and roaring.

Beachmaster shouted, at the top of his considerable *basso profundo* voice, "Into the water, everybody! Watch the young-uns! Stay together, blast you!"

Douglas popped to the top of the long-shore ridge waving his arms and sending loose stones and a cloud of bright sand flying into the air, there to burst into vivid, crackling flames.

He caught a quick glimpse of an eagle wheeling close to where Serenit was hidden. Turning to the south, he flung a spell of great force against the side of a towering cliff.

Slowly at first, then with increasing speed and a tremendous thundering, half the cliff slid, crumbled, tilted, and crashed into the ocean, sending up geysers of salt spray and boiling clouds of sand and mist twice as high as the cliff from which the avalanche had been calved.

Augurian set a large, crystal-clear ball of brook water on a square of blue watered silk in the middle of the hearth before the fire.

"At least we can see what's going on," he said, glancing at his friend Flarman.

"No harm in looking," agreed the Pyromancer.

Behind them Bronze Owl perched on the back of a chair and Black Flame curled comfortably on the seat, bracketed by his wives—Party, chubby with her latest pregnancy, and a slimmer Pert.

Beyond the circle of light from the fire in Bryarmote's great stone fireplace, the entire High staff ranked themselves on the kitchen table, on counters, and on cupboard shelves, silent except for occasional indignant whispers of "Down in front!" or "Ladies, please remove your tops!"

"Now," rumbled Augurian after a few moments of intense peering into the watery globe. "Myrn is . . . *ah!* . . . with the Sea Otter and . . . that little bird is Cribblon, I see . . , on some bare mountaintop."

"Those are the Darkest Mountains of Nearer East," Flarman declared, flipping hurriedly through a huge atlas nestled in his lap.

"Darkest Mountains . . . the hidden lair of one of the runaway Servants of Darkness, I believe," said Lithold, smoothing her skirts and leaning forward to see the water ball better. "Can you make it work more clearly, Water Adept? Or should I send for my crystal?"

"No, no," muttered Augurian. "It's just warming up. *Yes!* There's my Journeyman girl! That great Sea eagle is actually Myrn, and the smaller bird *must* be Cribblon. Where's that silly Otter? Run off somewhere, I suppose."

"Not Marbleheart!" protested Bronze Owl. "Soul of bravery, when the chops are done!"

"You mean 'chips' " muttered Flarman distractedly. "*Ah!* Now . . ."

"Chips! Chops! The same thing when it comes to our Sea

Otter,'' someone in the kitchenware crowd giggled nervously.

"Silence, now!" warned the Water Adept sternly. "Watch!
Don't talk!"

He reached out to tap the side of the globe of water with a
fingernail, very delicately. It gave off a crystalline *ping* and
the scene pictured in its depths shivered and shifted.

"What's that!" gasped Lithold, pointing at the image of
Tallest Peak.

"You've never seen the minions of The Darkness in person," said the Water Adept. "That's one of their Servants, for
sure!"

"I believe I can name him," said Flarman, snapping his
fingers.

"Ah, the duel over Endless Steppes!" crowed Augurian,
nodding. "I remember it well. Thank goodness it's not one of
the Overgray. If it were . . ."

". . . we'd be on our way there right now," finished Flarman, bobbing his bald head. "We may have to shoot off eastward anyway, friends. Be ready, Lithold, my dear!"

"Wait a bit," cautioned Augurian, clutching his friend's
sleeve. "So far not much is really happening!"

They hunched forward, staring at the scene shown in min-
iature in the ball of clear water.

"There!" whispered Bronze Owl, whose eyes were sharper
than anyone else's. "There's Douglas and the great-great-
grandnephew of Great Golden Dragon!"

"Yeah, Douglas! Go! Go! Go!" a line of Salad Forks
cheered, jumping up and down.

Table Knives clashed their blades together and Cups and
their Saucers rattled up a noisy tattoo as Douglas tore down
half of a sea cliff and dropped it into the ocean with a most
satisfying splash.

Blue Teakettle held her steamy breath, her lid jiggling with
suppressed excitement.

Myrn the eagle swooped along the two-hundred-foot vertical
cliff at the foot of Tallest Peak.

A distance below her flight path Marbleheart slid with sur-
prising speed, for a water animal, among loose stones and
broken chunks of splintered mountain.

Behind them the gyrfalcon whipped his wings up and down,

dodging about taller pinnacles of wind-carved rock, keeping as many of them as he could between himself and the top of Tallest Peak, on which he glimpsed the vague outline of a squat, evil-looking shroud of gray dust and black smoke.

"He hasn't seen us . . . *yet,*" Cribblon called, catching up with the eagle at last. "Not yet!"

The eagle spun about on one wingtip, screaming in sharp urgency.

"Where *is* Serenit?"

The air, shortly before clear as a bell, was quickly dimming and turning dun-colored and dirty. Great clouds of mottled mist, shot with short angry lightning bolts, rolled down the eastern side of Tallest Peak, gathering pebbles and stones at first, then boulders, and finally whole sheets of the rock face. It roared across the pebble beach below, where a few moments before Beachmaster's family had been sunning.

Myrn swallowed an urge to shout a warning to her husband. Douglas shot into the clear air over the descending bank of debris, plucking short bolts of lightning from the thundering rubble and sending them back up toward the top of Tallest Peak.

Cribblon, following Myrn, drew up sharply.

From a narrow crack halfway up the south-facing side of Tallest Peak, he'd caught a momentary flash of white.

Whipping into a tight vertical turn, grazing the mountain with his right wingtip, he hugged the wall to retrace his path, looking for a second glimpse of white.

There it was! A handkerchief?

Waved through a narrow crack in the stone wall?

The Journeyman Air Adept slammed his chest and stomach flat against the cliff, scrabbling for purchase with his claws and beak. For a terrifying moment he felt himself sliding away into thin air. In his mind's eye he saw himself dashed onto the scree of sharp stones fifty feet below.

"*Serenit!*" he shrieked, and at that moment his left claw caught on a tiny projection, his right claw struck a minute horizontal crack in the wall, and his slide to destruction halted.

"Who are you!" a voice called from within the rock.

"Cribblon," the Journeyman gasped, not stopping to weigh his words. "We've come to rescue you from . . . *whatever* it is, up above."

"Cribblon!" Serenit replied from within the fissure. "Good man! I wish I could help, but . . . well, you know?"

"Myrn is nearby," coughed the gyrfalcon. "She just disappeared around the edge of the mountain. Wait!"

At risk of losing his grip, Cribblon twisted his neck and wrenched his shoulders around, seeking a sign of Myrn or Marbleheart. The Otter, too, had disappeared from sight, probably beyond the cloud of debris that had been shed from the mountainside.

"If I try to fly," Cribblon said shakily, "I'll fall to my death before I can get my wings to beating!"

"Listen to me!" came the First Citizen's urgent voice. "Listen, old chap! How many words in the spell to make you a smaller, lighter bird?"

"Ah . . . five! No, four! Short ones," Cribblon groaned. "No time!"

"Listen, young Cribblon! You've got to chance it, for your own sake as well as mine! Let go, say the spelling words as fast as you can, and when you transform into a wren or—"

"A desert sparrow," gasped Cribblon. "I know that shape already!"

"Sparrow, then. At that size and weight, you can pull out of your dive in plenty of time."

"I understood you'd lost all your Wizardly Powers," Cribblon said hoarsely.

"Yes, but I haven't lost my common sense," replied the First Citizen. "Cribblon, my boy—do it, *now!*"

Chapter Seventeen

Half the Battle

AS Douglas circled above the flat-topped formation under which he and the Dragon had spent the night, he studied the crest of Tallest Mountain.

Where in morning light it had been sharply clear against the deep blue of the sky, now it had become muzzy and distorted. A brownish smudge streaked with jet black had replaced the morning's misty banner. When you watched it closely for a minute, Douglas realized, you became aware of movements in the cloud, of swirling, of . . . life of a sort.

Lesser suddenly appeared from the other side of the cloud of sand and dust, blowing puffs of hot, pink smoke and swishing his scaly tale to steer himself clear of the last of the falling boulders.

"How're we doing?" he bellowed to the Pyromancer. "Got any idea what to do next?"

"Keep on making a fuss of any kind, whatever!" Douglas called to him. "Myrn and her friends are up there, quite close by now, and we want the Darkness Servant looking the other way."

"Got a great idea!" exclaimed Lesser. "If you can keep him occupied for half a second . . ."

He flung his huge body down the east side of the roiling

cloud of debris, past buried Walrus Shingle, and straight into the waves that broke there.

A great cloud of steam mushroomed up. As the Dragon swam back and forth, the hot mist rose in the air, a hundred feet high or more.

"Good old Dragon!" Douglas cheered.

"Watch yourself," Lesser's voice came back. "Something's up!"

Douglas swung back to face Tallest Peak just as the hazy shadow near its summit launched a terrific bolt of purple lightning, aimed straight for Douglas's bit of space.

"Oh-oh!" he gulped, and just had time to fling a grounding barrier around himself before the electric jolt hit not ten feet from where he floated.

"Time to strike back," he cried aloud.

With a circling motion of his hands he gathered all the stray impulses from the Darkness's own bolt and juggled them into a ball of brilliant, crackling, blue coruscation.

Rocketing higher into the air, he drew back his right arm, launched the coruscating fireball, and shot away around the side of the southern mountain at top speed.

When he looked back from a strip of sheltered beach a mile down the strand, the brown pall that englobed the tip of Tallest Peak had been blown to shreds. All about the peak lightnings leaped and thunder rolled, dust glowing and sparkling even in the bright sunshine.

Douglas watched long enough to be sure none of the Enemy's fireball had fallen too close to where he'd last seen the eagle. Satisfied, he changed his position again, shooting along the narrow strip of wave-rounded pebbles into the shelter of a headland.

With a startling upsurge of water the Beachmaster suddenly popped out of the shallows nearby.

"Ho! Sir? A word, if there's time!"

"Quickly, then," Douglas called. "Wherever I happen to be is liable to get very dangerous all of a sudden. Take your ladies and babies well out to Sea, sir! It's dangerous here close inshore."

Beachmaster nodded and slid backward into the shallows.

"Can we help? I just realized what's going on here, m'boy!

I've been around enough to recognize Good Wizardry versus Evil Sorcery. What can we do to help?''

"Stay clear," Douglas shouted after him. "And, oh, make lots of loud noises. Distract the Enemy up top, there."

"We Walruses are very good at loudness," he heard the Beachmaster say with a laugh as he sank under the waves. "Noise it is!"

The unexpected return of his first volley had startled the Darkness Servant. For several moments everything was quiet atop the mountain and along the beach as both sides gathered their forces and planned new moves.

Ripping his claws from their anchors in the wall near Serenit's narrow window, Cribblon dropped like a stone toward the jumbled rocks so close below, screaming at the top of his gyrfalcon's voice.

"Cribblon!" Myrn, just then rounding the mountain, screamed. She tried to work her talons enough to form a magic gesture to stop her companion's fall, but an eagle's claws are too stiff and unbending for such fine work.

Thirteen feet from the nearest razor-edged, uptilted blade of blue-black flint, the gyrfalcon suddenly disappeared and in its place the desert sparrow shot out, away from the wall, narrowly missing the jumbled rocks.

The sudden switch of considerable falling weight to lateral movement, as Augurian later explained it, was released as a sharp thunderclap, which in turn shook loose the pile of sharp-edged stones and sent them tumbling and sliding over the cliff's edge to plunge into the foaming shallows at the foot of Tallest Mountain.

When the Servant glanced that way, it missed the tiny sparrow fluttering back up the wall toward Serenit's prison window. It assumed that the explosion and the resulting slide of tons of loose rock into the water had been another attack by the Pyromancer.

With a roar louder than the winds that lashed the peaks of the Darkest Mountains in wintertime, he flung an even larger bolt of lightning at the flat-topped hill over what had once been Walrus Strand.

When the acrid smoke cleared, the great rock was reduced to a great pile of clean white sand.

■   ■   ■

Douglas had, moments before, transferred himself to a shallow Sea cave beneath the foot of the next peak southward. The backwash from Cribblon's slate slide caught him unprepared, but he managed to reach higher than the waves and clung for a moment to a narrow ledge, out of sight of his attacker.

He paused to catch his breath and consider his next move.

From his vantage he could just watch the sparrow fling himself into the crack that served Serenit as a window to his prison. A moment later the eagle arrived and hovered painfully outside the First Citizen's cell, beating her wings back and forth to remain in place.

"Marbleheart!" Douglas gasped.

A monkey once again, Marbleheart was scaling the three-hundred-foot cliff to the spot where Cribblon had disappeared. He and Myrn exchanged a few quick words, it seemed to Douglas, and the great bird swung out and away, keeping the bulk of the mountain between herself and the searching Darkness above.

The monkey squeezed through the narrow slit and disappeared after the sparrow.

"Give us a good, loud diversion, my dearest," came Myrn's voice from a point just over his safe roost. "Keep the Being busy!"

Douglas waved at the eagle almost gaily.

He spoke a terse sentence to the Feather Pin on his breast, shot out of the seaside cavern, and angled high into the air at blinding speed. A thunderous explosion off to the north showed the Dark Servant still considered his enemy to be hiding behind the sandy pile there. A towering cloud of sand and stone shards was flung into the air.

Adding to the uproar came then the sound of fifty or more Walruses of all sizes and both sexes, plus nearly as many seals and sea lions who lived along the rugged coast, shouting and rumbling and singing at the top of their collective voices, although not necessarily in tune with each other:

> "By the Sea
> E-bon-y . . .
> By our beee-u-ti-ful Sea!
> You and meee . . .

You and meeee . . .
Oh, how happy we'll beeee!''

Douglas hung poised in midair, a hundred yards to the south of the very top of Tallest Peak.

"Here am I, Douglas Brightglade, Master Pyromancer, student of Master Pyromancer Flarman Firemaster, your old, old enemy from Last Battle! I warn you, Servant of Darkness, yield to me! Give way! Yield, Creature of Night! The time has come to surrender or flee!"

The whole top quarter of Tallest Peak shivered and shook, quivering like Blue Teakettle's famous Lemon Surprise gelatin. A great, whirling, ovate blob of blackest night appeared above the mountaintop.

As Douglas watched, it elongated east to west, and then snapped end over end with a shrill keening of fury.

Douglas performed a quick snap roll, over and back and down and then to one side.

A white-hot flash of something like lightning, but colder, harder, straighter, lanced through the very spot where he had been only fractions of a second before, curved up and over, and crashed headlong into a large, fluffy white cloud that had quietly floated up with the southerly breeze.

The cloud shook (Douglas later insisted that it hiccuped!) and absorbed the tremendous shock. Watching walruses and seals told later that the cloud turned brilliant purple, faded to palest pink, flattened out at the bottom and began to rain, a torrent of huge drops that churned the surface of the Ebony into greenish froth.

Fifteen thousand shore birds, any number of ocean fliers, and the vast herd of walruses, seals, and a passing school of bottlenose dolphins, attracted by the commotion and the singing, swirled happily in the rain and the foam.

"Don't look!" cried Myrn, circling closer to the First Citizen's narrow window. Marbleheart, having resumed his own shape, had poked his nose out to see what was going on.

"There's no other way out," he shouted to her. "The entrance to the cell is from the very blackest heart of the mountain, Myrn!"

"Take shelter deep inside there!" the Journeyman Aqua-

mancer screamed over the sound of the first volley aimed at
her husband. She didn't dare turn to look where Douglas had
gone, if indeed he'd escaped the terrible blast. "I intend to
blow your hole wide open!"

"Yes, *ma'am!*" was all the Otter squeaked before his face
disappeared from the window.

"On the count of five!" screamed Myrne.

In the silence following the Servant's greatest blast so far
she heard retreating footsteps on hard stone, three pairs, within
the mountain.

Then a greater silence.

"One . . . two . . . three . . . ," she began to count out loud.

From above came a scream of insane fury. The Darkness
Servant was plunging rapidly down from the peak, heading for
Serenit's cell.

Myrn clapped her wingtips together with a loud *pop!*

The eagle disappeared and in her place hung, for a terrify-
ingly long time, the young Aquamancer, unsupported by wings
or spell.

". . . four . . . five!" the three in the tiny cell, huddling as
far from the window wall as possible, heard her shout.

Douglas timed a splendid explosion of his own and the
spear-point top of Tallest Peak glowed red, then white, and
began to melt.

The Darkness Servant screamed in surprise and pain, as
much for the clear, bright light as the heat, and flung itself
away to the north, leaving a long, thick black-smoke trail behind itself.

Myrn, just beginning to fall toward the shallow surge at the
foot of Tallest Peak, sent a white globe of superheated steam
smashing against the mountainside just below Serenit's prison
window.

Then she disappeared!

The steam ball, the golden color of the sunlit shallows off
Waterand Island, struck the rock face and burst with a pleasant
plop and a long-drawn *hiss!* The steam condensed at once into
boiling water which began to run down the cliff. Where it
darkened the rock face, the very stone foamed and bubbled
furiously.

The wall began to crumble away, like a sugar cube in hot tea.

The high, twisted summit shook, rolled to one side, and collapsed slowly with a tremendous and growing roar that made every noise that had come before seem soft in comparison.

At the last moment, just as the section containing the window to Serenit's cell sloughed off, smoking and bubbling, three small birds shot from the crevice, out into the clear air and well beyond.

A pair of fork-tailed swifts and a rather scruffy-looking black raven cawed in fear, but in exultation, too: Marbleheart, Cribblon, and the First Citizen of New Land were free!

A few yards away they were met by a white dove. Together the four flew swiftly away to the west, across the high mountain pass.

Chapter Eighteen

On the Trail

DOUGLAS allowed himself to settle to the shattered dune gently, like a leaf dropping from a maple in fall. He looked weary but satisfied, smeared with black soot and wet with perspiration.

"What I need," he groaned to Lesser Dragon, who flew in from the open ocean to meet him, "is a cup of strong tea and a hot bath!"

"There's time for both," Lesser assured him.

The Dragon produced a large, battered tin teapot from somewhere about his scaled person, and filled it from a streaming spring that had erupted all of a sudden on the torn and haggled side of Tallest Peak. He blew his blowtorch breath on the pot-bottom, so that almost at once it began to boil cheerfully.

He produced from the same mysterious hidden pouch a pair of big, thick, white china mugs, filled them expertly, and handed one to Douglas. The companions sat wearily on a shattered stone shelf overlooking the Ebony and sipped hot tea.

The chaotic battleground was settling back into quiet. Out to sea a huge flock of birds made a distant racket as each bird exchanged impressions of the morning's battle with his neighbors.

"What a fight! And what a fright!" called a new voice, and

Marbleheart came *galumphing* up the beach in a manner that fairly oozed triumphant pleasure and pride.

"Myrn?" the Pyromancer asked quickly.

"Escorting Serenit the Jackdaw back to Farrouk's hollow fortress," Marbleheart explained, plumping down on the hot sand and breathing a deep sigh of content.

"Have a cup of Dragon tea and tell us everything you know," invited the Dragon. "We haven't been introduced, although I know who you are, Wizard's Familiar. I am Lesser Dragon, great-great-great-grandnephew of—"

"Great Golden Dragon, at a wild guess," cut in the Otter, laughing and eagerly accepting a steaming cup.

"Myrn will soon return," said Douglas, sipping from his cup. "Serenit was rescued in good shape? Wonderful! Good morning's work, I'd say."

"Best yet," Marbleheart insisted. "In the meantime, it's noonish. What's for lunch, Master?"

"Always thinking of his stomach!" groaned Douglas to the Dragon. "Well, come to think of it, I'm hungry, too. I don't recall getting any breakfast this morning."

"Let me order," begged the Sea Otter. "How about . . ."

In less than ten minutes the three companions sat down to a delightful luncheon of chunky tuna salad on dark, pungent rye bread, sliced cucumbers and spring onions in balsamic vinegar, and five huge four-layer yellow cakes with dark fudge frosting.

"All I like best!" enthused the Sea Otter, passing the cucumbers-and-onions to the Dragon.

"No, no thanks! Cucumbers give me gas. And you don't want to be around when a Dragon belches!" Lesser said, shaking his vast head with regret. "Although, to tell you truly, I dearly love cucumbers."

"We'll take our chances, then," Marbleheart insisted.

A delegation of sea and shore birds, followed more slowly by Beachmaster, looking quite proud of himself, and a party of eared seals and the pride-mother of the local sea lions, climbed up the shore to pay their respects to the Pyromancer and to find out what, actually, had happened that morning.

"Well, good friends," Douglas began, chewing his second tuna salad sandwich, "things should be peaceful again around here now, but the cause of all the trouble, a Servant of Darkness, is still at large and will cause us trouble sooner or later, I'm positive. My friends and I will be leaving shortly to finish the job. Did anyone note where and how far he—it—went?''

''Over the northern horizon, Fire Wizard,'' said Beachmaster in a low rumble. ''Out of our sight, from here at sea level.''

Several high-flying terns confirmed the walrus's words. They'd had a better viewpoint from aloft.

''What lies away to the north, I wonder?'' asked Marbleheart. ''None of us has ever been there, you see.''

''Nor have most of us,'' replied Beachmaster. ''Let me ask around. Somebody here must have visited those parts.''

He slid ponderously down the beach and into the surf, making a great, celebratory splash.

When they'd finished their picnic by watching the Dragon devour four of the cakes in short order, and Douglas was sending the dishes back to Wizards' High with sure gestures and a magic phrase, the walrus labored back across the pebble strand to report.

''The coast bends to the east after a day's swim as eared seals measure distances; it's about forty sea-miles according to your way of telling distance, I believe . . . and then swings sharply to the north again. The shore rises into towering cliffs for as far as anyone here has traveled. Even the birds know little of the inland area there. Evidently it's some kind of desolation.''

''I thought you walruses went far north to . . . er . . . mate,'' Marbleheart asked. ''You don't know what the land is like?''

''Actually, we go south to Stormy Strait, then west a bit to enter Warm Seas, then north to the cold waters off Everfrost to mate. None of us has ever gone very far north in the Ebony; few creatures from North Ebony ever come this far south. I've got a number of wives asking farther a-Sea, however. I'll let you know as soon as more information comes to my ears.''

''I deeply appreciate all your help,'' Douglas told him. ''I'm afraid the fighting here destroyed your pleasant beach. If you wish, I can attempt to restore it as it was yesterday.''

''Thank you for your most gracious offer, Wizard,'' replied the walrus rather formally, ''but I've already got scouts looking about for a new bit of comfortable, quiet, peaceful waterfront for the rest of the season. We usually move from place to place anyway, so as not to deplete the local fishing. It's no problem, believe me."

"Well, if there's ever anything you need in the way of Wizardly assistance," Douglas said with a pleased smile, "call on me, please! And tell all your clan how much we appreciated their help here this morning."

"We were delighted to be of use to the famous Wizard Brightglade," the Beachmaster announced.

He bid them farewell and slid down the gravelly shore to splash ponderously into the now-calm Ebony, followed by the rest of the saltwater beasts and birds, when each had received thanks on behalf of his own species and kind from the young Fire Wizard.

"What do we do now?" Marbleheart asked his Master.

"Wait for Myrn to return. As good a spot and time as any to give you some much-neglected lessons in Basic Pyromancy," Douglas said soberly.

The Sea Otter groaned at the thought of lessons, especially so close to the clear, cool waters of the Ebony, which invited a long, luxurious swim and perhaps would yield some tasty shellfish or shorefood snacks.

However, since he really was eager to add to his store of spells and useful enchantments, his groan was just for dramatic effect.

"Let's start with this business of quick transformations into monkeys and birds and back," Douglas began, settling himself against a cushion of soft white sand. "Why did you shed the handy form of a monkey coming down the mountain? And later abandon that of a swift as soon as you safely could, once you'd escaped the mountainside?"

"I-I-I was *uncomfortable* as a bird," admitted the Sea Otter, stretching himself out full length on the warm sand and blinking at his Master. "And as a monkey, too, although that was better than the bird. I'd rather pop around as an Otter, when I can."

"It could've been dangerous, and certainly took precious time and energy," Douglas admonished. "Tell me—what was so wrong with being a bird? A very beautiful and graceful little bird, the swift, I've always thought."

"Well . . . ," Marbleheart said slowly. "It seemed to be . . .

well, *uncomfortable.* I'd never flown so far or so high or so fast, you know.''

''A touch of *acrophobia*, perhaps?'' Douglas wondered.

''*Acro . . . what?* Oh, come on, Douglas! Use words a poor, stupid, unschooled Briny-born Sea Otter can understand!''

Douglas laughed aloud.

The Otter looked uncomfortable, but down on the beach the walrus clan began to sing a rumbling, shuffling kind of triumphal song in honor of the defeat of the Servant of Darkness . . . although before that exciting morning they'd had no idea such a Being existed.

The day flew pleasantly by, and as the sun backlit the mountains toward early evening, a bright star flashed over their crest, curved down, and came to rest beside their campfire.

''I'm ready to chase all sorts of phantasmagoria,'' Myrn announced, smiling as brilliantly as glowed the pearl necklace which had brought her. ''My wonderful, handsome husband! Serenit is safe with Harroun and Saladim. They took to each other at once. Where's the flying horse?''

''She went off to find her family and folk. Not a sign nor word yet,'' Marbleheart told her, allowing her to ruffle the soft fur at the nape of his neck as soon as she had kissed and hugged Douglas. ''King Priad seems to have gone missing.''

''Well, their home *is* on the far side of the Ebony,'' Myrn considered. ''It's not very wide, is it?''

''They'll be along,'' Douglas assured her. ''Meanwhile, here's a nice hot supper from Blue Teakettle and a comfortable place to spend the night before we start out after the Darkness Servant again.''

''No word from home?'' Myrn asked once they had eaten Blue Teakettle's supper by the light of the fire on top of the sand dune overlooking the rolling Ebony swells.

''No,'' admitted Douglas. ''But I'm sure Flarman and the rest are keeping an eye on us from afar. When they've something to contribute, they'll send word by Deka the Wraith.''

Myrn settled down comfortably into the crook of her husband's left arm, laying her dark head on his broad shoulder contentedly. She seemed quite pleased with him, with herself, with life in general.

''I *do* prefer this to life in the Sultan's *hareem,*'' she murmured sleepily. "It surprises me there are no fishermen here on the Ebony. I saw all sorts of signs of fish offshore when I flew in just now."

"It's something you might mention to Sultan Trobuk when we see him next," Douglas said. "There're a lot of wandering tribes on High Desert. Fishing might be the answer to their need. As a rule they're quite poor in material things and life can be chancy, I suspect."

"Very poor, but a proud, fiercely independent people." Myrn nodded. "*Hmmm!* They just might take to commercial fishing. Many of those I met would have liked to settle down to farming . . . or said they would," Myrn said, yawning, "if their desert weren't so dry. Which is a shame, for I know there's plenty of good water not far below the sand, Douglas."

Her husband gave her an understanding hug but said nothing.

"Sleep's not far beneath my eyelids! Do we sleep here in the open, beloved, or do you think a tent would be more comfortable?"

Douglas disentangled himself from her, fished out his best handkerchief, laid it on the ground on a flat, sheltered spot just over the dune-top from the winds, and spelled it to become a large, comfortable pavilion complete with a big, soft bed, a dressing table with a mirror, many lanterns on stands all about, and a double wardrobe.

When he turned from this task back to his wife, he found she was sound asleep, snuggled into the warm sand, smiling contentedly.

At dawn Douglas woke to the sounds of laughing and splashing. When he pushed aside the tent flap to admit the fresh breezes of an Ebony coast morning, he learned the commotion came from a delighted Sea Otter, twelve young harbor seals, a crowd of their parents, and Beachmaster's entire clan.

Marbleheart was teaching the seal pups to play water polo using a large, round, green sponge he'd plucked from the sandy bottom offshore.

The young seals were raucous, eager competitors and the spectators, including a vast circling flock of birds, laughed, cheered, and clapped whatever parts of their anatomy served best for applause.

Myrn, looking sleepily beautiful, came from their tent and Douglas led her down to swim out to watch the game and join in the cheering.

"Blue Team!" screamed the Otter. "Offside! Toss up! Toss up! C'mon, Blue Team! Jump ball! *Wheet—tweet!* Way to go, Red Team! Shoot! Shoot!"

The seal pups plunged recklessly through the waves, flipping the sponge ball from player to player, crying out excitedly and laughing with pure joy.

Marbleheart, seeing his Master and Mistress, swam over and bid them good morning.

"They're absolute naturals!" He laughed. "Learned the game in no time flat!"

"You've probably started a new craze on the Ebony," Myrn cried gleefully. "You'll have to teach someone else to be their referee, however. We should set off after the Dark Servant, don't you think, Douglas?"

"We can't wait any longer for Indra," Douglas decided. "We'll leave a message with Beachmaster for her to follow us."

He waved to the Walrus leader. When the great beast swam easily to his side, Douglas asked him for any news from his scouts.

"Last they said, well after midnight," the huge walrus reported, "they lost track of our Being where the ocean coast turns to the north. Headed inland, they think."

"We'll start there, then," decided Douglas. "He would not have gone far in daylight yesterday but would have moved at night. I've some charms that'll help us, once we've picked up his trail."

Within an hour the Wizards were off, mounted on the Dragon's broad back, accompanied by Marbleheart Sea Otter and Cribblon, who'd returned from Harroun's house in his normal shape, at last.

Skimming along fifty feet above the turbulent surf at moderate speed, they came less than an hour to where the coast turned sharply eastward.

"We'll drop down here," the Pyromancer directed Lesser, pointing at a high basalt headland they were approaching. "Check for signs and consult some spells."

"The Servant has been here." Marbleheart sniffed. "Smell his nasty fuming!"

Douglas and Myrn huddled over their spelling for a few minutes on the top of the headland while the Otter, the Dragon, and Cribblon walked off a few hundred paces, "Feeling the air," as Cribblon put it in professional terms.

When they returned to the Brightglades, they found Douglas looking a bit mystified and Myrn shaking her head in a worried fashion.

"The signs are both clear and confusing," Douglas told them. "What did you see?"

"*Smelled,* mostly," Cribblon replied.

"Our quarry was here late yesterday," said Lesser, "and he moved off northwest, leaving the coast behind him. Or so I surmise from what few signs still remain. He has taken steps to obscure his route."

Douglas nodded and then shook his head.

"We can't be very specific, either," Myrn said. "We'll just have to proceed by eyesight—and smell—for now. The Servant has managed to addle our usual Seeking Spells, I'm afraid."

"It'd take us hours, maybe days, to clear the air of his countermagic," agreed Cribblon.

"As long as we can *smell*," Marbleheart insisted somewhat impatiently, "we'll know we're on the right track."

"*Smelling* never was a problem with you, Otter," Douglas teased.

"Unless he's wise enough to stop to bathe," Cribblon speculated, not indicating whether he meant the Servant or the Otter by this.

"He's no amateur at obscuring his path, I suspect," sniffed Marbleheart, making a face at the Air Adept.

" 'Simple is best,' however," Myrn maintained, quoting Augurian. "Let's see if we can find anyone who can tell us of his passing or about the land to the north. I'd think the Servant would have a definite destination in mind, wouldn't you?"

"Let's hope so." Douglas sighed. "We'll go on foot, for now. Unless you can track the smell of his smoke while flying, Lesser?"

"Not too well," the Dragon admitted. "Too much depends

on unpredictable winds aloft and sudden updrafts and the local humidity. You'll be much surer on the ground, Douglas. Dragon noses are not very good at smells.''

"It's just their breath that smells," Marbleheart said, poking the Dragon playfully. "Well, I'll lead the way!"

"You're the expert at smelling! Let's go then," cried the Pyromancer. "Cribblon, keep an expert eye on the weather and the sky, too, please. Other than the smell of nasty fuming, the sight of smoke rising or fog blowing . . ."

"I understand, Douglas," replied the Aeromancer.

"And I'll watch for local creatures," Myrn decided. "*Someone* will have noticed the Servant passing this way, I'd think."

"That leaves me to be rear guard, then," decided Douglas. "I'll call Deka and send word homeward. Just in case. The Darkness, even just its Servant, is nothing to take lightly."

"Well spoken!" agreed the Sea Otter, and he set off at an easy lope, nose swinging from side-to-side, eyes bright for the hunt, for he was very good at this kind of tracking.

The huge Dragon mounted into the hot air and climbed until he was a mere dot against the metallic blue of the sky.

Cribblon paced solemnly a few yards behind the Sea Otter, letting his eyes and his sharp Aeromantic senses of smell and taste range to all sides, but especially ahead, watching the horizon for telltale signs of air movement, unusual clouds, or suspicious patches of darkness.

Myrn walked beside her husband silently, stopping now and then to bespeak creatures living hidden in the jumbled, rocky land. These were few and far between, and all were either reluctant to speak or ignorant of the passing of the Servant.

Douglas Brightglade thoughtfully considered the wording of his message to Wizards' High. If he urged Flarman and the others to come at once, they could not arrive much before late the following day. Instantaneous travel was well-nigh impossible by all the laws and powers of even the strongest Wizardry.

To await them here would be to risk losing the faint traces of the Being they followed. The acrid odor of the Servant was growing fainter by the hour as the hot sun blasted and moiled the air. They had to go on or lose it altogether.

By this time tomorrow it might be too late, Douglas thought
. . . *but on the other hand, if Flarman and the others were to
arrive tomorrow, they'd add greater experience to the search,
even though the trail has become cold.*

In the end, he composed this terse note:

"Magisters, all—

*Myrn has rescued Serenit and placed him in safety with
a good friend. We are pursuing the Servant of Darkness,
who was Serenit's kidnapper. He (she? it?) flees to the
north into the unknown land northwest of Samarca.*

*We will follow until we close with the Servant and seek
means to render him powerless. Any advice you can give
on this would be greatly appreciated!*

*If I knew what landmarks lay ahead in this empty land
I would suggest a rendezvous with you, but we are all but
completely in the dark. Full Wizard or not, at times I
greatly realize my lack of experience. Do what you decide
is best for all.*

*Love to all from Myrn and myself, Cribblon, Marbleheart,
Princess Indra of Tereniget, whom you'll remember as
the flying horse Nameless, and Lesser Dragon, who has
kindly joined our traveling troop."*

He scribbled the message on a rather dog-eared notepad he
found, after some rummaging, deep in his right sleeve. As it
was now after midday, he called to Marbleheart to find a cool
and shady spot for rest and lunch.

The Sea Otter chose a clump of upright, tree-tall cactuses
in the narrow midday shadow of a butte. It was extremely hot
in the sun but dry, with only the faintest trace of the fleeing
Servant's odor still hanging in the air.

Douglas summoned Deka the Wraith while Myrn arranged
for lunch. Deka and the lunch basket appeared at the same
moment. The basket was gaily bedecked with a checkered tablecloth of red and white, but the Wraith seemed uneasy and
rather faint, even in the deepest shade under the butte.

"Greetings, Wizard Brightglade, Journeyman Brightglade,
gentlemen," she whispered. "You certainly find the *worst*

kinds of places to visit, if I may say so. How may I serve you?''

"Deka, dear old friend," sympathized the Otter. "Sit by me here near the fire and well out of the sun. Share a bit of shade and lunch with us.''

''A pleasure! Desert sunlight is *very* hard on such as I,'' said the astral being, blinking even in the reflected glare. She sat with the Otter in the wide pool of shadow the Dragon cast.

''I've a message for Flarman,'' Douglas told her. ''I assume everybody's still at the High?''

''As of a few minutes ago, yes,'' Deka told him. ''Some *miscytwine*? Of course! A dry place you've come to, Myrn! A few of those cool, blue grapes would be nice, too. Thank you!''

They sat in the deepest shade to eat. Only now, looking about themselves, they saw the empty wilderness was not as ugly as they had at first thought. On every hand wind-etched rocks formed strange but rather pleasing shapes: columns, tables, spires, and even full arches.

Bright little red flowers graced the tips of whiplike cactus bracts, sending pleasant scents into the desert air. The shade felt surprisingly cool after the full sun in which they'd walked all morning.

Myrn busied herself fashioning a parasol from the tablecloth, and then made one for Cribblon and another for her husband. Marbleheart shook his head. He needed all four feet for walking.

''I think I'm getting used to these dry places,'' he remarked to Deka. ''Not that I'll ever really come to enjoy them.''

''Personally,'' answered the Wraith, sipping her third glass of the tangy lemonade, ''it must be quite nice here . . . at night. The Day Star comes as close to being downright painful here as anything in my experience. But I prefer—quite enjoy—still, warm, deeply shadowed places like this at night.''

Douglas read his note aloud to her. She would memorize and deliver his words to Flarman.

''You say,'' she said, rising to depart, ''that you are unfamiliar with the land to the north of here?''

''Never been there or read anything of it! Empty wasteland, I gather?'' Douglas replied.

''Well . . . perhaps,'' said Deka, beginning to waver in the bright light of the sun reflected from the rocks behind them. "It was once a very powerful kingdom of Men. Sandrovia, it was called by its warlike inhabitants."

"Do you know anything else of it? We need information, Deka!" Douglas called as she faded almost entirely away.

Her voice came as if from a great distance. "Sandrovia. Kingdom of the Sandrones. A full fifty thousand of your short years ago, Douglas Brightglade, they killed each other off. Their great city is a ruin, north of here a day or so at your present pace. You can't miss it!"

"The sort of place in which a Bit of Darkness might hide?" Douglas called after her.

But the Wraith was gone.

Chapter Nineteen

A Very Ancient Place

"I do recall a few fragments of tales, come to think on it, of the ancient Sandrones," Myrn said as they resumed their trek. "A fierce, warlike race. I don't recall anyone ever telling of their homeland. It may well have been here."

"The wickedest of Men!" Cribblon called back from his place second in line. "Frigeon spoke of them. Practiced Black Arts, he said, and banished all softer emotions from their hearts. They conquered a vast empire, enslaving native peoples and forcing them to work in mines from which they extracted cold iron for their swords and arrowheads. No, I don't recall he ever said where they lived."

"Must have been here. Deka's no fool," Marbleheart turned his head over his shoulder to say.

Douglas nodded. "What happened to them, then? If Flarman knew of them, he never spoke of them to me."

"According to old Frigeon," the Aeromancer replied after a pause to negotiate a particularly uneven patch of broken scree, "they destroyed each other in bloody civil wars. If there were survivors, they must have fled their city and their homeland."

The company plodded silently on in the terrible heat and rising clouds of fine dust, saving their energies for walking, breathing, and climbing over broken fields of shards and creeping up steep slopes of dangerously loose scree.

Only Lesser, gliding silently high overhead, darting off to this side or that to investigate alternate routes for those on the ground, seemed quite at ease.

When the sun's rays struck almost levelly across the tortured plain, they came to a sharp-edged cliff dropping away, straight down a mile or more, beneath their weary feet. The land below was shrouded in evening shadow, with only occasional sharp pinnacles of stone rising high enough to be lighted by the setting sun.

"Camp now," Douglas decided wearily. "Anybody got any idea where?"

The Dragon swooped down in time to hear his question.

"I saw a sort of cave over that way a bit . . . just below the rim. Actually, this hole thing is a crater. Perfectly round. Very wide and deep. Very, very ancient."

"Lead the way!" Douglas said. "It'll get more than a bit chilly here in the open after the sun sets."

"Deserts usually get cold at night," Myrn said from experience. "Shelter of any kind and a warm campfire—and a good dinner, too—will be most welcome."

"A cool bath would be even *more* welcome," growled Marbleheart, turning to follow the Dragon along the rim, which was as smooth and level as a road. "Watch your footing, people! With this sun in our eyes, a person could lose his step easily."

They carefully trailed after the Dragon along the very edge of the drop. Douglas noted that the stone on which they trod was glassy-smooth and darkly streaked in black, blue, and gray.

"A volcano?" he asked Cribblon.

"No, I think not," the Journeyman replied. "If we had the Lady Geomancer with us, she could tell us about this rock."

"*I've* never seen anything quite like this," Myrn said, shaking her head.

"I have . . . on a much smaller scale," declared Cribblon. "It's an impact crater, I think. Circular in shape and . . . oh, a good ten miles across. Very, very ancient! It's been thousands of years since something crashed down here."

"See! The very stone melted and ran like hot wax," Marbleheart pointed out. "Glad I wasn't near when *this* happened!"

Lesser spread his leathery wings and dove into the dark crater. When the party caught up and peeped over the edge, they saw him clinging to a narrow stone lip or shelf, fifty yards down the sheer crater wall.

"Cave here," Lesser called up to them. "Wait! I'll come up and ferry you down. The wall's mostly the same sort of black glass . . . too slippery and smooth for climbing, even for an Otter-turned-monkey!"

He flew back to the level above, loaded them all on his back, and dove off again, circling out over the black bottom of the crater, where the sun no longer shone at all, landing easily on the narrow shelf of smooth stone just before a long, low opening in the cliff wall.

"Water!" cried Marbleheart in glee, jumping to the ground.

He ran to a shallow basin just inside the cave mouth and sipped a mouthful of the water it held.

"*Pshaw!* Ooooh! *Nasty!*" he cried, spitting the water out again at once. "Besides, it's blood-warm."

"Never mind!" Myrn laughed. "I'll get some water from the great courtyard fountain on Waterand—the best water in the world!"

"Right away, I beg you, Mistress," the Otter cried mournfully, spitting and sputtering. "I think this stuff has poisoned me!"

Douglas scooped a palmful of the offending liquid and smelled, then tasted it.

"Nothing too very harmful," he assured his Familiar. "Smells and tastes rather like geyser's water, although not as boiling hot. You recall the hot springs in the Stone Warriors' valley? Same thing. Dissolved minerals and chemicals and things like that. Some would deem it quite healthful."

"The more fool, they!" coughed Marbleheart. "How could anything so vile be of any benefit?"

Myrn quickly imported, by means of a handy Aquamantic spell, a large crystal basin of cool, clear Waterand water. She also provided tall crystal tumblers fit for a king's table and a fifty-gallon silver tub for the Dragon, and soon they had all slaked their desert thirsts, including the Dragon, who could go for weeks, he said, without water of any kind.

"Good for you," sputtered Marbleheart, "but I'm a water baby myself, and I'd dry up and blow away if I didn't get fresh water daily."

"Hourly, rather," laughed his Master. "Let's look at our accommodations for the night."

The party followed him into the cave, ducking under the low ceiling at first. Once past that, even the Dragon could easily enter, and he breathed a long, steady yellow flare to light their way.

A few paces inside, the cavern floor dropped steeply to a huge room with a dark pool at its center that glittered in the flare's light.

"Something . . . ," Douglas began, but stopped when he reached the gravelly margin of the pool. The Dragon's light showed a perfectly flat, mirrored surface . . . and the reflection of his head and Myrn's as she stepped up beside him.

"It's not more bad water, is it?" the Sea Otter exclaimed. He tried to taste it but only succeeded in bumping his sensitive nose. "*Ouch!* It's hard as ice, but not as cold and not wet at all!"

Douglas laid his palm on the surface, fingers splayed.

"It's glass, I declare!" he exclaimed, drawing his hand back and examining it, as if he thought it would be blackened by the obsidian.

"Common substance around meteor strikes," declared the Dragon, who was something of an expert on such matters. "It bubbled up here as a liquid and hardened without anything to disturb it. Rather pretty, don't you think?"

"Well, if we sleep here," Myrn said, running her hands over the obsidian slowly, "I suppose it'll be no worse than sleeping on a marble floor. It's not cold, anyway."

Douglas agreed. The glass retained heat . . . perhaps some of the long-ago heat of the awesome impact.

Marbleheart found a beach of soft, black sand off to one side where they could settle in some comfort, eat their supper, and crawl under their blankets. Douglas was about to drift off to sleep when he heard the Sea Otter speak.

"Who are you talking to, Familiar?" he murmured.

"Bats," whispered Marbleheart. "They live here in a side cave and go out during the night, they tell me, seeking insects for their food."

Douglas sat up and listened.

Indeed, he heard soft fluttering above him and a high, almost inaudible squeaking. When he looked toward the slightly lighter mouth of the cave, he saw a great, slurred mass of rapidly moving specks of blackness flowing upward and out into the night.

"I'd have liked to bespeak them myself." He yawned. "Maybe we can catch them in the morning. Bats are shy but usually quite friendly and helpful. Remember the bat family in the witch-queen's dungeon?"

"I remember Tuckett and his family very well," his Familiar whispered. "These bats'll be back just before dawn, if I remember bat practices. Go to sleep, Douglas!"

Before long the entire party, including the Dragon, were sound asleep.

When she awoke, Myrn climbed the steep slope to the mouth of Bat Cave and found her husband and his Familiar studying the crater, now lighted by the risen sun.

"Quite a sight!" chirped Marbleheart. "I don't relish the thought of walking around down there. Hard on the feet! Bound to get pretty hot, too!"

"Beautiful in its own, special way," Douglas said, turning to greet Myrn. "But our Otter's right. We'll be better off now flying to the other side."

"What's on the other side?" wondered the Journeyman Aquamancer. "*Oh!* I see! A city of some sort on the far rim."

"The cave bats pointed it out to us or we might have missed it. Unless I'm completely wrong," Douglas said, "that's Sandrovia. Or what's left of it. What else could it be?"

"A place for a wicked bit of Darkness to hide," Myrn said. "The sooner we look at it, the better. Not particularly pretty, is it? Well, the Sandrones didn't sound like a particularly attractive race, from what Cribblon says. Do you think any still live there, husband?"

"No idea . . . but we'll soon find out."

"Breakfast first," insisted Marbleheart, turning to reenter the cave. "A good place for . . . what?"

"Black coffee and pumpernickel bread?" Myrn called after him. "No, I guess bacon and eggs and hotcakes would be better. I'll see to it at once!"

■   ■   ■

The broiling sun was well above the eastern rim by the time
the party mounted Lesser Dragon and was carried smoothly
across the vast crater to the silent, sun-bleached ruin on the
north rim.

Marbleheart peered curiously down into the crater as the
Dragon flew over it, commenting on the weird formations and
muted blacks, dark blues, and purples at the bottom. Rain for
hundreds of centuries had filled many of the depressions in
the floor with dark, greenish water but no plants grew there,
even now. The thin soil was largely a dusting of dark obsidian
sand and snowlike flakes of shiny mica, formed during the
tremendous heat of the original impact.

"I'm certainly glad we didn't have to walk." Cribblon
shuddered. "Oh, my poor old feet! And the way around
would've added a day or more to our journey. Hurrah for the
Dragon!"

"Hurrah!" Marbleheart added in a heartfelt cheer.

"Getting close," warned Lesser, blushing a brilliant crimson all the way to his ears. He coughed an embarrassed blast
of green smoke and shook his head. "Where do you think we
should land, Wizard?"

"Take your choice," Douglas said, after a glance at his
fellow travelers. "We'll look at the town first, then search for
signs of the Servant."

"Unless he finds us first," Myrn added, tucking her blowing
hair under her kerchief. Female Wizards seldom wore Wizard's caps. They resembled the witches' conical hats too much,
and Lady Wizards were careful to be distinguished from that
lesser (often antisocial) type of magicker.

"If he's *nearby,* we'll smell him out!" Marbleheart pointed
out. "How about the open square, Lesser? Room to land your
great bulk?"

"I can land on the head of a pin, if I've a mind to," grunted
Lesser. "Even a pinhead like yours, Sea Otter!"

If he'd had a thumb the Otter would have thumbed his nose
at the Dragon. He laughed delightedly, instead. The great flying beast dropped his starboard wing and curved down into an
open plaza before a tall, stark building with some remains of
a steeply pitched roof and a dozen thick, broken towers.

The plaza was paved with granite blocks evidently once

polished to a high gloss but now dulled by long centuries of weathering. In corners and doorways standing open to the constant winds, fine black sand drifted like coal dust, often several feet deep.

The scene was one of ancient ruin, empty for thousands of years. The low, round-edged buildings had a few high windows and a few wide doorways from which the wooden doors had long since crumbled to dust. Even their hinges had turned to faint, rusty stains.

"These windows were all heavily barred once," observed Lesser. He stood tall enough to look in at the high, empty openings closely. "Not much left to look at within, either."

Douglas stood in the center of the plaza, spinning slowly on his right heel until he'd turned through the entire compass. Myrn, meanwhile, drifted lightly back and forth, touching the rough walls and peering up at the remains of steeply peaked eaves far above.

"Not a soul around," Marbleheart declared, his voice echoing over the sound of the hot breeze soughing around the corners of the buildings and moaning softly across the empty windows. "Not even enough signs of life to seem spooky or feel haunted!"

Cribblon was the most active of them all, darting briefly into dark doorways and reappearing almost immediately, his head thrust forward and his hands clasped firmly behind his back. He reminded Marbleheart of a hound, casting for an elusive scent.

"Any ideas?" Douglas asked at last, sitting on a low wall in the shade of the palace shell.

"There're plenty of signs of Men," his wife said slowly. "But not for a very long time . . . centuries, at least!"

"What strikes me is not what I detect," said Cribblon, emerging from the palace itself, "but what I *don't*. Such a place, you would think, would have been taken over a long time ago by small animals, maybe even some larger beasts, and certainly flocks and families of birds. This is a perfect place for swallows, even for hawks and birds like owls, kestrels, and gyrfalcons. The air here should be a-buzz with wings, and the nooks and crannies crowded with nests. Not even the bats choose to live here in Sandrovia!"

"What do you make of that?" Douglas wondered.

Cribblon shrugged his shoulders and resumed his patrol about the square, entering houses and coming out again, breathing Airish Exploring Spells and shaking his head when he got no responses.

Lesser Dragon found a hot stretch of sun-washed pavement and dozed quietly. Wizardly doings were not his thing.

Marbleheart climbed to the top of the palace wall and peered from that vantage up and down the narrow curve of the city on the crater rim. Finally he slid down a remaining pitch of roof made of closely fitted slates, very smooth and even, and scrabbled down to join Myrn and Douglas in their spot of shade.

"Nary a sound," the Otter sniffed. "Nary a soul, neither!"

Cribblon came, at last, and sat beside them, too, his eyes still constantly sweeping the palace forecourt and the narrow plaza beyond, up the sides of houses and across their broken rooflines.

"There's something quite unnatural about this place," Douglas decided after a long silence.

"Too quiet," Myrn agreed.

"Not even bugs, nor even airborne plants!" murmured the Aeromancer. "If there were plants, you'd expect bugs, and you'd then expect small birds and lizards. If there were small birds and lizards, the larger raptors would be flying silently overhead in the morning light, hunting the birds and lizards. But . . . nothing!"

"Try a Calling Spell," Marbleheart suggested.

The Pyromancer sat straighter, reached into his left sleeve, and produced a worn leather pouch tied with rawhide strings.

Untying the strings, he placed the bag on top of the wall between his knees and studied the array of tiny bottles, tubes, vials, boxes, and bags fastened in place by red rubber bands.

He finally chose two small crystal vials.

Marbleheart, who'd watched him do Calling Spells many times before, hunched closer. Myrn moved to give her husband elbow room, and Cribblon nodded and watched carefully.

Douglas made a series of magic gestures. A brightly burning fire of sweet-smelling bits of dry wood sprang to life on top of the wall. After a few moments, he uncorked a silver vial and tilted a single droplet of milky liquid into the palm of his left hand.

From a second vial, he added three dashes of a white powder. A small marble of soft gray with pure white striations formed at once and, speaking a soft series of spelling words, Douglas dropped the sphere into the center of the fire.

The flames turned bright orange for a moment and, when they'd returned to a steady blue color, the watchers saw a bright-glowing pink, pearl-sized droplet in the middle of the fire, its surface slowly whirling and twirling in delicate shades of gray.

Douglas, adding another short incantation, added a single tiny drop of a clear liquid from a third vial onto the sphere. With a sharp *hissss* the liquid touched the hot bead, turning it at once a golden color, crackling and pulsating very slightly.

"Wait!" Douglas cautioned the watchers. "The call may take a minute or two to be answered."

"What . . . ?" Marbleheart said.

He stopped to scratch at his round right ear with a forepaw.

"A bee?" Myrn exclaimed. "Way out here!"

"Sit still!" Douglas ordered the Otter sharply. "He won't hurt you!"

Marbleheart froze.

The bee, which had circled the Otter's head twice after being swiped at, settled on his forehead and began cleaning his wings, humming softly to himself.

"Hello!" Douglas said to him. "I'm sorry if I bothered you. I can see you have to work hard to gain a living in this empty place."

The insect stopped his grooming and turned to face the Pyromancer.

"Been a very long time since any of my hive-mates has reported seeing a Man, let alone a party of them, if that's what you be, friends."

"A party of Wizard and near-Wizards," Douglas explained. "My name is Douglas Brightglade. I'm a Pyromancer."

He introduced his wife and Cribblon, explaining their origins and their magical specialties.

"Pleased to meet you, Wizards all!" hummed the bee politely. "What is this I'm seated upon, can you tell me? I've seen plenty of furry beasts in my time, but none with so rich a coat . . . or so strange an odor."

"Marbleheart Sea Otter, my Familiar," Douglas replied.

"From a distant part of Sea called The Briny."

"Briny!" the bee coughed. "Not a very pleasant name, I must say."

"A pleasant enough sort of place for an Otter, however," Marbleheart retorted, with an effort uncrossing his eyes while being careful not to shake his head. "Although I left there years and years ago and have never since returned."

"Wise Otter!" the bee chuckled. "But I don't mean to insult your homeland."

"You can't say you prefer *this* spot," Douglas said, waving his hand to include the whole crater. "Not a flower anywhere that I've seen."

"No, I came only at your call, Fire Master. Normally I would stay far away and well outside this barren place. Something in the soil prevents even the hardiest bramble or rankest dock from rooting here. Flowers never grow in Sandrovia. Never have . . . in memory of my people!"

"We appreciate your coming all the more," Myrn told the insect.

"I'm pleased to provide any assistance, of course," said the bee, bowing slightly to the lady. "Do you wish me to guide you out of this horrendous wilderness? Easily done!"

"No, we seek information about this ruined city and to know if you or your people have seen anything suspicious here of late. In the last day or two, in fact," the Pyromancer told him.

"We pay little attention to the old, empty city, or the crater, either, as I said," the bee insisted. "However, now that I'm here . . . *ummm! ummm!* . . ."

He appeared to be listening, turning, much as Douglas had done earlier, in several complete circles, vibrating his wings in a blur. "I hear strange sounds from deep below. Something moving very slowly about and softly snarling . . . or sniffling? . . . sort of. Deep under our feet, it is. *Hmmm!* Best to flit away while we can! Something's going on deep inside the crater floor, way down below."

"I don't hear anything," objected Cribblon.

"But *I* hear it, Air Adept," the bee murmured softly. "Deep. Low-down, constant, but coming from a Being of some sort. Not an insect, nor a Man, nor a Fairy, nor anything like that. Oh, dear! Not even a Near Immortal! Something harsh . . . and lonely . . . and fearful.''

"If you fear, we'll not detain you," Douglas said gently. "I think I know what it is, and it *is* dangerous, believe me."

"It's not been here very long," added the bee, preparing to flit off. "I never heard it before, friends and Wizards. Nor do I wish to hear it ever again!"

And he shot off on a beeline toward the low, grassy hills just visible to the north.

"I'm truly, truly stumped!" admitted Douglas Brightglade.

They had retreated from the blazing-hot plaza to sit under the arched entryway of the largest ruin, where there was now deep shadow as the sun moved across the glaring sky. Only Lesser Dragon remained in the broiling sun, sleeping peacefully, snoring wisps of yellowish steam.

"What interested me was the honeybee's description of the Being under the crater," Myrn put in. "Did you notice? 'Not Man nor Fairy?' Nor any kind of Near Immortal!''

"But we already knew that," said Cribblon. "The Darkness are certainly not Men, nor Near Immortals like a Fairy. What else is there? I forget!"

"An Immortal, then?" Douglas considered. "Not that either, perhaps? What do you think, Myrn?"

"I'm just the junior-most Journeyman here," Myrn protested, shaking her dark head. "Not much was ever said in Augurian's training classes about Immortals. Oh, that they exist and that there are Bright Immortals and . . ."

"Precisely!" Douglas nodded. "*Dark* Immortals!"

"We need some older and wiser heads on this, I guess," said his wife, sighing.

"You're right!" Douglas agreed. "I'll send for Flarman, Augurian, and Lithold, to come at once!"

"Meanwhile, we must stay here to keep watch, in case this pesky bit of Darkness decides he should flee somewhere else," Myrn said, setting her chin firmly.

"They'll be here, all three, as quickly as their combined Powers can bring them across the wide Sea," Douglas told the party a short while later.

They'd set up camp on a side porch of an ancient palace,

one which still boasted a half-roof for shade and some shelter from the constant, drying wind. Marbleheart and Cribblon went off to explore the rest of the city on the crater's rim and Myrn was preparing to order lunch.

"What has this Darkness Servant to fear?" wondered Myrn, setting places around a stone table for the party, including the Dragon, who'd just awakened from his forenoon nap. "For that matter, why did he—it—run from us when we came to Darkest Mountains?"

"I can't imagine, darling," answered her husband. "It's only a tiny part of the whole, old Darkness, of course. It may not yet understand how powerful it *could* be. I only hope our Masters can give us some assistance and more information. For example, how did the Fellowship of Wizards manage to defeat The Darkness at the end of Last Battle? Nobody's ever told me that."

"Nor me," Myrn admitted. "Well, we'll hold on—or hide like scared rabbits, if need be—until they arrive. Late tomorrow, do you say?"

"Flarman just said, 'We're on our way!' "

"Might as well make ourselves as comfortable as possible, then," Myrn sighed. "You like spicy dishes, young Fireman. How 'bout a nice curry for lunch? I imagine Lesser'll like that. And Marbleheart will eat just about anything!"

"Good enough! Meanwhile," Douglas said, rising and beginning to pace back and forth, a habit he'd picked up years since from Flarman Flowerstalk, "I need to think. There *must* be a way to control this ... *thing,* or whatever you want to call it. Some way ..."

At Wizards' High, far to the west, the three older Wizards prepared to answer Douglas's call.

Flarman said to Black Flame, "You and Stormy must come, too, Puss! We may need every bit of help we can get."

"Do you think this Servant of The Darkness is all that powerful?" the Geomancer asked, sounding rather worried. Of the three of them, she had the least experience with The Darkness or its Servants.

"We can't tell from this far away, can we?" Augurian answered for Flarman. He set his battered, water lily–patterned carpetbag near the kitchen door. "Ah! Here's my Familiar!"

The long-winged Stormy appeared in the kitchen doorway.

"I should come, too," said a new voice. Bronze Owl rattled and banged down the wide hall from his post at the front door.

"It means leaving the High unguarded!" Flarman protested. "Well . . . come along then, Owl. We can use another hard head, and you once were famous for your knowledge of The Enemy."

The Pyromancer went to the kitchen range and patted the round, warm side of Blue Teakettle fondly.

"You're in charge while we're away, Blue, my pet."

She puffed a short, reassuring jet of pale blue steam, saying, "Trust me, Magister! When you and Douglas and his Myrn return triumphant, we'll have a grand Victory Celebration!"

"*If* we return, there'll be cause for celebration," sighed Augurian, who tended to be a pessimist at times.

"Everybody ready?" Flarman called loudly. "Not forgotten anything? There won't be many toothbrush trees or washrag bushes handy in the wasteland northwest of Samarca!"

He led them out into the kitchen courtyard, where late spring had turned overnight into full summer. Equinox was just a few days away.

The Ladies of the Byre, the brown-and-white hens, their cocky rooster, and their yellow chicks, had stayed awake late to cheer the Wizards on their way.

Precious, who'd take care of the Wizards' High livestock and watch the cottage while they were gone, stood leaning on the meadow gate, chewing on a stalk of green oat-straw. Overhead the stars were popping out and the moon, just rising, was almost full, bright, and untroubled by clouds.

"Good evening for a fast flight!" cried Flarman cheerily. "Form a line, please. It'll make things easier for an old magicker if you touch each other or hold hands. Here's *my* hand, my dear."

He grasped Lithold's capable left hand with his right, reached for Augurian's hand with the other, waited while Bronze Owl flapped noisily up to perch on his left shoulder, and glanced down to make sure Black Flame was standing touching his right ankle, purring confidently. Stormy Petrel rested easily on Augurian's off shoulder, his wings furled and his eyes hooded.

"You really should find another Familiar of your own, my

dear.'' Flarman smiled at Lithold, squeezing her hand.

"When I find a suitable candidate, I won't hesitate, Flarman,'' she said, returning his smile. ''Do you think I should've brought along a warm sweater?''

"No, from where Douglas called it's hot enough for a swimsuit or less.'' The Water Adept laughed.

Flarman leaned forward to check. Glancing up and down the flight line. "Ready all? Get set! G—!''

A gust of warm, wet breeze rushed in where almost the entire remaining Fellowship of Light (lacking only the Choinese Magician named Wong) had a moment before stood near the courtyard well.

Rooster nodded importantly to his wives and began to *shoo* the excited chicks back into their chicken coop beyond the door to the Wizards' workshop.

Party and Pert turned to go in at the open workshop door. It was nearing Party's birthing time and she felt heavy and rather tired.

The old orchardman shook his gray head, thanking his stars he'd never been tempted to become a Wizard of any sort. He tossed his oat-straw to the ground, pushed the meadow gate closed, and stumped off down to Old Plank Bridge over Crooked Brook, on his way home to his bride and bed.

Chapter Twenty

On the Rim

"I'VE got it!" cried Douglas, sitting up straight on his blanket in the hot darkness of the palace porch.

The nearly full moon was well risen, and the desolate city was entirely quiet... ominously silent, Marbleheart thought with a sudden shiver. He rolled over on his back and stuck all four feet in the air, but said nothing.

Myrn stirred, blinked at her husband a bit as Bronze Owl would have blinked, shook her head, and said, "It can't wait, can it?"

"Doing some thinking." Douglas grinned at her fondly in the dimness. "Forgive the rude awakening."

Myrn sat up, pushing her lustrous black hair out of her eyes. "Need me...?"

"No, no! Go back to sleep. Dawn will come in about two hours. Flarman and the rest will be here by midday, if all goes well. Then we'll settle this Darkness Servant thing for good and all."

"A hint might make me go back to sleep out of pure relief." Myrn yawned.

"Well... I was trying to fill a void in my knowledge. How did Flarman and Augurian—Lithold'd left before Last Battle—finally defeat The Darkness and send it back into Endless Caverns atop World?"

"I *know* the stories, Douglas," said his wife, just a tad impatiently.

"But Flarman once—and one time only that I recall—used a word for how they'd finally bested the Darkness. It took me a long time to remember that single word, dearest, and it's just come back to me in my sleep."

"I promise if you tell it to me," Myrn growled, "I'll go back to sleep and let you ponder it the rest of the night."

" *'Unity!'* " Douglas pronounced. "Go back to sleep!"

"Unity?" asked the Sea Otter, several hours later.

They were walking on the rim at dawn, watching the sun slowly unveil the sea of dark glass at the bottom of the mile-deep crater and spotlight the chimneys of red flowstone scattered across its shining surface.

"We can defeat this . . . this Servant," Douglas explained, "if we act in unison, all together, with single purpose. That's what Flarman discovered in the terrible Last Battle against The Darkness, two centuries ago."

"Humph!" snorted Marbleheart. "I would have thought the Forces of Light were united from the very beginning!"

"Evidently not." Douglas shrugged. "As I recall, King Grummist lost his nerve and nearly cost them all their lives And brokenhearted Lithold had left the Fellowship when her Familiar was foully murdered. Some of the Federation of Light were distrustful of Faerie, you recall. And, of course, there was the selfishness of Frigeon. No . . . our side's Unity was rather ragged at the beginning of Last Battle, I fear."

He picked up a flat stone from the path and threw it with all his might out over the deep chasm.

It fell, and fell, and fell . . . until at last they heard it *crack* faintly, almost a mile below.

"So we wait for our Magisters to arrive?" asked the Sea Otter when the echoes had died at last.

"We wait. They should be here in a few hours."

"Meanwhile," Marbleheart murmured, cocking his ear over the edge, "I believe I hear bumblings and rumblings from below now, too. Do you catch 'em? Very faint, but . . . *something*!"

The two friends stood very still, leaning out over the edge, listening. Myrn came up to them.

"What's this?" she chided them cheerfully. "You look like you two are about to fall into the hole."

"We're . . . uh . . . listening. There are sounds coming from down there," whispered Marbleheart.

"I heard them as soon as I woke," Myrn agreed with a nod. "It shouldn't stop our eating breakfast, should it?"

"Never!" cried the Otter, swinging about. "C'mon, Master! Sensible commons make common sense, I say."

Douglas wished his wife a good morning with a kiss. Arms about each other, they followed the Otter to the palace of the ancient, doomed warrior race known as the Sandrones. Marbleheart detoured to call Cribblon from his resumed investigation of yet another of the empty, roofless, windowless ruins along the rim.

"Deka!" Douglas cried.

Under the porch, where the early-morning shadows were deepest, shimmered the form of the Wraith messenger, moving and wavering and looking ill at ease in the brightness of reflected light.

"Greetings, Wizard Douglas. Mistress Journeyman. Hello, Sea Otter Familiar and Journeyman Cribblon," whispered the Wraith. "I cannot stay long. Flarman bade me come and say they're but a few hours off, coming fast."

"Thank you, old friend! Rest with us while we break our night's fast," Douglas urged.

The ghostly messenger appeared as weary and wan as they'd ever seen her.

"Yes, do!" Myrn urged. "Tell us the news, if you can."

"No time now," replied the Wraith, already beginning to fade. "You understand? I'll be back at eventide. I really dislike this place by day. . . ."

And she was gone.

"Well, we'll eat without her," decided Myrn. "Ah! Here are cantaloupes from somewhere. Certainly not our garden at the High yet? I don't know how Blue Teakettle does it! And she even sent sweet pastries with cinnamon and sugar icing, such as certain Otters are very fond of."

"Coffee?" Marbleheart asked Cribblon, who followed him onto the porch. "What were we looking for, if a mere Familiar may ask?"

Cribblon sipped contentedly at the steaming black coffee before he answered.

"It occurred to me that this Servant had to have a way to enter the . . . crater, as I guess one should call it. I've been looking at openings in the surface below. It must have found a way under the crater floor, somewhere."

"The cave we slept in two nights back?" Myrn suggested. Cribblon considered.

"No, there was no trace of the Servant there at all."

"I quite agree," said the Otter.

"Scent is about all we have to follow. There's no way anything could leave footprints on that glassy rock below," Myrn also agreed.

She nibbled a cinnamon-dusted breakfast roll thoughtfully while her husband and the Journeyman Air Adept discussed possibilities.

"I can help you explore the floor of the crater," said Lesser, called from slumber by the smells of coffee, hot buttered cinnamon rolls, and raspberry jam on toast. "We may find a crevice or a cave down there."

"Have some food first," Cribblon said to the Dragon. "We may be gone a long time. The crater is miles and miles in each direction and it'll take us hours and hours to give it even a preliminary scrutiny."

"Whenever you're ready, then." The Dragon grinned.

"The other Wizards are due shortly. I'll stay here in the city," Douglas decided. "How about you, Myrn?"

"I've a few Water Spells might give us some information about our Enemy," Myrn said. "I'll need a nice quiet place with a good view and a few minutes to think and spell. I don't suppose Flarman is bringing our babies with him, do you think?"

"I very much doubt it," Douglas said with a wide grin at the thought of their twins. "Although, sometimes I think they have more enchanting powers as babies than we older folk will ever enjoy."

"They're Wizardly children and Faerie nephew and niece, as well," Myrn reminded him. "Who knows what they could—"

"We're off, then," called Lesser. "Yell down the hole if you need us. Sound'll carry a long way on that glass!"

The Dragon, bearing the Journeyman Aeromancer, shot into the air, then began spiraling down, down, around and around the mile-deep chasm.

"I wish there was something more I could think to do," worried Douglas.

Myrn used her Traveling Pearls to fly to the top of the palace's front facade, the highest point anywhere on the rim. Shortly they heard her speaking charms and chanting spellsongs, but too softly for them to recognize words or guess at purposes.

Douglas pulled a chessboard from his deep left sleeve, unfolded it, and laid it on the low wall between them. Marbleheart, who'd expected a morning of Familiar lessons, was relieved when his Master held out both fists, each enclosing a pawn, red and white.

"Red!" The Otter inspected his choice with some satisfaction. "My favorite color!"

"My move," Douglas claimed.

For considerably more than three hours he and his Familiar dueled over the ancient chess squares, first one and then the other gaining the advantage.

"Check!" chortled the Otter gleefully, at last.

Douglas moved a white knight two squares ahead and one to the left, protecting his king and threatening the red queen..

"*Arrrgh!*" Marbleheart growled deep in his throat.

He settled back on his haunches to ponder his next move.

For some time Douglas had been listening to sounds coming to them through the very rimrock. A rumbling followed by a long *shussss,* then a groaning, sometimes a faint *thump! thump! thumpety!*

Marbleheart lifted his ears to listen too.

"Sounds like Servant's moving furniture down there," he said to his Master.

"Something like that, I guess," replied Douglas. "Your move, Otter. Or do you resign?"

"Never!" cried the water animal, reaching for his single remaining rook. "This should give you pause!"

"Not a smart move, Marblesnoot," said a voice.

"Set the white king in check with your queen," advised a second, female voice.

"Never risk your queen," contradicted a third, unmistakably the voice of Augurian of Waterand.

"Magisters!" cried Douglas, looking up from the board. "Welcome to . . . whatever this place is called!"

"I recognize it, although I've never been here before," said Flarman Flowerstalk, settling easily on the low wall beside the younger Pyromancer. "The infamous ancient stronghold of the . . . ?"

"Sandrones," supplied Lithold Stonebreaker. "A very ancient, lost, long-dead and unlamented race of Men. People of the Warrior Kings. Some call them Aboriginals, but that's a subject of serious debate. What you see here is a small portion of the ruin of their great capital city, Sandrovia."

Marbleheart pushed the red queen forward to trap Douglas's white king. "Check and checkmate!"

"This Familiar's getting too good for me," said the younger Pyromancer, sighing and knocking his king on its side as a sign of surrender. "Hello, all! Who wants to play the Otter next?"

"You could have escaped his trap, however," Augurian considered, studying the board. "What's Myrn doing up there on the roof?"

"Trying some Aquamantic spellings and divination, I think And getting a sunburned nose, too!" said Douglas. "I'm relieved you're here at last, Magisters! I have to admit I'm quite stumped as to what should be done."

"Put your board away, then, and let's get to work," Flarman advised. "Is that your new Dragon-friend I see, down there below? Old Splash," he added to his best friend, the Aquamancer. "How about some nice, cool, clear water? It's a long and arduous journey from Wizards' High."

"My canteen is empty already, thanks to your borrowings," snorted Augurian. "Come down, Journeyman! Greet your elders!"

Myrn floated down from the top of the palace wall, gave all three older Wizards, the black cat, the white-and-gray bird, and Bronze Owl welcoming embraces, then handed her husband's rotund Master a frosty glass of ice water.

"From Waterand Island," she assured him. "Best in World!"

'Well, perhaps," said Flarman, sipping the drink appreciatively. "No water excels that of the High's Fairy Well, I claim."

Douglas went to the edge of the crater to recall the Dragon and his rider. When they arrived, they found Lithold Stonebreaker standing in the full midday sun of the courtyard, slowly turning about to examine the whole ruinous scene, eyes half-closed against the glare, humming to herself.

"Fascinating place," she told Myrn. "Even as ruins! I always wished I had known the Sandrones. Although I must admit their taste in architecture leaves something to be desired."

"I gather this city was here before the meteor impact, then?" Augurian called to her from the shade of the porch.

"Yes. Oh, by a long, long time! Actually, the meteor that caused this impacted here not too long ago. I was here three hundred and forty-three years ago, when it was still white-hot and the crater was filled with molten glass and boiling metals!"

"So!" cried Myrn. "I was right! The city *is* much older than the meteor."

"What you see is but a tiny fraction of what was once here. The meteor was called down by powerful Black Magic. By The Darkness itself, if I don't miss my guess entirely," Lithold Stonebreaker told them.

"The Darkness!" exclaimed Douglas. "That never occurred to me at all, Lithold. I assumed the impact came much longer ago than that."

"The Darkness was once again beginning to force its will on Men, Dwarfs, and Fairies—every thinking, caring race in World," Lithold went on. "The last of the proud Sandrones refused assistance from our First Alliance. They defied the Darkness . . . and sealed their own fate. Complete destruction of their empire, and of their whole people!"

"Extend your vision, m'boy!" Flarman urged Douglas. "When dealing with The Darkness, one must think in terms of *millions* of years or even more . . . *hundreds* of millions!"

"And The Dark Enemy has the patience to wait until Men and Near Immortals become unwary, and then attempt new depredation and conquest." Lithold sighed, sounding rather discouraged. "Is no one going to offer us poor wayfarers some lunch? Flarman didn't even allow us time for a decent breakfast!"

"Immediately!" cried Myrn, electing herself hostess. "Give me a few moments and we'll sit down in the coolest shade to a hearty luncheon . . . and long conversation."

Douglas introduced Lesser Dragon to the assembled Wizards, their Familiars, and Bronze Owl. The Dragon, it turned out, was already acquainted with the two older male Wizards. They spent lunchtime chatting of long-ago events and exchanging news of old acquaintances.

"I'm very pleased to be afield once again," Bronze Owl confided to Myrn and Douglas. "We left Blue Teakettle in charge, of course. She can handle just about anything that might pop up."

"Her cooking certainly hasn't suffered from added duties." Myrn laughed. "These hot popovers are the very best I've ever tasted."

"Appropriate for sitting on volcanoes or nestling near meteoric desolations," the bronze bird chuckled. "Where's our strayed bit of Darkness, eh? Under the crater glass, I would guess."

"So we believe. He, or it, is down below, even now. Earlier he was rumbling and grumbling and moving things about deep under the crater floor," Cribblon told him.

"Well, it's time we started doing something about him," said Lithold. "Gentlemen, please, and Mistress Myrn!"

They sat in a circle, some sipping a third or fourth glass of iced tea, others nibbling at the lime ice Blue Teakettle had sent along.

"This is my sort of place, so shall I chair the meeting?" asked the Geomancer.

"You have the chair and our ears," Flarman agreed, and Douglas and Augurian nodded their approval.

"First, we should review the whole matter for a moment," Lithold began. "You are all aware of the great age of our Enemy?"

"Eons and eons old," guessed Marbleheart.

"Even so!" agreed the Geomancer.

"But the Sandrones, we decided," Douglas put in, "ruled much of World *before* The Darkness arrived."

"When The Darkness last came to World, the Sandrone Empire was already old and weakening . . . rulers of all except those who lived within or high above Earth or in the great Primordial Sea. Few now remember those elder days—not Wizards, nor even the long-lived Fairies or Elves. Dragons go back that far—some of the Eldest Dragons, at least—and Sea dwellers such as Oval the Great Sea Tortoise."

"Oval!" exclaimed Douglas. "I knew she was old, but . . ."

"Older than even the hills to the north of here," said Lithold solemnly. "Water gave her and the other Sea dwellers safety from the conquerors."

"Ah, yes." Augurian nodded his head. "Water is ever the great protector of life."

"When it became necessary to oppose the wicked Darkness invader, fire was the best tool," insisted Flarman Flowerstalk. "In fact Fire Wizards—there were a number of them before our time, Douglas, as you learned at my knee—always took the lead in countering and driving back the Darkness. Not just in Old Kingdom, two hundred years ago, but at least three other times, ages before that."

"At Very Beginning," Lithold resumed, "at Eodawn, there were very few Beings yet in World. We call them *Prototypes,* for want of a better name."

"Earth, Air, Fire, and Water," Cribblon named them.

"And a few even older," the Geomancer added. "And the oldest of all were Darkness . . . and Light!"

"So, that's why we're called the Fellowship of Light!" cried Myrn.

"And our various allies—Men, Elves, and Faeries, all our friends—were called the Forces of Light. We together were at least partially successful in Last Battle in Old Kingdom, driving Darkness into the Polar Night, where it hid itself and its allies deep under World's frozen mantle. It has hidden there, ever since, awaiting its next chance."

"Then . . . they'll come back again, will they?" Marbleheart blurted in a disturbed tone.

"Maybe. Maybe not! Certainly, if the Forces of Light remain vigilant—alert and constantly on guard—then, no! Witness the Fellowship of these nearer times and the participation of most other races of Mortals and Near Immortals, other Beings . . . but primarily Men, Fairies, and Dwarfs.''

"Unity, then," said Douglas.

"Yes," Flarman nodded, rubbing his bald head, which already showed pink signs of sunburn. "In Unity there is Strength."

"And one might also mention the pleasures and satisfactions of Unity," said Augurian.

"We drove The Darkness off because we finally accepted the theme *Unity Despite Diversity.* The Darkness, on the other hand, preached *Unity Without Diversity.* No Diversity allowed, *ever!*" Flarman said.

Myrn bobbed her dark head thoughtfully, saying, "But how does this help us in our present crisis?"

"I see how it does," said her husband. "This bit of evil purpose, this Servant of Darkness, has become separated from the greater Darkness. He represents a dangerous Disunity!"

Flarman nodded. "When this Servant fled Last Battle, for whatever reason, he became what old Valley farmers call a *maverick.* He became, willingly or not, a Diversity, apart and on his own."

"He'd be striving to rejoin his kind, I would think," suggested the Sea Otter.

"No, for his *kind,* as you put it, will never accept his return to the pack. The Darkness would never trust it not to rove, stray off again. In fact, The Darkness will assuredly destroy it, given the chance!" Augurian told them. "The Servant has few options."

"Yes." Lithold nodded. "It can try to establish itself as a separate, lesser Entity. Then it might petition The Darkness for reunion later. Or . . . he can try to hide forever."

"Unfortunately for this Servant, The Darkness will never forget nor forgive," Flarman said, standing and looking out over the crater, where the air shimmered in the intense afternoon heat.

"So . . . ," Douglas thought out loud, "this Darkness Servant must be destroyed, or driven back to The Darkness, which would be the same thing, for it . . ."

"He will never willingly go back," Augurian interrupted.

". . . or," continued the younger Pyromancer, "it might be banished to where it can hide forever."

"Well, *forever* is a very, very long time," Flarman muttered, turning back to the group on the porch. "But even a few hundred or a few thousand years would be welcome respite. This maverick Servant would endeavor to sneak behind our backs while we were guarding ourselves from The Darkness. He'd cause all sorts of dire disruptions and dangerous distractions . . . as he was planning obviously, in the present case, by capturing Frigeon . . . or Serenit, rather."

The group sat in silence for some minutes, considering the implications of the problem.

"There is, however, a place this maverick could hide for a long, long time," said the Journeyman Aeromancer at last.

"Deep Sea?" asked Bronze Owl. "The fiery center of World?"

"No, Bronze Owl," replied Cribblon. "We must send him off World entirely."

"And foist him on some other poor planet?" Douglas said, not happy with the idea at all.

"No, no," cried Lithold. "Cribblon has it! We must send the Servant home. To Outer Darkness."

"Outer Darkness, it is!" cried Marbleheart, then added, "Never heard of it."

"It's the vast emptiness between and beyond all worlds," Lithold explained. "It's all but endless void, and deep enough that a bit of Darkness, cut off from his own kind, could hide forever."

"A terrible fate!" gasped Myrn, feeling sorrow at the thought of any Being wandering lost in such a place.

"Better that fate for it . . . better than bitter defeat from us . . . better than sure and complete destruction from his own fell Master!" declared Augurian.

"Of course," admitted the Journeyman Water Adept after a long moment of painful thought. "I can see that."

"Now!" cried Flarman Flowerstalk, sitting down again. "How to begin?"

Chapter Twenty-one

Deep Within Deep

CRIBBLON stood on the sharp verge of the crater rim, pointing down and out to where he and the Dragon had explored that morning.

"There are a number of possible entrances—cold fumaroles, actually—among that group of chimneylike spires. We were about to look at them more closely when you called us, Douglas."

"I don't see them," complained Flarman, squinting into the afternoon glare.

"When the sun moves down the western sky a bit more they'll show up better," the Journeyman Aeromancer replied. "I'm not positive, Flarman, but I think we detected the acrid scent of the Servant in that area. He may have dropped down one of those holes."

"It'll take further dangerous exploring, I think," Douglas considered. "Who'll go?"

"I'll lead the way," Cribblon said, firmly.

"We'd better have at least one Pyromancer in the search party," Flarman said at once. "And you, Lithold. You should be right at home under the surface."

"I'll go," agreed Lithold.

"And who else?" asked Myrn. "I . . ."

"You and Augurian can best serve by staying here and

watching. There may well be other escape holes to the surface. If he gets away unseen, it'd take us centuries to find him,'' Douglas told his wife.

''Cribblon, then, and Lesser, and Black Flame and me,'' Flarman counted them off on his fingers. ''And Lithold, as I said. Douglas, you're in charge up here. You two young people and Marbleheart and the Aquamancer must watch while we work.''

''I'll go below with you,'' announced Bronze Owl. ''I've the very best night vision and don't depend on breathing air. There may be foul gases and noxious fumes under the glass.''

''Agreed,'' nodded Flarman. ''No problems with that load, then, Sir Dragon?''

''None! Let's up and away while some light remains,'' cried Lesser.

''Watch for my signal,'' called Flarman, helping Lithold to a seat on the Dragon's broad back behind his leathery wings. ''Keep in touch, Douglas!''

''I'll wait for your call,'' Douglas agreed.

''We're off then,'' cried Lesser with a snort of yellow smoke and green fire.

He planed his great wings, plunged headlong from the rim-rock, and dove into the vast impact crater, heading straight for the tall chimneys that marked Cribblon's vents.

Douglas removed his cloak and spread it on the ground at the edge of the crater. A few words and a simple magic gesture, and the cloak rose over their heads and stretched flat to give them a wide, welcome shade.

''We'll retire to the palace roof,'' decided Augurian, waving for Myrn to follow. ''To watch the outside of the crater. There are some useful spells I know. . . .''

A few minutes after they'd left, glancing to the west, Douglas saw a line of dark thunderclouds forming, far away, over distant Sea.

'' 'In case of fire,' I suspect.'' Marbleheart laughed aloud. ''Well, why not? I could use some of that rain right now!''

The two companions settled down to watch—to listen, rather, for the scouting party was by then out of sight.

■   ▬   ■

An hour passed before the Dragon returned to the rim and settled beside their shelter.

"Pleasant day," he remarked, folding his enormous wings down over his back. "I'll help you watch. Rather too lonely down there."

"They went into one of the fumaroles, I take it?" asked Douglas.

"One showed signs—smells, rather—of the Servant passing down. Too small for me to follow, so I decided to come back up here."

Lesser shortly fell asleep in the full sun. Marbleheart sprawled on his tummy, legs splayed wide, three-quarters asleep himself, at Douglas's side.

"Pot of strong coffee would be useful," Douglas decided.

He plucked a coffeepot from the empty air and drank a steaming cup before he awoke the Otter to offer him a cup.

"Keep alert!" the Pyromancer reproved.

Another hour passed slowly. Myrn came across the shimmering square from the palace roof and sat down beside her husband in the shade of his cloak.

"Nothing moves on the outer plains. Nothing at all! Augurian can watch there and take care of the storm clouds, too," she announced. "Not much else we can do, until they find the Dark Servant and get him to move."

She and her Wizard-husband talked of home at the High, of their neighbors in Valley, but mostly of their children. Nothing stirred anywhere in the huge crater, nor on the rim, nor in the air above. Augurian's storm hovered on the western horizon, blinking diffused lightning from time to time, still much too far off for them to hear its thunder.

The sun dropped at last behind the thick clouds. The air was perfectly clear and still over the deep crater. Its colors, burning ambers and yellows and off-whites with deep black shadows, shifted to beiges and taupes and a hundred shades of cooling gray.

"Here's our old friend the honeybee," Marbleheart said, breaking the long stillness.

"Came by to tell you," the black-and-yellow insect said after turning completely about three times in a polite bee's greeting, "our honey scouts report something unusual on the northern edge of the crater desolation."

"Are there flowers there, then?" Myrn asked in surprise.

"Clumps of heather, flowering cacti, and desert succulents," explained the bee. "Worth the risk and the discomfort of the long flight for a few days of the year, you understand. Besides, we thought it might be helpful if we kept our eyes upon the flanks, Wizards."

"I can't tell you how much we appreciate that," Douglas thanked the bee. "I'm sorry! I should have asked your name last time you came to see us."

"I am Goldenrod, named so after my mother's favorite flower," replied the worker, quite pleased to be asked. "My hive is that of Queen Purple Sage. We're a sect of the Eastern Rhododendron nation, which is the second-oldest and largest tribe of all High Desert *Hymenoptera*."

"Goldenrod?" Myrn wondered. "Is that what your friends call you?"

"Not quite," the bee chuckled. "My friends call me Rod. You may call me that, also, for I feel we are already good friends, Mistress Wizard."

"Pleased to meet you socially." Myrn curtsied to the bee.

"Tell us about this disturbance to the north," Douglas asked the bee, inviting him to settle on the back of his left hand.

"Well, usually the cracks and vents there are just that—holes in the ground, filled with sand and small rocks, leaves and dried twigs and such. The scouts report that, an hour or so back, debris began to fly out of the vents. *Blown* out, would be more like it. Hollyhock said it was like some great beast snuffling out dust and sand and bits of leaves in loud sneezes."

"Hmmm! Interesting," Douglas commented, glancing at his wife. "Someone's doing housekeeping down below!"

"But, why?" Myrn wondered aloud.

"A while later," Rod continued, "Hollyhock's people noticed that the vents were clear and the air coming up was very warm. Quite hot, in fact."

"Maybe we'd better investigate," Marbleheart put in, anxiously. "Although goodness knows, I have no desire to crawl around inside hot air vents. Had enough of that on old Blue Eye."

"Remember, this is not a volcano," Douglas told him. "Rod, what is happening, do you think?"

"Another team of gatherers came back to the hive an hour

ago. They said the air coming from the fumaroles had become burning hot. They were setting fire to the dried leaves and such, blown out earlier. If you look closely, you can see the smoke of the fires, over there!''

They jumped to their feet and studied the northern side of the crater.

"Yes, I see columns of sparks, maybe a whiff of smoke,'' said Douglas, pointing.

"I see it!'' cried Marbleheart.

"But what does it mean?'' Myrn asked. "Any ideas, Pyromancer?''

"It's either our Wizards down beneath,'' her husband mused aloud, "or . . . something the Servant of Darkness is doing. The second is my guess. The Servant is reacting to Flarman's invasion.''

"Makes sense,'' Marbleheart conceded. "What should we do about it?''

"Is there a lot of brush and grass over there?'' Douglas asked Rod.

"The lower northern hills are fairly covered with short grass,'' the bee replied. "A fire there . . .''

". . . would burn downwind for some distance,'' the young Wizard guessed, sounding concerned. "I've seen it happen in Valley when a shepherd's cottage fire threw off sparks. With nothing to stop it, it could burn for miles and miles with this west wind to push it along.''

"It would destroy a lot of old, dried heather and stuff, but little else,'' the bee agreed. "It happens every now and again because of lightning. It seems to refresh the plant life, afterward, so we don't worry about it. Just keep well clear.''

"A good idea, where there's wildfire,'' the Pyromancer said. "But at this time and in this place . . .''

"Wouldn't Flarman or Lithold or Bronze Owl tell us if they were threatened by the heat or the fire?'' Myrn asked.

"They would . . . perhaps,'' her husband replied. "But I've heard no call from my Master.''

"No news being good news,'' Marbleheart muttered. "I hope!''

"Rod, can your scouts keep an eye on this fire and heat, without getting in harm's way?'' Douglas asked the honeybee.

"About to suggest just that,'' buzzed Rod, launching himself from the Pyromancer's hand. "Report back to you if . . . what?"

"If anything changes. It may die down. It may be a natural phenomenon, after all," Douglas told him. "As you can see, rain isn't far off anyway. Send someone to tell us if the situation changes."

"Pleased to do so," the bee hummed excitedly, preparing to fly. "The Hive of Queen Purple Sage is happy to serve!"

He shot off toward Queen and home.

The vent they followed down deep into the substrate of the crater narrowed steadily. Flarman was beginning to consider performing a Reducing Spell.

"It'd slow us down considerably, however," he said to Lithold.

"Not just yet," the Geomancer replied. "Hold it ready, just in case."

The Journeyman Air Adept, in the lead, slipped between two great, heat-glazed boulders. In a moment he called back that the tunnel beyond had widened into a fair-sized gallery.

"Air's clear of poisons, as yet," Stormy Petrel reported. "Even though it smells somewhat like badly spoiled oysters."

He rode Cribblon's left shoulder, sampling the very hot, dry air as they went.

"I think I can just about make it through here," grunted Flarman.

With a volley of grunts and some well-placed groans, he managed to pass the narrowing of the way. Lithold followed more easily—she was quite slim by comparison.

Bronze Owl and Black Flame came last. The cat sniffed suspiciously as he came through the gap.

"The Darkness's stench gets stronger by the minute," he growled. "*Whew!* You should smell it easily by now, Owl."

Owl's smelling was not his strongest sense.

They stood together in the center of the long, high passage in which they now found themselves.

"Everybody quiet! Listen for a minute," Flarman ordered. "Let's see. . . ."

The search party fell silent.

Since leaving the surface they'd used an old and useful Pyromancy spell to light their way. Tiny but bright magic flames burned over their heads with a steady yellow glow, sparkling off the glassy walls, floor, and ceiling of the tunnel. Distorted reflections of the party roiled and jumped, stretched and shrank, depending on the curvatures of the mirror-smooth surfaces.

In this, the first large room they'd reached, even the magic light failed to reach the far end. The ceiling was only dimly visible far overhead. Unlike familiar water-carved caverns, there were no stalactites nor stalagmites nor sheets of flowstone—just hard, black, mirror-smooth surfaces that made it difficult to judge distances and directions.

They stood quietly listening The silence was almost tangible.

"Nothing!" murmured Lithold at last.

"It's playing games with us," grunted the older Pyromancer softly. "Let me call out to it . . . him. Can't hurt . . . he knows we're here . . . and it might help."

"Dangerous, perhaps," Lithold warned. "But, well . . . go ahead, Flarman!"

The Pyromancer placed two fingers between his lips and blew a loud, shrill whistle, the kind used by shepherds in the hills above Valley to call their dogs or warn their flocks of predators.

The sound echoed, shrilled, swelled, and rebounded about them. Lithold and Cribblon covered their ears and Black Flame shook his head in feline irritation.

Bronze Owl seemed unaffected, but Stormy Petrel blinked quickly several times, a sure sign he, too, was bothered by the piercing sound.

"Well, at least it gives me an idea how big this cavern is," Flarman murmured when the echoes at last died. "Let's—"

"Wait!" hissed Bronze Owl, raising a cautionary claw.

"What is it?" whispered Lithold very softly.

"A sound . . . quite low," Owl answered, just as softly. "Can't anyone else hear what I hear?"

"Something moving?" asked Cribblon. "Scraping . . . ?"

"Step back!" Flarman barked sharply. "Against the wall!"

The group crowded close to him.

With a terribly loud *snap!* and *crack!* a huge slab of the floor before them dropped suddenly away, leaving a dark opening—large enough, Bronze Owl later said, to drop a small house into—gaping at their feet.

Air rushing up from the cavity crackled with intense heat. The edges of the hole glowed incandescently.

"Back!" shouted Flarman. "Spell us some protection, Lithold!"

The Geomancer was already waving her long, graceful fingers and muttering a Heat-shield Spell.

At once the heat seemed to lessen. But when Bronze Owl flapped out over the open chasm his wingtips glowed blue with the blast-furnace heat.

"Come back here!" cried Flarman. "You'll melt!"

"I'm fine," the Owl called back. "It'll spoil some of my usual bright luster, but it's not hot enough to melt good-quality bronze—not yet, anyway."

He flew slowly forward through the hissing inferno, fighting the tremendous updraft and examining the narrow path left beside the chasm. By the time he returned, the heat had begun to subside.

"We can go ahead, if you so decide," Bronze Owl reported. "The passage ahead is really rather cool."

"Was that an accident?" Lithold wondered. "Or a warning?

"Definitely a warning," Flarman told her. "Perhaps you should—"

"No, I'll go on with you, Fire Wizard. We're getting warm on his trail."

"Warm, indeed!" sniffed Black Flame. "No matter! Lithold's insulation is holding well enough."

The Familiars and the bronze doorknocker followed the three Wizards around the open pit into a much cooler tunnel beyond.

"How long can you hold your spell against burning, my dear?" the Pyromancer asked the Geomancer.

"Days, if necessary."

"That's a blessing. We may need it!" Cribblon sighed. "Follow me, troop! See? The tunnel changes just ahead."

Where they'd been following a smooth-walled, steeply inclined channel of heat-blasted, black-glazed stone without seams, branches, or side passages, they now entered a gallery of a different sort.

Its convoluted, warped walls were of burnished metallic

gray in places, a roughly pitted and blasted blue or purple in others, and sometimes a rich, crystalline green, broken into a million facets.

"Emerald!" gasped Lithold. "Only tremendous heat could do this!"

The way now was riddled with side passages ranging in size from as big as a horse to small enough to admit only mice, bottomless drop-offs in the floor, and ceiling vents that branched and rebranched away overhead.

They'd found the remains of the meteor itself, Flarman realized.

"Something's ahead," Bronze Owl cried softly.

Chapter Twenty-two

Heart of the Meteor

CRIBBLON, Lithold, and Flarman examined the exposed remains of the vast meteorite with great interest. In the light of the floating flames it looked like nothing so much as the interior of a vast, blackened Swiss cheese, with bubbles and holes and gaps and passages everywhere.

"I'd have thought it would have completely melted and become solid . . . iron?" wondered Cribblon, somewhat in awe.

"It might have," the Geomancer explained. "But the heat and the pressures were so intense that the material of the meteor bubbled and burst, roiled, and boiled, and burped—which explains the holes, you see."

"Hot enough, if you ask me, even now," squawked Stormy. "Not my kind of place!"

"Nor mine," hissed Black Flame, pausing to lick his front paw pads, which, he thought, ought to be sizzling in the heat, but were really quite cool, as though he'd been walking beside Crooked Brook in midsummer.

Bronze Owl was examining the pathway into the interior of the meteor. It was rough, twisted, and angrily stressed . . . but there were faint signs of the passage of the Servant, even so.

Flarman straightened from his examination of a sparkling patch of deep blue amethyst.

"I think we may be making a mistake, friends," he said, gesturing them all closer.

"Not a very usual thing for you, Pyromancer," said Lithold, slipping her arm through his.

"But it occurs to me, my dear, that having two full Wizards, a Journeyman, and a flock of Familiars on his trail may be making this Servant act . . . irrationally. I'm convinced he *fears* us to the edge of insanity. To him, we must appear rather loathsome!"

"Us? Loathsome?" Bronze Owl hooted at the notion.

"His reactions," murmured Black Flame thoughtfully. "Even a trapped mouse will turn on his hunter. You may have hit upon it, Flarman! He's terrified of us."

"And a terrorized magical Being is triply dangerous," Lithold agreed with a quick nod. "Fire Wizard, I believe you're right!"

"The solution is . . . ?" asked Stormy Petrel, fanning his wings to stir up some cooling air.

"The solution is to send just *one* of us forward to approach this panicked Servant. He is, by his own lights, young, inexperienced, and very frightened."

"Yes, I sense it now that you suggest it," Lithold slowly agreed. "We should face him on a more gentle, one-to-one basis."

"You're his greatest enemy, Flarman Flowerstalk," Bronze Owl added. "You were one of the fearsome Fellowship that drove back The Darkness beside Bloody Brook. He knows of you. And of you, perhaps, Lithold."

"That leaves me, then," decided Cribblon. "Good! I'm the one to bring a breath of cool reason to this young splinter of Darkness."

And before the older Wizards could further discuss or object, the Journeyman Aeromancer hitched up his robe, nodded to the company, and trotted off down the main tunnel into the heart of the meteor.

"Go with him," Flarman muttered quickly to Bronze Owl. "Take one of the lights, too."

Without a word, Bronze Owl spread his scorched wings and flew after the middle-aged Journeyman. One of the Wizardlights wavered, then followed, casting weird and flickering shadows on the twisted, blistered walls of the narrow passage.

■   ■   ■

Cribblon later said he moved forward in abject terror, hardly breathing. Bronze Owl would say he didn't believe it, judging by the sight of the straight-standing, firm-striding Journeyman following the Servant's traces into the middle of a fallen star.

Even with his relatively weak sense of smell—all owls, bronze or bird-flesh, depend on eyesight to hunt, rather than smell—Owl soon realized they were passing through an almost-invisible cloud of poisonous fumes.

Cribblon had detected the deadly gas and was shrouded, now, by a bluish aura that filtered the gas from his immediate space. He went on steadily at walking speed, never hesitating.

Owl followed, unaffected by the deadly atmosphere and intense heat.

"Now, if he tries *extreme* heat . . . ," Owl muttered uneasily to himself.

Cribblon gestured for the light to move ahead of them to guide their way, which had become ever rougher and more treacherous underfoot.

They came suddenly to a vast round space, a huge bubble within the meteor's tortured fabric, a great, globular room big enough to hold a half-dozen Wizards' Highs, with room to spare.

In its center hung a great, rolling cloud of intense, formless blackness, fully thirty feet across, spinning slowly around and around on a wobbling axis.

Cribblon stopped just inside the entrance to study the Enemy for a long moment.

Bronze Owl stopped under the entry archway.

"Come not one step farther, Foul Wizard!" crackled a hollow voice from within the black cloud. "Or I will destroy us all!"

"Not a particularly intelligent idea, I'd say," Cribblon answered calmly. "For one thing, it would offer a tremendous advantage to your former Master, The Darkness itself. Himself. Whatever. If you destroy us *and* yourself, Servant, you destroy not only me, a lowly Journeyman Aeromancer, but a Pyromancer and the Geomancer as well. Who *then* could distract your terrible Master from *you* . . . if you should manage to survive? Unwise, I'd say."

There was a long, shuddering silence in the middle of the meteor's empty heart.

"Well, at least you and I would not be around to suffer the consequences," rumbled the Servant at last. "We would be . . . annihilated! Utterly destroyed!"

"Most likely," agreed Cribblon, then he added slowly, "I've never thought much about reputation, about creating memories and legends. I suppose total destruction, followed by the enslavement of everyone who survived me, would destroy any place I might have won in history. The question I ask myself is—*Do I care?*"

"And do *I* care?" the Servant hissed. "About *either* of us? We are nothing in the Great Scheme of The Darkness!"

"You could go back to him, however," Cribblon responded. "Could you not? Having destroyed at a blow the entire Fellowship of Light—Flarman Firemaster, Augurian of Waterand, and Lithold Stonebreaker, not to mention Douglas Brightglade, the young Pyromancer. I'd think your Master would welcome your return with open . . . whatever you Beings use as arms."

"*Ha!* You don't know my Dire Darkest Master as *I* do," the black cloud snapped and crackled. "He'd accept my gift of destruction of his enemies . . . and add me to the list, as well! He'll *never* even *begin* to understand why I fled on the final night of Last Battle."

"I fled that field myself," Cribblon murmured sadly. "And my own Master, the powerful Aeromancer Frigeon, turned and fled also. I was ashamed for a long time, but finally came to realize . . . nobody was a hero that day. Not even Flarman Flowerstalk, sometimes called Firemaster."

"I suppose you're right." The blackness seemed to heave a tremulous sigh. "But your fellow Wizards evidently understood and forgave themselves and you. *My* Master . . . doesn't know what forgiveness could ever be!"

The two, the middle-aged Journeyman and the lost shard of The Darkness, fell silent. Bronze Owl couldn't be sure, but it seemed the poisonous atmosphere was clearing a bit.

"In any case . . . ," Cribblon began to say.

"What else can I do?" wailed the Servant mournfully. "*You* wish to destroy me! The Darkness would—will *certainly*—destroy me! If I could just stay hidden somewhere, perhaps he might eventually forget, if not ever forgive, my cowardly defection!''

"From what little I know of your unforgiving Master," the Aeromancer went on quietly. "I wouldn't count on ever being forgotten nor forgiven.''

The ebony cloud heaved another rasping sigh, one filled with self-pity, sorrow, fear, and utter frustration.

"I must *try!*" it said at last with a sound akin to grinding teeth. "Even if for a just little while I want to survive, Journeyman! Can you understand that?''

"I was in much the same situation for over two centuries myself," Cribblon admitted. "I thought everyone else had been destroyed or was in captivity or distant hiding . . . even Flarman Firemaster himself!''

"Well . . . ," the cloud said, interested despite himself. "What changed your mind?''

"One day I was kind to a complete stranger. He'd been severely injured by a Black Witch's magical burning. I nursed him back to health and some measure of sanity. He started me thinking that maybe others of my kind were still alive, doing what they could for themselves and their fellows, no matter how badly harmed, how wickedly savaged. In time I was able to go back and face them, and I found they had long since forgiven me my cowardice. In fact, they *understood* it, from what they had been through themselves!''

"B-B-But," objected the Servant, "in my case? Endless Darkness, I *know*, will never forgive nor allow me to come back to its service! *Never!* And . . . I'm not at all sure I *want* to go back!''

Another long silence between them. Bronze Owl would have held his breath, if he'd had breath to hold.

"What *do* you want, then?" wondered the Aeromancer.

The Servant of Darkness swung from side to side, as if pacing back and forth. Cribblon waited. Bronze Owl leaned wearily against a huge, clear, red crystal set half into the wall beside the entrance, waiting, also, and listening.

"My best course seemed to be to make myself strong. Then The Darkness *might* consider me as an ally. If I managed to overwhelm or even just to cripple your Fellowship—especially Flarman Firemaster and the terrible Water Adept—the Darkness might be forced to deal fairly with me . . . perhaps.''

"I may know your former Master's evil nature better than you," Cribblon sniffed. "It's totally selfish! Completely evil! It would accept your conquests, as you say, and then turn and destroy *you*. . . ."

"I know that!" screamed the Servant in anguish. "Don't you think I know that? But it would be a delay, and a tiniest atom of a chance to survive!"

"A friend of mine, a young Fire Adept named Douglas Brightglade, has an alternate suggestion . . . if you'd care to hear it."

"Brightglade! I've heard a little of him. He drove me from the Darkest Mountains, you know. Surprised me. Stole my prisoner. I never thought the Fellowship would forgive Frigeon, after all he'd done against the members of the Fellowship."

"Frigeon was once my own Master, you see," whispered the Aeromancer.

"I-I—well, no, I didn't know that." gasped the cloud. "Your own Master? But—"

"It's a very long story," the Aeromancer Journeyman interrupted. "But, if you'd like to hear it, I'd be happy to tell it."

"We've plenty of time," rumbled the Servant. "Tell me your tale."

"A long time ago, as Men reckon time, I was apprenticed to the Master Aeromancer named Frigeon. He was already involved in the struggle against your World-devouring Darkness. You don't need me to tell you more of that, do you?"

"No, I was there, doing my part, carrying out orders," admitted the cloud.

More than an hour later Cribblon stopped talking, for he'd reached the end of his story.

The black cloud hung very still now in the center of the great, round chamber at the heart of the meteor, neither moving nor speaking.

Bronze Owl remained as still as the crystal against which he rested.

"I wish . . . ," said the cloud that was the Servant, "I really do wish . . ."

Cribblon remained silent, patiently waiting.

"I've had a taste of a sweet, sweet freedom," the cloud said at last, settling slowly to the floor of the chamber. It flattened out wearily. "I could never go back to being a Servant of The Darkness. I think I realized it from almost the very beginning."

Silence.

"What does the Wizard Brightglade suggest?" the cloud asked, extending a tendril of gray-green smoke uncertainly toward the waiting Aeromancer.

"Douglas says there *is* a place where you could be free . . . perhaps forever. Perhaps until The Darkness is finally defeated. A place of peace and, yes, loneliness, too."

"I prefer to be alone, I find," said the weary Servant. "Where is this place?"

"You might remember," Cribblon said. "It's the place, Douglas says, from whence your kind came in the Very Beginning. You should be right at home there. The great open spaces between the vast wheels of stars?"

"Nice, empty, quiet, wide, timeless, peaceful place? I recall it, now you speak of it! Would I be safe there? Left to myself?"

"Nobody can guarantee that, of course. But your Darkness seems to have forgotten it, even if it was once its home. And, Douglas says it's great . . . huge . . . vast . . . very nearly unending!"

The Darkness Servant was silent again for a long time and, at last, sighed deeply. The sound, like a gentle forest breeze, was one of contentment, of hoped-for peace, and of a decision reached, at last.

"Well," said Pyromancer Flarman Flowerstalk. "How long has it been?"

Lithold consulted a watch pinned on her blouse.

"Seven and a half hours, figuring from when the noise stopped and the heat began to cool," she replied. "What are you thinking, Flarman my dear?"

"Either poor Cribblon has been utterly destroyed by the Servant . . . or it has flown," guessed Black Flame.

"But Cribblon would have sent Bronze Owl to tell us, to warn us, in either case," Flarman said, stroking his beard as he always did when he was perplexed. The heated air made his whiskers flay about and crackle with blue sparks.

"I don't think anything has happened to Cribblon," said Lithold. "Perhaps he's succeeded, after all. This silence is rather encouraging. Wicked things always have trouble staying silent, I've noticed."

The walls around them suddenly creaked, cracked, and shimmied.

Flarman sat down suddenly and Lithold grasped a bit of stalactite to keep from tumbling also.

"Earthquake!" squawked the Albatross. "Time to get out of here, sir and madam!"

"I won't leave Cribblon in there alone!" cried Flarman. "You others . . . get back to the surface, quick as you can! I'm going after the Aeromancer. . . ."

Lithold stooped, gathering the two Familiars, the bird to her shoulder, the cat to her bosom. The floor heaved and the walls creaked again as she strode back the way they'd come.

Flarman plunged down the twisted corridor into the buried meteor, the way the Air Adept had gone, calling his name.

Almost at once he ran into the Journeyman, trotting back toward him, followed by the Bronze Owl on the wing, clattering loudly.

"Back!" shouted Cribblon, spinning Flarman about and facing him the way he'd come. "*Run!* It won't be safe here for many more minutes, Magister!"

Flarman allowed himself to be hustled from the meteor, which was now quivering like a living thing and making frighteningly loud snapping, banging noises, as if someone were smashing china against a stone wall, piece by piece, and crunching the pieces underfoot.

Bronze Owl sent the bright watch-light shooting ahead of them. Almost at once they began to climb the fumarole vent, scrambling for foot-and handholds, gasping for breath. There was no sign of Lithold and the Familiars.

"They've flown on ahead," Flarman guessed. "And I'm too old for scrambling like this, friends. We must fly!"

He coughed a string of spelling words, spread his arms, and lifted his feet, snatching the startled Cribblon by an arm as he shot past him. Owl flapped his tarnished brazen wings with an urgent clatter and a bang and flew ahead, shepherding the yellow Wizard-light before them, up the steep passage.

"Better tell me what's going on," Flarman yelled over the tumult of their flight.

"No time! No breath!" rasped Cribblon. "Wait 'til we get to open air!"

It seemed like hours, but was really just minutes, before they popped out of the fumarole vent like a cork and shot high into the cool air, just behind the hurtling Lithold and her passengers, and just ahead of a great, roaring cloud of incandescent gases and glowing, white-hot cinders.

Flarman took the Geomancer by the arm and they followed their bronze guide north to the empty city on the rim.

They spotted Douglas, Myrn, Augurian, and Marbleheart with Lesser Dragon, standing and watching, not yet fully aware of their danger.

"Load up! Clear off! Head for the beehive hills. Get clear!" screamed the Pyromancer and the Journeyman.

Douglas, Myrn, and the Water Adept, followed by the Sea Otter, dashed to board the Dragon, who spread his long wings at once and leaped high into the air to follow the hurtling Pyromancer.

Ahead of them Stormy carried Black Flame in his claws.

"We should be safe on the shortgrass hills," shouted Cribblon over the rising thunder behind them. "The Servant . . ."

Before he could explain, they'd cleared a low, sandy valley separating the crater from the grass-clad beehive hills.

Flarman pointed at a rounded, low hillock ahead, and flew straight to it, with the others following.

Douglas was off Lesser Dragon as soon as the Dragon's claws touched the ground.

"What is it," he shouted to Flarman.

"I have absolutely no idea," the Pyromancer panted. "Ask Cribblon!"

"We're safe now, I think," the Aeromancer gulped. He spun on his heel and flung out his arm, pointing. *"Look!"*

The Wizards' party faced south. From this height they couldn't see the floor of the crater, but they saw, suddenly, a brilliant, hot, red-orange glow shooting out of its depths, high into the evening sky, piercing the looming rain clouds, lighting the entire eerie scene with a jack-o-lantern glow.

There came then a roar like ten thousand granite boulders

charging down a steep mountainside. An eye-searing column
of the brightest white light shot straight up, lighting the empty
desert for miles and miles around, brighter than full day.

From the depths of the crater erupted a rough, glowing,
green sphere, its lower surface ablaze with thundering jets of
fire, red and blue and eye-searing white.

"The Servant!" shouted Cribblon. "He's on his way into
farthest space!"

The ball of red-hot, white-hot, blue-hot glare seemed to
pause a timeless moment, orienting itself to the just-risen
moon.

With a roar greater than any before, it rose higher into the
night sky, curved gently to the east and a bit to the south . . .
and in a blink became an arrowing streak of light.

In three quick heartbeats its roar died away to a murmur
and it became an attenuated line of fire pointing straight for
the moon.

"It'll miss the moon by a finger's breath," Cribblon estimated once the hum of the meteor's flight faded to a distant
throbbing, then to a low whisper.

At long last the trace disappeared into the crowded field of
background stars. Still the watchers stood on the grassy hilltop,
saying nothing, just watching.

A new crash and a flash burst suddenly upon them. The
thick thunderclouds had moved over the scene and a pelting,
cold rain began to fall, soaking them all.

"Augurian! Master!" Myrn screamed.

"No fear!" said a voice from the darkness. "I saw no reason to turn off the waterworks. Cool things down."

Myrn flung herself into the Water Adept's arms in relief,
hugging him fiercely. Douglas and Flarman rushed to embrace
them both. Augurian's Familiar shook the raindrops from his
tail feathers and gave a shrill whistle of relief.

"What happened, if I may ask?" wondered Marbleheart,
the first to recover his breath and wits.

"Not here!" Douglas said. "Look, the crater is boiling."

A vast cloud of superheated steam shrieked from the depths
of the hole left by the departing meteor. Already the white-
hot edges of the pit were cooling to cherry red. The city of
the Sandrones had disappeared completely in the blast of the
relaunched meteor. Hot steam mingled with the rain clouds.

Sheet after sheet of lightning flashed across the crater in constant thundering.

"My Queen wants to know if it's safe to stay here," a worried voice hummed in Douglas's right ear.

"Oh, Rod, old boy-bee!" Douglas greeted him. "I should think *perfectly* safe! Wouldn't you, Flarman?"

"Not only that," added the older Pyromancer, "but the birds and the bees and the beasts will find Sandrovia Crater a much more pleasant place to live hereafter, I should think, once that new lake cools down a bit. Plenty of hot bathwater for all!. Good for daisies and bluebonnets, as well as lilacs and rhododendrons and azaleas, too."

"Thank you, Wizards," hummed Rod. "That was quite a fireworks show!"

The rain continued in a torrent, showing no sign of stopping anytime soon. Climbing aboard Lesser Dragon's broad, wet back, the nonfliers in the party settled down for a wet trip to Indigo Deep.

On the way, although everyone was tired and ready for sleep, Marbleheart insisted Cribblon explain what they had just witnessed.

"It's all very simple, really," said the modest Journeyman. "The Servant remembered his home between the star-clusters. He decided to take your advice, Douglas, and go home.

"The hurry he . . . it . . . was in to leave was not because of fear, but because the most direct path to the spot in the outer firmament he wished to reach was about to set behind World. He was afraid if he waited longer, he'd have to go the long way round, y'see. Sorry if it frightened anyone! He thought it was necessary."

"Who's frightened?" snorted the Sea Otter. "Great show, taken all in all! You weren't scared, were you, Tomcat?"

Black Flame pretended to be peacefully asleep in Flarman Flowerstalk's large and comfortable—and thoroughly damp—lap.

A herd of forty magnificent winged horses waited for them at Indigo Deep.

Failing to find the Wizards' party on the Ebony shore, King

Priad and his daughter had led their people south to Sheik
Harroun's hill fortress.

"It was a hard decision," Princess Indra admitted to Myrn.
"We weren't sure if you needed us to help capture that . . .
what did you call it? . . . Servant of Darkness?"

"By the time you could have gotten there, my pet, everything was resolved, but we certainly appreciate your concern,"
cried Myrn, hugging the pretty winged horse about the neck.

"Now, we've got together a coterie of powerful Wizards—
and some great Journeymen and Familiars, too," Douglas said,
once they'd told their story to everyone's satisfaction. "It remains to do at least one more bit of magic here, and the sooner
the better!"

Priad, who was a strongly built chestnut stallion with flashing white wings, looked at his wife and his daughter fondly.

"We . . . er, ah. . . ." He hesitated. "Well . . . if I may, good
sirs?"

"What do you want to say, Majesty?" asked Myrn, hugging
the filly fondly for the second time.

"My father and my mother and my people . . . well, they
wonder if . . . by any chance . . . they could remain *as they
are?* When it comes down to it, you see," Indra said hesi-
tantly, "my people prefer to remain beautiful, strong, flying
horses and poets . . . rather than mere king and queen, knights
and ladies!"

Flarman laughed aloud in both delight and surprise.

"You can make that choice, of course," he chuckled. "If
you change your minds, we can always send someone along
later to de-spell you."

"The life of a flying poet," said King Priad seriously, "has
much to say for itself. I have to say, however, that my daughter
Indra . . . well, she's not so sure."

"Indra!" exclaimed Myrn Brightglade. "You wish to return
to your former shape? *Ah!* I begin to understand! Well, and
good!"

"I see," Douglas said slowly. He also had observed the
reunion of the flying horse and the High Desert Sheik's poet
son. "Magisters? Would it be possible to restore just the one
little flying horse?"

"No problem!" Flarman chuckled. "If Princess Indra is
sure she wants it that way."

"I have no doubts at all" the filly insisted most firmly. "I love Saladim, and wish to marry him. And he loves me, and would even if I remained as I am, but . . ."

"Say no more," Lithold told her, clucking sympathetically. "We ladies must sometimes leave close family and faithful for love! There are worse reasons, I can tell you from hard experience, my dear. Shall I handle the special transformation for her, Flarman? I have some little knowledge in such spellings, you remember."

"*Do* it, for goodness' sake," Flarman insisted. "I'm eager to kiss the bride myself."

"There's the matter of poor little Hana. And her father, who had me kidnapped," Myrn said to Flarman. "And I should like to thank so many of the people who helped me . . . especially Shadizar and her delightful children . . . and I've never even met her husband, Farrouk, you know. So many loose ends to bind up! Perhaps I should delay my testing?"

"Delaying an Examination is *never* a good idea, unless you're just not ready," said Augurian. "And I know you *are* ready, stepdaughter!"

"We must return to Samarca," Douglas insisted. "I'd like to help Sultan Trobuk with the problem of his Grand Vizier. And thank Shadizar and Farrouki and Farianah, and meet Farrouk. But your Examination . . ."

"I know—it's *important!*" Myrn sighed. "Well, I can't seem to postpone it, can I? We will just have to hurry!"

"There's Brand and Brenda," put in Marbleheart. "I must admit I miss their pulling my fur out by baby's fistfuls and smearing my handsome muzzle with cold porridge, and pulling my tail when I'm trying to study . . ."

"You're a dear, dear, beloved Sea Otter!" Myrn melted. "For no other reason than to see my darlings, I ache to go home. But my husband is quite correct. Douglas and I must go back to Balistan to clear up one more mess and then thank everyone properly for their help!"

"I have never learned to say no to my wife," Douglas said with a sigh to Flarman Flowerstalk.

"It's why there are Wizards, my boy," chuckled Flarman, clapping his former Apprentice on the back. "To grant wishes where they're deserved."

■   ■   ■

The Supreme and Highly Revered, the Sultan of all Samarca and the High Desert tribes, the handsome and intelligent Trobuk sat cross-legged on the sandy shore of the great, shallow lake.

In the clear, blue-greenish water before him swam two dusky nymphs, his beautiful wife Nioba and the girl everyone called simply Hana, the daughter of the Grand Vizier. Hana was holding the Sultana afloat with one hand, encouraging her to kick her shapely legs and paddle furiously with her arms.

"No, no! Highness, you must put your head *under* the water on each stroke. Otherwise, you'll sink!" Hana insisted, laughing.

"Head down!" agreed the Sultan, reaching for a sugary date wrapped around a toasted almond. "Bottom up! Kick legs! Stroke! *Stroke!*"

"What kind of language is that before a child . . . *ulp?*" sputtered his wife, stopping her earnest fluttering. With the end to her furious paddling, she sank abruptly beneath the surface.

Hana quickly pulled Nioba erect and pounded her on the back while she coughed water from her throat.

"You're getting it!" her husband enthused. "Bravo! Hoorah!"

"If I didn't love you so much, I'd learn to hate you very quickly," coughed the pretty Sultana. "Keep my head down! Keep my . . . tell me, what kind of language . . . ?"

"Better call it a day, my sweet," advised her royal consort. "A few more lessons from our water *houri* here and you'll be swimming like a fish!"

Nioba waded out of the clear lake water and accepted a warm, soft towel from the Sultan, trying to scowl but laughing despite herself.

"Look! Here's an old friend," called Hana, who'd gone up to the pavilion to get their robes. "It's Myrn! Welcome back, Mistress Aquamancer!"

The Water Adept waved and came down to the beach from the road.

"Mistress!" exclaimed the Sultan. "We're making wonderful progress. My wife will shortly be a sea nymph, just like you . . . if she can remember not to breathe water!"

"Don't tease her, sir." Myrn grinned. "The first rule of

learning to swim is to forget how you must appear to those who watch.''

She hugged Nioba and then Hana, despite their dampness, and bowed gravely to the Sultan.

''No bowing!'' he ordered. ''I'll accept a hug, in its place! Tell us—did you rescue your friend from . . . whatever it was that snatched him from his northern land?''

''My mission was completed and, happily, it ended as I wished it to!'' Myrn answered.

They walked up to the pavilion and, while the Sultan went off to don his own clothing, Myrn regaled the ladies with her adventures in the north.

''We saw some interesting fireworks from that direction,'' said Trobuk when he'd returned, fully clothed, and the story had to be told all over again.

''That was the poor old Servant, or whatever it was called,'' explained the Journeyman Aquamancer. ''He's escaped to his original home in the empty space between the stars.''

''Your Journeying is finished, then.'' Nioba sighed. ''And you'll wish to return home. Don't you have an Examination to take very soon?''

''Just a few hours hence,'' Myrn answered with a nod. ''We came back to finish up one last bit of business with you, Lord Sultan. If you have time to meet with my husband and our friends . . . ?''

''There'll always be time to talk to friends,'' Trobuk promised. ''Where is Douglas? And the Aeromancer—is that right?—and my friend the furry Sea Otter?''

''When I heard you were swimming I asked them to wait for us up the road at the first cafe inside the city gate,'' Myrn explained. ''I knew Nioba would not want all those men watching her swimming lesson.''

''Perfectly correct!'' the Sultana agreed, laughing. ''But who else have you brought to meet my husband and me?''

''My Master, and Douglas's Master, too. Powerful Wizards, both of them, but very sweet and kind.''

''We'll walk to Gateway Cafe, then,'' decided the Sultan, waving off his squire, who'd been waiting to bring up their magnificent mounts.

''We're just plain tourists here,'' explained Flarman after he'd been introduced to the Sultan, the Sultana, and young

Hana. "Douglas and Myrn have told us of their warm welcomes here and we wanted to thank you, in the name of the Fellowship of Wizards, sir."

"Nothing to thank me for," cried the Sultan. "We both loved Myrn from the first evening she set dainty foot in our palace, and Douglas was a fascinating guest . . . though for too short a time, I must admit. Welcome all, to Balistan!"

They were seated about a large, round table under a gaily striped awning stretched over the side of the main road near the southern gate of Balistan. The cafe's proprietor was rushing breathlessly about in wild excitement and his waiters were bringing fruit drinks and almond cakes and savory kabobs on bamboo slivers, highly spiced but delicious, to the royal party.

"They came riding up on a *monster*!" squealed a street urchin, eyes wide in awe. "It's still there, behind the cafe, eating orange sherbet by the tubful!"

Most of the passersby only looked politely at the Sultan's guests . . . and at the Sultan and his Sultana also, it must be admitted. But a crowd of children on their way home from school gathered on the walk before the cafe, ogling and goggling unashamed.

"If you'd rather move inside, Lord Sultan," said the cafe's owner. "This crowd . . . !"

"Nonsense," cried Trobuk. "They're all my subjects and close friends and good neighbors. I like to ogle them while they ogle me and my wife!"

To prove it he waved to the children and grinned while Nioba walked over to them and greeted them in a most kindly manner.

"Sultana Nioba," asked a girl of, perhaps, six. "Will you bear a royal heir soon? My mama says . . ."

"Soon," Nioba said, laughing. "I promise!"

"What will his name be, then?" one of the little boys asked eagerly.

"What's *your* name?" the Sultana asked him.

"Bomba, Your Majesty," replied the lad, blushing brilliant red. "The son of Bomba, the best weaver of rugs in all Samarca!"

"I've heard about your father, then," called out Trobuk. "Many of his rugs grace the floors of my palace here, and at Port, too."

"*If* our first child is a boy-child, we'll name him for his great-grandfather," Nioba told the children. "Does anyone here remember his name?"

"I know! We know!" several children shouted. "He was the Magnificent Sultan Fadouzal!"

"Correct," cried Nioba, nodding her head. "And, my dear, what is *your* name?" she asked the girl who had asked about the coming baby.

"I'm Maida," the child said shyly. "My father is Alibab. He's a soldier to the Sultan's Guard."

"A truly beautiful name," murmured the Sultana. "If my husband agrees, we shall name our first girl-child after you, pretty little Maida. And you shall come to the palace after school every day, if you wish, to play with her and help to bathe and dress her and teach her her first words."

The girl, although nearly overcome with joy, remembered to say, "Thank you, Your Majesty!" to the beautiful Sultana.

"We came by," Flarman was saying to the Sultan under cover of the conversation at the edge of the road, "to tie up the last loose end of Douglas's and Myrn's adventures in Samarca, if we may."

"Ah! The matter of Mistress Brightglade's kidnapping?" Trobuk asked, serious at once.

"Exactly." Douglas nodded. "It was a perfidious and, what's more, entirely selfish act! But it's up to you, Sultan of Samarca, to judge the culprit and set his punishment."

"I suspect who you'll name." Trobuk sighed sadly. "It's been in my mind ever since Myrn disappeared, but I'd no proof."

"We have no proof, either," said Myrn. "Except the desert men who kidnapped me told me they were paid by the Grand Vizier to carry me away."

"I suspected as much," cried the Sultan, laying his hand on Myrn's arm in apology. "What will you have me do? Death by strangulation is the sentence meted out to those who steal young girls and sell them into slavery. Shall I order the wickedly ambitious Kalinort arrested? Say what you desire, my dear Lady Brightglade."

Myrn shook her head.

"No, we but wished to make sure you understood who did the deed, and why, Sultan Trobuk. The three kidnappers said they'd been paid by the Grand Vizier to carry me off. Kalinort feared I would assist my friend Nioba and strengthen your resolve to have only one wife. Kalinort wanted to marry his daughter, Gerhana, to you, to cement himself to you more strongly than ever."

Trobuk nodded, looking very solemn.

"It's as I suspected. Kalinort is a very ambitious man . . . but also a very capable minister. As far as anyone here knows, he's been an honest one"

Nioba said quietly, "We can't have our servants kidnapping our dear friends to influence your decisions, husband."

Trobuk held out his hand to his wife, who came and sat beside him.

"I would exile him to the deepest desert," she suggested. "We must not give anyone else the idea he can commit such a heinous crime for his own—or even our—benefit."

"I agree with you," said the Sultan.

"It's your decision, of course," Myrn said. "It seems to me such . . . activities are not unheard of in the history of Samarca."

"Nor in our own, if it be honestly admitted," put in Flarman. "People remain people, for all their fine manners and fancy dress. Perhaps this Kalinort, acted in the belief that he and he alone was responsible for the safety of the kingdom . . . the Sultanate, rather."

"That makes it difficult, Master Wizard, because I agree with you. I have no reason to consider Kalinort a wicked self-seeker planning to replace me or my line. My rule represents a new day in Samarca. The bad old ways *must* be eradicated. A Grand Vizier has no license to kidnap *anyone*, or enslave them, or have them killed, no matter how worthy his purpose. Not even the Sultan, I am daily telling my people, has the right to take life or livelihood or freedom without due processes of law . . . which applies to the lowest water carrier as it does to the Grand Vizier, or the Sultan himself!"

He thought silently for a while, and the rest of the group about the table were very quiet, too, allowing him to ponder.

"Let us," Douglas spoke at last, "talk to this Kalinort and see how he reacts to what you know of his crime. Then, I'm positive, it must be you who decides his fate, Lord Sultan. You'll have to live with your decision."

"As for me, it was no real hardship . . . in fact, the kidnapping was very useful to my purposes, sir." Myrn smiled softly at her memories. "I'd not condemn him too harshly, to tell the truth."

The young Sultan smiled dazzlingly at the beautiful Aquamancer.

"You are more than kind! A condemnation of my Grand Vizier is a condemnation of his Sultan, I'm afraid. Politics enters into this, of course. Kalinort springs from a rich and powerful group of Port noblemen. Yes, let us adjourn to the palace. I'll call for Kalinort and I'll listen to the man before I judge him."

"No execution, however," begged Myrn. "I don't want blood on my conscience, Lord Sultan!"

"It's *my* decision, remember. Everybody finished? Then we'll go up to the palace," the Sultan said firmly.

He rose from the table, gesturing to the host to come and receive his reward for a pleasant rest under his awning.

A member of the Sultan's Guard came to the Grand Vizier's apartment as Kalinort sat at dinner with a dozen of his close followers and relatives.

"Our Lord Sultan bids you attend him at once," announced the Guard, politely. "I am to accompany you to his presence, Excellency."

"I'm going to him in a short while, at any rate," Kalinort objected.

"Sir, His Sublime Majesty bids you come *at once!*" the Guard insisted calmly.

"I'm at my Sultan's command, of course," replied the Grand Vizier.

The Guard led the Grand Vizier, unaccompanied by any of his followers or servants, through the palace halls to the Royal Suite. If Kalinort felt apprehension at the sudden summons, he didn't show it.

"Ah, Kalinort!" said Trobuk as they entered his presence. "Come sit with us, sir. You know Douglas Brightglade, the Pyromancer, of course. And you know his wife, the beautiful, and powerful, Aquamancer?"

At the sight of Myrn, the Grand Vizier's face lost some color and his smile turned to stone.

"And the others here are . . ." The Sultan smoothly introduced the older Wizards as well as Cribblon and the Familiars, all of whom sat at his table.

"Sire . . . ," began the Vizier, coughing slightly. "I—"

"Let me state our situation baldly, so we will know where we stand," Trobuk went on, ignoring the attempt at interruption.

He clearly but quickly told of Douglas's mission, then of Myrn Manstar Brightglade's Journeying. When he described how Myrn had been carried off into slavery at Stone Trees, the Grand Vizier lost the rest of what color he had and shrank into himself, bowing his head.

"These are the facts as I've learned them," finished Trobuk. "What have you to say of this matter, Grand Vizier? Did I hear it a-wrong? Is there anything missing?"

Kalinort sat, head bowed, for a long minute in silence.

Everyone at the table watched him in equal silence. When the Otter picked up a fruit knife to cut a plump orange, the Grand Vizier shrank back in sudden fear.

Douglas shook his head at his Familiar.

"Sorry," Marbleheart apologized.

He dropped orange and knife with a loud *thump* on the tabletop.

"Your information, Sire," began Kalinort softly. "Well . . . it's right as far as it goes."

"Tell us how far it goes, then," requested the Sultan, leaning back against his cloth-of-gold pillows.

"I *did* order the lady—of course, I didn't know she was a Wizard, Sire, at the time—to be carried off into slavery at Stone Trees."

"So much we know," murmured Trobuk.

"I-I—did it to strengthen your government! T-T-To strengthen your rule," the frightened Grand Vizier stammered. "The Lords of the Coast, you know, are unhappy that you, a High Desert prince, had chosen for wife a lady of the same High Desert tribes!"

"I'm aware of their feelings," said the Sultan, glancing at his wife.

Nioba said nothing but gazed calmly at the Grand Vizier. Hana, seated at her side, glared angrily at her father. Tears coursed down her cheeks, but she also said nothing.

"Well . . . ," Kalinort mumbled. "Well . . . as your Grand Vizier . . . I believed it was my duty to solidify the base of your rule by incorporating—"

"I know all that," said the Sultan. "Did you order my guest snatched—there is no other word for it, sirrah!—and sent off into the desert to serve in slavery?"

"Ah . . ." Kalinort hesitated, his eyes swinging wildly from side to side.

"An answer is required!" Trobuk snapped. "At once!"

Kalinort sank to his knees before the Sultan.

"Yes . . . I admit I had the lady stolen away. I did it for *your* sake, beloved Sultan Trobuk. You must believe me!"

"I *do* believe you, Kalinort," grunted Trobuk angrily. "The question is, can I forgive you? You may have had a good purpose in mind, Kalinort, but your means—especially when you did this thing *in my name*—were totally wrong and very wicked!"

"Sire!" cried the Grand Vizier, who didn't strike the onlookers as particularly *grand* now. "Sire, Sire!"

"I cannot fault your loyalty, Kalinort," the Sultan went on, allowing his anger to subside. "But neither can I find anything but great fault in your attack on a guest, let alone the fact that she's a powerful magicker!"

"Sire!" cried the wretched minister, bumping his head on the floor.

"Saying 'Sire' does no good!" snapped the young ruler. "I hereby remove you from your post, to which I myself appointed you!"

"Oh, please, Sire . . . !" sobbed Kalinort, wringing his hands. "Oh! Sire!"

"Never before saw anyone actually 'wringing' his hands," clucked Marbleheart to his Master.

It was the following morning. The party from Wizards' High was preparing to depart by Pin and Pearls.

"Poor man," Myrn sighed, shaking her head. "Oh, I know he brought it on himself. But . . . what's to become of him?"

"Word is, among the Sultan's Guard," said Hana, entering with an armful of colorfully wrapped gifts, "that Father will be sent to the Northwest Land. His task, which will take him some years, is to survey the area for the Sultanate around the great new crater lake, to determine if it's worth developing, either as a place for the Sultan's people to farm or raise flocks or as a possible mining site.''

"That was Lithold's suggestion,'' acknowledged Flarman. "Just put those presents in my bag, my dear. I'll hand them out when the time is right, you may be certain.''

"What's to happen to you, Hana?'' wondered Myrn.

"Weep not for me,'' the girl said, giving Myrn a warm hug. "I'm to remain with my beloved Nioba and learn to be . . . whatever I am fated to be, I suppose.''

"And forsake your papa?'' asked Marbleheart, who was not all that sympathetic to the former Grand Vizier, if the truth was known.

"It will be my responsibility to keep an eye on Father. He's really not a bad sort, for all the times he neglected me for his ambitions. I still do love the old rascal! Between us, Lady Nioba and I hope to mellow his haughty ways and bring him home in good time. He really was a splendid Grand Vizier, everyone agrees. But he was brought up in ways that modern Samarca has rejected, you see. He'll have to learn to change!''

"Kalinort's nothing if not intelligent,'' Flarman added. "If anyone can reform his ideas and make him useful to the Sultanate, it will be Trobuk and his goodwife. And you, my dear child!''

"I'll try very hard, Lord Wizard, for all our sakes,'' Hana murmured.

"Well, I've an idea, then,'' said Myrn, perking up at the thought. "In a half-year or so the Camel Merchant Farrouk and his wife, my very good friend Shadizar, and their lovely children plan to voyage to such fascinating foreign places as Waterand Isle, dear old Flowring Isle, New Land, and High-landorm . . . and of course, our beautiful Valley of Dukedom. I shall suggest to Shadizar that she bring you with them. You're of the right age, just, for foreign travel, my dear! And you should get away from all this business of being alone so much of the time. You'll love the children, too, I know.''

"I can hardly tell if she's pleased or disappointed,'' chuckled Marbleheart after the delighted young lass had turned four unladylike cartwheels on her way out the door, chortling gleefully as she went.

■   ■   ■

Two of their party had decided to remain in Samarca for a while.

"I know Myrn will pass Examination with flying colors," Cribblon explained to Douglas. "Serenit wants me to accompany him on a visit to Port, of which he saw virtually nothing. He hopes to arrange for selling New Land timber to the Merchant's Guild. He could do it just as well by himself, but . . . well, we both feel we've some catching up to do on an old friendship."

"You're not jealous of Cribblon?" Douglas asked the First Citizen.

"Not at all! I've never been so happy as I am as First Citizen. And Cribblon really needs some experienced guidance. He's surprisingly naive for one who will become a powerful Air Wizard."

"He's eager to assume the burdens of Wizardry," Douglas agreed, nodding his head slowly. "As for you, Serenit . . . to be blunt in the most friendly possible way, some people just don't have what it takes."

"No one knows it better than I," the First Citizen said with a hearty laugh. "And even without my old spells and magicks, perhaps I can help Cribblon on another task. The good Sultan has asked him to study the great wind-and-sand storms that plague his eastern provinces."

"Maybe we can at least provide some way to *predict* them better, further in advance," added Cribblon eagerly. "Nobody should fool around with the Powers of Air . . . as my Master once taught me."

"Your own Examination for Advancement to Full Wizardry . . . ," Serenit said to the Journeyman.

"A while off, yet, I fear." The middle-aged man sighed, smiling shyly. "I'll learn . . . but I always seem to take a long time for that."

"Nonsense!" cried Myrn, who'd returned to hear this last bit of conversation. "I'll speak to the Examination Board about you, you may be sure. We couldn't have succeeded here without your sure craft, your wisdom, your gentleness, and . . . so much more!"

"I'm deeply grateful for your words, Myrn," the Journeyman said, bowing deeply in the manner of the Nearer East to cover his pleased blushing. "I'll come to Wizards' High after a while. We'll be busy until then."

"So will I," Myrn Manstar Brightglade assured them all.

As they stepped into the hot morning sun in the Great Entrance Courtyard at the front of the Sultan's palace, Myrn saw a familiar face in the crowd of courtiers and their ladies.

"Groat!" she cried out. "I thought you were with Shadizar in Port!"

"No, the Sultan . . . well, I've been offered a new position on the Sultan's staff."

"Marvelous! I'm so happy for you, old friend. Here's my husband, Douglas Brightglade. Groat is a very good friend from Port," Myrn explained to her husband. "I've told you about him."

"Many times," said the younger Pyromancer with a laugh. "Most pleased to meet you, Master Groat . . ."

"Grand Vizier Groat," said the young man, grinning enough to split his face in twain. "His Supreme Majesty, the Celestial, the Ever-merciful, the Sultan . . . and so on and so forth . . . has asked me to serve him in place of the old Grand Vizier, who left to seek a healthier climate last evening."

"You? Grand Vizier!" cried Myrn. "Well, I think Trobuk has made a very wise choice. You'll do perfectly, young Groat! Grand Vizier Groat, I should say."

"I sense a fine, Aquamantic hand behind that promotion," said Douglas to Myrn as they prepared to join hands with the rest for the fastest possible flight home.

"You think that I . . . ? Really, Douglas! Trobuk is completely capable of picking his own court officials."

"I'll not be too far away, so if you like I'll keep an eye on the young Grand Vizier," said Lesser Dragon, who had heard the exchange.

"Very nice of you to offer," murmured Myrn, patting the Dragon's cheek-scales fondly. "No, I think Groat is the perfect choice for the post. He'll have few, if any, political connections with the Coastal Sheiks, for one thing, to distract him from his duty. Good-bye, good old Lesser! Where are you off to, if we may ask? Back to the buried temple in the desert?"

"Eventually. A very cozy and suitable house for a Dragon, I always found," replied the great beast. "No, I've promised Princess Indra I'd return to her at Indigo Deep. She and the young poet Saladim will marry next spring, and I am to be her chief sponsor after her father, the flying horse!''

"A strange wedding party, that," chuckled Marbleheart. "But a wedding I would love to attend, Masters!"

"Might be!" said Douglas with a pleased nod. "If my wife can pass the Examination for Advancement to Full Wizardry. Or maybe, even if not!"

"I will hold you to that, husband," teased the Wizard-candidate. "Be sure of that! Give little Indra my deepest love and tell her we'll stand with her when she's married, Lesser, fiery old friend. A promise!"

"I certainly shall tell her that," the Dragon told Myrn. "Now, farewell! I see the older Wizards are awaiting you. Call on me anytime, dear friends—I'll come to you! Great-great-great-granduncle Great Golden has often told me of your very pleasant Valley."

Chapter Twenty-three

Home Is Best!

MYRN paced beside midsummer-quiet Crooked Brook and crossed the ancient, rickety Plank Bridge to walk into the fragrant shade of Precious's apple trees They were already heavily laden with green fruit.

"Mama sad?" little Brenda asked Marbleheart.

The twins, having spent several early-summer weeks with their paternal grandparents on Farango Waters, were as brown as berries. They were paddling their bare feet in the cool shallows just above the plank bridge. Marbleheart had been naming the fishes for them, mostly brook trout, which swam nearby . . . but not *too* near.

"No, not sad! Not at all. It's called *apprehension*. Or is it *anticipation*?" explained the Sea Otter. "Look, you cubs! There is a school of pan-sized perch. Delicious fired with butter with a pinch of salt and a dash of pepper."

Brand lay on his back on the grassy bank, watching the bright bluebirds in the willows overhead.

"Mama *looks* sad," Brenda insisted.

"Go across to her, then, and make her smile a bit," suggested the sleek Otter. "How about a swim, Brand, old man? You need some work on your backstroke."

"Swim!" chortled the boy, leaping up to strip off his shirt and short breeches. "Come, Brenda!"

"No," said his sister, rising. "I want to give Mama a hug and tell her we love her."

"I'll come along shortly, then," Brand promised, unwilling to give up his swim. "Where's Papa, Marbleheart?"

"Auditing the Examination Board," the Otter answered. "That means he's *listening,* not being a member of the Board himself."

Brand said, *"Ummmm!"* not knowing what all the Otter's big words could possibly mean.

"They'll have their decision before too long, m'boy. Not to worry!" Marbleheart said confidently. "I've known your beautiful, smart mama for a long, long while, and there's just no way she could fail her Advancement to Wizardry."

Douglas came from the double front door, spoke briefly to Bronze Owl, who was hanging sleepily (although, in fact, bronze doorknockers never sleep) from his favorite nail in the center of the right-hand leaf, and walked down to watch his Familiar and his son splashing in Crooked Brook.

Nearby a class of Neriad children—newly come with their families to live, at Flarman's invitation, along the Brook that watered Valley—chanted lessons about bugs and butterflies and midsummer flowers.

Douglas gestured to their instructress, a brown-and-gray robin hen, not to stop for him. Concentration was broken, however—as you might expect when a famous Fire Wizard comes along in the middle of a class—and the tiny beings waved and called to him as he passed.

"Well, then," said their teacher, bobbing her head. "Perhaps we've been at this long enough, nestlings. Who's for a visit to the Fairy Well?"

"Oh yes! Yes, let's," the dozen tiny sprites cheered.

In a moment they were off, flying behind their plump teacher and calling out to friends they met along the way.

"Where's your mother, fish-boy?" Douglas called to his son, who was riding Marbleheart's back in the deeper water under the bridge.

"Over among the apples," Marbleheart replied for the child. Brand was wholly preoccupied with a family of water-walkers skating by on the stream's smooth surface.

Douglas crossed the bridge before he saw his wife and

daughter seated together on an old wooden wheelbarrow Precious had left in the orchard.

"Green apples make the *very best* apple pies of all," Precious was known to say. The barrow stood ready for the time when the apples were more fully formed.

"Green apples . . . ," Douglas said, standing before his wife and daughter. "I love 'em, but they've been known to give little girls the *golliwogs*!"

"Never!" Myrn laughed. "Not old Precious's apples! I made a total mess of it, didn't I?" she added sadly, looking off toward the orchardman's pasture and the low, blue southern hills beyond. "Well, I can always try again. Flarman took his Examination *four* times before he finally passed, Augurian told me. And my Master admits to *five* attempts!"

"True. But you won't have to take it that many times. You and I are lucky, love—we've had the best Wizardry teachers in World."

"Well . . . maybe next time," Myrn said with a sigh.

"There will be no next time," Douglas said firmly.

"What? No second or third testing! Why not?" cried Myrn in sudden consternation.

"No need, passed-Water Adept!" Douglas laughed, kneeling to embrace and kiss both his daughter and her mother.

"Oh!" Myrn sobbed, sudden bright tears starting from her lovely Sea-green eyes. *"Oh!"*

"Now you've been duly bussed and unofficially informed, I'm to bring you up to the cottage for official notification," her proud husband said.

"In a moment!" sniffled Myrn, accepting his handkerchief and wiping her happy tears away. "Thank you, my oh-so-wonderful Douglas!"

"No thanks due to me, m'lady!"

"I mean for helping, but I really mean for being such a good friend and lover and husband and father to our children. All of the above!"

He pulled her tight into his arms and dried her salty tears of joy and relief with several more kisses.

Brenda giggled and tugged at her father's long tunic sleeve.

"Me!" she begged. "Kiss Brenda!"

Douglas swooped and bore his daughter aloft, placing her on his broad shoulders, despite the rather grimy fingers she wove into his fair hair. She smelled of summertime childhood, of applewood, the lush green grass growing along the Brook, and of sweet milk, and oatmeal cookies, too.

So burdened, Douglas took Myrn by her arm, then went to pull their naked son from Crooked Brook and hustle him into his blouse and breaks.

"It's all over," Douglas told Marbleheart.

"Which means," Marbleheart chuckled, "knowing things around here, that new things are just about to begin to happen.

"Dinner first, however," the Sea Otter added, following the Wizards Brightglade and their whooping children across the lawn to the front door.

"Congratulations, Water Adept!" Bronze Owl called to Myrn. "Here's the whole cat family, fresh from a new littering and eager to say they knew all along you'd pass, first crack out of the box."

"It seems everyone knew except me," Myrn sniffed happily. "Thank you all! I could never have—"

"Aquamancer!" shouted Flarman Flowerstalk, erupting from the front door like a cork from a bottle. "I must say you did even better than your rather dense husband did. Ask your Master! He's the best teacher of us all."

Lithold Stonebreaker came out to embrace the newly passed full Wizard, and helped her shed a happy tear or two, smiling all the while. Then tall, stately Augurian came down from abovestairs and added a dignified tear or three to the occasion, and a loving embrace and several kisses, too.

From the High's cool and cavernous kitchen came the sound of Blue Teakettle leading the kitchen utensils in a rousing cheer.

"Pecan pie and vanilla ice cream now," announced Flarman. "Full banquet tomorrow night! Marbleheart's already invited everybody for miles around and, he says, Queen Margot and Prince Aedh and the little Faerie Princeling are coming, too."

"It'll run rather late, I'm afraid." Augurian sighed, "I should get back to my studies at Waterand . . . but another week or so won't matter."

■   ■   ■

The two young Wizards watched the sky begin to turn light gray over Far Ridges as they sat close together on the stone curb of Fairy Well.

A deep purple predawn quiet held Valley in its lap.

Somewhere a meadowlark trilled, far off toward Trunkety Town. In the byre next to the Wizards' workshop under the High, the cows and their calves, always early risers, were beginning to stir, waiting for milking, for breakfast, and for their day in the sun.

In the deep blue western sky, near the horizon, above the setting Morning Star, a single, red dot of light flashed brightly for a long moment, then disappeared forever.

"The Servant's reached his ... her ... its safe haven, I see," Douglas murmured to his wife.

But Myrn was sound asleep, dark head on his broad shoulder, hands clasped in his, still smiling.